Embracing Scandal

By

Suzi Love

Dedication

To all my writing buddies, friends, and family --
This book is dedicated to you in gratitude for all
your support while I worked toward becoming an author.

Special thanks to Cathryn Hein, Rebecca Withnall, and
Louisa Mack who helped get this book started.

I'm truly grateful to all of you.
-- Suzi Love

Copyright

Embracing Scandal

Table of Contents

Embracing Scandal 1
Copyright 2
Table of Contents..3
Chapter 1 4
Chapter 2...19
Chapter 3...32
Chapter 4...45
Chapter 5...59
Chapter 6...70
Chapter 7...76
Chapter 8...84
Chapter 9...100
Chapter 10...114
Chapter 11...128
Chapter 12...141
Chapter 13...152
Chapter 14...159
Chapter 15...169
Chapter 16...173
Chapter 17...180
Chapter 18...198
Chapter 19...208
Chapter 20...220
Chapter 21...231
Chapter 22...242
Chapter 23...263
Chapter 24...279
Epilogue 290
About Suzi Love 293
Excerpt from Scenting Scandal 294

Chapter 1

Martin House, Mayfair, London, 1843

Curse the city and its constant interferences. Secluded in his fire-heated library, Cayle St. Martin, Duke of Sherwyn, attempted to block out all things British by imagining himself back on a Mediterranean beach, unfettered, unhurried, and warm.

The brandies he'd downed didn't guarantee peacefulness but they fired his blood and ensured a few hours of deeper sleep. No doubt they, and several glasses of wine at the ball, would also earn him a pounding head in the morning as well. His butler's shoes echoed on the marble tiles in the hall, the reverberations making it easy to trace Jenner's progress to and from the front portico as he opened, closed and secured the heavy oak doors, twice.

At the first knock on his front door, Cayle had listened and dismissed the disturbance as inconsequential. After the second knock, a long silence had been shattered by solitary footsteps as the butler strode towards the library where Cayle sat, comfortably sprawled in an overstuffed armchair.

Despite now living in theoretically peaceful England and not having heard a stranger's tread, old habits of mistrust died hard. Cayle eased up his trouser leg and gripped the hilt of his thin bladed knife, an assurance in case his butler wasn't alone.

Jenner tapped and pushed the door open. "Your Grace."

"Yes, Jenner." Cayle relaxed his grip on the knife and sighed. He flicked his tongue around the rim of the crystal goblet, savoring the last drops of brandy. If only his new ducal status, with its never-ending demands on his time, was as palatable as his late father's well-aged liquor. "Who was at the door?"

Displaying his habitual unruffled demeanor, his butler crossed the library and deftly plucked the glass from Cayle's lax fingers before he dropped it onto his stepmother's latest extravagance, a thick Persian carpet.

"A person who demanded an audience with the Duke of Sherwyn." His butler's nose raised another notch, a seemingly impossible feat, as he placed the brandy glass on his silver tray without even the tiniest clink. "The individual was informed that

His Grace was not at home."

Cayle rubbed a hand over his tired eyes. On occasion, Jenner's puffed-up snobbishness drove Cayle mad. Yet when he wanted to be left alone, Jenner's inflexible stance at the front door was a blessing. His butler could sniff out beggars and pretenders at a hundred yards and only the highest-ranking members of the ton were invited inside these hallowed halls. If the St. Martin's lofty address failed to deter unwanted visitors, Jenner's haughty manner generally succeeded.

"Did he say why he wished to see me at this ungodly hour?"

"No, Your Grace, *she* did not enlighten me."

"She?" His feet hit the floor. "What sort of woman comes knocking on doors at this hour?" He studied his butler's stern expression. "Obviously not any of the ladies of my acquaintance."

"From her shabby attire and her insistent manner, I deduced that she was in dire need of employment. Either as a maid, in which case I advised she present herself to the housekeeper at the tradesman's entrance later in the morning, or by attracting a richer patron than her present keeper. As her appearance would offend the sensibilities of any Mayfair gentleman, such as yourself, I insisted that she immediately remove herself from Your Grace's doorstep or I would summon the watch."

"Ah, well done, Jenner," Cayle said. He hid his grin as he pushed himself to his feet with the assistance of the wide chair arms. "So, if our first visitor was so easily disposed of, who knocked the second time?"

"Of that, Your Grace, I am uncertain. The street was empty apart from a street urchin running along the pavement. I assumed the boy had knocked on our door as a prank."

Cayle strolled to the doorway and stared down the dimly lit passageway. Nothing moved. He couldn't detect any sound apart from the final sputtering of the last candles burning out.

"Most likely some boyish lark. A dare." Yet the hairs on the back of his neck stood to attention. "Though I don't doubt your capabilities, Jenner, I shall recheck the locks before I retire. It's long past time we were both in our beds."

Jenner dipped a small, stiff nod. "Indeed, Your Grace."

Cayle had privately spent three grueling months untangling the family's finances while publicly pretending to be one of his peers, lazy and without direction or ambition. But even now he had no inkling as to how Jenner regarded him. As the black sheep who'd been booted out by his father after an incident at a ball. Or the heir who'd not returned in time to stop his father send the family close to ruin when his wits became addled.

He hoped perhaps their old retainer had forgiven him and they could return to a more acceptable relationship. Though Jenner's bending spine appeared to be from a bone-deep weariness, the equivalent of Cayle's own exhaustion, rather than forgiveness of past sins.

Jenner walked with his measured steps towards the servants' quarters. He stopped halfway down the hallway and turned back. "One hesitates to speak out of turn, Your Grace, but you appear to be suffering from more than an excess of brandy and overwork this evening. Before your time abroad, your disposition was generally regarded as steady and cheerful. However, your recent somberness has been noted by the staff."

Cayle froze at such candid observations from his reserved butler. According to his stepmother, fraternizing with underlings was a sin as horrifying as dressing oneself without a valet's assistance.

Jenner spoke quietly yet his words resonated down the tomb-like passageway. "The staff has asked me to thank you, Your Grace, for working so tirelessly to restore the household and the estates to their former glory. They ... All of us, pray that Your Grace will resolve the family's difficulties quickly. Once the reputation of the St. Martin name has been re-established, we hope you may find time, once again, to see to your own happiness."

Household servants knew everything that happened and often before the inhabitants became aware of events. So it came as no surprise that the coldness between Cayle and his stepmother had been discussed below stairs. His brothers regarded Julia as Satan reincarnate and she'd certainly helped ignite the feud between Cayle and his father that had seen him dispatched to the Continent, out of sight and out of everyone's mind.

Since his return, he and Julia had made a pact. An agreement that he hoped would see her out of their lives once and for all. But she was determined to see her title of Duchess of Sherwyn returned to its, and her, former glory before she'd remove her talons from his hide. Being chained to her side on public occasions was sending him further into hell.

His brandy-mellowed mind could easily envision her so-called friends, the pretend elite of London's society, being the ones to pound on his door. Each time he attended a societal event with Julia clinging to his arm he was reminded of his responsibilities to the St. Martin name and what he owed his brothers. Julia sent ladies to his side at these events. Whispered in their ears the long list of his titles. Dangled him in front of their lemon-bleached noses like a carrot to be awarded to the greediest and grasping donkey.

Julia believed herself subtle and congratulated herself on selecting a ready-to-breed duchess who would be under her command. Under normal circumstances, Cayle would respond to these fast ladies with their none-too-subtle sexual advances with a few seductive moves. Stolen kisses at a ball that might, or might not, lead to a few pleasurable romps in the lady's bed.

He regarded his self-enforced celibacy as a temporary inconvenience, nothing more. But his stressful months were not only tormenting him mentally. His ignored physical needs had started clamoring for more attention. Solitary relief was too brief to truly satisfy him.

He missed the feel of a woman's soft body wrapped around him, and each time those women brushed his body, accidentally or on purpose, he imagined arranging an assignation. They'd meet in the conservatory. He'd lift the woman's satin skirts, push aside the layers of petticoats, and plunge, without ceremony, into her sweet body.

Then sanity would return. Julia's hawkish eyes followed every move he made as she waited for him to make another stupid mistake. To drop his guard and find himself trapped by another woman in a compromising situation.

To secure his brothers' futures, he needed to stick to his plan. That plan included avoiding women; all women.

Jenner cleared his throat. "And as an older man, might I also be so bold as to suggest that solutions to a gentleman's troubles often present themselves after a good night's sleep and without a sick head and heaving stomach."

In the half-dark, Cayle grunted his agreement.

"Apart from which," Jenner's voice rose a notch, "mindless swilling of your father's perfectly aged brandy is a gross injustice."

Jenner left and Cayle slumped against the wall. His battles with both the accounting ledgers and his ghastly stepmother must be disconcerting his staff, if his lofty butler had lowered himself to dispensing fatherly advice.

He started towards the street door, instinctively walking close to the wall and avoided the open middle path. His senses warned him of another presence, mystical or physical. As he'd made peace with the house's resident ghost when still a boy, the likely explanation was a material presence.

Well, then! He dealt with physical combat better than emotional or physic stresses. With fluid movements, he retrieved his knife, slipped past the portico doors, and edged towards the medieval laird's chair. From the dark corner came the scent of flowers, faint yet appreciable. A small shape huddled in the depth of the chair, half-concealed by the wooden arms and with scuffed boots hanging at least a foot above the floor. His uninvited visitor must be either a woman or a young lad.

His nostrils filled with flowery scents and reminded him of happier times when bouquets were picked in meadows and tied with ribbons and love. Definitely a female and one possessed of enough coin to be wearing a tantalizing and expensive fragrance. Memories stirred but he pushed them aside. Pleasurable recollections didn't belong here, in his cold hallway on this miserable night.

He peered at the chair. An old coat engulfed an undersized frame and a soft brimmed hat dipped over her face. He lowered his blade and rested the steel's tip against his thigh.

"You can come out now. We're alone."

Quiet, even breaths purred from the stationary figure. He frowned. Ridiculous idea that any she-thief would sneak into his house and fall asleep in the entrance. He bent closer. Without warning, she sucked in a breath so deep it hissed like a blacksmith's iron sizzling in water.

He jumped back and every muscle clamped like a vise as his

error, his own greenhorn foolishness, registered like a slap in the face. She was awake.

"Stand up." He raised his knife and waved it in a circle between them. "Let me see the person audacious enough to break into my house."

Taking her time, she slid off the chair and stood. The cloak, more decrepit than any respectable housemaid would wear, fell into soggy folds over her skirt. A damp dark veil drooped over the hat's brim, while from beneath the hat, bright auburn hair tumbled like a waterfall to her shoulders and wet strands clung to her cheeks. He reached out to lift her veil but she leapt back, skittish as a new foal, and banged the backs of her legs against the chair.

"I won't harm you if you behave."

Silence.

As a sign of trust between them, he lowered the knife. "But I am intrigued. Many people try to slip past my butler. Before you, they've always failed. You've obviously had a lot of practice at entering houses illegally."

No comment.

"You must be an excellent thief."

Her hands clenched at her sides. Her cloak was pushed aside when she planted her fists on her hips. "I. Am. Not. A. Thief."

Though he'd finally goaded her into speaking, her indignation barely registered. His eye was drawn to the feminine form she'd unwittingly exposed when the thin fabric of her skirt pulled tight across her stomach.

"If you're not here to steal, why go to such lengths to get inside my house."

"I needed to see you." She flicked clumps of wet hair over her shoulders. "Alone."

"And I would definitely like to see more of you."

For a second time, he tried to lift her veil. She flinched. He waited. Frustration rose as he pondered her need for obscurity. Was she a ruthless robber avoiding detection? A harlot trying to appear exotic and mysterious? Or worse, a husband-hunting miss pretending coyness to ambush a duke.

He let his eyes drift upwards from an ill-fitting brown skirt to hover where her full breasts strained against bodice fabric thinned with age and moisture. After a long appreciative look, his gaze meandered up and over those never-ending cascades of bright-colored hair.

His scrutiny might unnerve many women but this mysterious female merely huffed, stiffened her spine, and waited. Her breathing sounded louder, a little faster, yet she stood squarely and anchored her gaze around his upper chest. And took the offensive.

"I'm relieved you discovered my face at last. I was beginning to think I'd need to draw you a map."

He treated her to his most roguish and unrepentant grin. "Ah, but you see, my sweet, if you haven't come here to rob me--"

"Don't be ridiculous."

"Then, you're a puzzle. If you were better dressed, I'd assume you'd come to entertain me." He stared at her sodden and shapeless cloak and dull clothing. "Ladybirds tend to dress like peacocks. Even my maids dress better than you. And though I approve of what's on display--"

He nodded towards her chest, where her breasts squeezed up and over her ill-fitting bodice like fruit spilling from a basket. She glanced down and gasped. She tugged the bodice's folds together but managed a mere thumb's breadth. That garment obviously belonged to someone far less endowed.

"Your speech is far too refined for any street walker." He tapped a finger to his mouth. "Did my well-meaning brothers send you?"

A crease dipped between narrow brows the same hue as her hair, reddish-brown but leaning more towards red, and the coloring blend he'd always preferred.

"Your brothers?" Noticing that his eyes were roaming over her body again, she huffed and tried to tug her bodice upwards. "I wish you'd stop speaking in riddles. You're making my head spin."

With reluctance, he lifted his attention back to her face.

"I thought they might have sent you to cheer me up. Consolation for my fortitude in dealing with all this."

He waved his hand to indicate his house.

"Nonsense. You were trained from birth to take charge of all this."

Another moment of déja vu tugged at his mind. He ignored the off-putting and ill-fitting garments and tried to make out the female beneath.

His door knocker clanged for the third time.

"Bloody hell! Can I never have peace?"

He spun towards the door, eager to reach it before the knocker echoed a fourth time. Before it woke every servant in his household. Or worse. Before it roused the Dowager Duchess of Sherwyn, who'd retired an hour ago to her own expansive wing.

"No. Wait."

His still unidentified female ran behind him. She clutched the sleeve of his right arm, the one dangling his knife. As one, they looked down at the blade swinging beside his thigh. She made no sounds of terror. Nor did she recoil or tremble. He was struggling to sort out this female paradox when she tightened her grip on his arm.

"Don't open the door. Please."

"I must or they'll knock again and awaken my servants."

She clung like a limpet. "Please, I beg of you. Send them away. Don't give me up."

"Them? Who's after you? The watch?"

"I've broken no laws. Do as I ask, please. For your own safety."

He frowned at her in the dull light, trying to see past the hat and the endless hair to the woman beneath, to understand what she thought. What she plotted.

"Very well. But in return, you'll reveal yourself and explain why you're here. Agreed?"

The ugly hat bobbed twice, before she disappeared back into the shadowy corner. He opened the door, knife grip tightened, to confront the two men who stood in the rain wearing sodden coats and sheltering under black umbrellas.

The nearest of the two men stepped forward in a deliberate move to block his view of the other, raising Cayle's shackles and rousing him from apathy after his tedious night. With a quick flick, he raised his knife, circled it inches from the chest of the first visitor.

The man's loud catch of breath was music to his ears and

suited his disposition to unnerve others tonight, especially if these men threatened the woman.

"Your Grace, I'm Lord Mitchell."

Cayle ignored the extended hand. The second man pushed forward, attempting to wedge his shoulder into the doorway beside Cayle. He shifted sideways, blocked the intruder, and again waved his knife. "I know you." He pointed the blade near the man's neck. "Lord Bennett. Arthur Bennett. It's been some years since we met."

"Sherwyn." The man gave a short nod, careful to keep his neck well above the knife's reach. "Why are you opening your own door? And with a knife in your hand?"

"Why are you pounding on my door at this hour?"

"We're after the woman who was seen coming into this square, sneaking into one of the houses. We think it was this house." Bennett edged his shoulder into the small gap between Cayle's upper body and the door supports, using weight to try to bully his way into the house. "Let me inside, Sherwyn, and I'll remove her before she causes you any bother."

"Woman? What woman? Is she someone I know?" Cayle reached across and slouched against the opposite jamb, knife twirling.

Bennett flinched, and moved his umbrella into an offensive position. "Just a whore. Her name's not important." He flinched when the knife met him on eye level. "Damn you, Sherwyn. You'll cut me."

He chuckled. "No, no, no, Bennett. Not that I'm loathe to pierce your loathsome hide, mind you, but the maids get upset when I spill blood across the Italian tiles."

"Now see here, Sherwyn. You've no right to mock me. We've not even been in contact since you left England. Haven't spoken since that night." Bennett's sneering look made Cayle itch to lean closer with the blade. He'd avoided this cowardly sneak at school, and detested the namby-pamby man as an adult. Bennett leaned in and smirked. "You caused quite a scandal by seducing Lady Sybila on Hetherington's desk."

Cayle clenched his teeth, bit down on his habitual retort. No point defending himself against that charge now, not after his father died believing the lies. Hopefully, his younger brothers now knew the truth, and their opinion mattered, and no one else's.

Lord Mitchell used his elbow to forcibly shift Bennett aside. Pity. A few red drops to scrub off white tiles didn't compare to the satisfaction of pricking Bennett's self-opinionated bubble. Mitchell's mouth turned up at the edges. A peace-making smile?

More the grin of a rabid dog. "Please, excuse Lord Bennett. Overeager to locate our lost friend. We were to be entertained by a ... female acquaintance tonight."

"I take it you mean a light-skirt."

Mitchell's laugh was forced, grating. "Well, yes. A trifle embarrassing really. This agreeable ladybird promised all sorts of delights if we could offer a warm and dry gathering place nearby." He laughed, self-consciously, and again forced. "My fault. Muddled the directions. You know how it is when you've overdone the wine with dinner. Head and stomach rebel."

Cayle, his eyes pinned on Bennett, nodded at Mitchell. Jenner's ironic words of wisdom echoed in his head. 'Gentlemen who seek mindlessness by over imbibing frequently suffer embarrassing afflictions of their anatomy the next day.'

"-- agreed to meet at our friend's house." Mitchell gestured vaguely. "Down the square. Blow me down if Bennett doesn't sight the silly girl entering the wrong townhouse."

"It was this house." Bennett dipped his umbrella, wielded it like a battering ram.

Cayle scowled and stood his ground. "No, not this house."

"B-but I saw her. She slipped inside. Through someone's open door."

So, they weren't positive which door she'd entered. Excellent. Plus, Bennett's habitual cowardice could be played upon.

"Brown cloak. Brown hat," Mitchell said, using his hands to indicate the woman's size. His tone of voice had sped from conspiratorial to annoyed, in a matter of moments.

"I-I was certain she came through this door," Bennett said.

Better and better. If he was to shield the hiding woman, so near he could smell her floral bouquet, he needed to sound convincing over Bennett's confusion.

"Gentlemen. I too may have over imbibed on the brandy this evening, but not so much that I wouldn't notice a harlot walking through my door. A delightful one at that."

"Where's your butler?" Bennett said. "Perhaps he let her in by mistake."

Cayle drew himself upright to stare down at Bennett using his most ducal scowl, and was delighted when his adversary looked away first. "My butler makes no mistakes. Besides which, he's retired for the night. Only me here, and I'm for my bed." He grasped the door handle but Bennett, in a rush of bravado, thrust a booted foot into the opening. Cayle snorted, shifted his knife forward to touch Bennett a few inches above his trouser-clad knee. "Step back, or I won't be held responsible if it slips."

Bennett sucked in a loud breath. "You wouldn't dare."

He laughed. "Ha! Remember, I'm now Sherwyn. I'd dare anything."

He shoved the door closed though he resisted the temptation to slam it in their faces. He listened with his ear to the door until he heard their footsteps on the pavement. He spun around and bumped into the woman who stood directly behind him, oblivious to the water dripping from her lank hair and forming a puddle at her feet.

"Are they gone?" Her breath caught a little on the question.

"I think so." She heaved a heartfelt sigh.

"Thank you for not giving me up."

"Apart from loathing that particular man, I'd not let anyone take a woman against her will."

"There were two of them. One of you."

"I've a knife."

"Oh, please," she said in cultured tones that dripped with sarcasm. Though her hat shielded her face, he sensed that his visitor was rolling her eyes. "As your breath reeks of brandy, I suspect that you are foxed. Fortunately, I came prepared to protect myself."

Something jabbed his thigh. He looked down, squinted, frowned, and then grimaced. Cursed himself again. Ignoramus! Lack-wit! Dunderhead! From between her cloak's front folds, he caught the bright shine of metal.

A pistol, the type men concealed in coat pockets when traveling, pointed directly at his groin. Held by a small, yet remarkably steady, hand. Blind-sided by a slip of a girl! How his educators on the Continent would laugh at all his novice missteps tonight.

"So I see." Every nerve jangled and his body readied for fight, or flight. "As I value the sector of my anatomy at which your weapon is pointed far too much to argue, I'll remove my weapon. I trust you'll follow suit." He slipped his knife back into its sheath. "A gun-wielding woman makes me nervous. Mistakes happen."

"I never make mistakes." Her demeanor was far more self-assured than any thief or prostitute had a right to. "I was taught to shoot by an expert when I was a girl."

She retracted her pistol and secreted it on her person, probably in a concealed skirt pocket, and a hiding place any well-trained spy should have considered. Whew. He hadn't realized he'd been holding that breath until it whooshed out.

"Now. Who are you and what do you want?"

"You really are foxed. My disguise didn't fool those two." She waved a hand towards the street. "And whoever they had following me. Yet you! You still haven't recognized me."

He frowned. "Despite what Lord Mitchell inferred, I'm positive you're not a light-skirt. I'm guessing you're a lady of the *ton*, perhaps after a re-enactment of some amorous night we spent together in the past." He waved her away from the door and ushered her into the hallway. "But I'm mortified to say if we *were* together, it's so long ago I've forgotten."

She sighed. Disappointment or resignation? "You've forgotten all about me."

He halted her under the wall lamp. "If you're looking to renew an old friendship," he said as he trailed a finger across her décolletage, "we may be able to arrange something. But at a time when my wits are more collected." He shifted his lower body closer to her legs and leaned into her.

She raised a hand between them and backed away. She shook her head. "No, no, no." She spun towards the door. "I made a mistake in coming here. To *you*. I must leave."

She tripped, stumbled. He caught her by the arms and swung her around to face him.

"Hey. Not so fast," he said with a chuckle. "Stay and we can discuss it."

When he slid his hands down to encircle her waist, a shiver rippled down her rigid length. Fear? Why now and why from a brazen and gun-carrying housebreaker?

Two tattered leather gloves pushed in the center of his chest. She gave an ineffectual little shove. "Release me immediately!" Drawing herself up to her full height of a smidgen over five feet, she thrust out to force away his arms. She adopted her hands on hips stance and hissed out her warning. "Cayle. Saint. Martin."

"Ah, I'm touched." He put a hand to his heart. "You remember my name."

"You blind and intemperate dunderhead. Of course I know your name. As you should remember mine."

He adopted a soulful puppy expression. "Forgive me. I've had a long and tiring evening and struggle to recall my own name. Let alone guess at yours."

The little witch growled, then waggled her head. "We ... you and I..." The tiny tyrant waved an imperious hand back and forth. "Arggh! *You* were the one who taught me to shoot a pistol."

He squinted at the woman. Regretted the last brandy. And the three -- or was it more?--before it. He ripped off her ridiculous hat and pushed back the curtain of wet hair.

"Merciful heavens!" He stared, wide-eyed, at the distinctive green of her eyes and the red sheen of the drier hair on her crown. "Rebecca Jamison? Is it you? Really you?"

"Of course, it's me." She rolled her eyes. "How many girls, apart from my sisters and I, did you teach to shoot?"

"Apart from the Jamison girls?" A deep chuckle rumbled up. "None. Three of you created more than enough anxiety for any sane man." He touched her face, softly. "Good, Lord, you've changed so much."

"Of course I've changed. You've been gone for several years. In that time, I've grown. Become a woman."

He stared at the subject of his countless youthful erotic dreams. She was older, stronger, and even more defiant. Yet the lady that stood before him was a riper and more enticing version of the girl he'd known.

"Yes, you've certainly grown," he said, unable to resist another lingering look around the bounteousness of her matured figure. He swallowed, blinked, and dragged his gaze back to her face. "But what in heaven's name were you thinking, Becca? Making this hazardous, middle-of-the-night visit? Though my slightly inebriated side is enjoying the situation. You, Lady Rebecca, are an incredibly beautiful--"

A foot stomping on his tiled floor interrupted him. He dipped his head to hide his grin. Becca had always reacted that way to compliments. She'd never believed she was beautiful. Never understood that men were drawn to her as moths to a brightly burning flame.

"Please stop saying those idiotic things and allow me to speak."

For a long moment, he stood silent. Then he threw back his head and chortled, though even to his own ears his laughter rasped, sounding rusty with disuse. "Becca. Some things never change. You're the only lady I know who looks like an angel and insults like a navvy."

"Huh! Your conversations twirl more than a spinning top. They'd drive a schoolgirl to insults." She ticked off numbers on the fingers of one revolting brown glove. "First, I'm not a thief. Second, I'm not a courtesan needing coin. Third, I've never been your mistress." She looked down at her maid's drab clothes, shuddered. "And if the women you're taking to your bed dress this shabbily, I suggest you raise your standards."

He drew several shuddering breaths. "Correct, on all counts. Now, appease my burning curiosity. What deception did you employ to hoodwink my servant?"

One shoulder lifted in the semblance of a shrug. "Oh, that! A child's ploy. I laid coins on the fourth step and paid a street urchin to knock on your door and then run. When your gatekeeper bent to retrieve the coins, I slipped around the door and inside."

Incredulity, then infuriation, surrendered to mirth. The simplicity of her ruse, alongside her detached style of recounting her deception, startled him into a snort of amusement.

"Huh! My ever-vigilant butler diverted by the sight of a few pennies."

"Oh, no, not mere pennies. Gleaming new gold coins. Rest easy. Your servant's momentary distraction cost me a high price."

He lifted his hand to hide his smirk. Since he'd become Sherwyn, Jenner's behavior vacillated between extreme formality due a duke or nose-lifting disdain owed to the family's black sheep. This chink in Jenner's polished armor pleased him.

He dipped his head, and said, "I bow to your finesse as a trickster. Now for my next pressing question. Why are you here?"

"I need your assistance."

He grinned. "Ah, so once again your white knight is being asked to draw an imaginary sword and defend your ladyship's honor."

She groaned. "If only things were still as uncomplicated as in our childhood games."

He tensed, fists clenched. "Is it Bennett? That scoundrel always had a reputation for coercing innocents."

She shook her head.

"Lord Mitchell then?"

Another shake of her head. He loosened his fingers, unclenched his teeth, and forced himself to stay calm.

"No. Though as they followed me tonight, they've proved themselves to be mixed up in it."

Despite having no idea why Bennett was a threat, his fingers twitched with the urge to press his knife to the man's throat again. His instinct had always been to protect Becca. Nothing seemed to have changed there.

"Two nights ago," she said, "the woman we engaged at the Women's Betterment Society to tally the Stock Exchange ledgers -- our friend -- was murdered. The killer was still inside Peggy's house when I arrived. Her slayer stopped at the back door and stared directly at me, memorizing my features." Her pronouncement was flat-voiced, deadly calm. "Thankfully, his immediate concern was escaping with our two accounting books. But when the cache identifies me as the woman who saw their lackey's face, I am certain they will send him to dispose of me as well. They are peers, titled and wealthy, and cannot risk being exposed as members of an illegal group. If we cannot stop these men, brutes who employ cold-blooded assassins to do their dirty work, I will certainly be the next to die."

The Duke of Sherwyn's chilled blood turned to ice

Chapter 2

Becca watched Cayle. Under the rules of etiquette, she had to remember to address him as Your Grace or Sherwyn in public, despite knowing he'd abhorred the bowing and scraping as expected by dukes, including his father.

She tried to judge his level of inebriation and his reaction to her news, though she was wise enough to stay out of arm's reach. In the past, her knight in shining armor had constantly overreacted if he thought her adventures, or misadventures, placed her in harm's way.

"Please, my dear." His fists unfurled as he flung his arms wide in a dramatic gesture. "Go ahead and clarify that terrifying statement." His voice lifted another octave. "Before my hair turns completely white. Or my legs give out."

Neither Cayle's fury nor his towering size frightened Becca. But she was terrified that the city would awaken and the streets fill with people before he became calm and rational and listened to her plea for his help in collecting the final proof that would send at least a dozen of their peers to prison for illegal trading practices.

"Or even worse." He voice was a low snarl as he pointed at the floor. "I misplace the contents of my heaving stomach all over the duchess's prized carpet."

She winced. For the tenth time she listed to herself the reasons she'd bravely bearded this particular panther in his lair.

To protect her family.

To secure the nest eggs saved by the fallen women at the shelter.

To save her own life.

As the new Duke of Sherwyn, Cayle was her best, or possibly only, chance to do all that and to keep her promise to Scotland Yard. She hoped he'd listen with an open mind. Hoped he'd comprehend how much danger her family and friends were in without realizing how close she had come to also being murdered.

"I'd gone to Peggy's cottage to collect some letters she'd written on behalf of our Women's Society. The door was ajar. I knocked but Peggy didn't answer, so I went inside."

Peggy had been sprawled across the floor, her sturdy legs protruding at odd angles from her yellowing nightgown. Her hair had been matted with blood and tangled in the strings of her dislodged nightcap and her plait had been a rusty red mess instead of a neat tail of plain brown.

"I can't sleep. Every time I close my eyes, I see the murderer standing over Peggy's battered body. But he runs towards me. Not away." She shuddered and closed her eyes.

Fingers brushed her cheek. "Becca, I'll not let anyone harm you."

"If I'd only arrived at Peggy's cottage a few minutes earlier."

"Stop it. You mustn't blame yourself."

"How can I not? One life has already been destroyed because of me. My friend was killed. Her body discarded like a tattered rag doll."

His bloodshot gaze narrowed on her face. "So, knowing how your mind works, you'll try to focus the consortium on yourself, and thereby keep everyone else out of danger." He raised a brow. "Am I correct?"

Damned man was still a mind reading menace. "You're wrong. I've little wish to confront those men by myself. But neither will I allow anyone else to be hurt."

"And who protects you from the current set of fire-breathing dragons?"

She raised her chin. "I've outgrown such childishness." She lowered herself to the closest settee, a demonstration of ladylike maturity and a reprieve for her trembling knees.

"Pity." His forehead furrowed into a pained frown. "Ah. That's why you wore a disguise. And why you came so late at night."

She nodded. "The consortium watches our house and tracks our movements. In order to speak with you alone, I was forced to dress like this and sneak out the servant's entrance in the dark. Although luckily, the syndicate's inner circle doesn't want me dead. Not yet.

"Wonderful!" He glared at her. "Your blithe not yet offers such comfort to my nerves."

She glared back. "Oooh! I cannot explain if you interrupt with your sarcastic jabs."

He dipped his head, and then waved a hand. "I apologize for my uncertain temperament this evening. Please, tell me about Peggy, and what she did at your Women's Society."

"She writes -- No, she *wrote* the letters for women who wish to invest in stock ventures. We were trying to keep their identities, and their objectives, a secret."

"Why? Because they're women? Because jobbers stood for them in the Exchange?"

She raised a brow. "For someone only recently returned to London, you appear exceedingly well acquainted with the inside activities at the Exchange."

He shrugged. "I've spent every spare moment since my return settling the family's finances. Naturally, I've looked in at the Foreign Funds Room a time or two. Nobody in my position can afford to let bank balances sit idle, despite some labeling it as trade."

"I'm impressed, Cayle. You detested accounts when your father wanted you to learn."

Once more he shrugged, yet his show of nonchalance appeared overdone. "Perhaps it was more of not liking the methods of the educator, rather than the subject being taught."

She shuddered at her recollection of the late duke's disciplinary methods. "But you're correct," she said, pushing away images of birch rods twanging on bare flesh. "Some in our prudish society frown upon a gentleman of your caliber frequenting auction rooms. But, for a woman, it'd be an outrage."

His eyes fixed upon her, all signs of his earlier fatigue vanished. "I can well imagine."

"Though legally nothing prevents a woman from owning shares," she said, assessing his concentration by the tense way he held his long, muscled body. "Visiting members are vetted at the door. Bank managers and jobbers pay eight guineas a year to enter the main Exchange room, yet self-righteous men evict females."

"So, is it your gender that sees you under threat?"

"Not merely our gender. When the consortium heard we invested in secret, and often did very well, at first they became alarmed. Then, they became angry. Very angry indeed."

"I can well imagine men abhorring being bested by a female."

"Exactly. Therefore, we utilize Foster and Braithwaite as our agents and invest through them using the minimum identification on any documents."

"Impressive. I heard that Foster and Braithwaite's business grew twelve fold in the last few years by riding on railway stocks."

"Hence, our problem. Their profits, our profits, became legendary. People speculated about the mysterious names on share certificates." At his puzzled look she added, "Simple enough. We draw up letters. Ladies sign with their initials and family name, nothing more, so no one realizes the investors aren't men. Or rather, no one did before."

"And now?"

"Two weeks ago, some members of the outer circle approached my brother, Michael. They believe him to be personally responsible for our own change in fortune."

"How big a change in fortune?"

"Oh, nothing too major." She waved a hand in a vague manner and hoped her face didn't flush. "Modest successes. Dividend rates in excess of six percent in some situations."

His eyebrows shot upwards. "Six percent! Nobody I do business with calls that modest. No wonder they wish to obliterate all reference to your family, and your Society."

"Yes, if only we'd been able to keep our good fortune a secret. We take the uttermost care with our clandestine activities, as we value our privacy and our reputations."

He raised a brow and pointed at his clock. "Oh, yes. Great care with your reputation!"

She chose to ignore him. "Michael laughed it off. Refused to join their so-called group of friends who dabbled in investing. So they raised the stakes. If he refuses to hand over m ... his calculations for all the new railway share ventures opening, within the next two weeks, they vowed to destroy the members of his family. One by one, until he gives in."

"Ah, now I understand. That's why they're keeping you alive. They're waiting to acquire the records. They assume as eldest, and involved in a charitable society, you hold the most knowledge of..." When he mumbled, she stiffened. Did he guess? "Of Michael's future stock predictions. Then, when they have all they require, they'll kill all--"

"Yes, yes, I know. They'll dispense with us regardless." She lifted her chin a notch. "But I can resolve this situation. Given a little more time, plus a little assistance from you."

"Ah! Back to the crux of the matter. What you require from me."

He widened his stance, pushed back his coat tails and leaned on one hip, though the intensity in his eyes belied his casual pose. Eyes that shone as black and mysterious as an eastern sultan's eyes pierced, probed, and penetrated to the depth of her soul. She shivered. Against the backdrop of a richly embellished Mayfair house, Cayle appeared like a demon-god who could breach the defenses of mere mortals, including her, with one dark look. Ridiculous fancy.

"As the Duke of Sherwyn, you've entree into the best houses and social events."

After a scowl towards the ceiling, he muttered, "Thanks to my stepmother, I'm forced into it. But what does my recent social popularity have to do with your current predicament?"

"In daylight, with other ladies, I can stroll about the streets. Visit shops, sometimes slip unnoticed into the twice-weekly stock auctions at the Hall of Commerce in Threadneedle Street. And I've already searched the desks of many of the mere misters and lesser peers of the lower orders of the consortium, as their houses aren't guarded like fortresses."

"Do you mean to say you entered these men's homes and rifled their papers?"

"Well yes, but--"

"Are you mad?"

"I risked little, because those sort of houses cannot afford a footman guarding every passageway. Especially not on occasions such as those I attended, where every footman is needed to fetch drinks for belligerent guests. Slipping into those libraries was child's play." She sighed. "What I cannot do is visit the homes of the highest ranking peers to scour their correspondence for any that bears the special seal of the consortium. Nor secure enough privacy to copy any incriminating letters I may find. Someone always hovers, and watches, at those type of houses."

He paced before her like a restless panther, an angry scowl pulling his face taut. His fine looks had always turned heads, but this brooding beast carried a lethal combination of strength and menacing masculinity. She shivered. His newly acquired arrogance of bearing enhanced, rather than detracted from, his magnetism, although this time, she knew to avoid his magnetic pull.

"You intend searching the houses of every peer in the city who is making money from stock shares?"

"No, no, not all of them. We've done a lot of research--"

"We?"

"My family have become quite adept at research. We've narrowed our search to gentlemen known to invest in railway expansions in a large way. Our final list is of those we consider to be involved in the inner, and most secret, tier of the syndicate. It contains eighteen names, the majority of whom are high-ranking peers."

"Bloody hell, Becca." He ground the expletive out through clenched teeth. "You're out of your depth. I've been involved in similar commercial groups. They'll stop at nothing for the sake of money."

"Nevertheless, we need certain details you may overhear at clubs about certain gentlemen having sudden windfalls. Or things gleaned at certain balls and soirees.

"Unbelievable." Both hands went up in the air. "That's *certainly* as clear as muddy water."

"Clear or not, I'm asking you to trust me. To help me." She held out both hands, palms up, and hoped he wouldn't notice their tremors. "With your assistance, I can verify more names. Collect proof of each one's involvement and hand it over to Scotland Yard. Time is of the essence, as we've now less than two weeks."

She watched him absorb, assess, decide. In under a minute, he guided her to his desk and seated her before it. "Make a start. List the names of every man you suspect to be a member." He placed writing materials before her. "Then list those you consider inner tier, and include their ranking."

He walked away, leaned on the mantelpiece, waited, a too-poignant reminder of the last time he'd walked away in silence. In her naïveté, she'd imagined their carefree youth, their first love, predestined a lifetime together. Stupid, stupid fool.

This powerful new duke, stalked by every husband-hunting chit and matchmaking mama, and invited to prestigious social events, was far above her touch. Her chest pained with the sharp slice of loss.

Moisture pooled in her eyes so she squeezed them shut, rubbed them with closed fists. She focused on the reasons she'd entered his residence unchaperoned. To safeguard her family and, if possible, warn her childhood champion of his future entrapment. Nothing else.

He walked back, frowned, and pointed to the blank foolscap.

"Go on, then. Names, titles, levels. What do they call it? An alliance?"

"A circle or a coterie, with tiers of membership." She sketched a cartwheel with radiating spokes. "Larger rings of membership decrease to a smaller number of the inner elite, the ones who hold the real power. The most desperate and the most evil."

"Add a column for any specifics about each of them. Next, write what evidence the Yard requires as absolute proof to take these men to trial. If they hold titles, they'll demand exemption from incarceration, exclusion from public trial, and use every trick to avoid charges. Also, list the railway stocks you -- or rather -- Michael, plans to buy."

He grinned at her, pesky man. No doubt he saw through her ruse over who formulated their share plans, but for now she chose to ignore that, too.

"Time was obviously spent calculating the best mathematical outcome on each locality, and forecasts plotted for their suitability for expansion. I assume that's in those ledgers, the ones these men thought would be kept in Peggy's cottage."

"I cannot disclose details of the investments Michael is planning for the women. Not yet." She wrote details of the syndicate in her columns and then pushed the paper towards him. "The less you know, the less the danger. For you, and for my family." She folded her hands in her lap and adopted her best big-sister-do-as-I-say voice. "You may explain any further concerns you have to my family tomorrow morning."

"I'm to meet your family? Huh! Is that a request? Or another of Lady Rebecca's royal commands."

"Stop being difficult." He grinned. She stomped her foot but, despite heavy maid's boots, she made no satisfying sound on the dratted extra-thick carpet. His grin widened until every white tooth gleamed in the firelight.

Her jaw was so rigid she could barely spit out words. "You ... are ... still ... the most exasperating man I've ever met."

She marched to the settee and plunked down.

"Easily explained." He stalked after her and threw himself down beside her. "I'm the only man who's ever dared question your ladyship's orders."

She inched further along the settee and pointed a finger at him. "Regardless, you will present yourself at Jamison House in Grosvenor Square at precisely ten o'clock."

"So to satisfy my inquisitiveness, I must obey -- without question -- your ever-so-sweetly worded request? Despite the fact that I'll get no sleep tonight because I'll be imagining you being slaughtered in your bed."

Leaning forward, he angled his face closer until she was forced to scrunch into the corner. His nose came close enough to her neck that she could feel the warmth of his breath. It blew across her skin below her ear and goose flesh rippled in its wake. He inhaled deeply before giving a long and sensual moan.

Her throat constricted and her pulse raced. "Wh ...what...a...are...you..."

She couldn't finish her stuttered question. After five years alternately cursing him or forgiving him over his rushed departure and her consequent misery, she'd recently been congratulating herself on her more mature attitude. She spoke of the *incident* between Cayle and her cousin_as a strengthening exercise every young and naive girl should experience if she was expecting to find a suitable marriage partner.

"What am I doing? Why am I near you?"

She shook her head, vigorously, and resisted the childish urge to cover her ears so she didn't have to listen to his reasons. Her declarations to her sisters that seeing Cayle wouldn't upset her had quickly been proved to be false bravado. After this brief time in his presence, her head spun, her senses reeled, and old yearnings had revived with a vengeance.

"I remember your smell. Like the wildflowers you gathered. Strong and wild." His voice purred in her ear, a well-remembered seduction. She swallowed and prayed her shivers would pass unnoticed.

"Being near you calms my shattered nerves."

"More nonsense! Your nerves were always rock solid."

The tip of his cool tongue touched her heated skin. Shock, surprise, and wonder turned her into a wide-eyed statue.

"I also want to know if you taste the same."

She wriggled away and jumped to her feet, tugging at her skirt to free it from under his leg. "Of course I taste the same."

The disconcerting man stayed seated but lifted his hand towards her.

"If I touch your skin, will it still feel silky smooth? Soft like velvet?"

"No, no, no." She held up her hand, palm out, and backed away. "You cannot touch me. And you certainly cannot taste me. We may have been close in the past, but you severed our relationship. Rather cruelly, in fact."

He sighed. "I prayed that you'd understand why I had no choice. My father convinced me that leaving England would ensure that your family, and mine, could still hold their heads high. It was the only honorable thing to do. I hoped you'd forgive me. Eventually."

She nodded with as much emphasis as she'd shaken her head minutes before. "No. I mean, yes. I no longer care about the past. I learned from my mistakes. Moved on."

He flinched. "Is that all I was, Becca? A mistake?"

"Our kissing was a mistake. One never to be repeated."

He smirked. "On the contrary, my little innocent, we will repeat it. Soon, very soon." Rising to his feet, he gave her a taunting look. "Though I remember a lot more than kissing."

Memories had her body stirring and awakening. She clenched her fists and scowled but words failed her.

"Naturally I was referring to dancing and riding. Perhaps you mistook me to mean certain other things?"

Her face heated. Dratted revealing complexion! "If I recall anything else,' she said, moving backwards to prevent their torsos touching, "it merely reminds me that men are untrustworthy."

He groaned. "My intentions were honorable, Becca." He reached for her. "I could blame it all on bad timing and scheming women but I should never have left." He pressed nearer until her nostrils filled with his well-remembered aroma of musky spices.

His lips hovered a scant breath from hers. Dark eyes pierced her soul. "Please accept my belated apology."

Nothing was going to plan. She'd swallowed her damaged pride to ask for his assistance. Determined to be courteous, yet distant, in order to get the help her family needed. Instead, he'd offered a few repentant words, some soft touches, and she quaked.

If she was to avoid more heartbreak, she needed to bury any soft feelings and think rationally, like the men she pitted her wits against. Like the man standing before her. If she wanted to keep men at a distance, she should have approached another peer, any other peer. If she were sensible, she'd turn and run for her life.

But his large hands clasped her waist and held her motionless. He dipped his head and covered her lips with his. They were warm, enticing, coaxing her response. She shivered in his arms and he deepened and widened the kiss until she drowned in a sea of sensations.

Though she wasn't alone. All signs of Cayle's earlier foggy-headed lethargy vanished as he bent unerringly to her mouth for a second time. By the way his body hardened and responded, he was also remembering.

She twisted away and sucked in a deep breath. A feeble attempt at breaking his spell so she could uphold the vow she'd made years ago.

Never to let herself be fooled by a man again.

She circled the settee and shook her head. Undeterred, he followed.

"N-no, no, enough," she said, even as his long sigh of regret tugged at her softer side. Heaven help her, she was doomed.

Cayle moved with her. He blocked every one of Becca's meager attempts at escape. "Not enough for me, my reticent friend."

Without giving her, or him, time to think, he tugged her against him, too desperate for the feel of her to consider his actions.

"One taste is not nearly enough. Show me you remember how I taught you to kiss."

"I was younger then. I no longer enjoy such fripishness."

He spluttered. "Fripishness? Is that even a word?"

"It is a word, if I say it is," she announced, as she tried to wriggle out of his grasp.

Pretty little teeth popped out to worry her bottom lip. One front tooth was slightly off kilter, different like her. Her views were as unique as her wild mop of red curls or her freckled nose. Only she could add a completely ridiculous word to the English language, and make it seem as if it belonged. She raised her haughty nose.

"Within a month, the ton will be repeating it at every gathering."

He threw back his head and laughed until he shook.

"All right. It's probably not a real word and the likelihood of anyone of refinement copying it is remote. People will label it yet another strange thing I've done."

A well-remembered urge to protect her from cruel detractors, to bolster her self-confidence, struck him. "I, however, think fripishness is a delightful word. I shall use it whenever possible."

She snickered. "Society will assume Sherwyn has joined the Jamisons in Bedlam. If you're shrewd you'll deny acquaintance with me, especially if you wish to add new sparkle to your previously tarnished character."

The thought disturbed him despite the truth in her supposition. In order to reach his goals within the next year, he needed to remove any lingering blemish from the St. Martin name. Only by adhering to Julia's contract would they be free from her incessant greed.

Regardless, he yearned for a taste of Becca's passion. He edged closer and she retreated. "You're not really afraid of me, are you?"

"Of course not! Besides, I do have a gun, remember?" She shuffled backwards in tiny movements she thought unnoticeable. Unhappily for her, he was attuned to every movement.

"I'm not likely to forget a pistol pointed at my most valued assets. We're sharing a few simple kisses. Harmless."

"Kisses are never simple." She turned her head, not meeting his eye. "I've read treatises on bodily urges in the animal kingdom. Research shows males frequently behave in an inappropriate manner when suffering from unrelieved urges."

She'd rendered him speechless. Had society misses changed so much, become so brazenly outspoken, or was it only Becca and her inquisitive mind who researched such topics?

"Have mercy. Spare me your scientific opinions on my--"

"Masculine needs?"

The irritating woman was using scientific logic to rationalize his behavior. Though he'd heard the husky catch in her voice.

"You know nothing of my needs, physical or otherwise."

"Poppycock. I know more than you imagine."

He clutched his head. "I pray that's an exaggeration."

"Our second footman is cousin to--" She waved her hand. "I don't want to make things awkward--"

"One of my servants is a spy and you're worrying about it being awkward?"

"It's not as if we pay for our information." Her wide-eyed look of innocence didn't fool him for a moment. "That would be bribery."

Fascinated despite himself, he said, "So why do people spy for you?"

"Someone always has a female relative or friend who needs assistance from the Women's Betterment Society. A helping hand along a financially independent path."

"You get information by taking one of these women under your wing. Interesting. So what did your illegal source say about me?"

"Only that you're circumspect in your social habits." He raised a brow. "You accompany your stepmother in public. No hint of scandal." She held her head high and sounded strong and sure, yet her hands shook with tiny tremors. "Now though, we need more. We'd like you to collect information for us. When you receive invitations to certain upcoming social events, I'll inform you of certain items we need retrieved from those houses."

"Which *certain*--give me strength! Now I'm using that confounded word. And by retrieved, I assume you mean--stolen."

She frowned. "Stolen sounds so ... criminal. We think of it as paper slipping into coat pockets. By mistake."

He hid his grin. "Well, in exchange for wearing coats with large pockets for things to slip into, I shall require something. To compensate me for the risk if I'm caught."

"Ah, ha! Laura said you'd taunt me, or demand something, for old time's sake."

"Is your sister still outrageous and outspoken?"

"I'm afraid so." She laughed, a beautiful lilting sound. "Probably even more so than before. She's researching the habits of men regarding--"

"Regarding?" He raised a brow, intrigued by what caused that bright red blush to her cheeks now, whereas earlier discussions of courtesans didn't.

"Mmm. Well, um, she's studying how men conduct their affairs. Of the heart. And the bedchamber." Her small hands twisted her skirt into tight folds. "She strongly believes all women should understand what they are getting. Before they enter marriage."

"Testing the waters before she takes a leap of faith?" After her small nod, he asked, "And do you subscribe to her hypothesis? Perhaps already tested Laura's theories?"

"That is none of your business."

"Ah, but as recompense for stealing documents, you will answer my questions."

Her loud gasp was music to his ears. His smirk turned into a full-blown grin.

"Because you and I, Becca, shall test Laura's theories -- together."

Chapter 3

The Duke of Sherwyn groomed with care for his appointment in Grosvenor Square. Under his morning coat, he wore a deep blue waistcoat with an Albert chain securing his gold watch in the fob pocket and fashionably tapered trousers. A twice-about white neck cloth gave him a jauntier look, compared to the severity of dress he'd favored of late. Setting out, Cayle smirked in anticipation of the forthcoming battle with the formidable Jamisons, all of whom used to be as ramshackle and quick-witted as Becca.

After dispatching her in his carriage, he'd hailed a hackney and visited his three compatriots from the Continent, recruiting their assistance in unraveling the consortium. He'd allocated them tasks, relieving their boredom with their new English lives, and snatched an hour's sleep before their breakfast meeting. His friends had scurried about the City as busily as a pleasure garden doxy and many questions already had answers.

Discovering the names of the outer circle, the men advancing money into railway extensions, proved as simple for them as visiting clubs and striking up conversations. Gratifying. Because today he'd need to stay a few paces ahead of Becca in intelligence levels, or she'd treat him like an errand boy -- a foot soldier in her army.

Grosvenor Square, with quiet streets and parkland, spoke of inherited holdings, although not as salubrious as the colonnaded residences of Mayfair or as esteemed as Belgravia. Stately, not overstated. Peering up at the curtained bay windows, Cayle recalled his last visit to Jamison House when relationships had been harmonious. Anguish assailed him.

He braced himself, strode up the newly scrubbed steps and rapped the brass knocker, three times. Last night's lapse could be blamed on on-going tedium endured at Julia's hands, plus too much drink. Another strong knock. This morning, he'd present a firm front before forbidding Becca from placing herself in further danger. After acquiring the incriminating documents and freeing Becca from threat, he'd retreat with a clear conscience and no emotional involvement. Those excellent intentions lasted all of a minute.

The door was opened, not by the expected dour butler, but by the most dazzling beauty he'd ever set eyes upon. Beneath sea-blue eyes, the apparition's smile outstripped the brightest London sun, a muslin dress matched her eyes, and slippers, the same hue and embroidery-decorated, peeped out like shy children from a froth of petticoats. In absent-minded futility, he rubbed the ache in his chest and willed voice into his dry throat.

"Lottie, I've told you before," a scolding voice called from the house's interior. "When in the City, allow Thompson to attend the door."

Guileless eyes gazed up at him as she addressed the person hovering behind her shoulder. "Thompson is speaking with three of our men at the kitchen door. They're reporting on the latest movements of our suspected consortium members."

The owner of the awe-inspiring countenance and sweet voice stepped back to allow him a glimpse of the other speaker. Oh, heaven save him! He'd leered at a chit who must be Becca's sister, Lottie. Slavered like an adolescent at his first glimpse of a streetwalker's bosom while Becca lowered her brows and shot him a scathing look.

"Stop gaping like a gauche boy, so I may reacquaint you with Lady Charlotte Jamison."

The young lady bobbed a curtsy, smiled, while he stammered. "I-I'm pleased--"

"Sherwyn! Pull yourself together. Lottie is beautiful. Extraordinarily so. Even so, we've no time for you make a fool of yourself over my sister. My much younger sister."

Becca linked arms with her sister and, without a backward glance, marched down the hallway. He followed, cursing his stupidity in flaunting his reactions before Becca, of all people. When he walked into the drawing room, he noticed every face carried an identical expression of amusement. Ah! He was the brunt of a family joke.

The lone male grinned as he strode towards him. "Sherwyn." He extended his hand. "Michael Jamison. Grisham, if you prefer. Not sure if you remember me. I'd have been at Eton when you last visited our home."

"I remember all the family." He shook the proffered hand. "My brothers and I spent many happy hours in your woods. But let's dispense with formality. I still prefer Cayle."

"Though Sherwyn in public." The older lady was seated in an armchair that strained to hold her ample form. "You gallantly wielded the sword on Becca's numerous adventures. If you recall, I'm great-aunt to this unruly group. You may call me Aunt Aggie, as they do."

He bowed towards the cheerful older lady. She waved her pudgy hand towards the young woman standing nearby and gave a girlish giggle. "By your stunned expression, I assume you've seen our darling Lottie."

Schooling his expression, he turned to face their unorthodox door attendant. "Indeed, I have." Giving him a radiant smile, she dropped into a fluid curtsy. "Lady Charlotte." He dipped his head and fixed his eyes on the floor near her feet.

A pair of tiny boots appeared in his line of vision and one foot tapped a brisk beat. "Lottie, please stand a prudent distance away from the duke so he may regain his composure."

He shifted to allow Lottie to move past with a swish of blue skirts. From the corner of his eye, he detected a brewing storm in a pair of green eyes and inwardly groaned.

Michael stepped up and clapped him on the back. He was openly laughing. "Don't feel badly, Sherwyn. Lottie affects every man that way. We liken her to one of those fabled man-eating insects. Lottie entices men with her smile. Stuns them with her beauty. Sucks them dry."

"Michael." Aunt Aggie clutched her abdomen. "That vile image will destroy our appetites for luncheon."

The siblings shared amused glances. Their aunt's rotund figure belied the notion of anything spoiling her appetite.

Lottie spoke from her position near the window. "You cannot lay the blame at my feet. Men can be so stupid. They rush to divulge their secrets to me thinking I will be impressed." She clasped her hands as if in prayer and gave a much put-upon sigh. Every member of the family rolled their eyes. "Men refuse to see that women are intelligent, so I merely accept that and allow them their moments of self-delusion."

Her sickly sweet smile earned her a collective groan from her siblings.

"Lottie," Michael said, "you lure gentlemen like flies to a spider's web. Not that we're objecting. We appreciate every piece of gossip you extract from their numbed brains."

Lottie looked towards Cayle and smiled. She purred like a seductive jaguar. "I'll gladly listen to your secrets too."

Thankfully he was saved from more embarrassment when Aunt Aggie clucked her tongue. "Save your wiles for the gentlemen in the park. You'll have enough victims from our list there. Leave poor Cayle alone."

Before he had a chance to question that strange comment, an ear-splitting screech erupted. A whirlwind of skirts skidded through the door.

Aunt Aggie waved her arm towards the new arrival. "I'm certain you recall our resident bundle of energy, Lady Laura Jamison. Do make your bow quietly, Laura. Your ceaseless noise hurts my ears."

Laura stepped closer, forgoing a curtsy in favor of scrutinizing him from head to toe. "Cayle St. Martin. Or must I, Your Grace you to death?" With a cheeky grin and a lift of her brow, she said, "Goodness, you've changed. In a most flattering way."

He couldn't help but chuckle.

"Still, I recognized you instantly at the Murchison's the evening before last. Not that you recognized me, because I've changed, too. See?"

Laura lifted her skirts and twirled, almost landing on his toes. Despite having another tantalizing goddess standing before him, he blanked his expression and refused to react when she fluttered her long dark lashes, a deliberate taunt.

"Lady Laura. A pleasure to meet you again."

She laughed, a full-throated seduction in itself. "You're telling fibs, Cayle. You thought me a dreadful pest when I shadowed you and Becca everywhere you went."

"Laura, you're still a nuisance," Michael muttered. "Leave the poor man alone. Being subjected to you three girls en masse threatens a man's constitution. Jonathon and I describe our sisters as *raising the flag*." When Cayle looked blank, Michael said, "Their collective hair -- Becca's red, Lottie's white, and Laura's raven wing blue black -- resembles the colors of the navy's ensign. And they're twice as dangerous as the Admiral's fleet."

"Uh hum!" Becca cleared her throat several times, loudly. "Now that His Grace--"

"Becca." Cayle smirked. "We were far less formal last night. In fact, you--"

"Cayle!" Becca's eyes flashed fury. "Let Laura tell us what Thompson and the other men learned. Then we shall speak. Alone."

Aunt Aggie clapped her hands. "Tea first. I simply must have nourishment before we set to work."

Becca rolled her eyes, but the other ladies dispensed tea and food as seamlessly as well-rehearsed dance moves. Michael and Cayle accepted tea but refused sustenance so soon after breakfast. When Lady Jamison's eyes lit with pleasure at the selection of biscuits the girls placed on her plate, the men shared a conspiratorial grin over the older lady's larger appetite.

Michael quietly asked Cayle, "Did Becca explain about the Women's Financial Aid Society?"

"Only that the ladies assisted women in financial distress."

"Huh! That's Becca's simplistic view. She and Laura founded the Society, but now the whole family helps."

"Becca is terrified that Peggy's murderer will target the rest of you. If I'm to help you identify the ringleaders of this consortium, I need to understand your recent financial decisions. Why you began trading in railways stocks. Where you get your information."

He didn't mention the other secrets Becca seemed to be hiding. No need for Michael to know what else he was delving into.

Michael sighed. "Becca decided that if our father wasn't going to arrange for Laura and Lottie to have a season, we should do it. She didn't want them to miss out the way she had."

"Becca missed having a season altogether? I knew it hadn't been managed before I left."

"She and Laura entered society in a low-key way a year ago. Until then--" Michael glanced away. He met Cayle's eyes again and shrugged. "Our father's only interest in the household is making sure the budget stretches enough to pay for his next archaeological expedition. And now." He glanced over at his elder sister.

"Becca thinks she's too long in the tooth. That Laura or Lottie will be swamped with offers because they are beautiful. Then a man--" Michael shook his head. "A damned rogue. Treated her dreadfully. She forbade me from calling him out. Didn't want any gossip around her sisters."

Cayle loathed himself even more now. He should have ignored his father's orders and stayed in England. Stayed with Becca. He should have been keeping Becca and her sisters safe.

"This rogue, who was he?"

"Ahem." Becca's foot tapped a loud and impatient rhythm on the floor. She glared at Michael, making her displeasure clear and silently forbidding her brother from sharing any more of their secrets. She looked strong and ferocious and she wasn't ready to trust him. His grown Becca was a force to be reckoned with.

His Becca? Oh, no. A disastrous idea. They'd barely become reacquainted yet, as always, his instinct was to claim the impudent minx as his. And this time he wasn't running across meadows to slay dragons for a young girl. He had a clear picture of her attached to him in a different way.

A woman, naked and clinging. Their limbs entwined as they played adult games across silken sheets. And the sword that jumped to readiness wasn't hewn from wood but from his own aroused flesh.

His breeches felt tight and constricting. He swung his gaze away from the redheaded temptress and stared out the window. Instead of standing in a Mayfair drawing room, he imagined himself under a mountain waterfall. Icy cold water drenching him.

When he turned back, Laura was watching him with a far-too-knowing smile. Lottie gave him a tiny wave. He looked at Becca. Bloody hell. Her eyebrows were raised, her lips pursed, and she stared at him with a mix of interest and disapproval.

He resisted the urge to glance down and check his trousers, but instead widened his stance and readjusted his coat tails. Better to err on the safe side, his mother used to say. He hoped to God these ladies were too innocent to understand the cause of his discomfort, but all three were surveying him as if considering his potential as a stud stallion. Thank heavens, Michael took pity upon him.

"Would you three stop it? You're embarrassing Sherwyn." He turned to Laura. "I blame you for this unladylike behavior. You compare every man to the ones written about in those risqué sensational novels you buy. Men won't see you as innocents. They'll consider you women of the world and try to take advantage."

Laura smirked. "I, for one, am glad we're not ignorant girls. We've met enough cads, from both the lower and higher classes, that we'll not fall under the spell of any sweet-talking man. At least, not ever again."

Cayle's senses prickled as all eyes turned to him. He felt like a fox caught in the hen house. Or a lone duck surrounded by sharp shooters.

"Isn't that true?" Laura asked the question, but they all stared at their elder sister. Her normally pale complexion had washed out to the gray of bed sheets at a slovenly inn.

Lottie shuffled closer to her sister's rigid form. "Laura meant no disrespect," she murmured. She unfolded Becca's fingers, one by one, until they released their grip on the muslin folds of her skirt.

Cayle stepped closer to hear Lottie's soft words.

"You did nothing wrong, Becca." The sunlit color of Lottie's hair against her sister's cheek made Becca's face appear even whiter. "You couldn't have prevented what happened."

A small, strained silence settled. He took the chance to ask at least one of his questions. "What did happen?" No one spoke. "Is this to do with that scoundrel, Bennett?"

Aunt Aggie tut-tutted loudly several times and shot him a withering look. Mistrustful gazes speared him from every direction. Apparently, they linked him with Becca and Bennett. Accusation and blame showed on every face. Especially Becca's.

She'd been his best friend, the one he turned to when escaping his father's wrath. And he'd do anything to see her expression turn from misery to joy. Even perhaps, embrace another scandal.

Becca gave Michael a small nod. A sign to continue their discussion.

"The consortium wants our journals. Those stock forecasts

took us months to correlate. We need the income from them as desperately as the syndicate does. If Laura and Lottie are to--"

"Michael!" Becca snapped at her brother. "Cayle doesn't need to know every detail of our lives."

"On the contrary. The better informed I am, the better chance I'll have of insinuating myself into the outer coterie. And then, hopefully, the inner circle. Isn't that what you wish me to do?"

Becca glared at Cayle, not willing to give an inch.

Laura grinned. "I'm sure Cayle can be trusted to keep all our secrets. Our lists are predictions of new railway tracks being laid. When and where. In England or abroad. If the consortium uses those lists and beats us to the punch, it will be like stealing our money. And the money of all the minor investors."

"Those small investors will also become liabilities." Lottie shook her golden hair. "Expendable. Like us."

Tears trickled down Aunt Aggie's plump cheeks. "Dozens of families will be destitute. Thrown out of their lodgings. Children will starve."

"So what are those men you employ doing?"

Becca grimaced. "Visiting places that ladies are unable to go. Collecting information from banks, newspapers, and share record offices."

"Mr. Brown followed the Baron to his meeting with Lord Stevens and Lord Lindley at a tavern on the east side," Laura said. "There were three others whom Mr Brown labeled disreputable. His boys asked in the nearby alehouses. Those roughnecks dig into the pasts of everyone who defies the syndicate. Gambling debts. Mistresses. The consortium then blackmails people into joining them, or keeping quiet."

Michael scowled. "Which is why they've allowed me some breathing room. They searched Peggy's cottage, not only for the ledgers, but to find some scandalous information. About us. Or her."

Becca's moan cut Cayle to the quick. When he caught the killer, and he would, the man would suffer. For Peggy's murder and for tormenting Becca.

"But our dear, dear Peggy held no horrid secrets." Aunt Aggie sniffed and groped for her soggy handkerchief. "She was another innocent pawn in their nasty games."

"We're now sure the inner circle started this blackmail scheme," Laura said. "People are coerced into handing over money. With no written security. In exchange, their secrets are supposed to remain hidden. I doubt that legitimate share certificates are even issued."

"Aunt Aggie and I learned on Bond Street that the leaders target a wide range of the community," Lottie said. "They visit all the major shopkeepers to coerce them into investing their nest eggs."

"The syndicate will be pressuring the Exchange." Cayle addressed the room in general. "Have they bought any stock certificates before the official release dates?"

Becca eyed him with suspicion. "Such a large group may be forcing the Exchange to bend the rules. Or bribing them. We don't know yet." Becca walked over to him. "So how do you know so much about it?"

Michael eyed Cayle with mistrust. "Yes. You seem to have plenty of ideas on what the syndicate is doing."

Cayle shrugged. "Becca and I have already discussed your journals. And the battle over share certificates."

"I don't remember saying--"

"You were a little flustered at the time."

Becca scowled at Cayle. Damn the man! The cad was daring her to retaliate in front of her family. He'd thrown her into a spin with talk of kissing or tasting her.

She'd trembled when he'd sniffed her neck and touched his lips to hers. Heat was creeping up her neck. Again.

"I was not flustered." She willed her flush to cool and recede.

"Very well, I lied." A collective gasp sounded around the room. "Becca revealed so little that it aroused my suspicions. So I asked some friends to do more investigating after Becca left."

"But it was the middle of the night." She heard herself admit that aloud and wished the ground would open up and swallow her.

Aunt Aggie squawked, a cross between shock and horror. "Young lady, we shall discuss that impropriety later."

Becca glared at Cayle. Aunt Aggie wasn't a true stickler for propriety but she insisted that her nieces adhere to some of the rules of good behavior in order to protect them. An unchaperoned visit to a gentleman's home in the middle of the night broke every rule. The duke smiled at her. The manipulative man was fully aware of the hornet's nest he'd stirred.

"I know your major income comes from transport. Factories building engines and railways."

"How did you find that out in the middle of the night?" Becca forgot that her family were listening and adopted her most sarcastic tone. "I imagine you were compelled to visit several brothels before you found enough drunken gentlemen to speak with. Or perhaps the prostitutes were willing to share things with a wealthy duke."

"Rebecca!" Aunt Aggie cried. "Please remember your innocent sisters are present."

Michael snickered. "Innocent--" he began, to be cut off by Aunt Aggie's withering look. "Beg your pardon, aunt. But one can hardly call Laura and Lottie innocent."

Cayle edged closer to Becca to murmur so only she could hear, "And no, my green-eyed friend, I didn't visit any brothels in person. I left that entertainment to my friends."

She gasped before whispering back to him, grateful that the attention of her family was focused on her aunt. "If you're insinuating I'm in any way jealous, you're mistaken. You may visit as many women as you feel necessary to relieve your --" She waved a hand. "Your problem."

"My sweet, my interest is focused entirely on one woman. You!" Becca shook her head and then stepped away from him as he resumed the discussion by announcing to her family, "I've just assured Becca that it was my friends who called in to Scotland Yard for the latest details on Peggy's death. And who informed me about your railway interests. So now, I'm eager to know more."

Four sets of eyes watched them with concentration and four sets of ears followed the conversation with amusement. "It was wrong of you, Becca, to downplay the danger. When I mistook your disguise to be the costume of a common street walker--"

Aunt Aggie waved her damp handkerchief. "Pray continue. You mistook our innocent Becca--"

"Innocent!" Cayle spluttered. "She led me on like--" He had

the grace to look embarrassed. "I'd over-imbibed and my judgment was a trifle skewed."

Aunt Agatha replied, "And, yet, you still kissed her."

Ignoring the collective gasps, he said in a strained voice, "Yes, I kissed Becca, after I realized who she was. Inexcusable behavior." He bowed to Michael. "I request an audience to discuss your sister's future." Ignoring Becca's outraged gasp, he added, "In private."

"No need for that," Michael assured him. "I trust you."

Becca's irritation escalated threefold when Cayle attempted to take Michael's arm and maneuverer him towards the door. No doubt he sought a private discussion between gentlemen.

Employing her most mocking voice, she halted his departure. "Good gracious, Cayle. When did you become such a stickler for propriety?"

With a grim expression, he turned back to face them. "When my father died. When I inherited a title. When I became a duke."

Silence reigned. Her family watched him with anticipation. When he failed to fulfill their expectations of information, Aunt Aggie began an animated recital of his recent family history for the benefit of Laura and Lottie.

"Growing up, you thumbed your nose at such conventions even more than the rest of us," Becca said. "What happened?"

"If you must know, my stepmother happened." He straightened his shoulders and tightened his jaw. "She alone is responsible for the unwanted changes in my life. My dedication to clearing the St. Martin name and improving the estates."

From where she sat on the couch beside her sisters, Becca watched Cayle with sympathy. His back was plank straight, his chin held high. Yet his clenched fists and tight jaw told a different story. She'd grappled with other's taunts all her life and practiced the very thing Cayle faced now, the need to protect oneself from ridicule. As anxious to end this conversation as he was, she drew attention away from him and back to her.

"We've no time to dwell on past events," she said. "Laura must go to Green Park. Contrive some accidental meetings with anyone who attended Viscount Morrow's dinner party last evening. We need proof that the Viscount is part of the outer coterie. Aunt

Aggie and Lottie--"

"Yes, yes. We know," Lottie interrupted. "We must endure tedious morning calls with every boring lady who attended the dinner. You are indebted to me for this, Becca. I detest morning calls that involve our loathsome cousin."

Becca risked a sideways glance at Cayle, knowing the instant he registered just which cousin Lottie referred to. Always quick witted, his astuteness had probably increased tenfold in his years abroad. Another thing she must guard against. Avoiding him was the wisest course unless she needed specific information from him.

The last thing she wanted was to reveal all the Jamison family secrets. Or, to once again fall under the spell of his magnetism. His next question was inevitable, yet Becca was not prepared to answer it. The Jamison family were almost convinced of Julia's involvement with the cache and its master planner, but she was, after all, part of the St. Martin family and therefore owed some latitude. At least until they could prove, or disprove, that Cayle's manipulative stepmother was involved in illegal dealings.

"Is that it? Is it Julia? In all likelihood," he said, "she plans on me being discovered in a compromising situation with her. She's tried it before."

"No," Becca reassured him. It appears that Julia is content with her present paramour, whoever he may be, though she is most likely trying to control whom you marry. She needs a continuing flow of money to pay her debts."

"You seem to know everything. So, can you tell me -- is she gambling beyond her means again? Because I'd like to catch her at it. It would solve many of my problems if I could discredit her integrity."

"From our observations, her gambling seems to be very circumspect when she attends balls and soirees."

"That's one relief, I suppose."

"However, she has also visited gaming hells on several occasions. As unmarried ladies, we aren't permitted the same access to them as a widow with a male escort does."

"No, they're not the sorts of establishments unmarried women can visit without damaging their reputations. So who is escorting Julia to these places at present?"

"She seems to use several gentlemen as escorts, yet--"

"Yet?"

"The man who is her current lover remains a mystery. For some reason, she is determined to keep his identity a secret."

Becca watched Cayle puzzle over the depth of Julia's involvement, then transcend from bewilderment to full consciousness was a revelation. She'd no doubts that, with his quick reasoning, he had participated in many investigations and skirmishes and emerged unscathed.

He moved with the lithe grace of all the St. Martin men. Yet, as she'd discovered last night, his large body was hard and unyielding. His snug coat had undoubtedly been fashioned in France, for it stretched across his broad shoulders and enclosed his muscled arms like a second skin. Trousers of the finest cloth hugged his thighs so closely that the fabric remained perfectly smooth despite his energetic movements.

After hours spent poring over Michael's anatomy books, she and her sisters considered Sherwyn's well-endowed form a prime example of the male species. To her dismay, even their roguish aunt had preened when Cayle made his bow.

While bent at the waist, the duke had unknowingly treated them, front and back, to an intriguing display of breeches stretched over strong thighs, a muscled derriere, and given them all a glimpse of other intimate areas. The male parts well-bred young ladies were forbidden to notice.

However, the inappropriateness of her sisters' and aunt's stares hadn't caused the scowl now plastered across her face, because she'd reacted in exactly the same way to his display. For some unfathomable reason, the blatant admiration firing from three other sets of Jamison eyes had stirred Becca's ire, seen her stabbing fingers claw a small hole in the settee's upholstered arm.

In addition, her insides were stirring rather unpleasantly, her stomach rolling until she feared she'd have to scurry out the door. Feared her distressed stomach would require an embarrassing dash to the water closet.

Ridiculous for someone who never suffered a day's sickness from one year to the next. Unbelievable for someone who'd never been troubled by missish upsets in her entire life

Chapter 4

Cayle turned away, fists clenched at his sides. He should have guessed the haute ton would have gathered like vultures to pick over the bones of the St. Martin family. And as it had been Becca's cousin who'd deliberately trapped him at a ball, Becca would have heard every detail a hundred times over.

Queen Victoria believed that gently bred young women should pretend blindness when confronted with the seedier side of the city. Hard to do when scandalous literature was sold in the Bond Street bookshops they visited and the girls lived with brothers who reeled in at all hours stinking of wine and cheap perfume. Preachers of morality might stand on every street corner, but the only ones close enough to listen were the prostitutes who hawked their wares in the same places.

Becca clapped her hands. "Go on. We haven't much time."

She waited until her sisters and aunt had set out on their allotted tasks before she said to Michael, "And you must return to Oxford. I promise we won't take any risks."

With a grim look, Michael muttered, "Easy for you to say. I'll be four hours ride away if anything happens. How can I not fret?"

"Your university papers are due. Right now, your priority is finishing your degree. We'll send for you and Jonathon if things get worse."

Michael looked grim. He shook hands with Cayle and said, "Glad to know you'll be around."

"Rest assured, I'll watch over your family. I'll set more guards around the house at night. If the women must leave the house, they will either be under my escort or followed by my men."

Becca rolled her eyes and clutched her chest. "Please. We're only helpless ladies. We need a duke to save us."

Anger roughened his voice until it sounded like wheels grinding on train tracks. "I understand your resentment. However, men are expected to protect. Women are expected to forgo independence and accept protection. You asked for my assistance. Therefore, Michael has my solemn promise that no harm shall befall you under my watch. Hate me if you must, but I intend taking charge of this operation."

Michael said, "Be warned, Sherwyn, Becca can be prickly at times."

"Michael! I am standing right here."

Her brother chuckled. "But my sister will do whatever she is told. With good grace and as little argument as possible. Will you not, Becca?"

Becca, once again, rolled her eyes before sketching a curtsy. "My feeble female mind is relieved to have such an intelligent man take over."

Michael groaned.

"But as I don't want to worry my fretting brother any more, I will bend like a willow to Your Grace's will."

"Heaven help you, Sherwyn. When Becca becomes sarcastic, we all scurry for safety."

After a commiserating look and a slap on the back for Cayle, Michael strode out the door.

As soon as they were alone, Becca fired the first shot.

"Thank you for your concern, Your Grace."

Cayle cringed. Michael was correct about Becca in a haughty frame of mind. She was like a train engine, a compact red-headed steam-blowing version, who'd have the bravest of men shaking in their Wellingtons. He risked a small smile. This passionate parcel befuddled his senses and yet he felt more alive than he had in months.

"However," a finger stabbed his chest, "if I require a guard, I'll engage a Metropolitan Policeman. A professional in trapping criminals. Which you, on the other hand, are not."

He was tempted to contradict her but this was neither the time nor the place, so he swallowed his confession. He watched Becca's rant with amusement and admiration. Fiery, flaming red, and in full steam. His blood heated, roiled, and matched her vibrant hair color.

"Therefore, your only task will be to collect some records. Only when I'm certain there will be no danger to you. At the first sign of suspicion from one of your peers, you'll stop."

With the fluidity of a cat, he straightened to his full height and looked down at her. "I've been in precarious situations more times than you're eaten kippers for breakfast. No termagant in a redheaded temper will dictate what I may, or may not, do. You're in my hands, whether you like it or not."

She scowled. "I. Will. Not." Stabs to his chest accompanied her words. "Accept that."

"You either accept my protection, or I refuse to gather the evidence you require to convict these men." Anticipating victory, he displayed a smug smile.

Though his ultimatum silenced her, her foot tapping resumed. Drat the woman. She was probably pondering how best to prick his momentary bubble of swollen-headedness.

She tapped a finger to her front teeth. "As you've declared open warfare, I'm forced to reveal my trump card." His attention skidded away from her mouth and his smile slipped a little. "You require our assistance as fully as we need yours. It has come to our attention--"

"Laura or Charlotte? Who was eavesdropping this time?"

"How we gain our information isn't important. What matters is that you are about to be besieged."

His demeanor changed as quickly as a jungle animal that had scented a predator. "Besieged. By whom?"

"We feel reasonably sure we know the identity of your foe but, despite intensive inquiries, we can't confirm the identity of the person who is orchestrating the plan. We're narrowing the events down. Estimating times and locations the plot will be executed."

"Damnation! Your convoluted explanations tie my thoughts in knots."

"I'm surprised I need to explain. I expected that a man of your ilk would detect a trap long before it snapped shut on him."

"Just tell me how and why I'm about to be trapped?"

She gaped at him. "I thought it was obvious. You're a duke. Someone wants to force you to marry."

"Marriage?" Sweat dotted his brow. Not another of these schemes. "I can promise you I'm not marrying anyone. Not for a long time."

"No matter your wishes, if we can't stop it, you will be caught."

He swiped at his damp forehead with his coat sleeve. "If your aunt thinks she can force me to marry one of your sisters, she is very naïve."

"Oooh!" Her hands went to her hips and his eyes followed every movement. "Your ducal conceit is beyond ridiculous."

He met her angry eyes. "Perhaps it's you! Maybe you're after my title."

"Certainly not!" Her hands flew upwards. "A married woman is a man's possession. Marriage would rob me of the control I've worked so hard for."

"Husbands could shoulder the burdens. Instead of you ladies."

"Ha! Relieve us of our burdens while they rob us of our fortunes?"

"Not all men think that way, you know."

"Most do. And Laura certainly isn't after you. She cares little for titles. She's studying the aromas men emit. Their differences. If a man's scent attracts us, draws us to be with him, then he could be the perfect mate to provide companionship and to give us children. I advised her to attack the problem scientifically. List each gentleman's qualities, good and bad, and according to Madame Faberge's summations. Unsuitable gentlemen are quickly eliminated. Some will be given further tests."

"Rather a cold-blooded scheme." He considered the idea. "Unless of course," he said with a smirk, "the final test is bedding each candidate in turn. Comparing their virility."

"Ridicule Laura's methods if you must, but I agree with Madame Faberge. If men constantly think about --"

"Women's bosoms?"

"Marital relations. Wives should know how to please their husbands in bed. Otherwise, married men will keep mistresses. Or visit brothels."

Images of a willing Becca catering to her husband's every whim burned his eyes. The notion that some nameless man-about-town would benefit from Becca's well-researched sexual activities burrowed like a maggot into his brain.

Though their selection process seemed methodical, detached, and even vaguely humiliating for a candidate, he could easily picture himself auditioning. Could see Becca's red curls rioting across his pillows. Feel her small feminine body spread beneath him. Within seconds, he was hard and aching and sure as hell not thinking clearly.

He'd forfeited any right to see Becca's body, unclothed and glorious, when he'd left. Even if he was prepared to fall to his knees and beg her forgiveness, he couldn't give up his vow of celibacy.

Not if he wanted to show his peers how well he was managing the St Martin's estates and reclaim his position as a respected social leader. Dukes were supposed to set gentlemanly examples. To avoid gossip and scandal. Sometime in the future he'd no doubt keep a mistress but he'd ensure his liaison was so casual and so discreet that none of the ton's tabbies would notice. For the present, he was doomed to a private and celibate hell.

Visions of hell flames engulfing him still didn't prevent him asking, "What have you learned from the infamous Madame Faberge, font of all lovemaking knowledge?"

In his smugness, he'd failed to notice her eye color deepening to a stormy sea-green and her face reddening. Oh, hell. She licked a finger and dragged the moistened tip along the scooped neckline of her morning dress. He tracked its path with breathless attentiveness.

"Men don't regard it as making love." Her seductive murmur sent fiery shocks through every nerve and centered them in his groin, like sharp stabs from heated prongs. "Rather, as satisfying lust. Women are vessels to receive--"

"Enough!" He swung to one side as his erection, hovering the past hour at half-mast, swelled to full arousal. After an attempt at tugging his coat flaps together, he mistakenly glanced her way. The infuriating minx had the audacity to grin.

"But I haven't described all the ways Madame's girls are taught to pleasure men."

"Dammit, did they also explain that taunting a man in this wanton fashion stretches his restraint?" His voice deepened. "If you don't cease, right now, I'll toss you on that rug and demonstrate the numerous ways I know to pleasure a woman."

Becca gulped, glanced down, and the bulge in his trousers swelled to an even more uncomfortable size. She stepped forward with a hand outstretched.

"Cayle, I'm sorry. May I do something to help?"

The mixture of seductress and innocence drove him over the edge. Thrusting her hand away before it touched its mark, he turned his back. For two long minutes, he surveyed the limited merits of a country painting on the far wall before he could face her.

"Becca, never, and I repeat, never, ask a provoked man if you can assist him. Men ... even many gentlemen ... will take advantage of you." He scrambled for a distraction from a situation he should never have allowed. Where the hell was his mind? "Do you know when, and where, my hypothetical entrapment into marriage is to take place?"

"At Lord and Lady Hetherington's house party in two weeks' time."

Shock and horror paralyzed him. He needed to digest the implications of this. If indeed Becca's information was correct. And, if he trusted what she told him.

"Coincidental that my stepmother insisted I accept that particular invitation, and that I not ride my stallion, but journey with her in the carriage." Becca frowned, looked worried, but stayed silent. "Is that who's involved? Julia? She's as cunning as she is greedy."

"That is why you need our protection from this marriage net."

With a sigh of resignation, he nodded. "Regardless, I alone will question the inner circle, while you confine yourself to discreet questioning amongst the ladies."

"That ... that is patronizing, unreasonable, and--"

He pressed his fingers to her lips, firmly. "On the matter of your safety we shall agree, here and now, that I'm in charge. Or, I shall exclude you entirely."

As soon as he freed her mouth, she blurted out, "Exclude me, you arrogant--"

Once again, he covered her mouth. "Calling me names does not alter the fact that you need me, the Duke of Sherwyn. Now, agree to my terms so we may decide how to proceed."

"Oooh! You're the most annoying, conceited --"

By covering her mouth with his lips, he cut off this tirade. Not a kiss of passion, or even desire, but a warning as to who owned control. For one pleasurable moment, she relinquished power and relaxed into him, clutching his lapels as he tugged her closer. Victory, however, was short lived. Her breath coming in small pants, she shoved him away, while his senses remained addled after her surrender to his body. Momentary as it had been.

After gulping air, she launched into speech. "And remember one more thing: I don't want you flirting with my sisters. Because they're so beautiful--"

"Staggeringly beautiful."

Her shoulders hunched, as if protecting her sisters from a stampeding bull. She glared at him. "They learned at an early age to recognize fawning behavior from men."

"Do you also recognize it? Or are the compliments paid to you more sincere? As when they speak of your hair being the color of sunrise or that--"

"Cease! Gentlemen don't pay me such excessive compliments."

"Why not? You're as beautiful as your sisters." He stepped closer and appraised her face and hair. "With your vibrant coloring, you're infinitely more dazzling than either Laura or Lottie." She gave a telltale squeak. The little minx was not as immune to flattery as she'd like him to think. With each rising breath, her breasts brushed his clothing. How could she not know what she did to men? To him.

"Don't talk nonsense to me, Sherwyn."

"Ah, I've offended you. We're back to Sherywn. Soon you'll be Your-Gracing me." She stepped closer and her nipples rubbed his coat, heated him, and mocked his attempts at control. Her figure was too ripe, her energy too unbounded, for her to hide her attributes. "My sweet temptress."

He traced her décolletage with one finger.

"I'm not offended, nor do I believe you," she contradicted in anger, her arms now crossed under her breasts in a way that thrust them even further into his eyesight. His downward view allowed him full sight of lush breasts straining above what should have been a discreet neckline, although nothing would look demure on Becca's curves, despite her attempts to dress circumspectly. The woman aimed to kill him.

"So, when I tell you that every time I anger you, your eyes flash the most brilliant shade of green, you'll not react."

"Nothing you can do or say will offend me." Those amazing green eyes narrowed and the air between them sparked with emotion. "I refuse to respond to anything you say."

"Or, if I tell you that every time I watch your dainty little tongue poke out to wet your lips, I want to lick them again."

"I ... I already know what gentlemen say of me. Even the women."

"And what is that?"

Her expressive eyes clouded with pain. "They think me too much a bluestocking to be of any consequence."

"Your intelligence is a factor in your favor, sweetheart, not a drawback."

"It's not my only drawback as far as men are concerned. Moreover, do not call me sweetheart. I loathe false endearments."

He ignored her reprimand. "What else have these gentlemen been telling you?"

"I'm too headstrong."

"Only milksops want a woman without spirit. One who doesn't challenge their manhood?"

"Lord Ben ... a certain gentleman informed me on more than one occasion that expressing passion was common. Only women of the night exhibit such emotions. Ones that are paid to appear exuberant."

"If Lord -- whatever his name is -- was a real man, he'd want a woman with heat. With passion."

"Well, he didn't want me. He said he couldn't risk marrying a woman who acted the harlot, as he would never know if she performed the same way with his friends."

"Hell! Lord what's his name disgusts me. Any man would be proud to have you as a wife, Becca."

"Even you?"

She gasped, and then covered her mouth with her hands. "Forget I said that, please."

Drawing her hands to his lips, he kissed the backs. "I'm not in a position to take a wife. But if I could, you'd definitely suit me, or any sensible man."

"Huh! Not the sensible men I'm acquainted with. They happily quiz me for advice yet, if asked, they deny taking heed of anything a woman told them."

Becca jerked her hands away and walked to the tea tray to pluck up a biscuit. Her small retreats intensified his determination to uncover the identities of her detractors. From the table near the fire, he picked up an open book.

"*The Idea of Progress* by Francis Bacon. Hmm. Interesting reading." He glanced at her. "Yours, I presume?"

She nodded. "Bacon is a great social visionary. He believes that if learned persons, armed with new methods and insights, would open their eyes and minds to the world around them, then social injustices could be righted."

"Ah, yes. Something that appeals to your profound sense of right and wrong."

"Knowledge is power." She waved her half-eaten biscuit in the air as a prop to her speech.

"Bacon has been criticized for underestimating the role of imagination and overestimating the value of observation in new scientific knowledge. You shouldn't make that mistake, Becca."

"It's not a mistake to depend on tangible evidence when making decisions."

"I'd rather see the vivid imagination of a young girl unleashed again, one who believes in fairies and dragons. Burying yourself in accounts and ledgers to help your family is a noble cause, but you're also a woman." He stepped closer to run a finger down her cheek. "A remarkable one who should be courted by gentlemen who appreciate both sides of your nature. The pursuing and the pursued."

"I fear you may be the only man in England who feels that way. My sisters are pursued. Not me. I'm happiest pursuing information, researching ideas, not chasing dreams."

He studied her in silence. "I've decided how to claim my recompense."

She sighed, her shoulders drooping. "You've decided on money after all."

"Uh, uh." He shook his head. "Not money."

"What then?" Color flushed her pale cheeks. The other thing

he'd claimed last evening must have occurred to her. He laughed.

"Ah! You're not as brazen about these matters as you'd like me to believe. You're thinking about bedroom pleasures."

"Madame Faberge says that's all men think about."

"Except for me." He waggled his eyebrows and grinned. "Not at present. I've had no time to think of pleasure for many months. Although, re-encountering you has reminded me of what I'm missing." Her cheeks pink tinge deepened and she gnawed her bottom lip. "However, I'm unable to entertain such thoughts until I've settled my family matters. That may take some time. My short-term solution to both our problems is for you to accompany me on my jaunts around London. I shall gather your information. You shall safeguard me."

"That's impossible. My sisters are being brought out, at long last, and I assist Aunt Aggie in providing chaperonage."

"And who chaperones you?"

She sneered. "I'm long past the age of requiring one."

"Rubbish. You're still a young woman and an extremely desirable one."

"Nevertheless, I'm the eldest and therefore responsible for my sisters' safety."

"And who is responsible for yours?"

"My pistol keeps me safe."

"Michael also told me you missed experiencing your own season."

"My brother had no business discussing my personal affairs with you."

"He was concerned for your wellbeing. You've no more experience than your sisters with men whose sole reason for attending balls is to seduce innocents."

"You'd know all about that of course," she sneered.

He flinched but ignored the stab of pain to his heart. "The obvious solution is to join forces. If we attend the same events, our search will proceed faster. And you can't dispute that your sisters would benefit from being accompanied by a duke. Plus, I would be on hand to protect all of you."

"What a ridiculous idea. If you are constantly in our presence, it will cause gossip. People will assume you are courting one of my sisters."

He gave her a smug smile. "Not if we announce that you are my betrothed."

"Betrothed? Me?" Becca gaped at him. "Preposterous. Who would believe such a thing?"

She glanced down at her morning gown and frowned. Having recently been in Paris, he recognized it as not being of the latest fashion. The Jamison's strained finances might have restricted the ladies spending on their gowns recently, but their garments were tasteful and of good quality.

Somebody in the family knew how to stretch their money while still keeping up appearances. Probably Becca.

"I'm me and you're Sherwyn, a man of importance and wealth."

"Nonsense. You're the daughter of an earl and your pedigree is as blue-blooded as mine. If it's the outlay stopping you, I'll bear the expenses for you and your sisters. For gowns, shoes, and such."

Her eyes flashed. "No. You. Will. Not. I've made-" She swallowed hard. "Michael recently made a tidy profit on some investments. Our family is not short of coin."

"Good, then it's settled." Having enticed his prey into the trap, the hunter moved in for the kill. "You, and your family, will purchase all the finery necessary to attend various social events as my future bride."

"Absolutely not. If we must attend, it will be as family friends. We will inform people that you are kindly escorting my sisters in lieu of an available male family member. Not as your future anything."

"Very well. I'll make it known I'm courting you in an attempt to win your hand."

"I said escorting. Not courting."

"A fine distinction that doesn't signify. I'll arrange for all the necessary invitations."

Her hands went to her hips. "I'll need to see them in advance to decide which I'll have time to attend. Pressing matters of finance for the Women's Society require my attention."

He ignored her and kept talking. "We shall be attending two events this evening. Then the Townsend's ball on Thursday. Next of course, the ill-fated house party."

"Impossible! We cannot be ready by tonight."

"I'm sure that four industrious Jamison women can produce something suitable. I'll collect you at eight. Don't be late."

To hide his smugly satisfied smile, he turned and strode to the door. His disagreeable friend had been so busy arguing the larger points that his small victory slipped past her defenses.

He lengthened his stride, eager to escape unscathed. He'd dearly love to see the look upon her face when she realized he'd tricked her, but his life would be in peril.

"Oh, and Becca--" He halted and turned to look over his shoulder at her, unable to resist delivering the last word straight to her face. "Any man that prefers either of your sisters over you, is a complete fool." He waited, enjoyed her gasp of surprise. "And I ... am not a fool."

Closing the drawing room door behind him, Cayle raised a finger to his lips to silence the footman. Waited. Listened. A loud crash signaled a piece of china hitting the door. He hoped it wasn't priceless. The language emitting through the wood paneling turned the rough-looking footman's face red and he offered an apology.

"Lady Jamison shows a right foul temper when roused, Your Grace. She learned such language from doin' business with them trollops. Most of a time, my lady is as cool as still-room ale, but 'appenings in this 'ere 'ouse at the moment, be enough to try a saint."

Cayle grinned. "By the sound of that--" They flinched as another piece of china shattered. "I'd say I've provoked her ladyship beyond endurance."

"Yes, Your Grace. You must 'ave said somethin' powerful provoking for 'er to toss the china. Last time was a year ago after her papa went travellin' and left 'er ladyship with them unpaid bills."

"I think Lady Rebecca just realized I bested her. I'm quite certain that doesn't occur very often."

"Lady Rebecca be the cleverest of the Jamisons, by far."

The footman was far overstepping his position by confiding in a visitor, ducal titles withstanding. Yet from his observations, the Jamison employees behaved in as unconventional a manner as the employers. Nevertheless, they appeared loyal to a fault.

He couldn't resist prodding further, "Cleverer than even her brother, Michael?"

"The Jamison men -- not the old earl I don't mean -- may be at Oxford gettin' educations as befits gents, but our Lady Rebecca, she's the one what attends to matters 'ere. Thompson, our butler, he says the gentry fun our good lady for being so clever with her mind. Begging your pardon, I mean no offense, but some gents think a woman's only good for two things."

Before Cayle could stop him, the footman went on to explain a concept that was self-explanatory to any man who frequented low class inns. "In a kitchen, or on their backs, if you takes me drift?"

He groaned. "Yes, believe me, I do understand. But you think Lady Rebecca is destined for more?"

"Too right, sir. She talks to us 'bout our wages. How to save it, like. And she 'elped Thompson open a little sewing shop for 'is wife."

The footman opened the door and Cayle swung down the steps at Grosvenor Square, whistling a merry tune. He tucked away those fascinating snippets of information to ponder later.

Two weeks was ample time to investigate the consortium and lay charges if he uncovered any criminal activity. If a group of powerful men used blackmail or coercion to squeeze money out of innocent investors, he and his friends would delight in collecting enough evidence to hand them over to the magistrate. Under no circumstances could he allow the Jamison ladies to continue their dangerous inquiries, when he was able to settle the matter for them with little effort.

He'd be glad of this chance to repay the family, especially Becca, for past kindnesses. As a young woman, she'd allowed him more freedom to break free of his father's constrictions, to laugh and be himself, than anyone else in his life. However, he was astute enough to understand that one fiery bundle of energy in the form of Lady Rebecca Jamison might make a complete mockery of his careful planning. Her mind was a conundrum he itched to unravel, just as the marauder in him ached to unwrap the lush body under her unorthodox packaging.

It had startled him anew to discover how small she was, with her unruly head of curls barely reaching his shoulder. Her vitality and constant energetic motion made her appear bigger, braver, and more capable. She was as hot as a noonday sun and as sensuous as the most experienced girl at Madame Faberge's brothel.

Although, the extent of her understanding of the intimacies conducted in brothels remained up in the air because they hadn't concluded that conversation. Upon reflection, he realized they hadn't finished several discussions due to Becca's practiced skill in avoiding direct answers.

With his head, he understood the need to exercise rigid control. One tiny slip and he'd fall under Becca's spell as easily as her girlhood stories of woodland fairies and fire breathing dragons had captured his imagination in the past. In his heart, he knew reining in his emotions where she was concerned would prove difficult, if not impossible. His intention had been to state his case, order Becca to leave all the inquiries in his hands, and make a dignified exit.

He'd been a complete novice when his father had suggested, forcefully, that he'd be of mores use to the family trading and bartering on the Continent than being embroiled in scandal in London. He'd resolved to prove all his detractors, including his father, wrong.

Cowardice hadn't been the reason he's left England. Dueling for a crime he'd not committed would have proved nothing. Perhaps it would have pacified the Viscount but neither his family, nor Becca, needed the scandal. But he was now experienced in economics and espionage. A gaggle of women would not best him.

By extricating himself from Becca's situation as quickly as possible, the St. Martin name would be untarnished and his agreement with Julia honored. Avoiding personal entanglements would be easy for a man of his experience. A feeling of foreboding sent a shiver up his spine.

He shook his head and groaned. It was too late. His mind and his treacherous body were already involved.

Now he merely needed to keep his heart intact.

Chapter 5

The Duke of Sherwyn whistled as he strode up the white marble steps of his Mayfair house. Jenner admitted him before he knocked, offering the information that his two brothers played pool in the games room and awaited his return.

Cayle managed to retain his smile as he inquired, "And where is the duchess?"

"Her Grace is partaking of a light luncheon in her room before paying afternoon calls. She has requested the carriage as she is dining out and attending a soiree."

"Do you know where she is committed for this evening?"

"I believe they are dining with Viscount Brimley. They shall then venture on to dancing at Mrs. Simpson's."

"They? Who is escorting her tonight?"

"Your brothers have been requested to accompany the duchess in your absence."

"Ah. I imagine I'm to be boiled in oil for not making myself available."

Jenner nose lifted to indicate his extreme reluctance to become involved in family squabbles. "Her Grace appeared somewhat disturbed that Your Grace departed before she arose. I gather she expected to discuss the day's activities with you over breakfast."

"I can well imagine," Cayle remarked with dry humor.

Six months into his marriage to Julia, their father had recognized his mistake. While the duke's health had deteriorated, Julia, her eyes firmly fixed on wealth and titles, had increased her overtures towards Cayle. Yet, when the scandal with Sybila had erupted, his father had bowed to his wife's whims and banished Cayle, forcing him to leave his home and his brothers.

He could never forgive her for his years of exile, never forget that Julia was a social climber, albeit a beautiful one, who would walk across the backs of royalty if it would help her reach her self-serving goals. Julia presented a front to society. An obsessively groomed lady of not many more years than his own age, with artfully arranged blonde locks bobbing beside her ears to give the artificial impression of youthfulness and sweetness.

A woman who went out of her way to be pleasant, but only as long as the person she had selected for her attention could gain her something of importance. Otherwise, her claws were sharpened on whomever happened to be in her road. He much preferred a woman with true spirit and motives. Someone to be trusted. Someone with red hair perhaps?

Striding to the billiard room, he pushed aside his niggling worries over Julia's growing dependence on him, or more importantly on his increasing prosperity. After greeting his brothers with an amicable smile, they ensconced themselves around a small table to enjoy luncheon without the stifling presence of their stepmother. When he'd returned, Brian and Anthony had barely recognized him. Cayle had become his own man, one no longer beholden to the whims of the old duke and his second wife. Stealth and craftiness had kept him alive and one step ahead of commercial competitors. Taking control had become second nature.

"Remarkable! You actually appear to be happy," Tony said. "We despaired of you ever emerging from your dark gloom."

"Huh! Have I been that bad?"

Brian, never known for his tact, blurted out, "We've been worried about you. And your sanity. With so much weight on your shoulders."

"We were going to get you drunk. Or pay a light-skirt to relieve your stress."

Cayle's mouth dropped open. His brothers were stunned when he burst out laughing.

"What's so amusing?"

"You were saved the effort. A female visited me last night, here, in this house. And I thought that my two misguided, but well-meaning brothers, had sent her. I mistook her for a prostitute."

"She wasn't a street walker?"

He grinned and shook his head. "She was Lady Jamison."

His brothers looked horrified. "Which Lady Jamison?"

"The eldest, Lady Rebecca."

"You mistook Becca for a harlot?" Tony demanded.

"But..." Brian spoke at the same time. "But she's a lady."

"When she arrived," Cayle said, "I was two sheets to the wind. She was wet and grubby and hiding under a hat. I didn't recognize her."

"Good Lord!" Brian said. "Hard to miss all that luscious red hair."

"And those green eyes," Tony added with a knowing grin.

He scowled, annoyed that his brothers could describe Becca in such detail. "I recognized her when she removed some of her disguise. She asked me to help her with a small crisis and I then sent her home. As discreetly as possible."

"What sort of crisis brought her running to you after all this time?"

"More importantly," Tony asked with a knowing smirk, "why at night?"

Pleased to have a chance to get his brothers' opinions, Cayle explained the consortium's threats. Tony studied at Oxford so he'd probably had recent contact with Becca's brothers.

"Michael's a good friend," Tony said. "Good man to watch your back in a fight."

Cayle raised a brow. "Fight? I thought you were at Oxford to learn." His brothers shared a glance before pantomiming their mock horror.

"God's truth," Tony said, "you sound exactly like our father. We thought our days of being lectured on the evils of wine, women, and gambling had died with the old duke."

Brian shook his head. "For pity's sake, Cayle, you've become old before your time. It's not good for a man's health, you know, to go so long without bedding a woman."

"No women. I only have to keep Julia happy for two more months. By then, we should be in a better position financially. I'll give her a generous allowance if she agrees to live somewhere else. Anywhere else."

Brian sighed. "We appreciate your sacrifice, Cayle. We'll be glad to be rid of Julia and her airs of importance. Though we hate having to strain the estate's finances even further to be rid of the obnoxious woman."

"Then pray that our ships arrive on time next month. And that their cargoes make us a large profit."

"Then, good riddance to our scheming stepmother," Brian muttered. "I never understood why our father didn't see through her lies."

"At least, Cayle," Tony said, "Brian and I needn't worry about you making the same mistakes as Papa did with Julia. As you're so determined to avoid women, no self-obsessed cow will be leading you around by the nose. As for me, I'm too smart to fall victim to a pretty face and an enchanting body."

Brian smirked. "Ah. So you're no longer accompanying me to Madame Faberge's tonight, Tony?"

Cayle picked up on the name. "Actually, you'd be doing me a favor if you went there tonight. Apparently, Madame is a friend of Becca's.

Brian spurted red wine across the tablecloth. "Friends."

"I want to know when, and how, Becca met a brothel madam."

"Most likely through Laura." Brian grinned. "She's outrageous. Always getting into scrapes. Then flaunts her beauty, those luscious dark looks, to convince some poor naïve gentleman to come to her rescue."

Tony grinned. "Give it up, Brian. Laura won't give a pup like you the time of day. Besides, Lottie's fairer coloring is far more arresting."

Cayle smiled. "You appear to know the sisters very well."

Brian sighed. "My tongue nearly hits my boots every time I see the girls together. And I'm also partial to the tiny redheaded fireball."

Cayle scowled. He didn't like any man, even his brother, commenting on Becca's looks. "Leave her alone."

His brothers exchanged knowing glances. "It's been less than a day and you're as possessive as ever of Becca."

"Not possessive. Merely ensuring she remains safe, as I promised Michael. My focus will be on stopping Julia from acting the bitch when she finds out that I secured the invitations the girls needed to this week's balls."

"What? No time to snatch a kiss or two from Becca?"

"I'm warning you--"

Brian held up his hand, palm out. "Only teasing. Becca intimidates me. Though you'll have other competition for Becca's attention."

"Who?"

The two were silent for a moment before Tony answered. "You were gone. Becca was vulnerable."

Cayle scowled. "Michael told us that Becca was devastated when you left. She held her head high and tried to ignore the gossip."

Cayle looked from Tony to Brian. "I heard at least twenty exaggerated versions of the story. But there's more isn't there? Something you're not telling me."

Tony gave a resigned sigh. "The story doing the rounds of the clubs was that you preferred Sybila to her cousin because Becca was too much of a book worm. The rakes around town decided that if Becca was your leavings, she'd be grateful to have another protector step forward."

"Christ! Why didn't you tell me?"

"Because Father forbade us from contacting you. Or to try to stop the gossip. He believed that if Becca was stupid enough to become your mistress, she deserved the stones people threw at her. Julia was so convincing in her stories of you sniffing around her skirts, Father declared you a rogue of the worst sort. And Becca nothing more than a permissive slut."

Cayle groaned and dropped his head to his hands. "I had no idea of the true situation. I thought that by leaving, no one would blame Becca and her reputation would remain untarnished. Seems I made a mess of everything." He glanced up at his brothers.

"You know I never would have dishonored Becca and then deserted her. I did kiss Becca." His brothers raised their brows. "Fine. More than kissing. But nothing that would ruin her."

"That's why we defied Father. Helped Michael squash the gossip before too much damage was done. But Bennett visited Jamison House. Leant Becca a shoulder to cry on. Became her staunchest supporter when others ostracized her."

Bennett had always run with a wilder group than Cayle and had a reputation of using people, especially young women. His title, and influential parents, ensured that he emerged blameless after any unsavory incident. The thought of Bennett following Becca chilled Cayle's blood.

"Bennett appeared to be courting Becca, but Becca suddenly refused to see him. Refused to explain why. Michael believes

Bennett offered carte blanche instead."

"I'll kill the bastard."

"We think Bennett pressured Becca. Hard. Said she was ruined for marriage. But you know how hot-headed Becca can be. A few days after she argued with Bennett, he announced his betrothal to the daughter of country neighbors, Margaret Johnston."

"Johnston. The heiress?"

Brian nodded. "Bennett's motives stink worse than a City sewer. Margaret's dowry includes land in Sussex. A large slice that connects both family's properties. Productive land that brings in a large income."

"So Bennett's sudden switch was motivated by greed. Nothing to do with Becca herself."

"Bennett's attentions to Becca stopped around the time rumors started that his father was financially overextended. The Johnston's are a nice solid family. Not titled. But they hold rights to several profitable tin mines. A verbal match was contracted when Margaret was still in the schoolroom. Though Awful Arthur conveniently forgot these prior arrangements. No mention to Becca or any of the other girls he's purported to have misled."

"Michael hinted at something. When Bennett banged on our door in the middle of the night, Becca begged me to keep him out. Though she said nothing of her experience with Bennett."

His brothers looked grim. Brian rolled his eyes. "Becca pretended she was happy for Margaret. And Arthur."

"No wonder Becca distrusts men. She approached me for help only because she'd run out of options." He groaned. "And I've now made things worse for her. I arranged for the Jamison women to accompany us to the ball tonight. Becca will face the tabbies who gossiped about her and the greedy bastard who tossed her aside."

Brian rolled his eyes. "Julia will refuse. She detests the Jamisons. And she'll be furious if you take up with Becca again. Though, for some reason, she's Sybila's bosom confidante."

Tony glanced at Brian. "Though it turns our stomachs, Cayle, we'll pretend to be Julia's devoted stepsons and escort her. You can take the girls in the town coach."

Brian nodded. "But we cannot stay. Madame's salon calls us."

"And I'll spend another evening dodging scheming women.

Becca thinks I'm about to be snared in another marriage trap." He groaned. "These women want titles. Don't give a damn about the husband."

Brian snickered. "Not Laura. She tells everyone. Often. She's not a sheep. She'd rather not marry than marry someone she loathes."

"And Becca?"

Tony shrugged. "Says she's too busy. With Jamison House, the Women's Society, her mathematics. Would rather travel than marry."

Cayle's selfishness was going to cause Becca more pain. He'd wanted her to shield him. To save him from two more months of dodging toadying females, including Julia.

Because Becca needed opportunities to sneak into his peer's libraries, she'd have to be thick-skinned enough to survive dozens of jibes from Julia and her cronies.

"Michael's biggest worry is how Bennett's bizarre behavior is affecting Becca," Tony said. "Those hurly-burly servants at Jamison House would kill Bennett rather than let him hurt Becca again. But she still goes to extreme lengths to avoid him. Wears disguises. Sneaks out through the mews. And he visits brothels. Frequently."

"You two are going to one tonight," Cayle said. "Most men, unmarried or married, visit brothels."

Brian handed Cayle a large brandy as they listened to Tony.

"Gossip is that Arthur only wants one type of girl. Red hair. Smallish. Green eyes."

"Becca fits that description." Cayle banged his fist on the table. He frowned. "But so did his mother. And even when he was at Oxford, his attachment to his mother seemed almost--"

"Perverted?"

"Hell! What have I done? He'll no doubt be there tonight."

"At least the girls will be under your protection. Use your ducal stare to scare everyone away. And their house is guarded by ex-criminals."

"I promised Michael that I'd send more help. Our footmen will follow the girls, if they insist on leaving the house during the day."

"Good. There've already been two house-breaking attempts.

The staff have seen Bennett in the gardens in the middle of the Square."

"How much does Becca know?"

"Not the redheaded prostitutes. Only about being followed. A few gents became concerned about those brothel preferences. Voiced their opinions around the clubs."

Cayle paced around the dining table. "Becca cannot go near anyone she suspects of belonging to the syndicate consortium. Especially not the inner ring. I'll insist she leaves for the country straight away."

"Ha! You're deluding yourself. She won't let you take over. And she won't leave her family."

Cayle barked out a laugh. "I'll tie her to her bedpost if she tries to go anywhere without me."

He'd missed the thrill of facing, and defeating, an enemy. But the thought of roping that fiery woman to a bedpost, his bedpost, made his blood run hot. He pictured Becca spread across his bed, limbs spread. Imagined how quickly her objections would stop when he aroused her passionate nature. Could feel their bodies meeting, skin to skin.

"I'm deeply in your debt," Cayle told his brothers.

Instead of the yawning rift between them that he'd feared, their bond had strengthened, despite his absence. He explained what he wanted them to do while he caught up some old business friends.

"My friends are more than willing to help. I spoke to them last night and they're finding London life as constricting as I am. They can befriend Bennett. Find out if he's involved with the men threatening the Jamisons. Or if he's fixated on Becca because he suffers from compulsions and obsessions, like his mother."

"Take care," Brian said. "At the very least, the man's barmy."

"And madmen are dangerous," Tony added.

His brothers looked to be debating what else to reveal.

Tony spoke first. "Your exploits reached our ears, even at school. So we contacted Winchester. Our cousin keeps abreast of things. The three of us exchange news. Shares bought and sold. Your business expansions."

Cayle stared at them. "This conversation is the same as the one I had with Becca last night."

"We're not as directly involved in share trading as her family. Though our paths cross. We share snippets of gossip from our chums at Oxford. Winchester invests. Michael does the same."

"Half the city seems to have taken up espionage."

"Things changed after you left." Brian looked at Tony, who gave a tiny nod of agreement. "Father cut our quarter allowances. In half. Julia convinced him it was for our own good. Our pockets were often to let."

Cayle groaned. "I'm sorry. My actions caused you repercussions."

Tony shrugged. "It ended well. Forced us to support ourselves."

Cayle looked at them blankly.

"Winchester predicts which transport companies are ready to expand. We look at the competition. Check viability. If he buys well, he shares his profits."

"Good Lord. First I learn that Becca's family is now filthy rich. Spend their time researching railways and upcoming share markets. And my brothers, and cousin, are doing the same. Why didn't I know?"

"We knew you'd return, as the new duke if not before. Thanks to Julia's gambling, Father couldn't help you financially in Europe, so we weren't certain how flush you'd be when you came home."

Cayle sank down onto a chair. "You did this for me?"

"For all of us. Julia's extravagances were bankrupting the family. We wanted to secure Martin House, at the very least."

Tony grinned. "Plus, it's been a lot of fun."

"But how many of these fun times turned dangerous?"

Tony shrugged. "An occasional drama. But nothing as perilous as the Jamison's present situation."

"Tony and I have grown up," Brian rushed to reassure him. He shot his brother a grim look. "Thanks to Julia."

"We enjoy what we do. And it means we can help Michael. We understand the new railways. Know the track designers. Engineers."

As the eldest, Cayle considered himself responsible for his brothers. When his father had demanded Cayle remove himself from his sight, decided Cayle's punishment was to rebuild their flagging trading business on the Continent, many lives had been changed. He'd done well in Europe, but he'd neglected his brothers and turned Becca's life upside down.

Tony thumped Cayle on the back. "Don't worry. We still need our big brother's advice on how to deal with the fairer sex."

"I haven't set good example. Instead of staying when Sybila accused me of seducing her, I left in a rage. To punish father for not believing I was innocent. Now it's hard to make amends, especially over the pain I caused Becca."

His brothers looked worried. "We have bad news about Sybila. You're going to meet the lady, or rather the widow, very soon, because she returned from their country estate last week."

"I never want to set eyes on that conniving bitch again. Surely she wouldn't be stupid enough to approach me? Not after I refused to marry her."

Brian shrugged. "Every woman in London wants to sink her claws into a duke." He looked at Tony and grinned. "Better him than us."

"Don't be so smug," Cayle said. "These ladies, and their mothers, target all eligible man. They'll do anything to snare husbands."

Cayle remained uneasy after his brothers tackled their allocated tasks. His brain hadn't been brandy-soaked during his carriage ride home with Julia the previous evening. He'd had no more than a glass or two of wine at the musical recital.

Julia had blamed her tumble into his lap on a swerve of the carriage, but she'd only retreated to her seat when he'd showed his utter revulsion at having her touch him. His stepmother may be young, beautiful, and the sort of passionate widow any hot-blooded man would eagerly bed, but he could never get over his disgust.

Years before she'd filled his father's ears with those final disgusting lies, Julia had tried to seduce him. After she'd persisted in cornering him, he'd been forced to lay his cards on the table. Apart from her being his father's wife, she repulsed him.

From that moment on, Julia had set out to destroy him. In his father's eyes, and in public. And he trusted her less now than when he was younger. She might enlist empty-headed Sybila into her vile schemes a second time.

He was now older and wiser and, after dealing with sexually aggressive women in the Mediterranean, he knew how to outfox schemers. His false modesty amused him, because one woman could always outwit him.

One redheaded bundle of energy and passion that would never bend to his will. He laughed again. Staying one step ahead of Becca was more challenging than anything he'd done in years.

Chapter 6

Becca paced across her newly decorated bedroom. Laura was perched on her bed sipping a late afternoon cup of tea. Their recent changes in fortune had allowed them to redecorate several bedrooms. Becca, though not overly concerned with frills and fripperies, was secretly delighted with her feminine retreat.

There'd soon be enough money to redecorate the other rooms. The sooner the better. Their house needed to be shining before Laura and Lottie fully re-entered society and gentlemen callers streamed into their drawing room.

"You should be dressing," Becca advised her sister.

"So should you." Laura made no move to stand, or leave.

"I've a headache coming. I shall have a quiet night and allow Cayle to introduce you and Lottie."

"You, my dear sister, are afraid of being seen with the duke again."

"Rubbish. I'm not afraid of anything."

"You're brave about most things, though not all. The streetwalkers at the Society never faze you. Last month, you saved the widow Armstrong from marrying that disgusting Mr Blake. The cad was married. With children. Without your help, he'd have run through Mrs. Armstrong's fortune long before his bigamy was discovered."

Becca smiled. She'd formed the Society because she couldn't bear to see other women lured by men with pretty faces and sweet talk. Too many were left destitute by callous men who stole their money and ran away. With the help of Laura, Lottie, and their many friends, women were shown how to protect themselves and their precious savings.

She nodded. "A most successful operation."

"And Miss Carter the month before. She suspected Mr. Mackenzie of lying about his income. But she hadn't known that creditors chased him from Scotland to London."

Becca smiled again. "Yes. Miss Carter would have scrubbed floors her whole life to pay the man's debts."

Laura patted her sister's hand. "Those bounders have taught you to mistrust men. All men. And you'll become ill if you spend all your time worrying about others." Laura gave her a sharp look. "Not a pretend headache."

"It's the truth. My head does pain."

"From poring over account books. And you've lost weight."

"I could do with shedding some pounds."

"Nonsense. Your figure is nicely rounded. Men like a little meat on the women they cuddle. They loathe stick women in bed."

"You've been eavesdropping on men's conversations again."

"How else can a woman learn about men?" Laura grinned. "Our married friends are forbidden from sharing their secrets. I refuse to go to my marriage bed unprepared. That's why I'm researching lovemaking now."

"Keep your voice down. If Aunt Aggie hears, she'll ban you from every place men gather. No more listening to them gossip about their amours."

"Need I remind you, you were the first to read father's anatomy books?"

"Fine. I admit I'm inquisitive too."

"Women should understand what will happen on their wedding night. Know what to look forward to."

"Or to dread," Becca muttered.

"Those bitter old spinsters are jealous of women like Maggie. That's why they only mention the horror of a man bedding a woman."

"Maggie is madly in love with her husband. She's the exception."

"Becca, I know Lord Bennett hurt you when he announced his marriage to Margaret Johnston."

"I won't discuss that man. Or his betrothed."

"Glare all you like, big sister. Your withering look sends men scurrying at balls, but it's wasted on me."

"Aunt Aggie is wrong. I don't try to wither men."

"Of course you do. And it's useful for discouraging rakes and rogues. But not for all men."

"I won't waste time dancing with men who've no interest in me as a person."

When Laura charged off on her favorite hobbyhorse, Becca listened with only half an ear.

"Men choose women with childbearing hips. Treat brides like brood mares. A woman's expected to arrange hot meals, pop out an heir and a spare, and otherwise remain silent." Laura frowned. "I'll not put up with a husband who visits his wife for the ten minutes needed to implant his seed and then disappears."

Becca laughed. "Ten minutes? Maggie says her husband spends hours making love to her."

"Oooh! Lucius is a real man. A robust lover. The way he looks at Maggie, I feel all shivery. Warm inside." Laura pressed a hand to her abdomen. "Just here."

"Be that as it may, men no longer look at me as a potential bride. Because one man rejected me," her breath caught on a little hitch, "they assume I'll be grateful for a small morsel of their attention."

"Disgraceful," Laura agreed. "Rogues who imagine gratitude will make a lady lower her standards. Beg rakes to bed her."

"If I become desperate enough to exchange my freedom for marriage, I'll choose my husband for his intelligence and stability."

"You mean a staid and malleable man who you can control. You're afraid of feeling passion. Afraid another man will desert you."

"Passion drives women into trouble. And despair. That's not for me. Never again."

"I want excitement. And love," Laura exclaimed. "I long for a man who makes my knees tremble and my heart pound."

"Knees only tremble at soirees from the oppressive heat in rooms too small for the crush. And from the appalling lack of refreshments."

"There you go again. Pretending cynicism. Deep down, you long for romance, as I do. To find your perfect match."

"No man is perfect."

"My ideal husband will be handsome, though not conceited. Masculine yet tender. Intelligent yet not boorish."

Becca considered her sister's requirements. "I once wanted that too, but I'm wiser now."

Matrimony was a secondary to her primary responsibility of

caring for her siblings. Nevertheless, her thoughts turned to Cayle.

Strong, capable, able to shoulder heavy burdens, plus so devastatingly sexy that her pulse raced whenever he glanced her way. But they'd missed their chance to be together. Her immediate concern was two brothers who threatened to renounce their studies and return home. Two sisters who stayed by her side rather than have their seasons.

"Deny it if you will, Becca, but Jamison blood runs hot in your veins. One day, you'll meet a man who makes you burn."

She scoffed at her sister's fantasy. When Lord Bennett had turned to Miss Johnston, a woman more endowed physically and financially, she'd lost confidence in her own worth. She'd tried to hide her despair, but despite her bravado she'd been humiliated because two men had deserted her.

"I doubt such a paragon exists in the entire world," Becca announced with dramatic flair.

"On the contrary," Laura said, giving a huge grin. "Such a man prowled our drawing room this very morning. And he couldn't drag his eyes from you."

"Rubbish," Becca muttered. "A new duke has no interest in a bluestocking. He can pick and choose between all the beautiful women. Plus, blonds are fashionable. Not redheads."

"Then there's no reason to hide at home this evening. Besides, who'll chaperone us if you don't attend?"

Laura smiled serenely but Becca wasn't fooled.

"Neither you nor Lottie need my help. You can open any locked drawer faster than I can."

"But you need to distract our host. I almost got caught today examining papers that William Hardy left on his desk."

Becca shivered. She dreaded the evening ahead, despite teaching women to adopt strong and positive attitudes. She should heed her own advice.

"Nothing ventured, nothing gained. Or so Aunt Aggie says."

"Auntie uses that to prod us into attending boring recitals and suppers, in the hope that some eligible aristocrat will become enthralled with us. With you, actually. You're the eldest and should marry first."

"Heaven forbid. I'd rather be boiled in oil than marry some

hound obsessed country squire. Or a fortune hunting scoundrel. If our next railway ventures come to fruition, I'll have enough money to travel."

"It may be several years before you're able to go."

"I don't mind."

"Of course you mind. If not for rearing four siblings, you'd have set sail already."

"By the time Jonathon completes his studies, you and Lottie may be married. Michael may have found a bride."

"If Papa doesn't leave Scotland before the snow sets in, we'll not see him for another year. Not that he's any help. He barely notices us when he's here."

"I love being with all of you. My turn will come soon enough."

"Speaking about wanting, what will we do about Sybila and what she wants?" Laura asked. "Or rather, who she wants."

"We need proof that, once more, she's set her cap at Cayle. He agreed to help us in exchange for uncovering his current foe, though he doesn't know we suspect Julia and Sybila. I'll not mention them until we're certain."

"Cayle's suffered enough through our horrid cousin. Refusing to duel with a viscount three times his age was very noble."

"Why would any man fight over our horrible cousin?"

"She trapped Cayle. He had no say in what happened. Sybila is like a dog with a bone when she wants something. "

"I remember only too well," Becca agreed. "Sybila lied and cheated but our parents punished us."

"Whatever Sybila wants she gets."

"Those poor unsuspecting gentleman she flutters her eye lashes at are enticed into her web."

"When she thrusts her enormous bosom under their noses, they've no chance of escape."

"Some of them, though, are skirt chasers anyway. They deserve who or what they get."

Laura smirked. "Does that include Cayle?"

"No, he didn't deserve Sybila's nastiness. She ruined his life, yet showed no remorse when his father banned him from England."

"Things have changed. Cayle is old enough to work out what he wants. Or get what he deserves."

"What exactly do you think he deserves?"

Laura headed for the door, stopped, and said, "You, Becca. He deserves another chance with you. Wear your green gown. It matches your eyes. And Cayle remarked on their color to Michael."

Before Becca could protest, her sister was gone. And Becca doubted Cayle had said any such thing.

Her old blue evening dress was perfectly suitable for tonight's entertainment. She reached into the wardrobe. A tiny spot marred the sleeve of the blue gown. Her hand crept towards the green. Her choice was practical, nothing more.

Because next to her sophisticated cousin, Sybila, Becca felt gauche, naive and inadequate. Her main asset, her intelligence, was ridiculed, though Cayle had always appreciated her mathematical skills. Insisted that her preoccupation with statistics and calculations was perfectly normal for a young and titled lady. And he'd thrived on their heated debates over logic as much as she did.

While girls her age visited village shops, Cayle had ridden with her to Roman ruins and enacted dramas around fallen walls.

The Bank of England, Lloyd's of London, The Exchange; in fact all the places she loved were considered a man's domain. Cayle had changed, so would he be shocked by her all-consuming interest in share trading and manufacturing and her secret visits to places closed to women.

Her deepest wish was to share these parts of her life with someone. A man who accepted her as an equal.

She lifted the green dress out of the wardrobe.

Chapter 7

At eight o'clock, Cayle paced the foyer of Jamison House.

The same insolent footman eagerly informed him that Lady Rebecca had taken an hour to calm down after their morning argument. Becca would be furious, but he could manage her. He'd matured. Grown. Even his ducal powers sat a little easier on his shoulders.

The four Jamison women began their slow descent from the upper level, the hems of their gowns daintily lifted. The butler and the footman audibly gasped. Cayle's breath caught in his chest before he hissed out a sound of stunned disbelief mixed with pure masculine admiration.

Instead of congratulating himself on tricking his prickly and prideful opponent into attending the ball, he should have prepared for her aggressive response. Pride had spurred her to outfit her family in the most fashionable manner. Resentment of his offer of monetary assistance had goaded Becca into going to extremes. Like a teasing mare that holds her tail high and prances before a stallion.

The women weren't dressed in the pastels expected of blushing and stammering young ladies making their come-out, but in rainbow-hued fabrics normally flaunted by lusty widows on the prowl, or by courtesans with generous protectors. Their aunt, in deep plum with a plumed headdress to match, defied her middle years by descending with a lively, yet majestic, stride. Laura's springing steps made the soft lavender fabric bounce around her shapely ankles. Lottie appeared ethereal when yards of palest blue satin swished and swayed around her captivating shape.

Cayle groaned, not caring who heard. The evening was going to be a disaster and he had only himself to blame. These *last-minute* gowns were so spectacular that every expensively clad lady, especially his stepmother, would spit like jealous cats. Cursing himself for his naïveté, he longed to turn Becca around, send her back upstairs to change into less flattering attire. Perhaps a burlap sack. Anything but this mossy green silk, shot with silver threads, which shimmered brighter than her flashing eyes. Any gown that didn't cling to her curves, and have every rogue and rake lusting after her, or dry his mouth and rob him of speech.

As she walked towards him, he blanked his expression. He'd taken care to look appreciative, not leering, when her sisters had walked past. Still, Becca impaled him with a look. Issued an unspoken challenge.

Unable to stop himself, he glanced down. Followed the line of her bodice to the crossover vee between her breasts, past her waist and onward to her hips. Fabric flowed like a meandering rivulet around her curved body and swung in a soft arc around matching dancing slippers. Contrary to the current penchant for an overabundance of layers, a sparing amount of green fabric was cut in long and simple lines that suited Becca's petite stature and generous curves to perfection.

Cayle could barely breathe. Could only stand and stare.

Thompson recovered first. He handed a shawl to the older lady and the footman moved forward to do the same for Laura and Lottie. Cayle lifted the last shawl from the side table and moved to Becca. He dipped his head before moving behind her to drop the covering across her shoulders. If he touched her, she'd notice his shaking hands. The last thing he wanted was Becca believing the nearness of her sisters had caused his chaotic nerves. Or taking him to task over it, again.

He spoke quietly beside her ear. "You're breathtaking. Every man in England will want you."

She looked up at him. "Apart from you, of course, Your Grace."

He frowned. Was that dismay, or derision? Despite his brain understanding why intimacy was impossible, his lusting male side longed to see his own regret reflected in her eyes. Her minuscule bodice strained to contain her magnificent white breasts. With so much skin displayed mere inches away, it was impossible to concentrate.

"... Keeping your eyes, and thoughts, away from my sisters."

"Believe me, I wasn't thinking about your sisters."

Becca eyed him suspiciously before marching down the steps but, rather than faze him, her irritation made him smile. He'd charmed his way into the beds of some of most beautiful women in Europe, and with ridiculously little effort. Perhaps he was being arrogant, but working his wiles on four Jamison ladies seemed simpler by comparison. Paying attention to Laura and Lottie would anger Becca, but he considered it only fair when his own emotions spiraled out of control whenever he was within two feet of her.

Like now. She leaned forward on the opposite carriage seat and the neckline of her revealing gown dipped. His gulp was audible. Aunt Aggie reprimanded him with her eyes, before alerting Becca to her gaping neckline with a finger motion.

Becca gave a small gasp when she looked down. She slipped her fingers inside her bodice and tugged. He mentally groaned. The bodice, though now high enough to be decent, still sagged. If she touched herself again, he'd be forced to sit on his hands. Time spent sitting across from her in the coach, plus an evening closely attending to the ladies, was going to be torture.

Laura addressed Becca in an amused voice, "I knew that neckline would cause a sensation. The men won't be able to raise their eyes above your breasts."

Aunt Agatha snorted. Cayle growled. Laura laughed. She touched Cayle's knee with her gloved hand. "Do you think Becca's décolletage is too revealing?"

Before he could manage a reply, Becca interrupted. "If my gown causes a scandal, it will be Cayle's fault. He insisted we attend this evening."

Lottie corrected her sister. "Then we should thank Cayle, not embarrass him. Mrs. Simpson invites only the cream of society to her recitals. Queen Victoria and Prince Albert often attend. Cayle cannot be blamed for Hettie's mistake with your neckline."

Cayle smiled at Lottie before turning to a seething Becca. "If you'll allow me to assist?" He settled Becca's shawl higher around her shoulders. "We don't want you to catch a chill."

Lottie smirked. Laura clapped her hands and laughed. "Well done, Cayle. How very sensible of you."

Aunt Agatha thankfully rushed to his defense. "The duke is a gentleman. He is therefore a better judge of what men consider acceptable dress."

With a smug look he turned to Becca, only to find her glaring at him. Then Aunt Agatha took the wind out of his sails, "Especially if Becca is dancing. This latest fad for overly energetic polkas is certain to cause scandal for some young lady when she has a mishap with the bodice of her gown. I only hope it doesn't happen to one of my darling nieces."

Visions of Becca losing her bodice in the middle of a dance were enough to make Cayle squirm. He was prudent enough to remain silent and stare out the window for the rest of the journey. At this stage of his life he couldn't marry, but he had a clear picture in his head of tearing off Becca's bodice and watching her ripe breasts spill into his hands.

Last night, he'd felt an entirely masculine and primitive satisfaction over her eager response to his touch and now it would be difficult to keep his hands to himself. He wanted to touch her, to taste her again. Despite his personal turmoil, he needed to put leading strings on her in order to protect her. He didn't want her to stray far from his side each evening until the threat to the family had been relieved.

Taking the initiative and knowing he would be stirring an ant's nest, he announced his demands. "Rebecca," he addressed her formally, "if we give the impression that we are somewhat more than friends, it will provide the perfect excuse for us to remain close this evening."

Becca looked askance at him. Her face looked such a picture of horror that he felt mildly insulted. Her gaze narrowed on him as she matched his formality for the sake of the family, who were agog with interest.

She opened her mouth to speak but Aunt Agatha smiled her delight and overrode any scathing reply Becca wished to utter.

"What a splendid idea. Your attentiveness to our darling Becca will preclude any unsavory gentlemen approaching her. And Laura and Lottie will benefit from your superior knowledge of the suitability of any possible suitors."

Becca's mouth opened again but Cayle interrupted. "Becca, think about it. We'll be expected to spend time together. It's what courting couples do."

"Courting? I insisted we'd be introduced as old friends, nothing more. Nobody will believe you've any other sort of interest in me."

Cayle had no chance to further his cause as the coach slowed in the drive of Mrs. Simpson's establishment and he was kept occupied helping the women alight. He presented his arm to Becca, forcing her to place her fingers on his sleeve.

Bending closer to her ear, he murmured, "No one will think it odd that I pursue you. I'm a duke of marriageable age and you're a beautiful young lady of impeccable breeding. Our families have a long history together."

She shot him a withering look. "Anyone that knows me realizes I've no more thought of marrying than of jumping off--"

"On the other hand," he interrupted sharply, "a man can't be too careful. One false step and I could find myself actually married to you." He gave her a tight smile and ignored her astounded look.

"However, if we're to convince the world that we're engaged to be married, or courting if you prefer, you will need to blunt your sharp tongue."

Her look of outrage rewarded him. From this moment on, he intended keeping her with him. Leading strings worked that way. Where he went, she went. But also, he enjoyed being with her. Sparring with her and firing the heated passion that hovered just beneath her controlled exterior.

Waiting in the receiving line to greet their hosts, Cayle was forced to forgo that plan and shift a discreet distance from Becca. Because of the crush, she'd been pressed against his side, close enough that the scent of flowers wafted up to him. He inhaled deeply and then inwardly groaned as his entire body tightened in response to the scent of wildness she emitted. Simply breathing the same air as her unnerved him.

Good Lord, what had he done? In his arrogance, he'd assumed he could bend Becca to his will while still remaining impervious to her attractions. Making a slight revision of that plan became imperative in order for him to retain his sanity.

By introducing the Jamison sisters, Becca included, to every eligible gentlemen attending tonight, he'd ensure they were surrounded and protected. Physically, it would keep the ladies safe. Emotionally, he doubted any man was safe from their enticements.

Therefore, he'd take steps to ensure he didn't become one of the captivated throng. He had enough fortitude and inner strength to resist their allure. Despite his friends thinking him oblivious to the sensation his presence created amongst the fairer sex, it was in fact quite the opposite. As a sought-after bachelor with a title and wealth, he was acutely aware of the ravenous eyes of matchmaking mamas and fresh faced chits fixed upon him.

However, he'd created strategies to avoid them having no wish to raise expectations when he held no intention of succumbing to their efforts. Most evenings, he accompanied his stepmother and danced a maximum of three country dances with married women with no designs on him, then disappeared to the gaming room.

Four hours later, and with his previous escape plans in tatters, he cursed a hapless Jenner for not refusing admittance to Becca the prior night. He refused to acknowledge that some of the blame for his frustration fell to his own behavior in taking her in his arms and kissing her. If he were honest, he would concede that any and all intimacy with Becca was a mistake. When it came to that infernal woman, he was weak willed. He always had been and it seemed he would continue with the same behavior that pattern.

Moving on to the second of the evening's entertainments, the same pattern occurred. No sooner did they enter a room en masse, then more gentlemen than he could count bombarded them. Every man in London clamored for an introduction, or if he refused that, they claimed an association through another source. Many of the gentlemen were already well acquainted with the sisters with some far too familiar for Cayle's comfort.

Upon overhearing one conversation at the edge of the crowd, Cayle's mild irritation escalated into full-blown annoyance. Viscount Lindley was a known womanizer and always short of funds. His words flung Cayle into an instant awareness of how stupid he'd been in offering, demanding actually, that the Jamison ladies be presented under his support.

"But be warned," Lindley was saying. "While all three are a delectable morsel, I intend gobbling up the oldest."

His companion, Mr. Boswood, argued, "But she's a true bluestocking."

Lindley smirked. "I'm willing to overlook that little fault in order to get what I want." At his friend's inquiring look, the Viscount said, "That fiery little handful will not only look sumptuous spread naked across my sheets but after a night in my bed, she'll reveal all the secrets of how her brother turns metal into gold. Or rather, steam engine iron into currency. Lots of lovely wealth."

"You must be desperate if you're willing to marry such a bookish woman in order to acquire investment advice."

He chortled evilly. "Who mentioned marriage? There are other less permanent means of encouraging a woman to share a few morsels of gossip."

Barely able to reign in his temper, Cayle tapped him on the shoulder.

"Step outside with me, Lindley. I want a private conversation with you."

Ignoring the order, Viscount Lindley looked Cayle up and down before remarking in a loud voice, "Sherwyn, cut your step mama's leading strings at last."

Cayle fought for control, understanding that losing his temper in a crowded room would feed Julia's greedy purpose by showing him to be an unfit Duke of Sherwyn. However, Lindley had deliberately insulted him and he couldn't ignore the taunt.

His fists clenched at his side. Before he could raise one in retaliation, a soft hand circled the middle of his back. Becca slid around beside him and wrapped her gloved hand about his, folding his arm firmly against his side. He could easily have shrugged off her unwanted interference and her attempt to restrain him, but it would serve no purpose to brawl like street ruffians in Mrs. Simpson's elegant rooms.

Smiling at his companions, Becca said, "I believe my aunt is ready to depart, Your Grace."

Pulling himself together for her sake, Cayle relaxed his tense muscles and nodded his acquiesce to Becca. "Of course. The poor lady will be tiring by now."

Leaning in to the two men, he warned, "We'll continue this discussion at a later date. At a more private location."

Viscount Lindley sneered again. "When you're able to escape your domestic duties with the Jamison horde, Sherwyn, you'll find Julia at my uncle's house. However, they won't appreciate interruptions. He'd several exotic games planned for their evening. Games involving another dozen like-minded hellions and perhaps a footman or a maid or two."

Cayle sucked in a breath. Only Becca's firm restraining hand on his arm kept him from doing violence to the arrogant man making such crude taunts to his face. And, in front of a lady.

"You will speak with respect of every member of my family, Lindley, or we will be meeting at dawn."

Becca jerked on his arm to regain his attention. "Cayle, no. He's not worth endangering your reputation."

Then she turned to the Viscount to address him with rigid formality, yet in a quiet and earnest voice. "Viscount Lindley, I know the extent of your borrowings and your debts."

He stared at her aghast, his expression a mixture of disbelief and horror. "How would you, a woman," he spat out the words, "know anything about my financial affairs?"

Becca stretched up to whisper in his ear. Cayle leaned closer to hear as she recited a list of figures that was incomprehensible for him. The effect on the Viscount, however, was quite different. Lindley's face blanched to the color of a sheet on washing day.

Becca patted his hand as if he were a wayward child and added, "You may call on me at Jamison House on Thursday. At precisely ten o'clock."

The sagging Viscount nodded and bowed. "Of course, my lady."

"And there will be no talk of duels, do you understand me?"

To Cayle's amazement, Lindley hastened to agree.

Then Becca fixed the Viscount's friend with a haughty look and he too shriveled under her piercing stare. "Mr. Boswood, I fear your grand-mama will be greatly distressed to learn you're acting as less than a gentleman. She spoke to me only yesterday about a new will."

Becca leaned in closer to emphasize her point. Boswood's hand shook slightly when she clasped it between her gloved fingers.

"A visit from her favorite grandson may influence her in a favorable manner. However, a word in her ear from a concerned friend, namely me, may influence her in an unfavorable way."

Boswood paled even whiter than his ally. He visibly trembled. Neither he nor Lindley spoke. With a nod at the two chastened men, Becca steered a bemused yet seething Cayle to the door to execute a polite departure from their hosts.

Chapter 8

After assisting the ladies inside at Grosvenor Square, Cayle politely requested a few moments to confer with Becca. A tired Aunt Agatha blithely waved a hand towards the sitting room without even asking for the door to be left ajar.

Becca was right. Her family saw her as a chaperone for her sisters. Not a beautiful woman who'd tempt any man to sin. Her aunt must be batty, blind, or pretending oblivion if she hadn't noticed his reaction each time he was near Becca. His mind filled with lustful reveries of how and where he'd like to have her. Spread wide on a picnic blanket in a grassy meadow. Hair glowing sun-red while he licked tiny droplets of perspiration running between her breasts. Lips tasting of fresh air and sunshine and warm skin smelling like wildflowers.

"Yes, Cayle?"

He started when Becca interrupted his dreams. "You shouldn't have interfered tonight. In future, you'll stay well away from those men. I'll deal with them."

"I saved you from a public brawl." Becca faced him, hands on her hips, eyes flashing. "You were jeopardizing everything you've worked towards. Salvaging your family name, your reputation. Lindley is a half-wit. You're too stubborn for your own good. Besides, I left them with exactly the impression you wanted. That you and I are close."

Cayle paced the length of the room. He sighed. Striding back to Becca, he lifted her hands from her hips and soothed her taut fingers.

"Thank you. A fight in Mrs. Simpson's house would be the top gossip for a month." He stroked her fingers. "I can't let Julia gain the upper hand."

"Our situations are similar. Protecting our brothers and sisters. Avoiding scandal, at all costs. I want Laura and Lottie to do well this season."

He grinned. "Not an easy task. Your sisters have been painted with the wild brush. Like you."

"This isn't amusing. And I'm not wild. Merely enthusiastic."

"Enthusiastic." He almost choked. "You're reckless. And Laura and Lottie are following in your footsteps."

She glared at him. "You infuriating man. I need their help. But when the syndicate members are behind bars, Laura and Lottie can return to gentler pursuits."

"Hard to imagine your sisters stitching handkerchiefs or paying afternoon visits. They're too ... ah ... enthusiastic." He raised his hand and stopped her retort. "Sorry. I should be thanking you for calming the waters with Lindley. Not making you angry."

Becca's rigid posture relaxed. "Yes, you're in my debt."

"I promise," he said, letting his eyes rove lingeringly over her curves. "To find the perfect way to repay you."

Her breath hitched, deep in her throat. He hoped she was picturing all the ways he might repay her, just as he was. Ways involving his mouth and hands on every crevice. Good Lord. Conversations between them streaked from inane to sexual faster than lightning strikes. Her breasts rose and fell with each heavy breath. He knew where her accelerated awareness could lead them in an instant, even if Becca didn't.

Better to issue a lecture on future meddling. "I don't want you to be hurt."

Even as he spoke, he knew the person who could hurt her most was him. He couldn't live with himself if Becca was hurt a second time by his stupidity. Her softer gender, diminutive size, and inherent bravery stirred his masculine and gentlemanly instincts. Though Becca would swallow nails from her own factory rather than admit she needed physical protection, especially from him. After he'd dealt with the syndicate, perhaps Becca would look at him differently. See him a mature and responsible man. And see that not all men were as unreliable as her father, or Arthur Bennett.

While he marshaled his wayward thoughts, Becca was waving her hands while she talked. "Tonight's episode has proved that Viscount Lindley is one of the main troublemakers."

So many things were as he remembered. Becca leaped into conversations, and life, while he tried to keep her safe. The consortium had watched her for two weeks and now, thanks to him, the worst rogues who hunted the ballrooms looking for young women to prey upon had Becca in their sights. She and her sisters might imagine themselves capable of dealing with every type of man, but only another man of the same ilk could understand men like Lindley.

Titles and wealth spoilt them. They assumed the world was theirs for the taking. If he'd remained in London, who knows, he may have become like them. Shallow, self-obsessed, and lazy. He hoped he had more integrity, more moral fiber, than his grasping peers.

"How do you and your sisters know so many gentlemen when you've been avoiding society?"

She shrugged. "Many of my friends joined me when I started the Society. I don't discriminate. I show women of all classes how to manage their banking, to understand investments. We share luncheons, teas, and they have male relatives." She gave a little laugh. "Several of those men even consult me before spending their money. Mind you, they'd never admit to their associates that they are helped by a woman."

"What hold do you have over Lindley?"

Her reply was deliberately vague. "My family hears things."

"How do you hear these things?"

She shrugged. "Laura listens. Lottie flatters. And I--"

"You what?"

"I think. Analyze."

Becca's evasive answers weren't helping. If she kept playing games with these dangerous men, they would run out of patience and dispose of her with or without her knowledge. "For once, you stubborn fool, answer me truthfully. What do you analyze?"

"Investments. Inventions."

"And men accept a woman's advice, your advice?"

"Well, no. Not publicly, at least. But privately, they ask me to calculate the profits on investing in specific inventions. Or railways."

"I thought that was Michael's area of expertise." He frowned. "You're keeping things from me."

Her mischievous smile reminded him of the carefree girl she'd been. His heart ached.

"Who me? Would I do that?"

He laughed as she intended. "You're as slippery as an eel. But tonight was only a taste of things to come. You may have subdued Lindley and Boswood, but more the consortium obviously wants you rather badly. And as you refuse to be honest with me, our agreement is finished. From now on, I go about in society and you remain at home. Safe and secure."

"If you recall, I'd intended avoiding high society. That's why I needed you. However, I realized tonight that mingling with those people, seeing and hearing for myself, will help me collect our proof much faster."

She lit up like a bonfire when she spoke about mathematics and accounting. He smiled. This tiny bluestocking with her fire and passion made him feel more alive than he had in years.

"You give so much of yourself. To your family, to others. When do you take?" He trailed his fingers over her face. "When do you let yourself feel, or enjoy?"

He stepped forward. She edged backwards until her back touched the wall and he stopped. He'd sooner die than frighten her. But when her breath hitched and her eyes went wide, he recognized it as arousal. Not fright.

"Stop me, Becca."

She shook her head. Her bright eyed gaze followed his movements. He ran his fingers down her cheek, brushed across her lips, and then slowly, tantalizingly back again. Her tongue touched his finger, lightly moistened it. He jerked his hand back, but his lower body had a mind of its own, leaning closer.

"Hell, Becca. Stop me."

Once again, she shook her head.

With an agonized groan, he melded his body to hers. Every lush curve wrapped like the softest leather glove around his harder length. He ran his tongue around the circle of her lips until she opened for him. Until hunger took over. Latching on to her pliant mouth, he feasted again and again until her body trembled and he felt her knees give way. He pressed her flat against the wall as an unstoppable tide of need swamped him. Desire had never felt so intense.

He wanted to devour her, to suck her up like a ripe peach. Warm and pliant, this woman fitted his arms to perfection. His normally rigid control flew out the window.

"Becca, Becca." He chanted her name as he kissed and nuzzled her face and neck. One hand hovered over her swollen breast where it strained at the thin lace. "I need to see you. To look at you." He met her gaze and held it silently, waiting for permission.

Becca felt none of Cayle's hesitation. She smiled and nodded, willingly gifting him her consent. "Touch me. Show me."

Two thumbs eased down her gown's neckline. Firelight reflected the emotions racing across his face. Awe, amazement, reverence. The power of it made her soar and fly. She could do this to him, create such craving and hunger. Make him cry out with wanting her.

She watched his hands cup her bared breasts. He tested their size and weightiness with his palms before rubbing his thumbs over her puckered peaks. Eyes fixed with desire lifted to meet her gaze and his voice was husky and reverent.

"You're so beautiful." He jiggled her breasts a little. "These are incredible. Soft, and fuller than I remembered, pale yet lustrous. And you have tiny freckles sprinkled like fairy dust over their tops."

The poetry of his words melted her, inside and out. Several men had paid homage to her beauty, although in comparison to Laura and Lottie her coloring interested rather than stunned. And of course, her family paid her compliments for her intellect and soft heart. Yet now, this man, this darkly handsome man who'd known many women, appeared enthralled by her curves.

All of a sudden, she felt proud of her woman's body. Proud that hers was so different to his that he sought to worship it. Despite her avid declarations that she didn't need a man in her life, she did want one. This one. She wanted Cayle to worship her body.

His head dipped and surprise caught her as his sharp teeth gently nipped the tip of one nipple. Then a lathe of his raspy tongue soothed it. Combined sensations of pain and pleasure were almost unbearable. He sucked one erect nipple into the warmth of his mouth and she shook. He tweaked the other with his fingers and she panted. Between her legs, she felt a rush of fluid and a curious ache started there. She knew that only he could stop the yearning and ease the pain. She needed everything he could give her.

"More. More."

"Sweetheart, you are astonishing." A hand slipped lower to catch the hem of her gown and warm fingers trailed up her calf and over her knee, pulling up her satiny gown as he went, until her whole leg was exposed.

"If you had any idea what I want to do to you, you would be stopping me. Without hesitation."

"You're wrong. I do know."

After a moment of surprise, he shook his head and laughed. "Madame Faberge again I suppose."

"Yes. She told us that when a man, the right man, touches you between your legs, it feels like heaven. I want to know what heaven feels like."

"Oh, little one. Heaven is touching any part of you." Long fingers stroked softly over the outside of her undergarments. Close to the center where she ached for it, yet not quite reaching the source of heat ignited in her body. "Heaven is here."

One finger found the opening in her drawers and intruded slightly. She moved forward with an impatient wiggle until the tip of his finger nestled in the opening to her swollen passage. Not enough. Oh, not nearly enough.

The books had shown her where on her body it happened, but not the rush of sensation that had her shuddering in seconds as his hard tip rotated gently, back and forth. She felt hot and swollen, restless in her desperate need for relief. The plunge of his finger into the deeper recesses of her heat nearly caused her to swoon across the strong arm that still held her firmly to the papered wall.

"I've got you, sweetheart. Just let yourself go."

She grunted, and then said, "If I let myself go any more, I'll be a puddle at your feet. Perhaps you'd better position me someplace else."

"Are you giving me orders on how to seduce you?"

Bending his head to her chest, he started to laugh. "You're probably analyzing the situation, using your mathematical skills to calculate the best position for me to put you in."

Realizing that the rumblings and shaking coming from her chest were he and not she, she grabbed his hair and lifted his head to meet her at eye level.

"Oh, really. This is too much. Serious minded Cayle St. Martin finally lets himself go enough to laugh, really laugh, and it's at my expense. When you have your...part of you..."

His laughter quieted. "My finger moving, moving inside you."

For another moment, he remained motionless inside her while the tight heat of her inner passage squeezed around his finger, clamping down. Her body followed every tiny motion his finger made. Followed it, tightened on it and enjoyed it. When he started to withdraw she clamped her thighs around his arm.

"I know there's more. There must be more."

Her breath came in ragged gaps as she watched him fight to regain control of himself. Straightening and pulling away, he dropped her skirt to the floor and pulled together her bodice. He stepped back, putting some distance between them.

Clutching his head in his hands, he let out a long low growl.

"I shouldn't have touched you like that. I had no right."

"Don't you dare leave me like this." The fiery side of her was imperially annoyed. "Finish it, Cayle."

He shook his head. "It should never have happened. I'm not the man you need to introduce you to such things."

Frustrated, disturbed, yearning for she knew not what, her body burned hotter than a blazing fire. A fire that ignited her temper and made her want to flay him with his words.

"Oh, and once again you've decided what's right for me. What I need. Who I need. Well, I disagree. If you," she poked a finger in his chest, "aren't able to relieve me of these feelings, I shall ... I shall find another man. Yes, that's it."

She nodded in agreement with her own statement while he stared at her in bewilderment.

"You wouldn't dare."

"I do dare, and I will find another man. One not so high and mighty as the Duke of Sherwyn."

"No, you will not. I'll not stand for it."

"You've no right to stop me. You just gave up the right."

"You are the most irritating female I've ever known. And you're speaking through clenched teeth. It amazes me how you manage that when I know how dearly you love to talk. To lecture me."

She understood that he was deliberately trying to goad her. He wanted to fight with her, and to have an excuse to leave, but she refused to let him.

"And you," she poked him again, "are trying to be a saint. And I won't stand for that. If you leave me frustrated like this, I'll appeal to Madame Faberge for help." She glared at him. "So there."

"So," he said in a slow and considering tone, "you want me to show you what comes next."

"Yes. I want you to teach me everything."

He gave an agonized groan and moved back to her. "No, I won't take your innocence, not now, nor in the future. That delight should be left to your future husband. But I'll relive your frustration. Show you how to turn your body's desires into pleasure."

"But what pleasure will that give you?"

He gave a snort of laughter.

"I've become accustomed to the strains of celibacy. Although, it wasn't a problem until you blew back into my life. Watching you come apart in my arms will be agony and ecstasy combined, torture no man should inflict upon himself. So, don't ask me for more than I'm able to give, sweetheart. It'd be dishonorable to you, to me, to my family and yours."

Taking her hand, he led her to the settee. He sat with her on his lap and pulled her back into his arms and with the first touch of his lips on hers, lurched her back to their shared passion of moments before.

Kissing and touching until they both panted and gasped, she was aroused to the point of pain. Pulling apart a little, they gazed at each other in wonder.

"Oh, Cayle."

His head lowered to press heated lips to her forehead. "I know, sweetheart. Jesus, how I know."

For a long moment, he simply pressed her tightly against his chest while she absorbed the comfort of being held so close to his heart. He felt solid, and safe, and she wanted to stay there forever.

"Believe me when I tell you I wish my life was different. Until I rid my family of the threat Julia holds over us, I am beholden to obey her every whim. That means no scandal, no involvements, no entanglements of any kind."

Cayle brushed his hand in a tender sweep over her head in an attempt to smooth down the fly-away curls dislodged from her upswept hairstyle. His breath was warm as he nuzzled kisses into her hair before pulling away with a deep sigh and a worried shake of his head.

"I want your promise that you understand this is purely physical relief I'm giving you. You need to understand that at this time in my life, I can't envisage any permanent emotional attachment between us. I'm not ready for a woman, any woman, in my life."

A shaft of longing shot through Becca for a tiny taste of the emotional involvement he dismissed so callously. However, she was a strong woman. Knowing that Cayle was too honorable to touch her again if she didn't agree, she washed any emotion from her face and nodded silent agreement.

Right now she wanted the release, which tantalized just out of reach, far too badly to object. Later, she might regret her decision but for now she would take whatever he was prepared to offer.

"Touch me again, Cayle. I need you. Now."

"Open your bodice for me, sweetheart."

Mesmerized by the growling tone of his voice, Becca complied. With eager fingers, she slipped her already unbuttoned bodice over her shoulders and loosened the tie of her lawn undergarment. Once again, her breasts were presented to his eyes as a ripe feast on a dinner plate, yet she felt no embarrassment, no shame. In her deepest thoughts, in her old dreams for an ideal future, she had imagined this moment countless times.

His tongue flicked across to wet her dry lips, once, twice, before his mouth descended to settle over one nipple and give a strong tug. She arched up, hands threading tightly through his dark locks, clasping him hard to fix him where she needed him most. He reached down to raise her skirts and his fingers unerringly found a sweet spot between her thighs.

"Oh, my goodness. That feels so, so good," she murmured when he pressed down and then released.

He repeated the movement several times, up and down, until she lost all sense of anything except where the finger went and what it touched. Just as she believed she could stand no more of his teasing, he changed the rhythm.

The new circling motion of his index finger around the most intimate, most tender part of her body made her blood rise and sing. She felt hot and wet and the ache increased with relentless intensity. When his finger swirled the bud swelling in her cleft, the pressure escalated so quickly inside her that she thought she'd burst. She jerked, her moans and groans growing louder and longer as her body demanded more. The escalating sensations pulsing through her body were astounding and energizing.

He whispered in her ear, "Oh, my sweet, you're so incredible when you do that. Yes, reach for it, my love. Take what you want. Take it all."

His finger continued to alternatively push inside or twirl the sensitive outside until with a dazzling burst of power, she screamed and bucked. Over and over. She rose repeatedly off the settee to thrust against his taut body, riding out the spasms that wracked her then left her collapsed backwards over his arm. From her toes to her head, she continued to twitch and tingle whilst he feverishly licked every exposed part of her upper body.

He held her like that until the tremors subsided and she groaned out the downward spiral of her pleasure. His finger remained snug inside her and he continued to lathe tiny licks over her ear until she finally stopped, completely spent. When she returned to consciousness, Cayle was perched on the edge of the settee regarding her tenderly and her clothing had been righted. She blinked lazily and fixed her dazzled gaze on his face.

He groaned and looked away. "For God's sake, Becca, don't look at me like that."

"Like what?" she asked, still floating in a state of dazed happiness.

"Like I just rode in on a white charger to save a damsel in distress."

She smiled, a wise female smile. Because she now knew what all the fuss was about. Knew why some of her married friends had that same far away private look upon their countenances when they spoke of attentive husbands. Of course, having aided many not so fortunate women, she understood that bliss was not always obtained with a man.

It took the right man, Madame Faberge would say. A man who knew how to please his lover, putting his own needs second to the needs of a woman. Cayle stared at her with reverence, his hand caressing the side of her body. Yet, at the same time, he looked ready to jump up and run.

"I'm no hero."

She reached up to trail her fingers down his cheek. "To me, you're everything heroic. You may deny it, but your continuing loyalty to your brothers, even to Julia, all speak of a noble nature."

"No, you don't understand. I've done things. Things that prevent you casting me as a hero riding to your rescue."

Keeping her face purposefully blank to appease his rising alarm, she said, "You didn't rescue me, Cayle, but you did show me why women risk everything to conduct love affairs."

Sitting upright, she kissed his warm lips and hugged his tense body once before swinging her legs to the side. She placed a hand on his thigh to steady herself to stand, already regretting that their moments of intimacy had passed.

"Thank you for showing me."

Cayle looked at her with open-mouthed bafflement. While she stood and smoothed the creases from her skirt. While she fiddled with her bodice. He stared. Frozen in his seat. And silent. His demeanor slipped this evening from angry protector over her confrontation of Lindley, to an aroused man, and then to a bewildered lover. He seemed confused as to what to do with her next. It was up to her to direct the next step in their relationship.

With an emphatic nod of her head, she announced, "In order to educate my sisters completely, I am compelled to conduct many more experiments on this incredible phenomenon."

Cayle gaped at Becca in stunned disbelief, unable to form a coherent reply to her outlandish statement and horrified by Becca's suddenly brisk, scientific manner. He'd made the decisions, called the shots, told her it was a once only moment of intimacy. Of madness.

Becca becoming clingy was the last thing he wanted, but this matter of fact approach to what they'd just shared, exasperated him. And for the life of him, he couldn't pinpoint why it aggrieved him so much.

He stood on shaky legs to confront her. "Let me understand, I just gave you your first female pleasure--"

"No!" She shook her head. "Not my first, Cayle. You forgot the stables four years ago."

He nodded his head in agreement. "Your second..."

He considered for a moment. "No, your third orgasm. A very enjoyable and profound release if I may say in all modesty, yet you intend treating it as the commencement of a scientific experiment?"

"Oh, yes. I must now collect more extensive data before I make a scientific decision."

"Collect data. Where? With whom?"

The questions exploded from him before he had time to think. He glanced away, trying to haul back his raging emotions. Control was everything.

"Not that it's important to me, of course."

"No, of course not," Becca agreed amicably. "You, as a man with considerable experience in these matters, matters of the bedroom, or drawing room, as the case maybe, as is the case in this instance, our being in a drawing room just now when it happened, have made it as clear as crystal that while our paths must cross, in order for us to resolve the immediate situation with the gentlemen involved in the consortium--"

"Good grief! Stop that infernal babbling. Get to your point. If there is one. Although, by the devious, convoluted and completely incomprehensible way your mind works when approaching a problem, I doubt there is one. A point, I mean. Not a mind. Damn! Now I'm babbling. Your idiosyncrasies are catching."

He growled deep in his throat several times and ran his hands through his hair in frustration. He wanted to put his hands around her pretty little neck and throttle her. He wanted to throw her on the settee and finish what they'd started. Finish it in a way that ensured she would be fully his and wouldn't contemplate allowing another man to touch her that way. He wanted ... everything.

"What just happened," she said, in the sort of pompous voice she used to deliver a scientific treatise, "in no way entitles either one of us to interfere, or even question, how the other conducts their private life."

His arousal sagged, and shrank, although he doubted it would ever completely desert him while Becca was near. Or even, in the same city. Now, the only thought he had when looking at her was how to escape this situation with a shred of pride intact.

"I have no interest in knowing how," he snapped, "or when, or with whom you do ... well, anything."

"Oh, good."

"Not now, nor in the future."

"Then you will feel no affront when I don't share my methods of research or my conclusions with you."

"I have no wish to know," he said, lying through his teeth.

"You may remain oblivious because I will exercise the uttermost discretion."

"You, discreet! That's like saying the British monarchy has been a model of decorum."

"The gentlemen I have in mind are known for their diplomacy."

"Gentlemen!" Incredulity turned to fury. "You mean more ... more than one."

"A truly trustworthy study is required to be conducted over as broad a continuum as possible. And as these men are all very experienced at conducting illicit affairs, they therefore must be very knowledgeable about pleasing a woman."

Once again, she'd rendered him speechless. Earlier, the determined look on her face had been his undoing. A man didn't often get begged by a woman to touch her in such an intimate fashion. Or, to do even more. And idiot that he was, he'd refused.

Or at least, he'd attempted to refuse. Endeavored to turn and leave. But, she seemed so alive, so vibrant, so uniquely Becca, that he couldn't force his feet to the door.

Currently however, she wore a forced air of innocence that he knew was at odds with her true character and which was an unnatural expression for her elfin face. Her virtuous look worried him even more than her absurd announcements. With a comforting pat on his arm, his nemesis turned and scurried away. At the door, she flicked him a little half wave over her shoulder and then strode out without another glance. Or, without explaining which gentlemen were going to be experimented upon. The mere thought of any other man but him touching her as he had just done, left him angry and shaking. Glaring at her retreating back, he was unable to believe she'd left him standing, without so much as a decent good bye. He yelled in the direction of the empty doorway. "Rebecca Jamison. Come back here and finish that discussion."

However, the only Jamison to appear was Laura, grinning. "I thought family members were the only ones Becca abandoned in the middle of discussions."

"Your sister is the most infuriating, most frustrating--"

"Annoying. Devious. Confusing."

"All of those and more. Does she never stop to think before she hurtles into rash acts?"

After pretending to ponder the question, Laura replied with glee, "No, not often. Becca often doesn't think the same way as others. Her energy is poured into arranging stratagems to make life easier. But she becomes so engrossed in her schemes and experiments that she forgets the hazards of everyday life. She sees it as her duty to help everyone, gentry or commoner so she unwittingly steps into danger. And that's why we all help make her life run smoother. So she can continue her journeys of discovery unhampered."

"Yet, she thinks she's guarding all of you. Her family."

"I know. We allow her to think that. In return, she does an extraordinary job of managing the important things. It's the little things she forgets, like wearing a bonnet to protect her complexion. Or changing out of wet shoes before she becomes chilled. Plus, there is her terrifying tendency to trust the wrong men."

He flinched. "Does that include me?"

"Perhaps. If the shoe fits. You were part of the reason she has vowed never to marry."

"While you advocate that before committing herself to any man, Becca employs the famous Lady Laura Jamison's theory of sampling the wares before she buys."

"Better that than be lumbered with some fop who doesn't know his left hand from his right. Who will never please a woman in bed." She smirked at him, making Cayle squirm under her knowing regard. "But we all know that you know exactly how to please a woman, do we not?"

Afraid to consider just how she knew these things, he was

searching for a change of subject when the answer suddenly occurred to him. "Bloody hell, I forgot. You listen at doors." He felt weak kneed at the implications of that, horrified at the thought. "You were listening? Just now?"

Laura smiled a knowing smile and agreed, "Perhaps. Probably. Oh, well, all right, of course I listened. I need to research lovemaking using specimens who are no threat to my reputation."

Cayle threw back his head and groaned. "Damn all Jamison sisters and their research to hell." Looking at Laura with calculation, he asked, "Will you inform Becca that you listened?"

"Of course. We discuss everything. Every detail, no matter how big, or how small." Her gaze wandered over his tight breeches and nodded. "I can see this will be a particularly lengthy discussion."

As her meaning sunk in, Cayle involuntarily glanced down to where a remnant of his earlier arousal lingered. He felt as embarrassed as an untried youth. With an even more agonized groan, he hastened to the door, muttering a curt goodnight over his shoulder.

"I will return in the morning to escort you on your morning ride."

Rushing out the door to the pavement, Cayle heaved in gulping breaths of cold air but still it wasn't enough to dampen the rush of emotions. Nor was it enough to quell the lustful ardor that had swamped him at the feel, the sounds and the smell of Becca in full-blown orgasm.

The womanly scent of her arousal tugged at him still, a siren's pull. His ears still rang with her screams of completion. He feared bringing his palms to his face because he knew the scent of her lingered upon hands that had invaded her innermost secret places.

He wanted to suck the musky flavor of her juices from his fingers but he forced himself to remain in control of his urges. There was no time in his life for weakness, no time for the temptation of a virginal seductress.

Becca had no idea how close he had come to ravaging her on the soft carpet, or the firm settee, or bent over the hard desk. Still, he'd conquered emotional turmoil before and remained untouched and he would again. If only the lure had not come wrapped as one female package topped with a fiery red ribbon.

Even a saint couldn't endure such torture as being able to look at Becca and not touch, not taste her, and not devour. Despite Becca's accusations, he was not cut out for sainthood.

Hell, he was doomed.

Chapter 9

For the next week, the Duke of Sherwyn and his brothers donned elegant attire to pay calls with the ladies and escort them to the most fashionable events. To Cayle's amazement, the wild girls he'd played with at the Jamison's country house had emerged as London's most stunning women. What made it worse was that, to Cayle's eyes, Becca's vibrant beauty was by far the most enticing.

By his resolve that Becca present herself as befitting her new image of a lady of wealth, he'd drawn the attention of countless bucks to her attractions. And to those of her stunning sisters. Now, the group could not ride, nor stroll the park without being hailed by gentlemen of vague acquaintance angling for introductions. It was enough to drive him mad.

The only consolation was that his brothers suffered alongside him. Tony was blatantly smitten with golden-headed Lottie and Laura had Brian firmly under her thumb. Night after night, they endured the social round, standing on the edge of overcrowded ballrooms and drinking tepid beverages.

The silver salver in the foyer of Grosvenor Square groaned under the weight of calling cards piled high each day. By enlisting the aid of the Jamisons' butler, and stealth, Cayle appointed himself guardian of the sisters' social calendar. Any gentleman he or his brothers considered as too let in the pockets, of too scandalous a reputation, or just too damned handsome to compete with, was ostracized without reason.

And, all without their awareness. Until the day Cayle was caught hovering near the door by their brother, Michael, during his brief visit to the family house to be updated on developments.

"Sherywn! Does Becca know you are vetting her callers?"

Another man might have feigned ignorance but Cayle's nature was more straightforward. He enjoyed confronting a problem, puzzling over possible solutions and applying himself to fixing it, so he presented Michael with the truth.

A portion of the truth, in any case.

Cayle would never disclose to Becca's over-taxed brother what had occurred between him and Becca that night in the sitting room. Nor would Michael be pleased to hear the details of Becca's latest research, or the methods she intended using to conduct it. Although, thanks to Cayle's interference, no man had spent long enough alone with Becca to become her research subject. It became an all-consuming occupation, accompanying Becca, following Becca, protecting Becca. He'd little time to think about anything else.

"I decided--"

"You decided?" Michael laughed, amused by that idea. "Oh, dear, my friend. I would not like to be standing in your shoes when Becca finds out that you are sneaking around rearranging her affairs."

"It's for her safety. You've no idea how much trouble she attracts in a single day."

Michael chuckled and nodded. "Oh, I think I have some idea."

"Why, today alone, I had to forcibly rescue her from attack when she stepped between a chimney sweep and his master. The man beat the boy, a child a quarter of his size."

Now Michael laughed, a full-throated, head thrown back howl of amusement. "Let me guess, Becca jumped in to save the child?"

"Without a thought to her own safety." Cayle shuddered as he remembered his horror at seeing the master's whip coming down towards Becca's exquisite face. "And then she insisted I take the child to my house, in my carriage, feed him in my kitchen and, on top of that, give the little devil a position in my stables."

Michael stared at him intently as he asked, "And did you follow her orders?"

"Your bothersome sister left me little choice. She refused to budge until I gave in and, by then, quite a crowd had formed. Some wanted to call the police to deal with the man and some wanted to join him in his argument against Becca. The situation was becoming out of hand. I had to remove both Becca and the boy quickly before a full scale riot erupted."

Michael shook his head and groaned. "Oh, no. You too."

"Me too what? Why are you looking at me like that?"

"Oh, hell, I've just lost my blunt."

"You made a bet over me?"

"Jonathon and I wagered on how long a man like you'd last."

Cayle became irritated with this confusing conversation. "How long I would last with what?"

"No offense, but you made it clear from the start that any sort of female involvement wasn't in your immediate future."

Cayle stiffened as he said, "That's still the case."

"So, we wagered on how long you could be around Becca and not get involved in her causes. Her problems."

Cayle felt uncertain whether to be offended or not. "And Jonathon won?"

Michael nodded. "He said you'd not last a month without Becca irritating the hell out of you."

"It took a lot less than a month for your sister to exasperate me."

"We also wagered over how long it would be before you fell into your old patterns and, like us, spent every day worrying if someone was on hand to rescue her."

"She told me she no longer needs a knight in shining armor to rescue her."

"I'm afraid that the opposite is often the case. She is rather unique, our intrepid sister. And, eventually, anyone who comes into contact with her gets caught up in her adventures."

"I'm not caught up, I simply admire Becca as a friend."

Michael's eyebrow rose in question.

"All right, I concede that I think of her as more than a friend. And although I insisted we be seen about together, to pretend I courted her to allay suspicion, I'm still not in a position to become involved with any woman."

"So, are you're happy for Becca to conduct investigations with any gentlemen who takes her fancy?"

Cayle looked stunned. "You know about that?"

Michael laughed. "As the oldest male in this madcap household, I employ devious methods to keep watch over my sisters. When my spy network reported you were sieving the post, filching invitations, and ensuring that certain gentlemen were consistently refused admittance, I realized I needed to return home."

"You knew all that?"

"Laura isn't the only Jamison who can pry into everyone else's affairs." He grinned at Cayle's obvious discomfort. "I could modestly say that Laura learned much of what she knows from her brother."

"So you know of Becca's research? And Laura's?"

"Sampling before purchase."

Cayle stared at Michael, irritated with his casual attitude. "Then why do you allow it?"

"Ah, there you are again, Cayle. Assuming that any mere male would be able to control my highly intelligent sisters. Each of them is extremely capable in their own line of expertise. So my aunt and I decided that it's better to let them assume control, as long as we're there to diminish any unfavorable outcomes."

"That must be a full time occupation."

"Yes, well you can see why I am anxious for one, or all of them, to find husbands who can relieve Jonathon and I of the responsibility."

"It'll take a strong man to willingly bind himself to any one of them."

"A very strong man indeed." He continued to scrutinize Cayle.

"Oh no, Michael. Don't look at me like that. I've enough problems with my stepmother, and the estate. I can't be anything other than a friend to Becca."

Michael nodded in agreement. "Nevertheless, you'd like to be more, wouldn't you?"

"Becca is amazing. Intelligent. Beautiful. So full of life. Everything any man dreams about."

"Dreams about as a wife?"

"I've no intention of marrying any time soon."

"So, when we have settled the matter of the consortium, you'll have no further interest in my sister."

"I thought the pretense of a courtship would explain my presence at her side. She emphasized that I was an old family friend helping launch Laura and Lottie. Nothing more."

"Ah, yes. Unfortunately, Becca avoids any mention of marriage unless it concerns the four of us. She's been harmed enough in the past."

"I promise I'll do my utmost not to upset her further."

"As her brother, I must warn you that if you toy with her affections, if you hurt her in any way, I'll be forced to act. Agreed?"

"Agreed." Cayle understood Michael's concerns. If he had sisters, he'd be just as protective, if not worse.

"In that case, Becca is better off remaining under your protection, as a friend, while I'm hampered at Oxford. I've made enquiries into the role you played on the Continent, and Jonathon and I are satisfied that a man of your reputation is the best person to defend Becca from the consortium's threats."

Cayle frowned. Nobody was supposed to know of the part he and his friends played in keeping England updated on the politics of countries on the Continent.

"You made inquiries about me? From whom?"

"Let us just say that in the last two years we've made a number of powerful friends in government."

"Then, why have you not presented your fears about the consortium to them?"

"Because until we've written proof of each man's involvement, it's unfair to sling wild accusations around. Mud sticks, and the majority of these men are titled and from influential families. The Jamison family has been building a reputation of fair dealings in commercial matters. Our livelihood and our entire future depend upon it. So, before we uncover anyone's secrets, we must be positive that the men who are really in charge don't slip through our grasp. And that those who've only minor involvement, and no real knowledge of the depth of corruption in their ranks, aren't ruined."

"Yes, I agree. The innocent men have families depending on them."

"Unless anything changes in your association with Becca in the next week, we're leaving her welfare in your hands." Michael eyed him closely as he stipulated, "In the case of your relationship taking a turn, for better or for worse, I'll assume you'll do the correct thing and inform me of your intentions."

"Understood." Michael's warning was unnecessary. Cayle had no intention of stepping over the line he'd drawn between himself and Becca; no matter how prettily she begged.

"And, Michael, your contacts in our government must be powerful and put a lot of trust in you if they revealed anything about me. But now I need you to understand, I'll overlook your interference in my affairs in this one instance, given your concern for Becca. But neither I, nor my friends, tolerate anyone intruding in our pasts. Men have tried it before. And come to grief." Michael's eyebrows rose at Cayle's implied threat. He nodded his agreement.

***

Later that afternoon as he trailed the Jamison sisters, Cayle acknowledged that all three were stunning: strikingly beautiful, well-bred and far too intelligent for their own, or anyone else's good. Her Majesty's frequent walks through Kew Gardens to observe any new developments had made them the place to be seen, and therefore the best place to garner the latest gossip and rumors. Whenever they could escape duties with Julia, he and his brothers escorted the sisters on such outings, ostensibly so the women could mix with the cream of society.

But while most debutantes mingled to be seen, the Jamisons hunted information. Little by little, they were eliminating gentlemen definitely not involved in the consortium. Some had no spare money to invest, so the ladies politely dismissed them. Some were too lazy to be involved in commercial ventures, prepared to sit back and allow themselves to be supported by their families.

Cayle was constantly shocked at how much these gentlemen would reveal to Lottie, in exchange for one of her smiles, and how eager they were to impress her with anecdotes of their latest money making ventures.

"It's disgusting how these idiots hang on her every word," Tony complained to his brothers as they walked behind the ladies.

Brian and Cayle exchanged a grin before Brian teased his brother. "But, Tony, you can't deny that you also hang on her every word. You also are one of those drooling idiots."

"I'm not as bad as them," Tony protested. He looked at his older brother for adjudication. "Am I?"

Cayle laughed but decided it was more politic to ease his brother's worry a little. "Of course not. You've not written some sloppy love poem to her eyes yet, as your friend Theo has done, nor have you scattered rose petals for her to walk on like Clement."

Tony glared at Brian and said to Cayle, "The voice of reason, thank goodness."

"But you do become tongue tied every time Lottie asks you a question," Cayle teased.

Tony was about to protest but, at that moment the lady in question spun back to implore them, "Could one of you gentlemen kindly take Mr. Burnsbury aside and explain that I'm not interested in marrying him, no matter how many times a day he asks me. It seems my earnest pleas for him to cease are falling upon deaf ears and, while he hovers, I'm unable to extract any important information from the others."

"I...I..." Tony stuttered.

Cayle hid a smile whilst Brian stepped closer to Lottie to say, "I think my younger brother is trying to assure you he that he'll take care of the matter."

Lottie laid a hand on Tony's arm and his color heightened to a tomato red and he stammered once again. Deciding it was time to relieve his misery, Cayle said, "Never fear, Lottie. We will dispatch Mr. Burnsbury."

Lottie's eyes widened. "But, please, Cayle, do not appear quite so ferocious. You'll terrify him. He is a pestering sort of man, but harmless enough."

"Lottie, you're too kind hearted. The man is a nuisance," Brian remarked.

Cayle eased aside his two brothers while he reassured Lottie. "I'll personally attend to Mr. Burnsbury and no harm will befall him." She smiled up at him, that dazzling smile showing pristine white teeth, and placed her gloved fingers on his forearm.

In that instant, he was almost reduced to the same state as Tony. The same state he'd been in at Grosvenor Square the day he had become reacquainted with the sisters. Lottie had the ability to reduce every man to a quivering mass of jelly, although now that he'd kissed Becca, touched her, Lottie's pale beauty held no charm for him. His preference leaned towards something a lot more fiery.

"Lottie, do stop teasing the St. Martin men," Becca said from close behind them, causing all three men to jump.

Unrepentant, Lottie smiled. "Oh, Becca, I'm only tormenting

them a little. I know Cayle isn't susceptible to my flirting."

Lottie drew Brian and Tony back to the group of hovering men.

Cayle smiled at Becca and leaned close to her ear to whisper, "Were you jealous, my love?"

"Certainly not. Lottie's my sister. I appreciate how beautiful she is. How men are struck dumb by her looks."

"Becca, neither of your sisters is as beautiful as you. Lottie may be a more practiced flirt, but you don't need to flirt with me to enthrall me, my sweet. You've already done that."

Becca reddened at his words and dropped her gaze. Lottie drifted by them on the path, followed by her entourage. As she passed, she giggled and murmured to Cayle, "And Becca thinks you're her hero, her white knight. You're both equally smitten."

Cayle felt a great deal better now the tide had turned, and put a finger under Becca's chin to lift her head. He grinned when her color heightened even more. "So, you're smitten with me," he said in a smug voice.

"Your conceit is without equal. I'm smitten with all these wonderful gentlemen. It's simply a matter of deciding with whom I will conduct my next experiments." She gave a little wave of her fingers to dismiss him and merged with the group, leaving Cayle floundering with outrage.

How dare she make these outlandish announcements and then leave him standing gulping and spluttering? It wasn't to be tolerated any longer. There would be no experiments in the bedroom with anyone but him. She was ready for another lesson in pleasure and he was the only teacher who would be educating her, certainly not any of these drooling idiots. Perhaps tonight he'd demonstrate the next step in their liaison.

But, for now, they needed a confirmed list of which consortium members were pressuring the Jamisons. Time was running out. They needed to move faster. Becca was becoming impatient and in her present mood, he feared she would do something rash. And he had little or no chance of controlling her once she had made up her mind. Michael was correct. Controlling these girls was akin to ordering the wind to stop blowing or the sun to cease shining.

Looking at Becca now, surrounded by ardent admirers whom he planned on dispatching very soon, she resembled the sunshine itself. She glowed. She radiated warmth to everyone around her. No wonder these men clustered closer. Basked in her heat. Lord Stewart Meacham was basking in her heat now, leaning over her exposed bosom. Far too closely. Damn the rogue. Cayle strode forward to slip an arm around Becca's waist.

He inched Becca sideward away from Meacham's leering gaze. "Please allow the lady room to breathe, or she may faint." He coughed into his hand to hide his laugh at Becca's stunned expression.

"Faint? I've never--"

"Never been strong!" Cayle said. "Yes, we know. I'll escort you to your sisters."

Becca narrowed her eyes and all but snarled at him. He met her gaze and smiled, all innocence, as he led her away towards where her sisters were enclosed by another group of men. Laura and Lottie moved aside to allow her to join their conversation with a group of young bucks and Cayle resigned himself to another half hour of listening to mindless chatter.

Tony came to stand beside him and slapped his back and laughed.

"Thank God none of us are as dim-witted as them," Cayle muttered. He pointed to where Meacham leered at Becca. "Or as much of a rake as him, getting a thrill from peering down the bodices of innocents. The man is disgusting."

"Remove the scowl from your face or you will frighten away all their suitors," Tony remarked.

Cayle growled. "Those aren't suitors. They're a pack of animals circling their prey."

"Be thankful those women aren't susceptible to flattery and fribble. Their main intention here isn't to secure husbands, but to distinguish which gentlemen are desperate enough for easy access to wealth to risk offering marriage to a Jamison sister."

"And have any declared their intentions to you?"

Tony grinned again. "Do you refer to honorable or dishonorable intentions?"

Cayle scowled at his brother. "I expect that if you heard of any dishonorable thoughts directed towards Becca--" he corrected hastily, "or any of the girls, of course, that you'd inform me at once."

"Calm yourself. Few of these men are willing to take the risk of upsetting any of Michael Jamison's sisters. Or the Duke of Sherwyn. Talk is that the majority of them are anxious to ingratiate themselves in order to uncover the secrets of the family's new wealth. Michael is fêted whenever he shows his face at a London club. That's why he's taken to hiding out at Oxford and not venturing up to town very often."

"So, because Michael isn't around, these fortune hunters and scoundrels are targeting his sisters."

"That's why Brian and I promised Michael we'd watch over the girls as much as we're able. Everyone knows there'll be an increase in railway expansion very soon. However, it's beyond the arithmetical capabilities of most of the indolent men of our class to calculate where it's likeliest to happen first."

"But can the Jamisons verify it accurately?"

"In the past two years, they've invested without err in the right locale at precisely the right time. The family has made enormous profits, although they've taken great pains to hide the exact figure. Michael tries to protect the girls from these very fortune hunters."

"And by insisting they accompany me through the social whirl, I've exposed them all to these bounders each and every day." He groaned. "What the hell have I done?"

Brian tried to console him. "Cheer up, Cayle. If you'd refused to aid them, they'd have resorted to other means to finagle information."

"What other means?"

"Laura revealed they'd already searched four gentlemen's documents before they approached you."

Cayle groaned again. "Do I want to hear this?"

"No, but I'll tell you anyway. The girls have been taught the ways of housebreaking from experts."

"You mean they're criminals."

"It hasn't gone that far yet."

"Yet?"

"They've not needed to enter houses in an underhanded

manner because they gain entrance through the front door, like well brought up ladies. Several names were eliminated from their initial list of suspects because one or other of the sisters searched desk drawers for paperwork while paying afternoon visits."

"It's intolerable. Becca hinted that she may require me to steal papers, yet they've taken care of it themselves. Again. And she neglected to tell me. Again. They've become impulsive and reckless in their pursuit of these men."

"Ah," Tony said, "but they've more than enough reason. Their futures are at risk. Their father, the Earl, is still an amiable enough sort, but he's so involved in his historical diggings in Scotland that he barely remembers to take care of his own family."

"His five children have become very resourceful," Brian said in an admiring tone. "And, jointly, they protect their Aunt Agatha who has reared them since their mother's passing."

Laura and Lottie called upon his two brothers to settle a difference of opinion over which of the night's entertainments they should visit first.

Cayle cast a jaundiced eye over Becca's admirers. He admired her far too much to condemn her to life as a childless spinster, but amongst the fops, dandies and, worst of all, the rakes, clustered around, there wasn't a single one good enough for her.

Reading the desire on the faces of these men was easy. Once, his face had been stamped with the same looks of lust and desire when mixing with young widows and debutantes, the same male need to stalk and conquer.

For Becca, to be conquered would be to cut off all that was good in her, all which made her stand out. No man should ride roughshod over her intellect and enthusiasm. The man who gained Becca's trust would be someone outstanding. Someone who appreciated her as she was. Someone like him.

He couldn't stop thinking about her responsiveness. His thoughts always took him back to the same place. His bed. Her bed. With them both in it. No other woman he'd ever met was quite like her. She was intelligent beyond a level usually acceptable in the haute ton, even for a gentleman.

One moment, Becca was a fiery temptress, yet the next she was an unpretentious innocent. Soft, sensuous, delicious. At this rate, he'd never believe anyone suitable to be her husband, not while he could see only himself in that exacting role. The only man capable of giving her endless pleasure, of aiding her in her charity work, of being her accomplice in intrigue, was himself. She made him hunger for sex and dare he think it, love and commitment. However, he'd given his solemn oath to Julia.

Meacham once again edged the others aside and moved closer to Becca. Cayle's temper burned as Meacham dared to put his hand around Becca's waist. Stepping forward, he none too gently kicked Meacham's leg behind the knee, causing him to overbalance.

As he struggled to remain upright, Cayle took his place beside Becca and feigned an expression of concern. Meacham saved himself by putting out his arms but landed faced down on the grass, soiling his clothing.

"Meacham. Apologies. I fear I inadvertently bumped into you." Meacham recovered himself and glared at Cayle. A look passed between them, man to man, and Meacham understood that it hadn't been an accident. He stood and shook himself off.

"No matter, Sherywn. Accidents happen."

"Perhaps you should retire to your house and allow your valet to attend to your wounds."

"You haven't heard the end of this, Sherwyn," Meacham challenged. "Don't think that your title will protect you. Rumor has it that you're a marked man."

Cayle stiffened at the threat but had no chance to ask what he meant as inquisitive passers-by hovered around them. Meacham stormed off through the park, leaving them all unsettled. When Laura suggested the group disperse to prepare for the night's entertainment, they readily agreed.

"Ladies, my carriage awaits at the park's entrance. As the weather has turned inclement, I suggest we make a hasty departure."

Brian and Tony escorted Laura and Lottie along the path at a hastened pace, while Becca drew back to walk beside Cayle, tugging on his sleeve.

"What did Meacham mean about you being a marked man?" Her eyes were wide and her fingers dug into his arm through the weave of his woolen coat. He unwound her hand and placed it over his arm, smoothing out her fingers, enjoying the feel of her warm body pressed against him.

"Nothing. Nothing for you to worry about."

"Don't lie to me, Cayle. You know I'll discover the truth this evening anyway."

"Ah, yes. The Jamisons' famous sources of information."

He made a futile attempt at diverting her, but he'd be better trying to push back the tide than curtail Becca's curiosity. He sucked in a deep breath and exhaled slowly while deciding how much to reveal. "My friend, Devon, whom you met last week, informed me this morning over breakfast that my involvement with you has been noted. Unfavorably so. One of his informants brought to his attention that there is money to be made by any man willing to hasten my demise."

"Oh, no, Cayle," Becca exclaimed. "Why didn't you tell me? Oh, my goodness. This is dreadful."

"Calm yourself, sweetheart." He patted her hand and wouldn't allow her to withdraw it from his arm. "It probably has nothing to do with you or your family. Devon and I made enemies before we left France. It's probably a competitor in the markets over there wanting to rid themselves of competition."

Becca frowned and he knew he hadn't convinced her. When they reached the waiting carriage, Brian and Tony had already seated her sisters. Cayle handed Becca inside. "If you'll excuse me, Brian and I have pressing matters to attend to. Tony will escort you home."

"Becca, don't fret," Tony said. "Cayle can take care of himself. A lot better than he could before. His time away taught him a lot."

"It's also hardened him," Becca murmured. "I wonder what will soften him."

Tony grinned. "Oh, I think he may have already found what he needs for that." He nodded happily to Laura and Lottie. "Yes, my big brother may well have met his match."

After instructing the coachman, Cayle reached in to place a light kiss on Becca's gloved hand. "Don't fret, sweetheart. I'm a hard man to kill."

Ignoring her protests, he latched the door and he and Brian doffed their hats and strode away, knowing he was leaving Becca to fret and fume. Perhaps Tony could comfort her. But they had only walked five paces when he heard a voice behind him call out. He stopped and looked. A freckled face was peering out the carriage window.

"Cayle St. Martin, you will be at Grosvenor Square at eight o'clock tonight. Or I will shoot you myself."

Relieved that everything was as it should be between he and Becca, Cayle grinned and walked away. Somebody wanted him dead as well and he now had something important to live for.

Her name was Becca.

Chapter 10

"This crush is ridiculous," Laura muttered to Becca.

Cayle had arranged invitations to a ball given by the parents of his friend, Percy. The Duke and Duchess of Leicester eagerly welcomed the girls to their home as, according to gossip, they were terrified their son might waste another ten years carousing with his friends and being seen with Covent Garden actresses. Percy was expected to marry and produce a legitimate heir.

"As I said," Becca said, "knees only tremble at balls from being squeezed between a thousand other knees." She wore a fixed smile and curtsied, over and over, until her legs trembled as she greeted an endless clutch of guests. Many she knew, plus Cayle presented them to another forty or fifty couples and single men whose rank equaled his and were, therefore, richer society than the Jamisons had recently socialized with.

"Hearts only race," Becca murmured to her sisters when they had a small break from formal introductions, "when girls are fending off rakes who, out of sheer boredom, start a flirtation to pass the long tedious hours, while they oversee their pure-as-the-driven-snow sisters and protect them from men exactly like themselves."

"Becca, you're too cynical," Lottie said. "You should be grateful to Cayle for arranging this."

"Don't misunderstand. I am excited about being here. Because we now have a legitimate excuse for wandering through the Leicester's home. If I'm seen searching any of the rooms, I'll pretend to be lost."

They edged away from Cayle, and the ladies fighting to get closer to him, and surreptitiously made their way around the perimeter of the room to a less crowded area away. The area below the receiving line remained crowded with those of the ton, who scrutinized every new arrival and noted every name announced by the butler as they descended the stairs.

Footmen offered them glasses of chilled champagne and, as Aunt Aggie had gravitated towards her many acquaintances, the girls were happy to accept their drinks. Aggie had stayed in contact with dozens of her well-placed friends, even though the Jamisons' strained financial years, and retained many connections amongst the social elite. Soon after their arrival, she became embroiled in a heated discussion over the most eligible bachelor of the season.

"Soon the orchestra will play for dancing," Lottie announced.

"Which means men will gather around you like bees to a honey pot, Lottie," Laura remarked.

"Which also means a perfect opportunity for you to quiz them about the Baron," Becca added. "Michael can't delay the consortium much longer. The last names on our list are almost confirmed, but we need absolute proof that the Baron and his friends are the main organizers of the fraud. And we still don't know which man murdered Peggy."

"I'll try again with Lord Dermott and Mister Foster, but every time I mention the Baron, the gentlemen exchange speaking glances, become tight lipped and scurry away like scared mice."

Laura nodded, knowing she should feel grateful to be here at such a sumptuous ball. Other young women were joyous when shown the slightest attention from handsome men, and since Cayle announced that three eligible sisters were on the marriage market, men had flocked to their sides. On cue, Lord Dermott arrived just as the orchestra struck up and requested the first dance with Lottie, while friends drew Becca away. Watching her sisters, Laura knew the end of this continual social whirl would come when they solved the problem of the consortium.

Unfortunately for Becca, her days spent in the company of Cayle would also end. Despite her protests to the contrary, Laura was certain Cayle once more enthralled Becca. Tonight, Cayle accompanied his stepmother, having explained during their afternoon walk that it was necessary for him to continue to escort Julia. As soon as Julia disappeared to the card room he would find them, or rather Becca. They'd started to depend on the appearances of the St. Martin brothers in their daily life. To look forward to them.

A short time later, Laura paced at the side of the ball room while still keeping near Aunt Aggie for respectability sake, gnawing her bottom lip with her teeth in a fashion that if her chaperone turned around, would make her shudder.

"Where the hell is Becca?"

Aunt Aggie leaned closer. "Did you say something, dear?

With a fixed smile, Laura addressed her aging aunt and her equally ancient friends. "No, I was simply thinking out loud."

"Well, my girl, you would do better to leave your thinking for later and attract the attention of one of those handsome, young gentlemen standing near the door. I expect that with a teeny bit of encouragement, they'll be vying to stand up for the next set with you."

Laura muttered something that her aunt took for wholehearted agreement. It was in fact an observation that those gentlemen looked ready to bolt for their clubs as soon as they'd survived the hours required by their mothers or sisters at this, another boring event. Despite her glare, one of them approached. The rail-thin and extremely tall gentleman Laura didn't recognize passed by her aunt and, then, when close behind Laura, pressed something into her hand. Startled, she opened her mouth to speak but he continued right by as if nothing had happened. Not knowing what to think, she slipped the note into her reticule and made an excuse to slip away to the retiring room for privacy.

Nodding and speaking to several acquaintances delayed her and then, in frustration, she had to wait until the room emptied. She pulled out the note and read: *Tell your brother he has only three days to gather the remaining information we require. If he fails to deliver, harm will befall his entire family, commencing with his pretty sisters.*

Laura pushed aside her shock and rushed back to her aunt's chair. "Aunt Aggie," she said, trying to sound unconcerned. "Is Becca dancing?"

"She became a trifle overcome with the heat. His Grace kindly took her to the door for a breath of air. I'm sure she'll return in a moment."

Laura disagreed but smiled and murmured her thanks. If Becca was with Cayle, chances were they were outside, possibly alone, so it wouldn't do to bring attention to that fact. Sidling along the wall, she escaped to the doors, hoping no one would notice. Just as she slipped backwards out the open door, she slammed up against a body and judging from the rigid strength she felt, a male body.

"Damn!"

"A word I'd not thought to hear from a young lady this evening."

Turning, she faced the large immovable object blocking her exit. "If you would be so good as to move aside, I'm in urgent need of fresh air."

He smirked at her before he moved a scant six inches to the side, knowing full well that to pass she would be forced into close contact with his large, muscular body.

Giving him her fiercest glare, Laura said, "If you could just shift a little more to the left, I would be grateful."

"How grateful? Grateful enough to grant me your name?"

"My name is none of your business, you knave. Now step aside at once."

"Your obvious desperation to escape the ball has me curious. Why would a young lady be slipping into the garden alone? Ah! Perhaps you are meeting a lover."

Furious at being detained, Laura glared up at the man towering over her. Now that she could distinguish his features better, she realized he was not only a giant to her demure size, he was also the most handsome man she'd ever seen.

Becca preferred men of the tall, dark, and mysterious bent, but Laura was drawn to the more traditional idea of handsome. Fair-haired English gentlemen with lithe figures and blue eyes, conservative dress and a flair for flattery. The man standing in front of her, practically on top of her, was none of these things.

In coloring, he favored the St. Martin men, with dark hair and eyes. Studying him more closely, she discovered that he not only had Cayle's height and breadth of shoulders but his air of proud self-assurance as well. Eyes that were nearly as black as Cayle's regarded her steadily, waiting for the moment she finished her perusal of his form and looked up to connect with his gaze once more.

The gentleman waited in amused silence until Laura completed her inspection. Watching her, Winchester concluded this was no simpering or blushing miss inspecting him so carefully. Her eyes were not quite as dark as his but more the brown of an oak nut. Her regard was shrewd, as if she was studying some rare species of animal and must remember every detail to be later copied into a science manual. Neither did she have the brazen look of the married women who pursued him at these affairs, Sybila being a case in point. She was the reason he himself used the gardens as a means of escape until such time as he would have performed his duty and could reasonably excuse himself.

He'd next visit either one of his clubs or the house of his mistress. Despite the fact that he was bored with his current mistress after only a single month, the prospect of being trapped by Lady Sybila, and he used the term lady loosely, was even worse. As an older brother to several sisters, all coming of marriageable age, he performed his duty for the first half of most evenings by escorting them to the numerous balls and soirees they routinely received invitations to because of their revered family name and titled connections. Now the chit had finished her scrutiny, she seemed even more desperate to escape. On her dramatic features, he clearly read her indecision as to whether she would be rude and push past him or if she should return to the ballroom before her absence was noticed.

He couldn't help himself. He taunted her simply to see how she would react. "Indeed, quite a dilemma. Do you try to slip by me without coming into contact with any part of my body, a scandalous interaction considering we've not been introduced, or do you abandon whichever gentleman awaits you beneath the terrace? An agonizing choice. Which is it, my dark beauty?"

She gnawed her pouting bottom lip while she considered the impasse he'd deliberately generated. By now, she was running out of time. Whoever awaited her would become impatient.

"Damn," she repeated, louder this time. He raised a brow in question.

"Sir, I require your assistance for the next hour. But you may not ask any questions."

Good gracious. The chit actually thought to give him orders. Of course she had no idea of his identity, or of his reputation. His father had raised him to believe that the females of his family were to be cosseted, whether they appreciated his efforts or not. For the most part, his sisters chafed against what they called his excessive meddling in their daily lives and often chastised him for being conceited and overbearing.

But as they were family and he loved them dearly, he accepted that women should be allowed claim a modicum of control over their own lives. He would be the first to accede that his sisters were all extremely intelligent women. Mama had insisted upon it. She'd reviled weak willed women, believing all young ladies should have enough nonce to arrange their own lives to some extent.

As a kindness, he allowed his sisters the illusion of making their own decisions yet, behind the scenes, the reins remained tightly in his own gloves. Which, by the unwritten code of ethics of his immense family, was how it should be.

Amazed yet intrigued at the brashness of this girl, he countered, "You expect me to render assistance to you, a young lady I have not been formally introduced to, without you volunteering any information to me?"

"Yes, exactly. Now, come along. We have no time to waste."

Taking his arm, she attempted to move him from his intractable stance in the doorway. Irritated and frustrated, she glared up at him once again.

"Sir, you'll need to move. Quickly. Before he escapes."

"Before whom escapes from where? I'm going nowhere without at least that much information."

"Very well," Laura snapped. "A gentleman slipped a note to me in the ballroom but I was unable to identify him or give chase."

"Give chase?"

"Yes. It would be unseemly for a woman to rush through a crowded ballroom without an escort. But with you on my arm, it will pass for a leisurely stroll with an acquaintance."

"Ah, but we're not acquainted."

"Oooh! You are the most difficult man I've ever met."

"Careful, my lady, if you want my assistance you may want to temper your contrariness."

"My contrariness? You're the brute who refuses to budge an inch."

"Ah, now I'm a brute?"

She smiled up at him with overdone sweetness, even going so far as to flutter her eyelashes. "My good sir, would you be kind enough to escort me for a stroll around the room."

"Good God! You look even more dangerous when you are trying to sweet talk me."

"I've no need to sweet talk anyone. Ever."

He hid a grin. She was probably correct. With her looks and her determination she probably had half the toffs of the ton following her around like lap dogs. "It's high time you learned. Tell me your name at least or I'm not moving."

Bowing his head to hide his amusement, he waited while she held an inner debate. Obviously, the time factor won the argument for him as she acceded to his request with a sigh of reluctance. A gloved hand flashed out at him. The chit couldn't be haughtier if she tried, and he was sure she wasn't trying to be irritating but showing her natural nature.

"I am Lady Laura Jamison."

Memory assailed him. "Ah, of course you are. The middle one of the Jamison sisters."

Faltering a little at his unexpected recognition, she inquired, "You know of my family?"

"I do. I'm second cousin to Sherwyn. We used to visit your house with him. I remember a trio of hoydens--"

"Hoydens!" Dark eyes glinted with menace as her nose rose higher in the air. "My sisters and I were merely a trifle energetic in our youth."

"Energetic! You created mayhem everywhere you went."

Narrowing her gaze, she fixed him with her dark stare, one obviously intended to make grown men quake in their boots. He ignored it. "And now that you're past your youth, you still don't seem to behave as a well-bred young lady should."

"Ah, I now remember the uncouth family members Cayle used to have tagging after him. You're the infamous Earl of Winchester. Your scandalous exploits haven't improved with age, my lord."

Hiding his annoyance at being known for a few slightly scandalous escapades when he was younger, he felt a change of subject necessary before she had the audacity to speak of other topics he'd rather leave in the distant past.

"So, to return to your urgent problem, you need me as a decoy while you hunt for an unknown man. What was in the note he gave you?"

"I can't tell you that. Trust me when I say that it's a matter of life and death to not only my family, but yours as well."

"Now, I'm intrigued." He considered the matter for a moment before making a decision. "Very well. You'll call me Richard and we'll stroll the room, and if asked, we'll say that my cousin reintroduced us, as we're old family friends."

"Thanks goodness you are finally over your obstinacy. Becca must be warned that one of the men who's been following us, threatening her, is right here amongst us. In this room."

Placing her hand lightly on his arm, she once again urged him forward. He could never remember being led around by a female in quite the same way before. Usually it was he who did the leading, on his terms, in his own time. But this elfin creature demonstrated gigantic assuredness as she marched him around the perimeter of the dance floor, made a rapid assessment of the figure of every gentleman and with a few muttered words passed on.

"Far too short. Too fat. Too limp."

A snort escaped him at that description of Frederick Bundall, who considered himself the epiphany of fashion, his lithe form the mold for all the gentleman of London to copy. Being described as limp would send him to his bed for a week.

Being led around the room like a boy in short pants was such an unusual occurrence for him, he decided it was the most fun he had encountered at a ball since he and his cousins had added six frogs to the punch. The incredible beauty on his arm seemed totally oblivious to the envious looks flashed in his direction from practically every gent they passed. Nor did she seem to notice the waves of annoyance and almost hatred emanating from most of the young ladies present.

Richard had never a met a debutante like her. Far from preening like a peacock, as most were taught to do from birth, this vision of loveliness remained unaware of the impact she created, or of the people around her.

Her whole mind was focused on locating the man who'd slipped her a note, so he concluded that the matter must hold great urgency. Her tiny, gloved hand grasped his whilst her silken skirts swished as they strode, legs in a matching rhythm pressing close together. If it had been any other young woman, he would've made idle chitchat, produced an inane smile, and been secretly bored to tears.

But with the lithe body pressed close to his side in their hurry, he'd no time for conversation, no time to do anything but obey her silent commands. The audacious chit towed him through the crowd like a rowboat on a rope.

He might not be as highly ranked as his cousin, Cayle, a duke, but earls were customarily afforded more deference than this hoyden seemed prepared to show. He idly wondered if her father, also an earl, was shown this sort of disrespect by his wayward daughter.

A woman clinging tightly to the arm of a known rake would normally indicate to onlookers that they were in the midst of already enjoying a torrid love affair, or that the aforesaid rake was grooming the lady for his forthcoming seduction. That the man either knew, or was about to know, the woman intimately. But Laura Jamison gave no more thought to him than she would the stone pillars they were rushing past. He was a male body of large enough dimensions to clear a path for her and propel them around, or through, the multitude of people and acres of petticoats and skirts in the fastest possible time. And she appeared oblivious to the horrified stares they were attracting from people in the chattering groups they were forcibly disrupting.

Male friends, no doubt in search of an introduction to the exquisite creature on his arm, tried to attract his attention. If he wasn't moving fast enough to suit her purposes, she gripped his arm like a vice and urged him forward. Suddenly, she stiffened and came to such an abrupt halt that he took two steps forward before stopping an arm's length from her. Her gaze was fixed with intent upon the back of a tall, thin gent engrossed in conversation with a mixed group of socialites.

She whipped her attention back to him to ask in a fierce whisper, "Do you know him?"

When his answer was not forthcoming in a timely enough manner, she stepped around in front of him. Her jutting nipples grazed his coat buttons as she peered straight up at him, a cross look creasing her brow. He nearly gasped aloud.

"Hurry, you slow top. Do you recognize that man?"

She poked a hard finger in his chest bone.

"Ouch!" Richard rubbed at the sore spot, and dragged his gaze upwards from the sight of such lush cream breasts threatening to burst from their constricting fabric as the tiny whirlwind heaved deep breaths. At least she released his arm from her death grip as he swiveled to study the man she was watching.

"I believe that is Lord Kinsley. He was at Eton with me."

"Excellent. You can introduce us. I need to get closer to see if he is the man who pushed the letter into my hand. It was dark, yet I'm sure I can recognize him. If not by sight, then at least by smell."

"Smell?" he inquired. Did she really mean she was going to sniff the man? Knowing the Jamison girls as he did from past experience, he believed she would actually do it.

"Yes, I have a very sensitive nose and I've been training myself to distinguish smells in able to identify things, or people, more accurately."

"Pardon my ignorance on the nuances of scents, but how will smelling people help?"

"I'm testing a theory that gentlemen put out different aromas. Well, women do too, but I'm naturally concentrating on the male species."

"Why naturally? Why only the male species?"

Her strange conversation was making his head spin and her exasperated tone made him feel like the performing baboon his sisters had called commands to at the Natural Science Museum. African monkeys had a hard time following conversations of young girls much as he did following this one.

"I'm investigating to see if gentlemen who are more passionate have a different scent to those who are staid."

"And this will help, why?"

"No girl who has an ounce of passion in her soul wants to end up married to a man who is staid and boring. The marriage bed would soon become a chore."

Richard considered himself worldly in the extreme, as most rakes were known to be, but the incongruity of such blunt speaking issuing from the mouth of this girl he assumed was an innocent, was impossible for him to reconcile. A quick glance showed him that they'd not been overheard, but just as she'd been oblivious to the looks of the people they passed, she also was unconcerned that anyone might listen to their bawdy conversation. She obviously hadn't been out in society long enough to understand that the main reason for these ridiculously overcrowded balls was to be seen and to see. To gossip with and gossip about. And to listen in on conversations, in order to obtain more tidbits to gossip about the next day over morning calls.

The girl was a menace. Yet, an intriguing one.

"So, how do you rate my scent, Miss Nose?"

He treated her to his most winning smile, certain she would give him an encouraging answer, designed to flatter his ego. She inhaled briefly and her eyes widened, but she didn't answer.

"Do I rate highly on the passion scale?" He felt a tiny shiver in his neck and experienced an unused to flicker of anxiety as he waited for her anticipated affirmative answer.

He was a confirmed rake, a notorious seducer of widows and willing wives. Naturally, he would rate far higher in comparison than the majority of the insipid young whips present tonight. So why was she not reassuring him immediately that his assumption was correct? His scent seemed to be totally unnerving her, yet not in a good way.

Instead, she gave a little shake of her head and looked straight past him, to where Lord Kinsley moved away from the ladies he was with. Once again an imperative hand tugged on his arm and gripped his sleeve, dragging him along.

"I simply don't have time to spend conversing with you. Introduce me to Lord Kinsley before he escapes."

"He is hardly escaping." But when he looked again, it did indeed seem as if Lord Kinsley had spotted Richard's insistent companion and was hastening away from them. Spurred to action, he wove a path through the groups in front of them to arrive directly in the path of the departing lord.

Smiling broadly, he addressed the man as if they were the greatest of friends. "Lord Kinsley, it's been some time since we met. Allow me to introduce my companion, Lady Laura Jamison."

Laura extended her gloved hand so close to Lord Kinsley's chest, he had no choice but to clasp it lightly and execute a slight bow over it. "Delighted to meet you, Lady Laura."

To Richard's ear, the words seemed sincere yet the tone held a distinct chill. Interesting, he thought. Perhaps little Miss Nose was correct. For some reason, Lord Kinsley seemed in a hurry to leave them, even now edging away as if seeking a quick escape. But the diligent Lady Laura was not about to let him escape.

Inching even closer, Laura kept hold of Lord Kinsley's hand and leaned into his coat. And sniffed. Richard was horrified. Did the chit not understand the advantages of subtlety? Luckily, Lord Kinsley's face was so far above Laura's dark head that he couldn't see what she was about. Reaching out, Richard removed Laura's hand and placed it on his own sleeve, covering it with a firm hand when she tried to pull away. Laura looked up at Kinsley's gaunt face and smiled. Not a nice smile. More of a sneer.

"My Lord, I feel we've met before. Someone bumped into me a short time ago in the hallway near the retiring rooms. Could it have been you?"

"Certainly not, my lady. A gentleman would stop to apologize if he had bumped a lady. I am a gentleman. I've been involved in a discussion of the inclement weather with a wonderful group of friends."

Richard moved back slightly to reveal the group that Lord Kinsley had edged away from, recognizing several of the ladies. He groaned inwardly upon recognizing the more unruly elements of society that a young innocent like Laura Jamison should never encounter. At that moment, one of the women spotted him and welcomed him with a languid smile.

"Richard." Jemima King purred as she reached for his hand and stroked his fingers between her two palms. "How unusual to see you still remaining at one of these gatherings after the fourth set of dancing."

As she spoke, Jemima leaned forward far enough that her over endowed chest threatened to spring free of its inadequate holdings. The bodice of her gown was cut more than fashionably low, displaying for the men present an immodest amount of flesh.

The rest of the group closed around Richard, forcing him to acknowledge them and gain an introduction to his companion. With great reluctance, he presented Laura. By the way she eyed the women's attire and the caressing hands each in turn greeted him with, she recognized how close was his association with each and every one of them. He had no reason to feel embarrassment, yet under her scrutiny his face flushed and he had the ridiculous urge to run a finger under his now too tight collar.

"If you will excuse us, Lady Laura is anxious to find her family."

This time, Richard rushed them through the crowd with little thought for decorum. Finding a quiet spot behind a potted palm, he turned her to him. "What did you think you were doing to Lord Kinsley? If you'd leaned any closer in your sniffing endeavor, you would have toppled onto his chest."

With a scowl she answered, "If you'd leaned any closer to Mrs. King's bosom, you would have fallen in and never be seen again."

"You almost sound jealous."

"Jealous? Of an overblown woman with not a thought in her head?"

"Ah, she may not have a thought in her head but her other large attributes compensate for her lack of wit. Perhaps you looked at her and found your own," he glanced down to Laura's chest, "attributes, somewhat lacking."

Her irritation at his observation was plain. He had angered Laura Jamison and, for some reason, her hostility felt more welcomed than her indifference of earlier. Just as he congratulated himself on flummoxing her, she surprised him again.

"I must find my sister, and your cousin. Quickly." As he started to move, she halted him with a hand. "No, I don't require your assistance. I've learned all I needed. You'll only be a hindrance."

"A hindrance!" Never in his entire life had he been called a hindrance. "I assisted you. Guided you."

"No, you were merely a large body to clear a path for me. Now go away." She waved a hand to where Mrs. King and her group were plainly discussing them. "Go back and play with your friends."

"They are not my friends."

"No, possibly not friends. Although, you've bedded every woman." She delivered this statement as calmly as if they discussed the weather.

His mouth dropped open. "How could you possibly know that?"

"Their scents. Each of them oozed desire the minute you stepped into their circle. That sort of desire only comes after they've already sampled the treat then decided it was delectable enough to warrant another taste."

With that shocking pronouncement, Laura whirled away in a swish of skirts and left Richard staring after her, wondering how control of that interlude had slipped away from him. He needed to find his cousin, and he needed to warn him about Lady Jamison, both Rebecca and Laura.

***

Laura heaved a sigh of relief when she at last sighted Becca and Lottie. Her sisters stood on the other side of the ballroom four deep in enthralled men, paying their every word lavish attention. A discreet distance away, lounged Cayle; a tall, glowering Cayle. Before Laura stepped out towards them, her arm was grasped firmly and, in the blink of an eye, her hand was placed upon the sleeve of a recognizable blue coat.

"You again," she snapped. "I thought I told you to go away."

Not in the least intimidated, Winchester stared her down, something with which Laura had no experience. She threatened men, not the other way around.

"I'm afraid I'm not the sort to trot away like a chastised dog. You're looking to warn your sister. I'm similarly off to warn Sherwyn."

Her hand was held immobile by his strong clasp, so with scant good grace she conceded and they wove a line towards their family. Upon reaching Becca, Laura pulled her aside to inform her about the note.

Winchester was similarly engaged whispering to Cayle, but before he completed his tale, the Jamison ladies were already making a beeline for their aunt and to collect Lottie. By mutual agreement, the party bade polite farewells before the carriages were called for their departure.

By habit, Jamison Hall was nominated as the gathering place for a family conference.

Chapter 11

At Grosvenor Square, they gathered in the drawing room. Their great-aunt directed an intent look at the extra man who had joined them.

"Richard, Earl of Winchester, is it not?"

"Indeed, madam." Winchester bowed his head. "It's been some years since we spoke."

"You were always Cayle's hellion cousin. From what I hear on the rumor mill, not much has changed in that department."

Richard flushed but before he could reply Laura interrupted. "Yes, yes, auntie. I imagine a man of Richard's interests simply outgrew our girlish company."

Aunt Agatha chuckled. "If the broadsheets are to be believed, Winchester followed the path of all young men and moved on to more manly pursuits for a time." She smiled at Richard. "But your mother would be well pleased that you've taken responsibility for your family in a most able way now."

Laura shrugged, then said in off-hand way, "I will admit that, tonight, the Earl did render me some small assistance."

Richard had been moving away from the center of the room, and the attention, when Laura's words halted him. To Becca's amusement, he swiveled back to Laura, facing her with his hands on his waist under his coat tails and his elegantly shod feet planted wide. It wasn't often that a gentleman dared confront her outspoken sister.

"Some small assistance?" Richard's face was tight with outrage and his fists were clenched. "I cleared a path--"

"A trifle! Of no importance to our discussion."

Laura waved away his attempt at contradicting her. Becca held a hand over her face to smother her grin and realized that Cayle and his brothers were doing the same.

"So," Laura said, oblivious to the amusement she was creating for the St. Martin men, while Richard looked fit to explode. "I searched the ballroom to discover which gentleman had passed me the threatening missive. And I think I found him. But it only made me think that there are more gentlemen involved than we suspected."

"Yes, that's what's worried us about your list all along," Cayle said. "We knew more men must be involved. You've reported several different men visiting shops soliciting funds. Others have been at the Exchange every day coercing patrons into investing in their syndicate."

Becca watched Cayle pace the room in front of where they'd taken seats, impressed by his air of command and realizing he'd taken charge like this before. On the Continent, she assumed.

"Devon and I feel the second and third tiers of the ring are larger than you believed. More men involved. And that at the top level of the consortium, there's only one, or possibly two, who know what's going on. All orders are passed down the chain of command, so absolute secrecy is maintained."

"Cayle," Laura said, "I'm worried about Becca. She's in more danger than she'll admit. I'm sure these men have discovered by now that she often visits the coffee shops near the Exchange to update her numbers."

Cayle nodded his head but refused to meet Becca's eyes.

"I'm determined Becca will not endanger herself a minute longer. She'll retire to my country estate, at once. My brothers and I," he glanced at Richard, "and, I hope, my cousin, will continue inquiries in London. There's no reason for the Jamison family to continue placing themselves in such grave danger."

Becca jumped to her feet and stood in the middle of the room. "How dare you all talk about me as if I'm not here." She stepped close to Cayle and pointed one finger to his nose. "And don't try to tell us what we may and may not do. This started with the Jamison family and we, all of us, will see it concluded."

"No!" Cayle grasped her waving finger and shook his head. "I won't allow you to be a target any longer. I regret ever suggesting you accompany me to these events. I stirred this hornet's nest by thinking you'd be safe out in full view, with me. And I let you down. It's now up to me to resolve the problem."

"Ah, it seems to me," Richard said from his place resting on the wall, "this has become a wider problem than one concerning just your family, Becca. If what Cayle has told me is true, the consortium isn't only a threat to you but also to other families, including mine. And my sisters. Anyone who dares to defy them will eventually be placed in the same situation. It's time the constabulary became involved."

"No! Not yet," Becca said. "We only need another day or two. Then we'll have conclusive evidence to present to Sir Robert at The Yard. If we disclose ourselves now, we may not have another chance to finalize our list of those implicated."

Bang! They spun around to the noise in the hallway.

The drawing room door slammed open and Michael staggered in and collapsed on the rug in the doorway. The girls rushed to him though Cayle and Richard were faster, lifting him to the settee. Michael roused, grabbed his head and gave an agonized moan.

"What happened?" Becca cried.

"I was set upon at the end of the street by two ruffians." At the collective gasps from his sisters and aunt, he rushed to reassure them. "I'm fine. Just a lump to my head where they coshed me."

Becca ran her fingers over the back of his head and parted his hair to examine the wound. "There's a lot of blood but the cut isn't large."

"They weren't trying to do me permanent harm. It's another warning that time is running out. The thugs delivered a message. I must join them and hand over the journals, or there'll be another victim." He looked at the anxious faces of his sisters. "You have to leave London."

"Not you too, Michael," Becca exclaimed. "Cayle was just issuing the same sort of dictum. And Laura and Lottie and I agreed we'll fight this together. We won't retreat like meek and mild women."

"We can't run away and allow you gentlemen to execute the outcome for us," Lottie said.

"No," Michael said. "I thought we could outwit these men, but I was wrong. They've committed one murder and they'll do so again. And soon."

"I agree with Michael," Cayle said. "It's past time for the men to resolve this by ourselves. You women will either retire to my estate, or to your country seat, whatever suits, but I'm arranging constant guards for you."

As everyone started to speak at once, Becca yelled, "Quiet! Enough. Michael's head needs attention. And auntie is tired."

"We should retire and discuss this in the morning," Laura added.

***

Lottie rang for a maid who assisted their aunt to her chamber, and she instructed the butler to bring cloths for Michael's head wound, which bled profusely despite the wadded handkerchiefs pressed against it. Thompson hurried out to the hallway to assign the servants their tasks then returned to pour refreshments.

"Be warned, gentlemen," Laura said, as she handed out glasses of whiskey, "we'll proceed with our investigation for at least the next one or two days. If we haven't gathered more proof by then, we'll hand it over to our friends at the Yard. But we need the name of the man who devised this scheme."

"We need to know who murdered Peggy," Lottie said. "We promised our friends we wouldn't stop until her killer was brought to justice."

Michael patted his younger sister's hand. "I know. We all hate to see him escape punishment. Especially when we're sure he's a member of the highest rank of society."

Becca watched Cayle swirl his drink, a frown creasing his forehead. "What is it, Cayle?"

He shook his head. "I don't know. Something about the man at the top of your list still doesn't ring true. I can't put my finger on what we're overlooking about him. He moves through society with ease, unnoticed, so he's obviously titled, well-known, wealthy. So why this? Why now? What's made him so desperate?"

Brian exchanged a glance with Tony. "We've been working on that very idea. Along with Winchester, we've been following a line of inquiry regarding how deeply each man is invested in railways at present."

"And how much money each is in a position to part with in the future," Tony added. "You probably already realize that railways are the key to the plans the consortium's hatched. If they can secure all the future forecasts that you, as a family, have thought out, then purchase their shares early, they'll eliminate all other competition."

"That's assuming that I've either joined their group," Michael said, "or they've eliminated us by other--"

"Oh, Michael. Don't pander to us," Laura said, with an irritated shake of her head.

Richard gave a loud groan and strode in front of Laura. "Oh, no, never let it be said that the Jamison ladies are too sensitive to hear from their brother's mouth that someone intends to kill them, murder them all, one by one, over the next week."

There was a shocked silence as Richard realized what he'd been goaded into saying. "Damn. I apologize." He glared at Laura. "To everyone but you. We all know what Michael didn't say to spare your feelings, but he forgot that you don't have a feminine bone in you gorgeous body."

Another silence followed that outburst.

"Well, I suppose I should be grateful." Laura looked up at Richard with a perfect pout to her lips and a flutter of long dark lashes.

He eyed her with distrust. "Grateful for what?"

"At least you think my body is gorgeous. After you ogled all your castoff mistresses all evening, I couldn't be sure I'd even rate a second glance from such a connoisseur as you."

"Oh, please, God, save me from intelligent women," Richard said, dropping his head to his hands with a long moan.

Brian and Tony were nearly doubled over with laughter and Becca and Lottie, well used to Laura's antics, could only sympathize with his embarrassment. Cayle stepped in to save his cousin any more discomfort, although he too was laughing.

"If you'll let Winchester recover, we'd like to hear his thoughts on the syndicate members he's spoken with at Lloyd's and the other Exchange coffee houses."

Winchester looked relieved, but ignored Laura. "Between us, we know almost all the men and their commercial backgrounds. Some we've invested with before at Lloyd's Shipping."

When he smiled at Becca, he exposed two such charming dimples that she heard Lottie's long sigh and even Laura seemed a trifle bemused. Cayle frowned, first at his grinning cousin and then at her, when all she did was return his cousin's entrancing smile. A man, a duke, couldn't be jealous of his cousin, a lowly earl, who smiled at an insignificant lady like her, could he? To feel jealousy would mean that Cayle cared for her more than she'd allowed herself to wish for, to believe, to hope.

Becca gave her pitiable thoughts a nudge. Silly, silly ideas to hold onto. Hadn't she learned her lessons? She should never trust a man to not leave her, after her father left her mother continually to go off on archaeological digs and Cayle had deserted her without warning. Even that cad Arthur had turned away when a better woman had come along.

"And, thanks to the Jamisons, I made a tidy profit on that railway extension two years ago." Becca gave Richard a blank look, having let her dreams carry her away from his conversation. Cayle glared at her again as Richard explained, "When the eighteen miles from Basingstoke to near my home in Winchester was completed."

"Oh, of course."

"So, it's true that the three of you have made very sound investments, alongside the Jamisons." Cayle sounded a little put upon as he struggled to come to terms with his cousin's casual announcement of their collective assets.

Winchester smiled again as Brian and Tony nodded. "We certainly have, cousin. Though it's considered gauche to discuss monetary matters in mixed company."

Cayle laughed. "And I've been worrying myself into an early grave over our financial situation while I was abroad."

Tony looked sheepish as he admitted to Cayle, "Well, we had to do something. Julia had father refusing to even grant our allowances. Joining Winchester was a stroke of luck."

Winchester laughed. "It was a stroke of genius on my part to recruit you and form our little partnership. And yes, Cayle, it's become very lucrative."

"I can't believe I didn't know what my own brothers were doing. What my cousin was doing."

"We didn't know if we should confide in you or not," Tony said. "You were entangled in Julia's schemes and we thought it best to watch first. See how it would play out. Needed to watch how that'd play out."

"As soon as your agreement with Julia ended, we were going to tell you," Brian said.

"You didn't trust me enough to tell me beforehand."

Cayle's frown told Becca he was upset over his brothers' lack of faith in him and she grieved for the pain he was feeling. To her, family trust was everything and she knew Cayle longed to build a strong relationship with his brothers once again. That'd been the driving force behind his bending to Julia's demands, despite the torment he'd suffered from his peers over it.

"It wasn't that we didn't trust you, our big brother." Brian looked sheepishly apologetic. "More that we didn't trust Julia."

The women had been following the conversation with riveted attention when Becca interrupted. "I'm sorry, Cayle, but we believe Julia is involved with someone in the consortium. Her latest lover may be a member, or even the leader. She may be simply a pawn. Being used by this man to gather information at the balls the two of you attend."

"You mean I could be helping an illegal investment group collect information?" Cayle exploded. "Hell, if that is true, I'll finally have grounds to have the bitch--pardon my language, ladies. Have that woman expelled from Britain, and when I find out who she's involved with "

"Cayle, we don't know." Winchester looked grim, and worried, as he shook his head. "Not his identity. Brian and Tony have someone following Julia, but until we know what she's up to, we couldn't confront her. Nor inform you. Nevertheless, we're all in this together now, aren't we?"

He waited for the group's nods of affirmation. "Railways are the way of the future." He smiled at Becca and her sisters. "Do you not agree, ladies?"

Becca sensed that the shrewd look Winchester directed her way meant something. As if he'd already worked out who did the major calculating and planning before they placed money anywhere. She smiled. Best to not reveal anything until she could be sure.

"Railways are beyond doubt the way to accumulate wealth, if your nerves are steady enough to gamble on potential."

Cayle looked straight into her eyes, daring her. "If we're to finish this before hundreds of innocent people lose their bank funds, it's time we were all completely honest."

Becca's stomach churned but she remained silent.

"This is a chance for everyone to reveal all their secrets," he added, staring at her. "Everyone."

She looked down, picking an invisible bit of fluff from her skirt, until Cayle sighed and turned instead to Michael.

"I'd hoped that you trusted us enough to speak freely about what the journals contained. It seems my cousin and brothers are already major investors and I've explained that I was involved in the construction of railway tracks on the Continent."

Before Michael could sit up, Becca spoke. "No, no, Michael. You rest." She waved him back to the cushions and faced the men. "Very well, we'll tell you all we know."

"It's well past time you told me the truth."

Cayle glared at her with a grim expression that she tried to ignore. Despite their constant bickering, the thought of him being truly angry with her was sickening.

"We speculated a considerable sum of money into factories here in England that are building more tracks, at present for the Burgess Hill railway in west Sussex. Then we were given information that France doesn't have enough track to complete the line from Paris to Rouen, although the railway station at Rouen Saint-Sever is already under construction."

"Thomas Brassey is a good friend," Laura said. "When he was asked to build the link to Le Havre to join the Southampton ferry boat, Bec--"

"Laura! You mean Michael and Jonathon," Becca snapped.

"Oh, yes, yes of course." She gave Becca an apologetic smile. "Our brothers calculated the risks and decided it was worthwhile gambling a large amount of our recent profits into this one big endeavor."

Lottie chortled and rolled her eyes. "Becca thinks that having an inheritance will make Laura and I appear more attractive, as prospective wives."

"Lottie, neither you nor Laura need anything but your considerable beauty to attract a husband." Tony delivered his avowal with a flourish and his admiring gaze fixed on Lottie's cheerful face. The other men groaned at his overdone adoration.

"Thank you, Tony."

Lottie's words made Tony flush with pleasure. Laura's gaze went to Winchester, awaiting some similar comment but he looked away, refusing to meet her eyes.

"So," Becca said, frowning her annoyance at Winchester for hurting her sister, "we're about to invest a considerable sum there. Following that, we've been invited to join the development of the fourth line in Germany to extend an existing one from Leipzig to Althen."

Becca was annoyed also with Cayle when he nodded agreement.

"Damnation! By your expression, I see that none of this is a surprise. You already knew, didn't you?"

He inclined his head. "A lot of it, yes."

"And you said nothing to me?"

He shrugged, annoying Becca even more. "I suppose it's time I revealed the extent of my own involvement with railways."

"To use your own words, it's well past time you told the whole truth," Becca said after a little huff.

Cayle ignored her, something he did a lot of late and something she found increasingly annoying. The man was becoming insufferable. She had appealed to him for assistance, not domination.

"You knew we were investing in railways--"

"Ah, but there you're incorrect, my sweet."

"Do. Not. Call. Me. That."

The onlookers failed to smother their laughter.

"You, my prevaricating little friend, didn't tell me it was railway expansion you were involved with. If you'd told me the truth from the beginning, I would've been more forthcoming."

"Stuff and nonsense. Your patronizing male beliefs, your pompous dukeishness--"

"Dukeishness?" Cayle made a noise, half snort and half chortle. "I presume that's another one of your sham words."

"Your insufferable pride prevented you from sharing fiscal information with me, a mere... woman!"

Loud guffaws of laughter emitted from their amused observers. She glared at them all until they ceased, or attempted to stop, Laura placing a hand over her mouth in a vain attempt to stifle her giggles.

"Please ignore my ill-mannered sister, Cayle." Lottie nudged her sister hard in the side. "Pray continue."

Cayle returned Becca's glare but smiled at Lottie. "It wasn't only Britain suffering from railway mania two years ago. On the Continent, it was almost as bad. My three friends and I took advantage of that and did some forward planning.

"As Becca mentioned, several countries needed immediate supplies if they were to develop at the same rate as Britain and America. But they'd seen the spate of train derailments here, and wanted to expand in a safer fashion. We shipped experienced workmen and base products from Britain. The navies, the engine builders, all of them."

Winchester laughed. "When you told me you'd made some money on railways, I'd no idea how much. Now, I can see you've made quite a lot of money, probably as much as us, if not more."

"Several of us made a tidy profit, which we were at pains to keep hidden," Cayle agreed with a grin. "It's ironic that while I was expanding on the Continent my family and friends were here in London doing the same thing."

"I see nothing amusing in that," Becca snapped. "If you'd trusted me with the truth--"

"Me! You came to me begging for assistance. Yet you didn't confide in me. Oh, no. You told me half-truths."

Winchester made a show of clearing his throat. Michael groaned. Laura and Lottie exchanged knowing smiles despite the vile looks Becca shot in their direction.

"It's late. Shall we finish our earlier discussion," Brian said, trying to be tactful. "The majority on the list are minor investors. Mitchell has more money to play with and he wrings Melrose dry on a regular basis. But to trace this puppeteer pulling the strings, we need to follow the trail of money backwards. Discover where, and how, he works behind the scenes. Who else he's using."

"So you think your stepmother is having an affair with this man; a man with an elevated position?" Michael asked. "Are you certain?"

"No," Brian admitted. "But we think there must be another

man apart from the pathetic lovers she's flaunting, a far more influential man, because Julia only seduces men who are dukes, or not far below that."

Becca noticed that Cayle winced and looked at his brothers with pain in his eyes. "I didn't realize you two knew."

"Yes, we discovered that little sordid detail only after Julia had you driven out of England. She flung it at our father one night in one of her rages that she'd tried to seduce his son and heir."

"I'm sorry."

"Don't be," Tony assured Cayle. "Best thing to happen to us. Made us join Winchester."

Cayle swallowed and nodded his thanks at his brothers as Brian continued speaking. "He's a man who knows how to covers his tracks well. A man who has far more wealth, and possibly higher position, at stake."

"And therefore a far more dangerous man," Winchester said.

"Maybe a government man, a spy in a previous life."

"So far, we've been unable to uncover his identity," Tony added. "Despite pumping every acquaintance for even a hint as to his name."

"I'll start my contacts on that line of inquiry as soon as I leave here," Cayle said. All eyes were drawn to him, all understanding what he'd left unsaid until he gave a long sigh and added, "Very well, if you must know, yes, I asked some small questions for the government when I was visiting trade centers on the Continent."

They all looked at him in expectation until he groaned. "I can tell you very little more except that, no, I was not a spy, not in any official capacity, but my friends and I worked for those who ran a government service collecting various snippets of advice and ... "

When he froze mid-sentence, Becca knew he'd reveal no more secrets, amazed that he'd volunteered even that. Nods and shrugs and sipped drinks and fanned faces and unified silence, conveyed their message. Until Cayle understood. His mouth dropped open. "

"You all knew?" Around the circle, one by one, heads dipped. His eyes widened to saucers. "All of you?" Around the circle, together, variations of the same.

"I knew when my cousin--"

"I'm your brother, not some idiot--"

"We're not young girls--"

"Jamisons are intelligent--"

"I'm younger, I'm not--"

Cayle appeared to be suffering from shock as he turned to Becca. "Well? I'm sure you have something to say. Tell me what a fool I am, to not have known."

She shrugged. "This has been enough of a jolt to your ego. I doubt Her Majesty's government, nor you and your friends, ever imagined that a group of lowly London inhabitants could detect an expert spy hidden amongst us."

Cayle groaned. "I had no idea. What gave me away?"

"Mainly the way you issue orders. Like a man used to being obeyed," Laura said.

"And the stamp of your friends," Brian added.

Becca nodded. "Plus, there was the casual way you announced that your contacts would look into the names of spies. In the middle of the night."

"Damn. Have I been acting so dictatorially that others might have noticed?"

"No, only us," Becca consoled him. "We're family, more or less, so you've been more domineering with us than with others. And more demanding of me, than anyone."

"Only because I care about you. All of you. You know that, don't you?"

"We do understand, Cayle, really." Lottie gave him her sweetest smile and threw her arms around his neck in a warm hug, making Becca grind her teeth with annoyance.

She pulled her sister off Cayle's neck. "Now, let's finish up here and find our beds."

Very well," Cayle agreed. "We're all agreed that we need to end this uncertainty. If you ladies refuse to leave London--"

"We do!" Becca said.

"Then we'll increase pressure on the weakest links in the consortium chain. We'll announce that in three days the Jamisons will disclose their findings. Anyone who wishes to join their next venture will be free to acquire shares by adding their name to their list at the coffee house behind the Bank of England at opening on Monday morning. That means that over the weekend, the puppet master, if there is one, will be forced to act."

"Hopefully on his own initiative," Becca said, "Without involving too many others. So we may flush him out into the open."

"Tony and I will spread the rumor at different clubs."

"And we'll pay morning calls to as many friends as possible. Mention of our sudden influx of funds from new railway expansions should start a flurry amongst our friends' male relatives," Lottie added.

With arrangements in place, the men took their leave. Becca's sisters saw Michael to his room before retiring to their own beds. Becca stood at the door where Cayle hesitated.

"Don't fret over me. We'll meet again when we attend the theater tomorrow evening."

"Becca, this is my last warning. If you put yourself in danger tomorrow, I'll tie you up and send you off in my carriage. To somewhere far, far away."

He bent to brush a light kiss over her pursed lips before she could object to his arrogant orders.

Her body responded as it always did to his nearness, to his touch, and she forgot to reprimand him. As he turned and walked out the door, her heart asked the same question it had wanted answered for years. "But will you stay with me this time?"

Chapter 12

Cayle hurried towards the theater box, an unfortunate footman following him with a tray of drinks. First the man had dropped the glasses and then he'd poured their champagne at the speed of a snail. When the footman had finally started off down the carpeted corridor, Julia had stopped Cayle and her nonsensical conversation had delayed him an extra few minutes. The back of his neck prickled. Something was wrong. Though he sensed that this time it wasn't him in danger. It was Becca.

He grasped the box's curtain and tugged it aside. No Becca. He bent to Brian's ear and whispered, "Where is she?"

His brother misunderstood his urgency and merely grinned. "Can't stand Becca being out of your sight for a moment, can you? You, my dear brother, are smitten."

Cayle's glares shriveled most men, but his brother was oblivious to Cayle's rising temper and took his time answering. "The delectable Lady Rebecca--" Cayle snarled at him. "--and Laura, went to the retiring room."

"How long ago?"

Realizing Cayle was serious, Brian straightened. "Actually, some little time ago. They should've returned."

With a quick signal to Tony, all three men slipped out of the box. Cayle hissed in annoyance, "You should've accompanied them."

Brian looked stunned. "To the women's area? Not acceptable, Cayle. You know that."

Of course Cayle knew the rules of etiquette, but worry robbed him of rational thought. "Something has happened," he said. "Either to both of them, or to Becca. She's the one wanted most by the consortium."

"We'll find them, don't worry," Tony reassured him.

Ten minutes ago, Cayle had been perturbed. Now he was beyond worry. He was frantic.

From the moment Becca had approached him, she'd become his responsibility and he was an ignoramus for not taking more precautions. Part of him hadn't fully accepted that a large group of his peers were involved in crimes ranging from shady trading to murder. He should have insisted that Aunt Aggie lock Becca in her bedchamber until those men had been prosecuted. Hell, he should have sent her to a convent. Somewhere, anywhere, safe.

Laura hurried towards them and he almost bit her head off. "Where is she?"

"I'm sorry, but I don't know. We'd left the retiring room and were walking along the corridor when two gentlemen bumped into me. They tried to snatch my reticule and I struggled with them. I fell against the wall and by the time my vision cleared, they were gone. And Becca had disappeared too."

Cayle's cool-headedness had served him well in Europe, but now he was beyond reason. He was driven by rage. And fear for Becca. He had to find her, see that she was safe. And then, he'd wring her adorable neck for frightening him half to death.

The men split up, Anthony quizzing passing footmen, and Laura and Brian retracing her steps and looking into all the boxes. Cayle sprinted to the retiring room and with a shocking disregard for propriety, flung aside the heavy curtaining.

A footman called to him, "Hoi! You can't go there."

Ignoring the scandalized footman, Cayle rushed in, only to have his greatest fear recognized. On the floor of one of the curtained areas, Becca lay sprawled at an awkward angle. Her belongings were scattered around her. Dropping to one knee, Cayle gently rolled her and brushed back her disheveled hair. Thank the Lord. She was breathing, but very shallowly.

"Becca, sweetheart, speak to me."

When she didn't respond, his chest constricted. He could barely breathe. Sitting on the carpet, he carefully lifted her head into his lap. His hand contrasted darkly against her translucent skin when he brushed his fingers across her cold cheek. "Please, my love, say something."

Becca whimpered and made a slight movement with one arm. And though he loathed seeing her in pain, her groan was the most exquisite sound he'd ever heard. Her eyes flickered opened and she tried to sit up.

"No, lie still." He held her in place with a gentle hand.

"Hurts," she said in a raspy voice. "Throat."

He moved her fingers aside. Dark markings circled her neck. Man sized fingers had squeezed her slim throat tightly enough to bruise. And, if they'd taken more time, to have killed her.

"The bastards cut off your air. You must have passed out. When I catch them, I'll slice off their--"

"Cayle!"

Becca's glare stopped him voicing his intention but didn't stop him imagining how he'd deal with them when he caught them. And he would catch them. Very soon. He'd thought her kidnapped, or worse, and during those too long minutes, something had shifted inside him. He'd felt his hardened heart splinter. Crack with such force that he wondered why the others hadn't heard when they rushed to Becca's side. But his only concern was to remove Becca from here. Take her somewhere safe and have a doctor check her condition. He scooped her up slight frame and started for the door.

"No. Not outside." Becca's raspy words stopped him in his tracks. "Gossip."

Even when in danger, she only thought of others. Thought to protect her sisters from scandal. He nodded, resigned to carry out her wishes, despite hating having her here another moment. "Laura, fetch your aunt. Brian go with her. Tony, stand guard at the door. Don't let anyone enter."

He lowered her onto a chaise lounge and slid a cushion beneath her head. She was the most precious cargo he'd ever handled. But the strain of the last months--the horror of seeing Becca lying as if dead--was too much.

His shook with rage, angry with himself and furious at the men who'd attacked her. A man used to an arena of espionage would have listened more closely to a lady in danger. Understood her plans better and not underestimated her enemies. Especially when the woman was, in public anyway, his betrothed. He'd failed the person most important to him. While Julia waylaid him in the corridor, Becca had almost been killed. Julia! Once again his stepmother had conveniently, or inconveniently, waylaid him.

He stroked Becca's cheek with a light soothing motion and hid his true thoughts. "What happened," he asked softly. If she guessed he needed exert scrap of information so he could hunt down her attackers, tonight, she'd refuse to tell him anything. Or let him leave.

"Two men. Grabbed me ... from behind ... dragged me backwards ... retiring room ... snatched my reticule." She rubbed at her wrist and he scowled when he saw red marks encircling her fragile bones. He bent his head and spread light kisses around the raw-looking circle. He was blinded by fury at the thought of those men nearly breaking her wrist and almost choking her to death that he almost missed her whispered words.

"Looking for--"

"Looking for what?"

She hesitated, and then shrugged. "Money. Thieves. Looking for coins." She cleared her scratchy throat. "I carry few."

She looked at her wrist rather than meet his eyes. He raised her chin with a finger and stared directly into her expressive eyes. "When we were children you deceived me into doing your bidding with exaggerated tales of woe or half-truths. Remember?" The green of her eyes flashed with emotion but she gave a reluctant nod. "And though I never believed your larger-than-life stories, I always helped you?"

She shrewdly sidestepped his questions by going on the attack. "What? You don't believe me?" Her haughty look was another shameless trick, but rather than make him feel guilty, he was amused. He admired her steely backbone and her never-ending audacity.

"Oh, no, my sweet. Save your manipulations for someone more gullible. I can see through your fibs."

She stared at her clasped hands. "Which begs the question of why you're telling lies now. Something you've not told me about these men. Or what happened."

Aunt Agatha rushed into the room, red and flustered and Becca gave a sigh of relief, though he knew she only welcomed her aunt's fussing as it allowed her to avoid answering him. Again. Something was seriously amiss.

"Oh, my goodness, my darling," her aunt said. "How are you? I was so worried. We must get you home. You need to go to bed. I shall summon Doctor Simmons."

"No. No doctor." Becca forced words through her sore throat.

"Just bed." Her sisters helped her to her feet and she shuffled towards the door.

Cayle leaned close and whispered in her ear, "Our conversation is merely postponed. Not forgotten." Her eyes widened again and he heard her breath catch.

Brian arranged for the carriage at the theater's side door and, with a minimum of fuss, Cayle maneuvered them out. Brian and Tony would stay and question the footman. Becca's attackers had entered the theater without being noticed and Cayle wanted to know how, and why, they had arrived.

***

Once back at Grosvenor Square, the women trooped inside with Cayle snapping at their heels. With exaggerated politeness he asked Aunt Agatha, "May I have a private word with Lady Rebecca before she retires. I'll only keep her a moment."

Becca prayed her aunt would refuse Cayle's request. She'd spent the return journey trying to concoct a plausible story. But, to her dismay, her aunt urged her sisters to their beds and appeared quite happy to leave Becca alone with Cayle and his simmering temper. Though she did flick a quick questioning glance at Becca before addressing Cayle. "You're making rather a habit of requesting privacy with my niece. Is there any reason I should worry? Or inform Michael."

"No," Cayle and Becca snapped in unison, before turning to glare at each other.

"My goodness." Aunt Aggie raised her brows. "You remind me of an old married couple."

She laughed with glee at her own joke as she went out, though she was the only one amused at the idea. Cayle locked the door and then paced the room like an enraged lion. Becca's nerves fluttered. Not that she feared him physically, but because his volcanic anger, held in check during the carriage ride, appeared ready to erupt.

"Marry me!" He barked, as if bringing his hound to heel. She jumped in fright.

"I beg your pardon?" She'd expected a lecture for visiting the withdrawing room without a male escort, not Cayle demanding a wedding. She shook her head. No gentleman of refinement insisted on a two-week betrothal, with no thought to the woman's later disgrace. Nor did he order a woman to marry him with no more thought than ordering his dinner to be served. Several men had offered her romantic proposals, though all for business motives. Arthur Bennett had sunk to one knee in this very drawing room and begged her to accept him.

"I said," he enunciated slowly, his jaw tight and face contorted, "you should marry me."

"No. You demanded that I marry you," she corrected. "Not the most romantic of proposals. What possible reason could you have for wanting to marry me?"

"I don't want to marry you."

This was so obviously the truth that his words hurt worse than a knife plunging into her chest. She swallowed and straightened her shoulders. "This is becoming a habit. Proposals of marriage as a means to an end. Not because anyone sees me as a woman."

"No, no, I didn't mean to demean you."

"Then why ask?"

"I can't think of any other way to protect you. No man will dare lay a hand on you, or your family, if you become a St. Martin."

"You'd marry me simply to keep me safe?"

"If that's what it takes, yes."

"Huh! At least you're more honest than the others."

"Then it's settled. We're betrothed in truth this time." He announced their marriage the way a judge pronounced a life sentence.

"Nothing is settled. I'm still in the dark as to your reasons. Are you saying you love me?"

"No!"

"Well, that made your feelings clear. At least you're being truthful."

"Love isn't the issue. Your life is. You can't continue running all over London without my protection. So, we're committed to each other. More or less."

"Committed?"

"A figure of speech. A compromise until we sort out this mess."

"And as my committed future husband, will you continue my

lessons on physical pleasure?"

"No. I'm not a complete cad. I'll keep a respectable distance. Consider it a ... business association."

"Ah. So I'll be free to ask other gentlemen for more lessons on intimacy."

"No! You most certainly will not. I forbid it."

"I'm uncertain of the rules of such a business-like arrangement, but I doubt such a vague agreement gives you license to forbid me anything."

He scowled. "You're correct. You're a grown woman with a mind of your own. Nevertheless, I beseech you to refrain from engaging in any flirtations--"

"Flirtations?" Her raspy chuckle sounded like the squawk of an old hen. She absently rubbed at her sore throat. "I intend a lot more than flirtation."

"The idea of you flirting, or taking a lover, is ridiculous."

"How do you know I won't do it?"

"Because I know you. You won't do anything that brands you as a trollop. You'd never ruin your sisters' chances at making good matches."

The word trollop was supposed to shock her and rattle her defenses. Push her into acceding to his demands.

"And haven't I already taken risks?" She'd not back down from this argument. "With you?"

"Despite what we shared previously, I'll not take any further liberties." He shook his head and moaned. "God! Not unless you beg me, Becca. Will you beg me?"

What he asked struck too close to the truth. Cayle was part hero and part fantasy come to life. A knight she'd gladly ride away with, or beg for more lessons. She'd tasted bliss and now she craved more. Madame had predicted that she'd one day meet a man who was her perfect match. A man who encouraged her to explore, to learn and grow, even in the bedroom. For better or for worse, Cayle was her ideal man. Though his compulsive male side smothered her, his gentler side allowed her to fly free.

Changing the subject, she said, "You're a fool if you imagine those men will be deterred by some vague commitment between us."

"It was Tony's idea."

"Your brother thinks we'd suit?"

"No!" At his vehement reply, she scrunched down like a wounded sparrow avoiding a bird of prey. If Cayle noticed her pain, he gave no sign.

"Tony suggested that, as my wife, you'd retire to our country estate where you'd be more closely guarded."

"I see. A wife in name only?"

"Not necessarily. In time, I'll require an heir. Children."

"Let me understand." She searched for some hint of kinder, gentler feeling after their shared closeness in this very room only days earlier. "I'd hide in the country and wait for you to decide which year would be convenient to bed me. Waiting to become enceinte and provide you with an heir. Followed, I assume, by the requisite spare child."

Her calm exterior was a deception Cayle would normally have seen through. Yes, he'd been terrified on her behalf at the theater, but that didn't excuse his deliberate coldness when he spoke of marrying. She'd understood he'd marry primarily to beget children, and for that he'd need a wife. But she'd also imagined that he'd choose someone he cared for deeply. Her illusions were shattered. He, like his peers, saw marriage as a quick solution to an annoying problem. Nothing more. For both their sakes, she must hide her tumultuous feelings. Hide her new, and raw, emotions. If Cayle rejected her love for a second time, she'd never try again to find happiness with a man. Loving her siblings, and perhaps nieces and nephews, would be enough. She shuddered at the thought of committing herself without some small sign that Cayle's heart hadn't hardened to an unbreakable stone block while he'd been abroad.

"Precisely," he said, oblivious to her dilemma. "And when the time comes, I assure you that you'll enjoy being in my bed."

"Such conceit, Cayle. I've no doubt you're a skilled lover. Many, many women have sung your praises to me in the past."

He groaned.

"And your honesty is a refreshing change from my other proposals."

"Exactly how many have you received?"

"Oh, I think above twenty. Lottie keeps count."

A small sound of pain escaped him.

"And why did they want to marry you?"

His stupidity stunned her.

"Not ... not that your beauty and charm isn't enough."

"Naturally," she said sarcastically. "Several of them, I won't embarrass myself with a number, wanted my connection to Michael and his expertise. Some thought I'd make a decent bed partner so they gained twice over from the bargain. They mistakenly imagined I'd be content being a typical downtrodden wife, preferably residing in the country and producing offspring." She scowled at him. "Exactly the same thing you wish for me."

"My proposal is different. Mine is to protect you."

"How noble of you. Cayle St. Martin, once again slaying my dragons." She whirled from her pacing to confront him. "And what of your agreement with Julia?"

"As Tony pointed out, marrying you may solve all our problems. When you carry the St. Martin name, Julia will be forced to support you. Scotland Yard will be happy to inform me, as a duke, of any intended arrests and you can distance yourself from those members of the consortium before it happens."

"Rubbish. Prosecuting men of the British peerage will embroil our families in scandal and nothing you do can prevent it. Not even giving up the right to choose your own wife in the future will help me, Cayle."

"You're right. If you carry on as you are, prodding every man you suspect into revealing something, they will react. But not the way you imagine. They'll have you silenced rather than risk you speaking to Scotland Yard. I've heard you discussing, in the middle of balls, how close you are to handing over name to your friends. I'm worried for you, Becca. I care what happens to you."

"Does caring mean loving?"

His expression instantly hardened. "My father taught me that love is something people say when they want something from you. It never lasts. But as my duchess, you'll have everything you require."

"Except a man who loves me." Persisting with this conversation was crazy, yet she hoped that her goading would push him into an honest answer. Give her some small indication of his feelings. Something more than a lifetime business contract. She'd prefer to remain a spinster than settle for half a marriage.

"Love is a foolish notion." He gave a small grimace of distaste. "With your penchant for research, I'm sure you'll agree that love cannot be scientifically proved. Therefore, it's hard to believe in its existence."

A month ago, even a week ago, Becca would have agreed. All her life she'd studied information, analyzed it and accepted the conclusions. With her sisters, she'd researched lovemaking, not love. Now, when love had struck her like a bolt of lightning, she felt disorientated and unable to process the facts. Unable to think like a scientist and reach a reliable conclusion.

She only knew that she must hide her feelings from Cayle. Distance herself from him. Immediately. Remove him from this situation, and her life, without arousing his suspicions. Dismissing her friend would be hard. Being without the man she was now certain she loved would be like ripping out her heart. When she was an awkward child, Cayle's protection had been a blessing. As an adult, Cayle's strength had made her stronger in turn. But she'd been naive to think she could invite him into her life, even for a few weeks, without consequences. For both of them.

Saying goodbye would be like cutting off an arm. The alternative was unthinkable. He, and his brothers, risked their lives and their futures with Julia. She needed a plausible excuse for cutting Cayle loose. But, oh my goodness, the pain would be unbearable. Much, much worse than when Cayle had left without explanation four years before.

"While I appreciate your noble gesture, Cayle, it's nothing more than that. A gesture, and an empty one at best. One I've no hesitation in refusing."

The momentary look of relief on his face revealed everything. His spur of the moment proposal had been instantly regretted.

"I've vowed never to marry, never to become beholden to any man." To do Cayle justice, he appeared legitimately stunned by her refusal. "I'm quite happy to remain as I am. A bluestocking spinster." Becca turned and fled to the door.

In two lengthy strides, he caught her by the arm and spun her to him. "Are you crying," he demanded roughly, catching a tear on his finger.

"Of course not. I've never cried when I've refused a marriage proposal before. Yours is no different. Another way to control a woman's life." She bunched her already rumpled gown in her hands and fled the room, tearing up the staircase as if escaping a demon. Cayle, the angel of love and the devil incarnate.

She heard him snarling at Thompson before he went out the door. Fine, let him be angry. So was angry too. Angry that she'd gone weak kneed for a moment when insanity had possessed him and he'd ordered her to become his wife. She'd read the panic on his face the second he'd voiced the words. And the relief when she'd refused him. Freeing him, from an unwanted marriage and from danger, had been the right thing to do. The only thing. Though being fair didn't stop the ache.

In her body and in her heart.

Chapter 13

Cayle couldn't do it. He couldn't climb the steps of this brothel and bed another girl, after having had a small sample of the pleasure he could find with Becca. Despite the confounded woman's baffling rejection of his proposal, and him, earlier in the evening, he still wanted her. And her alone.

He'd accompanied three acquaintances from his club to Mistress Duval's as a way of avoiding Grosvenor Square, and Becca. By keeping busy elsewhere, he could ignore the voice in his head that prompted him to throw caution to the wind and scale the wall of Jamison House and visit Becca's bedroom. God knew he wanted to. With every fiber of his being he longed to see her, to touch her, and more importantly, to make love to her. He'd no one to blame for his unrelenting state of painful arousal but himself.

The other men had been well in their cups when they'd decided to round off their night's entertainment with a visit to a brothel. Having spent a boring hour pretending an interest in gaming, Cayle had valiantly tried to excuse himself. He'd wanted to take his misery home and drown it in some more of his late father's brandy. But the men had insisted. His second reason he'd ended up standing outside this brothel was more important. These three men were associates of Baron Mitchell and Viscount Melrose. Once they'd mentioned a rendezvous with them, and Bennett, at their favorite brothel, Cayle had allowed himself to be coerced.

Now, he felt only regret. And self-loathing.

Neither the Baron nor the Viscount had appeared by the time Cayle's three acquaintances had deserted him for three willing ladies who had taken them to another room. He'd refused the invitation to join their fun. Group romps didn't interest him. And watered-down wine didn't take the edge of his desires.

A redhead with green eyes and enormous bosoms spilling over her décolletage seated herself on his lap, attempting to entice him upstairs with soft words and brazen caresses. Nothing helped. The woman he wanted was tucked up warmly in her own bed, or at least he prayed she was, after returning from the dinner on the Jamisons' evening program. He ached to be in that bed with her. He loathed the idea that she'd test her theory and find a willing rake to experiment with. She wouldn't dare, would she?

Knowing the image of her with another man would niggle at his brain until he checked with the men he'd deployed around Grosvenor Square, he tried to stand. The woman wriggled suggestively in his groin. He gritted his teeth and tried again, determined to ignore her enticing body. A voice he recognized wafted down the steps. Cayle stilled. Bennett was bidding farewell to one of the house girls.

One he'd obviously had no compunction in bedding. A girl the image of Becca, and similar enough to the one on his lap for them to be sisters. Another redhead with green eyes who was young, very young. Cayle shifted the girl sideways off his lap and stood face to face with Becca's former betrothed.

"Bennett."

"Sherwyn."

Arthur visibly squirmed and glanced away. Then he straightened his back and turned back to Cayle. "I didn't know you frequented this establishment. Rumors tell me that your step-mama has your balls tied in knots. And that you must remain celibate or Julia--"

"Enough. My personal life is none of your affair."

Arthur chuckled. "Ah, I've found your Achilles' heel, Sherwyn. Your delightful stepmother."

"Once again, I recommend you mind your manners."

"Or what, you'll call me out. Everyone knows your reputation at dueling." He sneered again. "Or rather, your reputation at avoiding duels."

Cayle was a second away from lunging and pounding the bastard into the floor. But he'd no wish to see his name smeared across the morning's *London Tatler*. No wish to create more distress for Becca.

Bennett's shrewd glance took in the woman clinging to Cayle's arm. "Ah, I see your taste mirrors mine. Beautiful young girls with hair the color of sunset."

Cayle seethed at Bennett's assumption that they shared similar tastes in harlots. He untangled the girl's arm and moved away from the stairs before he spoke.

"I haven't been upstairs, as you have. The girl you are to marry, the delightful Margaret, will undoubtedly be angry when she hears that you still prefer redheads. Women with coloring exactly like the woman you were promised to before you met Margaret."

Bennett's face turned a mottled red. During their schooldays, he'd been jealous of Cayle's popularity, his wealth, and even his future title. Nothing had changed.

"Bennett, several sources have confirmed that you meet Baron Mitchell and Viscount Melrose here."

The man looked nervous. Scared. However, this spineless snake threatened the Jamisons and deserved no pity. "The gentlemen I do business with are no concern of yours, Sherwyn."

"I'm making it my business because it concerns my friends, the Jamisons."

"I've done nothing wrong." He glanced around the room, checking they couldn't be overheard. "All our dealings are fair and above board."

"You do realize that the consortium, of which you are a member--"

"You've no proof. Memberships are private."

"I do have proof. On several occasions, your meetings with Mitchell and Melrose have been recorded."

"You've been watching me." Bennett's high-pitched squawk sounded like a bird frightened for its life.

"I've had men following you for days, Bennett. I'm only surprised that a man of the Baron's caliber didn't know that. Careless of him, wouldn't you agree, to let his cohorts movements to be documented by the constabulary."

Shock marred his face. "Constabulary. I told you I've done nothing wrong."

"That remains to be seen. So, here's my proposal. If you want me to keep quiet about your predilection for a certain type of paid companion, you'll tell me everything you know about communication between syndicate tiers. Who decides which men are in each tier and how messages are passed."

Bennett grabbed his arm and drew him to the side of the parlor. "I can't do that, Sherwyn. You don't understand how dangerous these men are if crossed."

"Believe me, I'm beginning to understand all too well. They've gone beyond threatening Lady Rebecca and her family. They hired an assassin to murder the Society's book keeper, Peggy. I imagine you know that. Someone tried to steal their ledgers and Peggy disturbed him. The killer smashed her head in with a paperweight. Now, they're threatening to murder one of the Jamison sisters. Probably Becca."

Bennett visibly shook when Cayle took a step closer. "I never meant for Rebecca to be harmed. I told Mitchell about the Jamison's successes in investments in strictest confidence. I didn't know he'd then target Michael. But Jamison has an aptitude for predicting the most profitable manufacturing areas. Everything he touches turns to gold."

"Michael is the one doing this?" Cayle pretended confusion.

"Of course Michael. Who else? His brother is too young to understand enterprise. His sisters are, well..."

Bennett waved his hand vaguely but Cayle prodded him for more. "His sisters are what?"

"Ladies. Women." Cayle nearly choked. The dimwit had almost married Becca but hadn't understood that she was ten times more intelligent than him. Nor that her siblings were researchers and achievers, with or without Michael's input. Cayle chose his words with care, not wanting to arouse Bennett's suspicions.

"You don't see women as capable of understanding commerce?"

The fool looked askance at the suggestion. "You jest of course, Sherwyn. Everyone knows women are capable of running efficient households. Financial decisions, however, can only be made by men."

Smothering his urge to strangle this pompous ass, Cayle inclined his head in agreement. "A woman needs a man's guidance in everything but trivial matters."

Bennett visibly relaxed as they discussed the difficulties of dealing with females in general. Then Cayle led the conversation back to the Jamisons. "And you and the Baron are confident that Jamison will join your group."

"Mitchell thought a little pressure would show him that the

best way to protect his family was by becoming a member. He'll then reveal his secrets. In another two weeks, the Exchange discloses their upcoming releases. Jamison's insights will guarantee we make wise investments. He's preparing another railway prospectus. The syndicate wants to know which railway. Why should those whores benefit and not us." He nudged Cayle in a playful manner. "And what helps Mitchell, helps me."

"How is that?"

Cayle wanted to unleash the disgust welling up inside at the thought of this letch coming within thirty paces of someone as good as Becca. The swaggering show-off had guzzled wine, dallied with his redhead upstairs, and his mood had mellowed. His simple brain had softened until he imagined Cayle was his friend.

"If I play my part, Mitchell promises I'll live like a king for the rest of my life. Enough money to keep a wife and a dozen mistresses."

Although many of his peers kept mistresses, Cayle's skin crawled at the callous way Bennett spoke about adultery. Margaret wasn't destined for a happy marriage. Busy pitying Margaret, he missed what Bennett was saying.

"... And of course, I've asked before but she refused me. But soon, I'll be rich. Filthy rich. She'll beg me to take her."

"Do you mean the girl here, tonight? The redhead?"

"Heavens, no! My expectations are much higher. These sisters merely gratify me in the interim. I refer, of course, to Rebecca."

Cayle clenched his fist. "Rebecca," he repeated. "You expect Lady Rebecca Jamison to become your mistress." He wanted to kick the arrogant bastard into the street and pound him until he could never again speak her name.

Bennett's look was revoltingly smug. "Not at first of course. I'll offer her one last chance to be my wife--"

"But you're marrying Margaret."

"Margaret hails from a far better family. The reason I chose her over Rebecca before. But now that Rebecca's brother is joining the consortium, her consequence will be elevated. Enough that I'm once again willing to accept her as my wife."

"You're insane. Becca will never marry you after the way you treated her."

Bennett laughed, revealing the tinge of insanity Cayle suspected lurked just below the surface.

"Sherwyn, you misunderstand. Rebecca will either become my wife or my mistress."

"Rubbish!"

"Mitchell assured me she'd cooperate, one way or the other. The syndicate will cut off the Jamison's income, forcing the lady to welcome me, and my newfound wealth, with open arms. Thanks to you deserting her four years ago, Rebecca became the subject of gossip. With the Jamisons declared thieves and frauds, the consortium will once again control the majority of share trading in this City. I'll be rich and the Jamisons will be shamed by gossip."

"So, that's the plan."

"Ingenious, isn't it? Discrediting their reputation within business circles will destroy them. This time, the lady will view me as the savior of her family."

"You're insane." He grabbed Bennett's lapels and shook him, hard. He longed to do more but the brothel's parlor was busy and he couldn't afford to attract attention. "Mitchell is no more interested in Becca's future than he is in yours. When he's acquired the Jamison's investment knowledge, they'll no longer be useful. He'll dispose of all of them, and you."

"Nonsense," the fool blustered. "They need me. I'm of great importance to the inner tier of the consortium."

"I repeat--you're nothing but a dupe. Once they have Michael's forecasts, your miserable life will be snuffed out faster than a candle."

He paled. "You can't scare me, Sherwyn. The Baron will provide for me. We're associates, friends."

"Bennett, your friends are about to face prosecution. Help us and you might save your pathetic hide."

He gulped, swallowed hard. "How?"

"We need to know the Baron's next move. How long he'll wait for Michael to agree. And be quick about it, because Scotland Yard cells are worse than hell."

Bennett gulped again but nodded. "I'll carry out my own investigations. If I suspect things aren't as Mitchell assured me, I'll notify you. But in return, you'll not reveal to Margaret, or Rebecca, anything you've witnessed tonight."

Cayle needed Bennett's firsthand knowledge of the Baron and his cohorts, but dealing with the man turned his stomach.

"Agreed," he said after a moment's hesitation, though he ignored the man's outstretched hand. He might have allied himself with Bennett, but he couldn't bring himself to touch his hand. "Though if they are in danger, all bets are off. I'll tell them everything."

Bennett wiped his hand down his pants and turned for the door. Cayle watched him scuttle off like the rat he was. The girl who'd sat on his lap earlier sidled up to him, followed by her sister.

"Your Grace, if you're after the same things as the other lord, you can have the two of us. He says two redheads are better than one, especially if we both pretend to be pure girls. Like the woman he says we look like."

"Do you know who he imagines you are?"

The two girls giggled, showing clearly their young age.

"Of course, Your Grace. When his lordship is deep into his playacting, he yells her name. Is that your pleasure? To imagine we're that lady?"

"No, I'm sorry. There's nothing I want from you." Cayle hated himself. He'd thought Bennett loathsome, yet he'd almost given in to a moment's weakness.

Gone upstairs with a girl who looked like Becca. Bedded her. Imagined Becca writhing beneath him while he plunged into one of these twin girls.

Knowing he'd stopped at the bottom of the stairs didn't console him. He turned to the door with his mind spinning. He'd never felt so powerless to control his life, his emotions, or his desires. He wanted Becca, and her alone. And he didn't want Bennett anywhere near her.

Although, he had no inkling of what to do next, or how to proceed.

Chapter 14

At home at his Mayfair mansion, the Duke of Sherwyn slumped in the same chair, from which Jenner had roused him the night Becca had called. He'd done the honorable thing and offered her marriage. Nothing to blame himself for.

He groaned. What utter rubbish. He felt guilt and remorse. And shame. He'd ruined what should have been a happy occasion, possibly the most memorable of a woman's life. When Becca had recited the practical reasons men, many men, had proposed to her, her vulnerability was exposed. He'd wanted to sweep her into his arms and promise her the moon. Shower her with the romantic gestures she deserved. Be the man she merited as her husband.

Regrettably for her self-worth, he'd proved himself to be another arrogant bastard, who believed any woman several years past twenty and unwed should be eternally grateful for any proposal. Even an offer as cold and unsavory as his. He'd conceitedly assumed she couldn't manage without him. Needed him more than he needed her.

Becca had asked if he loved her. But he'd avoided that painful emotion after his father's harshness and his exile from his country and his brothers. Still, if these feelings for Becca were nothing more than neighborly concern and friendship, why did he feel so empty inside? Why did he ache when he wasn't near her?

When he was around Becca, he felt happy and at peace. He'd been confident they'd deal well enough together to survive marriage. Very few unions between people from their class were for emotional reasons. Becca was too damn stubborn to accept that marrying for practical reasons was a safer option. Marriage to a duke would benefit her, and her charity causes, not destroy her identity.

For two hours he brooded, alternately blaming himself for poor judgment and lack of tact and Becca for her ridiculous feminine reaction. He expected Becca, a theorist, to view her future as a duchess as a convenience and not romanticize it. Confused, perplexed and saddened, Cayle had no idea how to improve the situation. His indecision was unprecedented and unacceptable. By the time his brothers joined him, he was well on his way to drowning his sorrows in brandy. Jenner muttered about the stupidity of young men who couldn't see their noses in front of their faces.

Cayle glared at his brothers, annoyed they were interrupting his moments of self-pity and melancholy. Brian poured hefty slugs of brandy for him and Tony, before throwing himself into the nearest armchair. "You look like hell."

Cayle glowered and snarled.

Tony took a second look at his face and said, "Ah, I see."

Brian, always slower getting the point than quick-witted Tony, looked between his brothers. "See what? What am I missing?"

Tony chuckled. "At least we now know you're human. Brian and I were worried because you'd turned into a block of granite. Unbreakable, unbending and above all, stone cold."

"Glad my misery amuses you," Cayle said, glaring at Tony.

"I've no sympathy for you because you've wreaked this havoc upon yourself," Tony said. "You've no idea how to handle a woman of Becca's--"

"Don't finish that!" Cayle slammed his hands down on the chair arms. "I'm warning you."

Tony laughed again. "I was merely going to say, her intellect."

To Cayle's irritation, Brian caught on and joined in, both his younger brothers considering baiting their older brother fun.

"But Becca does have the most delicious body. Which you obviously don't know how to handle either."

Cayle's growl rivaled a tomcat's squalling.

"What have you done this time?"

"I didn't do anything wrong," Cayle said. "If you must know, I asked her to marry me."

"And we assume by your foul temper, she had enough good sense to refuse you."

Cayle pointed at Tony. "It's your fault that I proposed. You prodded me into it, saying she'd be safer under my protection."

Tony rolled his eyes. "Ah, but I said protection, not marriage."

"Becca is a lady." Cayle leapt out of his chair and grabbed Tony by the lapels, yanking him upright. "Not a mistress." He gave

Tony a little shake.

"So when she refused your offer of marriage, you didn't offer an equally mercenary carte blanche?"

"No," Cayle said, battling to control his outrage. "I didn't ask her to become my mistress."

Brian nodded sagely. "Though you'd like her to be."

Cayle couldn't deny this and his brothers knew it. Every time he looked at Becca, he saw beds, sheets, bathtubs. He pictured her naked and willing and those images were driving him insane. He released Tony's coat and his brother dropped back into his chair. Cayle ran his hands through his already tousled hair and shook his head in frustration before slumping back into his own chair.

Tony said, "Hard to imagine why Becca refused. A romantic proposal. Everything a young lady wants. Bended knee, betrothal ring, declarations of undying love."

For a short time, drinking had dulled Cayle's guilt over his slapdash proposal. He dropped his head into his hands and groaned. "I made an absolute cock up of it."

Brian laughed happily. "As we said, it's comforting to know you're not an infallible god. You make mistakes like the rest of us mere mortals.

"Have I been so unbearable?"

"For the first two months after your return, you were on an unrelenting crusade to prove yourself a better man than before. Better than our father ever was. You were so boorish we could barely stand you. But since you've been escorting Becca, you've changed. For the better. Everyone's noticed."

"Including our dear stepmother," Tony said. "She's displeased with you. And crossing Julia is dangerous."

"I know. Becca refused the protection of our name. What am I going to do?"

Tony's gift was studying people and their reactions. "If you want Becca so badly," he said, "go after her. Don't let Julia stop you. Her demands about the sanctity of our family name and avoiding gossip are ludicrous. Court Becca. Woo her."

"She wants a man who loves her. And she knows I don't."

Tony studied him. "Don't you? Then why are you here, drowning your sorrows, instead of celebrating evading the parson's noose? Think about it, Cayle. How would you feel if Becca had been seriously injured tonight? Or worse, murdered."

Cayle shuddered. His brothers nodded.

"Yes, you mightn't be ready to admit to loving her, but without Becca your life will be boring."

Cayle laughed. "And predictable."

"Humdrum and conventional."

***

Left alone, Cayle pondered the mysteries of Becca. With problems that he hadn't so far solved. His brothers were right. Her unpredictability brightened up his life, made him laugh, and whether he wanted it or not, made him feel again. Only, those feelings hurt. Worst of all, by hiding his emotions he'd hurt Becca. Unacceptable. He needed to fix that, now. He did something unthinkable in sedate Martin House. He hurried to the door and bellowed down the hallway.

"Jenner!"

The room spun a little but ever astute Jenner steadied him. Not that he'd actually over-imbibed, but he'd been too worried to eat.

"Jenner, it's past midnight. Do you think I should visit a lady at this hour?"

"Your Grace, the lady in question was intrepid enough to visit you in your residence at night. And from what I heard--"

"Listening at the door again, Jenner?"

"Indeed, Your Grace. And from what I heard, you've upset that lovely lady and you need to set things to rights. My good wife, God rest her soul, believed one should never go to bed on a quarrel."

Cayle agreed, ordering Jenner to arrange a hansom to take him to Grosvenor Square. It was past time to set things to rights. At Jamison House, Cayle pushed open the door to the servant's entrance and faltered. He debated if he'd imbibed too much brandy to be breaking and entering, or if being slightly inebriated gave him the impetus to do it. Creeping up the narrow stairs, he prayed no servants appeared before he discovered which room was Becca's.

At the next landing his question was unexpectedly and, for Cayle, miserably answered. The gut-wrenching sounds of sobbing tore at him as he stood outside the door, frozen with guilt. What had he done?

She'd laughed off his proposal as being the same as all her others, but they'd been for wealth or schemes. His wasn't. He'd trampled over her fragile feelings by committing the same sin. Like all the others, he'd forgotten that while Becca might have an intellect far greater than most men, she was still a woman with a woman's sensitivities.

Barefacedly, she'd lied that she didn't cry over proposals. Yet, he could hear her beyond the door still sobbing her heart out. And it broke his heart. That fresh crack in it widened by another notch.

Gathering his courage, he stepped inside and pushed the door closed behind him. For a moment, he stood still and watched her. She was spread face down across the bed, the top buttons of her gown undone with the remainder still fastened, long red locks tangled through them. Sob after sob shook her frame and rocked the bed. Lowering himself to the edge of the bed, he reached out a hand to stroke her back and said in a comforting whisper, "Little one."

Jumping with fright, she gave a little scream and turned her face towards him, but he gentled her with a caressing hand on the exposed nape of her neck.

"Sweetheart, it's only me. I needed to see you. To apologize."

She didn't speak but continued to watch him over her shoulder with wide eyes ringed with red. She hiccuped and swiped a hand over her eyes, smearing tears across her cheeks. While he'd attempted to numb his guilt with brandy and considered dulling his desire with a look-alike redhead, she'd been grieving. Alone and vulnerable.

Staring up at him with her green eyes so wounded and accusing, she reminded him of an injured animal caught in a trap. The last thing he ever wanted was to break her amazing spirit. Her feisty nature was the best part of this wondrous woman. The exciting part that called to the like part of him that he'd suppressed for his family's sake.

She rolled over and the shoulder of her gown slid down her arm to expose creamy skin with an adorable sprinkle of freckles wandering across her collarbone. He wanted to put his tongue there and he wanted to tug the rest of the gown away and press his mouth to all her hidden parts. She sniffed the air between them. "Are you drunk again?"

He snorted. "Possibly. Probably. Over-imbibing seems to have become a bad habit since I met you." But foxed or not, he couldn't sit beside her smelling the scent of her and yearning to inch her neckline just a little lower and still retain control of his sanity. He swallowed hard. Grabbing up her robe, he placed it in her hand.

"Could you put this on please? You're too much of a temptation."

For the first time, she showed a tiny fragile smile. "Really?"

Smiling now, he teased, "As if you don't know what you do to me."

She wriggled off the bed, causing her unbuttoned gown to slide further down her arm. With a low growl, he dropped his head to his knees. She turned her back to him and asked, "Could you unbutton the rest please. My hair tangled. I didn't want to wake anyone."

He came to his feet with his hand hovering inches away from her bare back, wanting to touch her so badly that he could hardly draw breath. One small touch was a luxury. Her skin felt like velvet, her hair smelt of lemons and he wanted her. With a desperation that made him shake. Talking would be safe. Somewhat safer, anyway.

"Becca, I want you to know..."

One button.

He could do this.

Control, that's all it took. "I meant no offense when I asked you to marry me."

"Demanded," she corrected.

"All right, I admit I spoke a little forcefully."

Two buttons.

"A little?"

"Perhaps too much."

Three buttons.

"But good heavens woman, I nearly lost ten years of my life when I saw you lying there tonight." He gripped the edges of her gown and leaned in to nuzzle her hair, his voice thickening. "I don't give a damn about the niceties. I can't have you in danger like that anymore."

He turned her to face him and, still gripping her upper arms, pressed his lips to hers, briefly, hard. "Do you hear me this time, Becca? No more. A man can only stand so much. You'll move in with me. At Martin House."

"I'm not leaving my family."

"You are the most immovable woman in creation, Rebecca Jamison, do you know that?"

"It may have been mentioned a time or two in my family." Trying for a light jest she smiled at him. "But surely in your travels you've met someone more pertinacious than me?"

"You'll not bamboozle me with vocabulary. Pertinacious is a real word, not one of your creations. And no, I've never met anyone as stubbornly persistent as you."

She eyed him as if debating how much to concede in order to get what she wanted. "Perhaps I was a bit hasty. What if I were to say you could sit in on all our family meetings. Hear all our new ideas."

"Not good enough."

"What about if I let you court me for real this time. Not just for appearances."

He was fully aware of her motives, but he wanted the outcome regardless of what he had to do to achieve it. Being closer to her meant he could see to it that she never risked her life like that again. But he'd also drive the willful little minx to the same limits she pushed him.

"And what else? I need more incentive than sitting in on Jamison family meetings that I already know the outcome of."

Crossing his arms he leaned against her dresser in a relaxed pose. "Winchester, my brothers, my friends, and I have taken control of all the meetings from now on in any case. And in society's eyes, I'm already courting you."

She let her gown drop further down her shoulders. Even when she wasn't trying to be a coquette, she enticed him more than any experienced woman. When she was practicing her newly discovered feminine charms on him, he was helpless to resist.

Yet, he held onto his control and waited. Years of ballroom flirting had taught him that a predator needed infinite patience to wait for his prey to be lured to him. Then, and only then, would he pounce. Let Becca think she was seducing him into doing what she wanted whilst he was letting her stroll into his snare.

The kiss his seducer brushed to his lips tantalized with a sweet mixture of innocence and beguilement.

His breathing shortened and his body leapt to attention.

So much for pretending he could retain control and remain unmoved. Beautiful Becca only had to glance down and she'd understand the effect she had on him physically. Only had to look into his eyes to see the desire he couldn't hide.

The little vixen knew exactly what she was stirring.

One of those capable little hands wandered down his body, skimmed across his waist and dipped lower. Grabbing hold of it before she could reach her obvious destination, he moaned. "God, what are you doing to me?"

"I want to let you see how good things could be between us."

She'd tied him up in knots wanting to do the right thing, the correct thing. While at the same time, he longed to throw her on the floor without preface and plunge into her as deeply as he could.

"Believe me, I know how good it will be between us, sweetheart. I lie awake every night thinking of that very thing."

Those magnificent eyes widened. "You do?" Gone was the innocent trying to play at experience. The naked longing in her voice told him she wanted him the same way he wanted her, desperately, totally. His response was crucial. No more mistakes.

"My love, I imagine myself poised above you while we kiss and then thrusting hard, deep inside your snug passage, your body welcoming mine. Embracing it and holding it." He laughed. "I imagine myself grasping scandal in both hands and reveling in the ride we'll enjoy together."

She gasped and her mouth dropped open. Her hands flitted downward between them to rest on her lower abdomen. "I imagine you sitting astride my legs, with me pressed tightly against that part of you that aches for me." He glanced down to where one hand was now circling in a restless motion on the outside of her skirt. "I'll move against you there until you can bear it no longer and you push yourself down over me in a frenzy. You'll be so wet, so ready for me, that I'll slide up into you and you'll cry out when you feel me touch your womb."

His hand covered hers to stop the movement of hers and halt the frantic circling that had scrunched her gown into a ball between her legs. Her breath came in small pants. The smell of womanly arousal scented the air, tightening Cayle's body even further. His erection hardened and throbbed, and his balls drew up in readiness for the explosion that was so close he could almost taste it.

"So why ... why are we waiting?" Becca clutched her gown again. "I'm offering you what you want. What we both want."

It took all his willpower to pull away.

The time wasn't right and he was now determined in what he wanted. And how he'd get it. With the greatest of difficulty, he extracted himself from their embrace and hurried towards the door. Still in control, still able to resist temptation. And his greatest temptation and greatest torment was Becca.

His hand touched the doorknob as the vixen spoke, her words flowing over his heightened senses and shooting his entire body to full alert.

"Cayle, turn around."

Helpless to resist her soft-spoken command, he turned. His breath caught in his throat. He shuddered down to his toes. She was naked. She was perfect. Everything he'd ever desired in a woman.

His first sight of her without clothes robbed him of breath.

When he'd brought her to orgasm in her drawing room, he hadn't disrobed her but only exposed the necessary parts. Her breasts were large enough for him to scoop them up in his hands and fondle them. Her narrow waist fanned out to wider, feminine hips and tapered down to legs that, despite her small size, were long enough to wrap his waist as he thrust into her. Dear God, he wanted her. He could think of nothing but claiming that luscious body. Finally, he managed to drag his eyes to hers. She looked apprehensive. Worried. She was staring at him as if awaiting approval. Intrepid Becca stood before him with all her raw vulnerability exposed and he wouldn't tell her anything but the absolute truth.

If he were a wiser or even a kinder man, he'd reject her once and for all. Walk away and leave her untouched. She deserved better than him. She deserved a man whose heart hadn't hardened and one who truly believed in love. Could declare his love openly, without terror.

But right now, in her bedroom and with her standing so still and silent before him, he could only want. And need. "You're so beautiful. So very beautiful. And you cannot imagine how much I want you." He sucked in a gulp of air.

"But I am a little drunk, a little overwhelmed, and a hell of a lot out of control."

She walked up to him and put her hands on his shoulders, looking up at his with imploring eyes. "Cayle, I want you."

"I know, my love, I know." He dropped his forehead onto her head, trying to draw the strength to depart. "Forgive me, sweetheart, but tonight I must leave before we both make a mistake. I couldn't bear to see regret in your eyes tomorrow."

"I won't regret it, Cayle. I want it. You. Now."

"No." He shook his head.

"When I become your lover, Becca, and make no mistake, I'll have you beneath me very, very soon, it will be on my terms. At my leisure. And not on the floor of your bedroom where your family may walk in."

It was gratifying to hear her little gasp as she remembered where they were. At least he knew that his practical little planner had been as caught up in their passion as he'd been and forgotten where she was. He took her face in both hands to kiss her gently.

"If you're sure, Becca, really sure, ask me again tomorrow after we've both had time to think about the consequences of such an action. A woman can only offer her virginity once. To one man. I'm not certain I'm the right man for that."

"I am, Cayle. Very certain. You're the man I want."

He gave a deep sigh of regret and released her. Once again, he turned back to the door, forcing himself to walk towards it.

"Tomorrow night we're attending Lady Moreland's annual ball. I will call here at eight for you. Goodnight."

Chapter 15

The next morning, the Duke of Sherwyn was eager to leave Mayfair, despite the little slumber he'd managed to snatch. After leaving Becca, he'd been restless, unable to sleep, so he'd used the time to scratch notes to his friends.

In the grey hours before dawn, he'd dispatched footmen to deliver them in the hope of catching all three compatriots before they began their busy days. As he rode to Devon's house, the streets filled with deliverymen on horse-drawn lorries loaded with foodstuffs bound for the markets. Housemaids swept front steps before their masters and mistresses ventured out for the day. Mothers carried baskets home to feed hungry children.

Life was carrying on as any other hectic day in overcrowded London and yet, for him, things seemed different. Everything had changed. For the first time in years, he felt lighthearted, as if an enormous weight had lifted from his chest. He could breathe again. Becca had done that, brought him back to life. He knew that walking away the evening before had been the right thing to do, the noble thing. And, yet, it had also been the hardest thing he'd ever done.

Her scent still filled his nostrils, visions of her made his head spin and her words rang in his ears. She'd wanted him. The same way he desired her. And when she came to him, and his possessive male side believed she'd come soon, he'd know she wanted him and not any lover with whom she'd conduct a scientific experiment. And that day, or night, would be the happiest of his life.

It took a moment for that thought to filter through his senses and for him to comprehend what it meant. They weren't simply friends, he and Becca. They were more, so much more. She was the only woman he'd ever wanted enough to be prepared to give up everything for. He'd find another way, anything to appease Julia, however he'd never give up Becca.

It was time to stare down old meaningless scandals in both their lives and embrace the freedom that could follow. They'd be released from the web of gossip that entangled them and tied their families to conventional rules. None of it mattered. Nothing except finding a way to have it all, everything he'd ever desired from life.

At Devon's house, Cayle flung himself out of the saddle and threw his reins to the waiting groom and raced up the steps.

As he rapped the knocker, he grinned. Then he laughed aloud in total abandon. Something he hadn't done in a long time. Throwing his arms wide, he practiced saying aloud the first words in the romantic string of vocabulary he now realized Becca yearned for. She needed to hear that he was sincere before she would further commit herself to him. His proposal had been a dreadful insult.

Strangely enough, it didn't perturb him as he'd imagined it would if he ever got close enough to another person to admit this feeling. The words came easier to his mind than he'd have believed possible a month ago. They flowed off his tongue.

Soon, he promised himself, he'd say them to the person who deserved to hear them. A neighboring window opened so the inhabitants could peer at Devon's doorstep to see who was making an unseemly racket at this hour, in their sedate street. He smiled. He waved. For once in his life, he welcomed the tittle-tattle, the gossip, the scandal and all that went with it. Anything was an improvement over the half-life he'd been living of late.

Too afraid to rock the boat with Julia for fear of consequences for his brothers. Too fearful of failure to risk falling in love. Too frightened of being hurt again to admit the depth of his feelings. He laughed again. He felt ready to embrace life.

Devon's butler admitted him with a look that said he was admitting this madman only under sufferance and he was directed to the breakfast room where Devon was enjoying a hearty meal. He signaled for Cayle to fill a plate and join him.

"Henry and Tristan will arrive directly. You'd do well to eat before Henry arrives and devours everything."

They both grinned at the thought of perpetually hungry Henry. He was lean and light on his feet, yet never gained an ounce of fat, despite eating every meal as though it was his last. His obsession with food was a longstanding joke among the four friends. As long as Henry was well fed, he was an excellent man to have at your side in a fight.

Devon looked Cayle up and down as he heaped his plate with food from his friend's buffet. "I see nothing wrong with your body, so it must be your soul that's suffering from this over exuberance of glee so early in the morning."

Henry strolled into the room before he could answer and walked straight to the food to heap enormous quantities of everything onto his plate. "What's wrong with Sherwyn's soul?"

Cayle continued to fork in food and grin at his friends at the same time. "There's nothing wrong with my body, my mind, or my soul. I'm simply happy to be alive on such a beautiful day."

"Good God!" Tristan's voice said from the door as he too entered and strode to survey the meal on offer.

"Sherwyn's happy. The sky must have fallen in."

"Oh, very droll," Cayle commented without looking up from his eggs. "I'm unfailingly cheerful."

"Rubbish!" Devon disagreed. "Since we've returned to England, your gloom has rivaled the cloudiest winter day in Scotland."

Henry, who'd stared at Cayle throughout the exchange, all of a sudden said,

"Well, I'll be damned. Sherwyn's in love."

"In love. With whom? I presume it's a woman." Tristan gave Cayle a smirking grin.

"Tris, once again, very droll." Cayle was forced into a snort of laughter. "And I didn't admit to being in love with anyone."

"Well, unless the situation with Julia has been resolved," Devon raised an eyebrow at Cayle who gave a vigorous shake of his head, "it can only be some fair young chit who has you in enraptures."

"Not a fair chit. She has flaming red hair with a temperament to match, and is without any doubt, all woman."

"Ah, the beautiful and buxom Becca," Henry said.

The others all nodded and made murmurs of agreement.

"If I catch any of you leering at Becca's bosoms, on any occasion, I will shoot you. One by one. Understand?" His three friends looked at each other then burst into gales of laughter.

"Oh, this is too much," Devon gasped between gusts of mirth. "Our world-hardened Sherwyn has succumbed to love after denying its existence for so many years."

"Why does everyone insist it's love?"

"Possibly because Becca is all you've talked about for weeks," Devon said.

"Although, until now, your comments have run to a categorizing of her numerous faults. Her redheaded temper, stubbornness, recklessness. Her ability to argue you into an early grave."

"Oh, we've no doubt a good healthy case of lust is involved, Cayle, but you're also showing all the signs of love."

"The question is, Cayle, what do you intend to do about it?" Henry asked. "The lust and the love. After all, she's a cut above the usual gullible debutante and she's an unmarried lady, not a beddable widow."

"Yes, she's all of those," Cayle mused. Becca's attributes and, as Devon pointed out, her many irritating qualities were well above any other woman he'd encountered. His next problem was how best to maneuver her brilliant mind into his way of thinking without her realizing she was being manipulated. To capture the wind and tame it. Bloody hell! An impossible task.

After a lot of pushing and pulling, Cayle managed to steer his friends away from the juicy topic of his love life and onto the pressing business they needed to discuss. Notes were compared on the financial stability of the men on the Jamison's list and new tasks assigned. Each of them had several avenues to follow up, several people to bribe to disclose even more information.

By the time they left Devon's house two hours later, Cayle had a better idea of who was involved and which men were so deeply involved and so deeply invested, that couldn't risk a failure. They had to have money. And they needed it soon or they'd miss the opportunity to become the major investors in the next railway track being laid. And in this instance, the missed opportunity would equate to several thousands of pounds of lost revenue.

Enough to make most men greedy. And a lot of them desperate.

Chapter 16

At nine that night, Becca stood with her arm on Cayle's, on the raised entrance of Lord and Lady Moreland's ballroom. From her bird's-eye view, she watched the butler announce them and the entire room come to attention and hold its collective breath. Every eye focused upon them. Some with amazement, some with maliciousness.

Although she'd dressed in the height of style to make a good impression, upon her worried perusal of the assembled crowd she realized that not a single female looked happy to see her there. To the women's eyes, she'd snagged the most eligible bachelor in town for her escort. That alone would make her as unpopular as a resurrectionist digging up bodies in a graveyard.

Additional to those transgressions, a great many suitable men had followed the Jamison sisters liked a cloud of locusts on their recent swathe through society. The mothers, daughters, and sisters prowling for eligible bachelors disdained business dealings and didn't comprehend that the lure of banknotes elevated she and her sisters to the status of season darlings amongst the men.

"Half of London is in this room and they're all staring at us. Whispering about us." She tugged on Cayle's arm in alarm. "What are we doing here?"

He peered at her from his imposing height and grinned. Gloriously relaxed, completely unrepentant. "Embracing scandal."

At such a loud and unsophisticated announcement, several people gasped and turned to look. They yearned for any ripple of excitement to relieve the tediousness of making inane comments on the weather in another stifling ballroom. A rush of unaccustomed fear and panic overcame Becca. Not for herself, but for Cayle. For her sake, he was taking an enormous risk. She squeezed her fingers hard into his forearm, trying to tell him to stop.

"You're supposed to be avoiding scandal." She tried to whisper but in her panic it sounded more like a wild cat's angry hiss. "Not announcing it, saluting it. Not before a room of conservative minded socialites."

"My sweet, I've reached the conclusion that scandal can't be avoided. Nor can it be outrun. It's far easier to welcome it with open arms. Embrace scandal. Then let others make of it what they want."

"Wonderful! And if that theory backfires?"

With an amused grin, he patted her hand.

"If all else fails, sweetheart, we turn and run for the door like cowards."

Shaking her head, Becca muttered, "You're not taking this seriously."

"I've been accused of being far too serious, far too often. My brothers tell me I'd forgotten how to laugh. But with you, Becca, I feel like the world is one large jest. And the only ones who appreciate it, are thou and me."

"And after this fiasco, I'm not sure about either of us."

"Come my love--"

"Stop! I told you not to call me that."

"Ah, but we're here to play a game. And endearments are all part of the flirting game."

"Yes, well, you'd have far more knowledge of that than I."

His hands clasped over his heart. "Ooh, a direct shot. You know how to wound a man.

Besides, I'm sure you must have engaged in more than flirting when you were betrothed to the almighty Lord Bennett."

She flinched from his insinuation. Did Cayle think her a hussy because she'd done more than flirt with him four years ago? She'd granted him liberties that young women of quality didn't allow, and tormented herself ever since thinking he'd left because she'd been too forward. From Madame Faberge, she now understood more. Men expected courtesans and prostitutes to be brazen in their seductions. Other women were expected to follow the example of Queen Victoria and adhere to conservatism, especially in the bedroom. Becca's belief in women's rights to freedom of thought and deeds often threw her into moral and self-conflicts as she tried to guide her sisters through the never-ending rules of society.

Despite long practice at shuttering her feelings, Cayle always sensed her emotional turmoil. Tucking her arm further through his elbow, he pulled her close enough to his side that the feel of his warmth and the strength of his muscled body distracted her from what he was saying.

"... Apologize. What you did, or didn't do, with Bennett is none of my business. I'll just say this. The man's an indiscriminate seducer and you're lucky he turned his attentions to another woman."

She looked at him as if he'd just uttered the stupidest comment of the century. "I beg your pardon?"

He enunciated each word as if speaking to a child. "Lord high and mighty Bennett is a cad who is destined for a fall."

"Do you know Arthur's business so well?"

"Ah, so it's Arthur, is it? If you were close enough to call him by his given name, what else were you were close enough to do?"

She gasped and jerked her arm back but he'd securely anchored it through his. "I don't want to talk about it. Especially with you."

"Nothing that happened with that rogue was your fault, little one. I was at Oxford with Arthur. Even then, he'd a reputation of engaging young women's affections, leading them to the brink of scandal and then deserting them, never to return. His reputation always remained intact and yet the ladies, ah, the poor ladies never came out of it quite so easily."

His steady gaze on her was as unnerving as his intuitive comments. "Is that how it happened with you, Becca?"

Drawing a deep breath of courage, she straightened her spine and looked him in the eye. "Yes, but it's in the past. Long forgotten."

"You can't lie to me. I always know. Your left eye twitches."

"Fustian. You're just baiting me. I'm long past worrying about the deplorable antics of so-called gentlemen."

To Becca's horror, her left eye gave a distinct spasm. When Cayle raised his own brows in silent gloating, she blinked and pretended it hadn't happened. "Except when they cheat gullible ladies, who are then forced to appeal to me for help recovering their inheritances."

***

Their party continued a parade of the ballroom and was soon rushed by eligible gentlemen. Brian, with Laura on his arm, and

Tony escorting Lottie, looked as annoyed as Cayle felt when men quickly surrounded Becca and clamored for a moment of her time.

However, this was their agreement. The two younger girls got the benefit of his patronage, whilst Becca gained wider opportunities to investigate who had him in their matrimonial sights. Several men were claiming introductions to the women and forced to comply, Cayle made pointed reference to their chaperone, Lady Agatha Jamison. These men should all know that the girls weren't easy targets.

Managing to get Becca aside for a moment, he said, "You and your sisters have many friends. You know many of society's elite and yet you've not caused this sort of sensation before. Why now?"

"For various reasons, we didn't venture about much for a time. It was easier to limit our socializing to paying calls and dinners with friends."

"And was I one of those reasons? My brothers told me what happened after I left. Becca, I'm so sorry about that."

Their conversation was cut short when several eligible gentlemen rushed to their side imploring dances with Becca. With mounting frustration, Cayle resorted to requesting her hand for a dance and then regretted it when she moved fluidly in his arms, reminding him of how good it felt to hold her. He held her closer than approved but the feel of her soft curves as they swung down the length of the floor together was worth the agony his body was forced to endure.

"Rebecca." Lord Bennett, with no compunction, interrupted them as they left the dance floor. Becca ignored him and endeavored to walk past but he grasped her arm above her glove, forcing her to halt. Cayle wanted to hit the bastard. Keeping his hands on Becca's arm, he held her a discreet distance from the letch and noticed with pleasure that Becca's tone turned icier than a Scottish stream in winter.

"How pleasant to see you, Lord Bennett." Her tone dripped with sarcasm. "Is your new fiancée with you?"

Ignoring her taunt, Lord Bennett carried on as if she'd welcomed him with open arms. "I tried to pay a call at your house, but your butler seems to have the misguided idea that I'm not welcome."

Her eyes narrowed and Cayle felt Becca's fingers tighten where he held them resting on his arm. "My butler is absolutely correct. I have refused you admittance. I am sure you understand why."

As she spun away, Lord Bennett's hand snaked out to grab Becca once again. "Nobody refuses to see me. You will dance with me."

Cayle used a strong grip to remove Bennett's fingers, taking great satisfaction from the pain he inflicted. "The lady doesn't want anything to do with you."

"What's between Rebecca and me--"

"Bennett. Please, show respect and address the lady by her title."

Lord Bennett shot Cayle a look of dislike before sidling closer to Becca. "Lady Jamison, may I request this dance?"

Cayle stepped between them but Becca forestalled him. "I will give you one dance, Arthur, but only because I don't wish to be the cause of a disagreement in a ballroom. I will suffer no more scandal on your behalf."

"You don't need to suffer even one dance with this scoundrel, Becca. We'll leave."

She placed a restraining hand on his arm. "Everyone's staring. I'll not be fodder for more gossip by refusing Arthur here." She took Lord Bennett's arm and they walked to join the set just commencing.

Cayle was standing at the side, scowling at the pair, when a lady joined him. "Your Grace, I am Lord Bennett's fiancée, Miss Margaret Johnston."

Cayle bowed over her hand, politely acknowledging her despite the lack of formal introduction. "Miss Johnston. Are you enjoying the evening?"

"Not especially, Your Grace. I do not enjoy watching my betrothed make a cake of himself over another woman in front of my acquaintances."

"It is only one dance, Miss Johnston." Cayle glanced to the floor to watch while Bennett clasped Becca far too closely as he swung her into each turn. He hissed in a breath.

"Yes," Miss Johnston said, "that is what I cannot allow. You must take care to keep your good friend, Lady Jamison, away from my fiancée."

"I am as dismayed as you are that he is persisting in claiming a close friendship with Lady Jamison." His eyes narrowed as he watched as the dance finished and Bennett attempted to steer Becca to the other side, rather than returning her to him.

The rogue had a grip on Becca's arm and was towing her towards the French doors to the terrace. Excusing himself from a seething Miss Johnston, he murmured, "I will inform Lord Bennett that you are desirous of his presence."

Wending his way to Becca's side was not easy in the crush and on the way he enlisted assistance from Laura, Lottie, and his two brothers.

"Arthur Bennett forced Becca into agreeing to dance with him. But he's led her to the other side of the ballroom, away from all of us. "We need to get to her before he touches her."

Upon reaching Becca and Arthur, whose escape had been thwarted by the crowds, Brian and Tony and Becca's sisters moved in closer so they formed a protective ring around Becca.

The low pitch of Cayle's voice did nothing to hide his fury.

"Bennett, be warned, if you ever lay a finger on Lady Jamison again, I'll kill you."

Arthur blanched under the attack but pulled himself up to reply haughtily, "And you, Sherwyn, should stay out of things that do not concern you. Lady Jamison and I have an arrangement."

Beside him, Becca gasped in indignation. "Lord Bennett, we have nothing of the sort. Any association we had in the past was severed. By you, I might add. I danced with you this evening to avoid further scandal. I no longer have anything to say to you. Goodnight."

As she tried to move past, Bennett reached out to grab at Becca. This time, Cayle gripped his wrist so hard that Arthur winced and paled.

"I warned you about touching Lady Rebecca. Never attempt it again."

Bennett laughed, a sneering jibe. "Or what'll happen, Sherwyn? You'll challenge me to a duel? You were shown to be a coward when you ran away from one with the Viscount four years ago."

The collected group gasped at the brazen audacity of the man.

In a deceptively calm voice, Cayle warned, "Yes. That's exactly what I'll do. Challenge you to a duel. And this time, I won't spare my opponent for any noble reasons. In fact, I'll take great delight in shooting you dead center in your black heart."

Becca held her breath as Arthur assessed the situation, willing him to leave without fuss. If he were dimwitted enough to make a scene, he'd garner no support from this group of Jamisons and St. Martins. With dawning horror, she realized she'd exchanged too much of her fiercely-won independence for the simple joy of spending time with Cayle. As a consequence of her self-indulgence, she'd forgotten how dangerous it was for anyone to become associated with her. How could she have forgotten Peggy's gruesome end?

Wisely, Arthur decided on a hasty retreat yet couldn't resist one last taunt over his shoulder.

"You'll rue the day you joined forces with this horde, Sherwyn. They're doomed."

He waved a hand at the St. Martin men and sneered his contempt. "Your entire family too, if they continue to associate with Jamisons."

With that parting jibe, he hastened away before the men gathered their wits enough to query his last sinister remark and chase after him.

Becca stared at the cluster of angry men, their dark protectors. Caught up in the whirlwind of recent events, she'd leaned too heavily on Cayle and put her trust in the capable hands of him and his friends. She'd listened to her heart, not her head, and her resolve to part from him had weakened.

Thank goodness her almost lover had walked away the previous evening. Now, she needed to be the strong one. If only it didn't hurt so much.

Chapter 17

Four hours later, Becca's feet ached from dancing and her voice was hoarse from endless discussions of inclement weather. The earlier incident with Arthur left her mind churning with the sickening knowledge that the St. Martins were being watched. All of them.

Somehow, she must convince them that she could control Arthur, and that their interference was unwelcome. The last thing she wanted was Cayle embroiling himself in another scandal or being challenged to another duel. Her limitations, her flaws, her neediness, had placed Cayle in danger. Disappointment that despite joining forces they'd failed to gather enough proof for Scotland Yard, increased her weariness.

Walking away from the dance floor, her shoulders were slumped with fatigue when a large male blocked her path, forcing her to look up. She sighed, unable to hide her exhaustion from Cayle's astute gaze. He shook his head, and then escorted her to where their hostess was engaged in chatter with Aunt Agatha.

"Lady Rebecca is feeling faint," he said. "With your permission, I will escort her to the terrace for a little fresh air."

"Oh, heavens, yes, Your Grace," Lady Moreland gushed. "Very considerate of you. Young girls these days are not as robust as we were in my day. Chits fainting at the slightest thing."

Before Becca could object, Cayle bowed to the ladies and turned. Thanks to his quick thinking, they escaped before Lady Moreland's meandering thoughts led to a dissertation on the faults of the young gentlemen of the day as well. Becca was led to the relative privacy of a narrow nook above the magnificent gardens, suffering the indignity with a fixed smile. However, inside she seethed. The moment they were clear of onlookers, she rounded on Cayle.

"What in heaven's name are you playing at? We're supposed to be enamored of each other. You're supposed to fetch me lemonade and escort me to supper. Look at me like a besotted fool." She clasped her hands and rolled her eyes in a theatrical gesture copied from Laura's repertoire. "Not fabricate a transparent untruth to drag me outside."

Cayle stopped, motionless, staring at her as if it was the first time he'd ever laid eyes on her, intensely, intimately. Then his eyes widened with some sort of inner revelation and he ran his hands up and down her exposed arms from her wrists to shoulders. When it appeared he wasn't going to stop, Becca squirmed out of his grasp to loosen his hold. In a dazed state, he stood and stared at her.

"What? You look like you've never seen me before."

"I don't think I ever have." She watched him swallow, hard. His voice sounded strained. "Seen you I mean. You're stunning."

She tilted her head to one side as she studied him, trying to decide what was wrong. "Are you foxed again?"

He shook his head. "Not nearly enough. I did sneak one brandy to keep me calm. Otherwise, I would've marched onto the dance floor and pulled you away from those lecherous idiots long ago."

"Oh, heavens. Please allow me some small intelligence. I know when someone is making a game of me."

"Has no one ever told you before how incredibly beautiful you are?"

"No, and I don't know why you're sprouting such nonsense now. It certainly isn't true."

With a small smile, he said, "Yes, it is true. You're truly beautiful."

She shook her head. "I'm not tall enough. I have freckles."

"Twelve."

She was even more confused. "Twelve? You've counted my freckles?"

"Yes, though I'd never realized it until now. I've counted every delightful one of them. And I know you screw up your nose in disgust when one of your adoring male followers utters something inappropriate."

"Male followers? Now I know you've been drinking. I'm not like the other girls in there. I've never had men falling at my feet."

"Becca, do you know the thing I adore most about you?" She shook her head in bewilderment.

"It's that you're totally oblivious to how wonderful you are."

He leaned in closer so his breath whispered over her temple.

"All those men, my sweet."

"What about them?"

"They already know what it's taken me this long to realize. You're unique. That's why they swarm around you like bees to a hive. They've all sensed that deep passion inside you. That sensual side you thought you kept hidden. But, you were wrong. It's there for every man to see. For every man to want, to desire."

"Cayle, you aren't making any sense. If any of this is true, why have I never noticed any of this? These men only befriend me for financial gain. They think I can pass on investment information."

"Does it make sense that I don't want you for those mundane reasons?"

His eyes glittered with a deep passion that she'd not let herself hope for before, but that she couldn't now ignore. The fire in his eyes matched the fire igniting in her.

Deep in her belly and spreading to warm her everywhere. Ever so slowly, without taking his eyes from her, he dipped enough that his lips could touch hers. The gentlest of caresses. Her heart stuttered.

She gaped at him, amazed at what he'd revealed. But his unguarded look let her see his feelings. He wanted her. Her. Rebecca Jamison. Perhaps ached for her as she hungered for his presence, his touch.

Without consciousness, she moved closer. Leaned into his warmth and male hardness. Pressed her breast against his chest until with a deep groan, he closed his arms around her and pulled her into his embrace. All the tenderness he'd shown for the past days evaporated. Left in its place was an unleashed male, dangerous, and past any semblance of his usual tightly controlled behavior. This time when his head dipped, his mouth folded over hers to take her with such ravenous hunger that her response was immediate and desperate.

Her sensual feminine side, often buried as she dealt with harsh day-to-day realities, was unleashed. When their lips touched again, she was out of her depth. Every touch of his warm flesh on hers had her enthralled. Held spellbound. Unable to move and worst of all, not wanting to move away as she knew she should.

His voice in her ear sounded rough with emotion. "I want you.

So much that seeing all those men dance with you, lust over you, nearly drove me to madness."

His lips brushed her temple and she shivered.

"Cayle, I'm not the sort of woman who lets herself be kissed by every man she meets. I wasn't about to let any of them touch me."

A laugh rumbled out of his throat. "Don't you think I know that? You were engaged to that idiot Bennett for almost a year and yet you kiss like an innocent. Or rather, you did until I recently restarted your education on that matter."

She knew Cayle didn't mean it as a dare, but Becca could never let a challenge go unheeded. "I haven't been in hiding since you left. Many men have flirted with me." She tilted her nose higher to give him her haughtiest stare. "So, if I want to kiss a man expertly, I will. I certainly know how. Arthur and I kissed often."

"Ah, so he did kiss you. You're too untouched, too untried for him to have given you anything more than fumbling pecks. No wonder you're so inept."

Fury made her draw herself up and point her finger in his face. "If I'm inept, it's you who made me so. As you delight in pointing out, you were the one who taught me."

Cayle grinned, white teeth shining against his sun darkened skin.

"At last. You've admitted you remember that last night behind the stable. How good we were together."

"What I remember is you kissing me, but it was of so little consequence to me that I've never thought of it again."

Feigning a devastation she was sure he'd never felt in his life, he clasped both hands over his heart. "My beautiful lady, I'm wounded. Of no consequence? I recall every detail. I've relived the moment in my dreams many times."

"Poppycock. Now you're being ridiculous in the extreme. Before you left, the gossip sheets were full of your exploits with Sybila, and others. And you did a lot more than kiss them."

"Careful, Becca." He chuckled. "You almost sound jealous."

"Jealous? Of Sybila Charmers. Rubbish."

"Perhaps you'll also now admit that after I kissed you, your first true kiss, you begged me to be your first lover." His voice was a soft, seductive murmur.

His words made her insides do crazy things. And not just her stomach. Her whole being sprang to full alertness. It was beyond her to remain cool and calm when heat spread to every part of her body. Her mind conjured an image of Cayle's long length, his tethered strength, entwined with her willing body as they lay naked in her bed.

Breasts that she considered simply a part, often an inconvenient part, of her female anatomy swelled and tightened until she was sure Cayle couldn't help but notice. She crossed her arms over her breasts and tried to relieve this unfamiliar feeling by applying pressure.

But Cayle was a sensual and aroused male. His attention went straight to her bosom, his dark eyes fixing there. Her body flamed as her nipples hardened and peaked and pushed against her bodice. His gaze was admiring and knowing.

"Ah, so you're not immune to thoughts of soon becoming my lover?"

"Your conceit knows no bounds, if you imagine every woman you meet is ready to throw themselves at your feet."

"Not every woman, Becca." His eyes twinkled with amusement as he teased, "As I recall, you were always the exception to that rule. Although, even you succumbed to my requests in the end."

Determined to hide how much his words and lusting looks affected her, she said, "Yet you've been blowing hot and cold every day since your return. You make me so confused."

"I know, and I apologize, sweetheart. It took me a while to understand what was important. But now I know. Though I'm unsure how I'll obtain it. And I can't afford to make any more mistakes. Not when my whole future is at stake. And yours."

"See! You're talking in riddles again and I don't understand. Besides, we've more important matters that need our attention."

His long finger stroked across her chest, slightly above the low neckline of her dress and again her breath hitched and her nipples pained.

"Sweetheart, what could be more important than exploring what's between us?"

"Don't call me sweetheart when we're alone. That's only for show. And I told you, there's nothing between us."

"Nothing. Then prove it. Kiss me, Becca. Kiss me with the same passion you did four years ago behind the stable."

"Cayle, you're doing it again. Talking in circles. Four years ago, I was a naïve girl who thought your kisses meant something."

"They did mean something. Then other things got in the way."

"You mean like being caught flagrante delicto with my cousin?" Cayle flinched.

The man he'd become wanted to yell out loud that he was tired of hearing that, tired of false accusations. Especially tired of Becca flinging the old lies in his face each time she attempted to retreat from him for some reason. This time, she was stirring a battle between them so he'd refrain from murdering lecherous Bennett and back away from their original agreement. However, he wouldn't allow it, wouldn't tolerate her retreat from him in a futile attempt to shield him. His clandestine skills acquired working for the British government ensured he was well able to protect himself. And her and the rest of her family. Becca would just have to accept that, with time running out for them, her stiff resolve must bow under his determination to remain her defender.\

"Sarcasm doesn't become you, little one."

"I'm not your little one. I'm not your anything. In your own words, we contracted an agreement of mutual benefit, nothing more."

Cayle absorbed that, knowing she was correct in essence. In his stupidest moment, he'd indeed said that. Hell, if he couldn't decide what was in his own mind, or his own heart, how could Becca be expected to? His indecisiveness in the past had baffled them both. Suddenly, inspiration struck.

"I'm willing to talk seriously, about business, in exchange for a kiss. A reward for being helpful to you, your family, and the women of your society. After all, you wouldn't be so much closer to finding Peggy's murderer without my contacts in every seedy sector of the city."

"We'd have managed somehow."

"No, you wouldn't. You couldn't have attended these elite balls and soirees. Or disappear for part of every evening into our hosts' private chambers, during which time I was forced to make excuses for you and your sisters. People must wonder if you suffer digestive problems after all the times I've said you were visiting the retiring room."

She opened her mouth to object, but he rushed to say, "In fact, by kissing me you'll support the notion that I'm so enamored of you that I'm to blame for your constant disappearances from under the noses of those watching us like hawks. And that you're not a thief who rushes about their houses opening safes and pillaging paperwork."

"Hauling me outside the ballroom with as much finesse as an overbearing oaf--"

"Goodness, dearest, you're slipping. Merely an overbearing oaf? What about being an arrogant pig?"

"Oooh! You're impossible. We can't hold a serious conversation while you poke fun at me."

"I promise, one kiss and I'll be serious." When she wavered, he added, "And you can halt it any time you wish."

Cayle nuzzled her hair, letting the warmth of his breath tickle her skin and incite those intriguing goose pimples over her neck. Becca glanced around for onlookers, while he prayed she didn't resist him. He needed to touch her, to reassure himself that what he'd discovered today was correct. That she fitted his arms to perfection. Becca alone made his heart race and his body heat with such a fierce hunger.

"What if someone observes us?" Taking her with him, Cayle stepped away from the light and pulled her behind a column.

"No one can see us here. One kiss in exchange for my undivided attention for the remainder of the night."

"Do you promise?"

Driven by the insistent push of his desire, Cayle was prepared to promise her the moon if she'd only press up against him again. The urge to grab her roughly and haul her against him was hard to damp down, but though she may pretend to be experienced she wasn't. His raging arousal would frighten her. The strategy he'd decided on was to tempt her, entice her, and lure her bit by bit into his arms. And hopefully, his bed.

The eventual prize was worth every bit of control he exercised. Having Becca in occasional rushed assignations wouldn't be enough. He needed more.

Four years ago, he'd been enchanted by her awakening sensuality but now he was overjoyed by the passion that lurked underneath her rigid control. Good Lord, how he wanted to be the one to unleash it. The idea of some other clumsy, wet behind the ears, scoundrel touching her and unleashing all that energy filled him with a fury he hadn't known he possessed. Looking at her tonight with her beauty and grace on display in a magnificent gown at a glittering ball, he knew she'd fill the role of his duchess to perfection.

He longed to strip that tantalizing gown from her shoulders, to peel down her chemise and feast himself on the succulent lushness of her breasts. How he'd stopped himself from planting his fist in the face of at least five gentlemen tonight he didn't know.

Being one of the male rogues himself for many years, he'd recognized their maneuvers for what they were, simple leering fools. Lords who claimed to be gentlemen, but who leaned in to peek down her décolletage. Who clasped her tighter than proper rules of behavior allowed when they danced with her, just to feel her body brush theirs as they twirled her round and round. Becca seemed oblivious to them all and yet the night she'd come to his town house, she'd known and had accused him of doing the same thing.

Now, blame it on the moonlight, blame it on animal attraction between male and female. Blame it on any scientific explanation Becca would come up with, but he could no longer help himself. Even a chaste kiss would be better than the aching hunger he suffered in his solitary bed each night, the burning in his body as fantasy after fantasy tormented him. Fantasies of the ways he'd claim Becca's curvaceous body if he was free. Allowing her to become accustomed to the press of his hard arousal, he leaned in, meaning to hold to a leisurely pace and seduce her with his expertise. At the first soft touch of her lips under his, control shattered, and then deserted him. He shuddered with too long denied desire.

Damn Julia and her stipulations. To hell with his self-enforced celibacy. He was a grown man with a man's desires and needs and right now, he wanted Becca. Hungered for her quite desperately.

Gathering her roughly to him, he claimed her the way he wanted, with passion, with lust. Oh yes, an enormous dose of lust.

Another thought sneaked in to his consciousness. This kiss felt different from previous ones. Deeper, more full of emotion.

But there wasn't time to dissect that idea when they'd only snatched minutes together in this secluded spot. Not one second could be wasted. There was only the here and now. A man, and his woman.

His next kiss was hard and fast, and then he settled into long and lingering caresses of her lips, her face, her neck. His hand crept towards her thrusting breast and she moaned, deep and long.

"Sherywn!" The loathing in the voice cooled his ardor faster than being doused with icy water. "Cayle St. Martin." Easing back from Becca, he reassured himself she was presentable. After adjusting the fall of his trousers over his painful groin, he turned to face his step-mother person. One of Michael's favorite adages sprang into his mind. If looks could kill, he and Becca would be dead.

"Julia, what may I do for you?"

"Let go of that ridiculous chit."

Cayle tucked Becca against his side. "Take care. To insult Lady Rebecca is to insult me."

"That conniving creature doesn't deserve the title of lady anything. I told you to stay clear of her and her entire eccentric family."

He heard Becca's shocked gasp. He took her hand and rubbed circles over her clenched knuckles. "The Jamisons are more my family than you've ever been, Julia, so please remember your manners."

Julia moved towards Becca, arm raised and palm open, but Cayle stepped between them. Becca, far from cowering, pushed past him. His stepmother outweighed Becca in the bitchiness stakes by a hundred to one, but Becca looked ready to do battle. Cayle couldn't allow either of them to make spectacles of themselves, or of him. Not when victory over his step-mother was almost within his grasp.

Julia, however, was hell bent on trouble. "Cayle, I insist you escort me inside. Before you make more of a fool of yourself over that troublemaker." She pointed a finger at Becca. "It's your fault people are watching Sherwyn. Again. You cause gossip wherever you go."

Julia's high color and wild look worried Cayle. With dangerous quiet, he told her, "Becca's done nothing wrong."

Julia waved her arms in a manner she'd label uncouth.

"Until you began sniffing around her skirts again, your past disgrace had been forgotten. You've membership to all the best clubs. Men ask your opinion on politics and investments. We're the envy of the Ton." Julia's face contorted with fury as she pointed at Becca. "I won't allow this ... this whore to ruin my plans. I'll not let the St. Martin name be dragged through the mud again."

Cayle glanced towers the balcony doors, hoping no one could hear Julia's ravings. She barely took time to suck in a lungful of air before saying, "I told your father that your connection to the mad Jamisons would bring us down. I arranged for you to be sent away four years ago and if you thwart me now, I'll do it again."

Her gaze swung to Becca who stood in rigid silence. "You're nobody. An insignificant bluestocking. You and your sisters will either return to the country with your tails between your legs or I'll do whatever it takes to stop your interference."

Cayle edged Becca away, before Julia's spewing venom pushed her to retaliate, verbally or physically.

"Madam, you've overstepped. You've a nasty habit of turning up at inconvenient times and I'd like to know why. First, the Chestertons' library four years ago, and now here. "

But Julia was beyond caring. She looked insane when she spat out at Becca, "Acting the whore and sharing Sherwyn's bed won't get you what you want. He's the Duke of Sherwyn. He'll never lower his standards and marry you."

Becca looked as stunned as he felt. When her knees sagged, he anchored her to his side with an arm around her waist. He'd never realized how Julia truly saw him. Yes, she loved that he was the duke and a means to her ends, but on a personal level she appeared to detest him, despite the numerous times she tried to manipulate him into her bed. "Julia, stop talking go back inside."

Not grasping how furious he was, Julia pointed at Becca. "He'll leave you as he did four years ago. You think I didn't know about your little trysts." When Becca's body shook beneath his arm, Cayle longed to deal Julia here, before the cream of society, and damn the consequences. "I permitted it because I knew he'd tire of you, as he does with all women. Except me."

Julia reached up to Cayle's lapel and ran a gloved hand down the length of his coat, her fingers hovering above his waist. "I'm the only one who knows how to please Sherwyn."

She gave a small brittle laugh. "He'll come crawling back to me, as his father used to do. As all men do."

Becca's eyes spun upwards to him, wide with shock. "Sweetheart, please," he protested, but she stopped him with a hand on his chest.

"No. I've often been forced to remain silent and not defend myself against malicious talk in order to spare my family from ridicule. But your stepmother has no right to misalign you, or me."

She faced Julia. "I don't believe that nonsense. You should be ashamed of yourself for voicing such wicked lies about your own family. Say what you will of me, I've heard it all before. But I'll not allow you to speak ill of my family. Nor, of your stepson. Cayle's bent over backwards to appease you, and to comply with your preposterous demands."

Dropping into a small curtsy, she added, "If you'll excuse me, Duchess, I find the air out here to be putrid. I'll rejoin my family and hope we never, ever, have occasion to meet again."

With her head held high, Becca stalked back into the ballroom. Cayle wanted to applaud her, but first he needed to rid himself of a menace. He escorted Julia to the door, so incensed he didn't trust himself to say anything except, "Madam, you'll attend me in the library at ten tomorrow morning."

Heedless of her protests, he hurried away to search for Becca. After he offered his apologies, he'd investigate Julia's uncanny knack of appearing at inopportune times. Had she arrived in Chesterton's library by coincidence? And at the very moment Sybila launched herself at him.

***

Cayle peered around the dance floor trying to glimpse Becca. A woman pressed herself against his side. With a start, he recognized the ill-mannered lady as Lady Charmers. He barely acknowledged her, giving only a very brief nod, and stepped away from her.

A hand on his arm stopped him. "Cayle, how delightful to see you. It's been too long."

Having no polite reply, he remained silent. Undeterred, Sybila charged on as if they remained friends, as if he wasn't spearing her with a look of utter distaste.

"I'd enjoy it if you'd call upon me at my home."

He struggled to maintain his calm. This bitch had caused his exile to the Continent. She'd lied about their relationship and caused the rift between himself and Becca. Being civil to her was excruciating. Being friends impossible. Though, by the way she pressed her breasts against his arm, he assumed this was an offer of more than friendship. He felt soiled.

"We've nothing to say to each other."

Sybila dropped her hand from his arm and took a step back. Like Julia, she appeared shocked that a man would reject her advances. "And if you come near me again, I'll tell the truth about your attempt at trapping me into marriage." He strode away without another word.

Locating Becca with her family proved easy. Trying to extricate her proved frustrating. As he waited with clenched jaw to gain her attention, Baron Mitchell and Viscount Melrose sidled up to him and pulled him aside.

With a conspiratorial whisper, Mitchell advised him, "Sherwyn, a word of advice from friends. While known to be an attractive wench, Lady Rebecca's reputation is such that if you continue to be seen with her, your own will suffer." Viscount Melrose, with his over-starched necktie, stood close by and nodded in time with the Baron's words.

"We're telling you for your own good, Sherwyn," Mitchell said. "The lady is sharp witted, though nothing to compare to her brother, of course."

Trying to contain his annoyance, Cayle said, "Of course?"

The Viscount stared at him as if the answer was obvious. "Well, because she's female." He pronounced the last word with such disdain that Cayle almost laughed in his face. The Viscount was known to have less intelligence than a block of wood, yet he denigrated Becca because she wasn't born a man.

"Naturally," the Viscount added, "her intelligence can't be as highly toned as her brother's. He'll one day be an earl."

"So being male, and titled, allows you more capacity for rational thinking. Is that it?"

"Exactly. You're also titled, and a man, so you're naturally intelligent."

His first instinct was to tell these two idiots what he thought of their reasoning, but this was his opportunity to lure them into revealing their associates' names. "And dancing with an opinionated lady may also do me permanent harm. Is that correct?"

"Exactly," the Viscount said again. "And we know you are supposed to be keeping your reputation clean at the moment."

With a cool smile, Cayle said, "You're referring to my stepmother, the Duchess of Sherwyn."

The Baron's smile was reminiscent of a serpent about to strike an unsuspecting prey. Cayle hadn't been home long enough for any stories regarding his time abroad to reach London. And having seen him escorting Julia, playing the lapdog, these fools had decided he would be easy to manipulate. A gullible man who'd heed their warnings about who to mix with. Or in Becca's case, who to avoid.

The smarmy Baron continued as if his every word was an absolute truth that Cayle should believe. The thought of this man influencing innocent people into making illegal investments made Cayle's gut churn.

"Come, come, Sherwyn. Playing doormat to your dissolute stepmother is the talk of the clubs. She has you by the balls." He smirked. "Unless your reputation remains as polished as a new pair of boots, your step-mother will continue to live in your house. Harangue you and your brothers, forever."

"What business is it of yours who I keep company with? Or if my stepmother approves?"

"I like to know everything about people who may interrupt my financial dealings in any way."

"And you think I'll do that, interrupt them?"

The Baron scoffed, "Of course not. Not you. If I was to be cruel, I'd point out that your reputation is for retreating, not fighting."

Cayle clenched his fists. Better to be seen the fool, if it would induce the Baron to reveal information which would help him keep Becca safe. He chuckled. "Yes. I'm known as a lover rather than a fighter. I'm uncertain if people still think that and I really don't care." He pretended to assess the Baron, to weigh him up as a confidant. "Although a man has needs, if you take my meaning. Perhaps you could point me towards the best gaming, or other establishments in town."

Mitchell visibly relaxed. The two men went into elaborate detail regarding the best places for Cayle to gamble, and the establishments best known for shady dealings. He said nothing to disabuse them of their notion that he was still wet behind the ears when it came to City vices.

But though he acted the fool for another five minutes, he discovered nothing of interest. The Baron was full of his own self-importance and believed himself invincible. The Viscount was an unwitting pawn in the game being played and believed himself a major investor in railways, yet Cayle was certain the Baron humored him simply because of his elite connections. The Viscount would likely be discarding when he'd outlived his usefulness.

He noticed Becca's glare arrowed at him, so he excused himself and moved to her side, placing her hand on his sleeve in a deliberate gesture of intimacy. A declaration that Becca was under his protection and a direct conflict with the act he'd performed for the Baron. He wondered who'd end up the most confused from these games, them or him?

"What were you discussing with the Baron?"

He chuckled. "And I missed your pleasant company too, my dear."

Suitably chastened, Becca bowed her head. "I apologize," she muttered. "When I saw you talking to them, I was worried."

He smiled, perversely pleased that Becca's thoughts and

feelings were as tumultuous as his. "You were worried about me," he teased. "I like that you care."

"I didn't say I cared--"

"It sounded like it to me."

"Oooh. You're doing it again." She stopped and pulled out of his grasp. "Deliberately being annoying just to avoid answering my questions."

"I've had expert tutelage from you in doing that, minx."

Even her stance was strong and confronting. He'd use that to his advantage; goad her into doing what he wanted. Right now, his desire was to have her. All of her. Any way he could manage.

Over the years, he'd seen plenty of more beautiful women. Yet this bundle of energy, this aggravating woman who was immune to his commands and resistant to his entreaties, tied him in knots. Becca was nothing like the simpering misses pushed at him during endless rounds of boring parties. Though his growing hunger for her was badly timed. He wanted to yell out loud.

His late father had bequeathed Julia enough money to live in comfort, yet greed pushed her to demand more, and more. Soon, he'd bequeath her a considerable amount of money so she could visit the Continent, or wherever she wanted to travel with her latest lover. He didn't give a damn where she went, so long as he never had to set eyes on the cheating witch again.

"I did glean one useful piece of information from the Baron. The group uses several higher-end gambling houses as a net to scoop up unsuspecting young men, ones still wet behind the ears. They coerce them into handing over their quarterly allowances in the hope of a rapid return."

"They're trying to raise capital. Major investors need money ready to give the government the moment the Exchange releases a new railway prospectus."

"It's a case of first in, first served?"

"Exactly," she said, grabbing his hand in her excitement.

"Which means the consortium controller might be combing the gaming tables. Looking for new prospects."

Becca's face glowed with renewed hope. She looked more beautiful than any woman he'd ever seen, making it hard to concentrate.

"Depending on how desperate he is, yes. Melrose let slip that the entire group is very tight for money. Mitchell stopped him from telling me too much, though he'd already disclosed a major holdup. They're waiting for their last venture to pay dividends."

Becca's brow creased as her active brain worked. "Which mightn't happen for two or three months." She tapped her forefinger on her bottom teeth. His eyes followed every movement as hungrily as a lion, imagining his finger being sucked between her moist lips. "Or, they may try to squeeze more money from their blackmail victims."

He shrugged. "Desperate men, desperate times."

"This worries me. If the ringleader knows he'll have a shortfall of funds at the start of the month when new shares release, he'll push his underlings to work harder. Find more victims."

"Don't fret. Their desperation will play out in our favor. They'll make more mistakes."

"They might decide not to give us any more time, like they did with Peggy. Try to take the journals by force, without waiting for me--for us--to finish our calculations."

"When they do, my friends and I will be ready for them."

"We're running out of time. Using me as a lure in the ballrooms didn't work. The ringleader didn't approach me. Didn't talk to me. We need to do more to draw him out."

He was so distracted by her slip of the tongue over who had made the calculations that it took him a moment to register what she was suggesting. "No, Becca. You will not put yourself in any more danger. You were nearly killed at the theater."

"But any day now, if we haven't handed over our lists, the Baron, or whoever's giving the orders, will hurt my family. I have to stop it. Anyway I can."

"We know Mitchell and Melrose are syndicate contributors, even if only low level. If we stop them, it could frighten others away."

"But we still haven't uncovered the leader. He's still unknown to us. Still the dangerous one. If we don't flush him out, he'll haunt us for the rest of our lives. I can't live like that. My family can't live like that."

He nodded. "We need to finish it. But you'll leave it to me. My brothers and friends can go places you can't."

Guilt flickered in her eyes. The stubborn woman was planning something, something that would put her life in jeopardy. Walking away from Becca now wasn't an option. He'd been attuned through his entire childhood to her schemes and, right now, she needed him more than ever. Fixing her with his most intimidating look, he asked, "What are you planning?"

She shrugged and turned away. "Nothing important. Just a little gathering of statistics."

"When, and where, will this unimportant gathering occur?"

He was determined to discover her plan. Determined to stop her before she decided to sacrifice herself. And if that failed, which was a distinct possibility as this was intractable Becca, he'd be there to protect and save her.

She tried to out-stare him but her silent war didn't dent his resolve. The years had made him stronger and more domineering than her softer nature allowed. He silently chuckled over how calculating and manipulative he'd become in such a short time, perhaps making him no better than the women who pursued him. Because now he pursued Becca in the same relentless fashion.

"Oh, all right. You'll force an admission out of one of my family anyway. When you get that ferocious look in your eyes, nobody can withstand you, not even my sisters."

"Regrettably, you see gainsaying me as a noble pastime. Your sisters, however, understand that I'm inflexible when it comes to your safety. They bow to my wishes. Now, stop prevaricating and tell me."

She sighed, as if badly put upon. "I'll ask Madame Faberge to arrange an entrée for me to the highest stake gaming establishments. Where the Baron meets his protégés."

He was speechless. Even for Becca this was too much. "Absolutely not. I forbid you to go to those places. You've no comprehension of the obsession, the debauchery, in those places."

"You're forgetting. I visit brothels regularly. Or at least, the kitchens of those establishments. The girls feel freer to speak with me if it is their place of employment. Gambling hells won't shock me either. I must do this if I'm to save Michael."

He recognized the fire in her eyes. Knew that by ordering

Becca to do something, she'd take the opposite road. Yet, the thought of her wandering the streets at night, flitting from one gaming table to another, was enough to turn his hair grey.

"And who's going to accompany you? Not Michael."

"No, not Michael. Every time he leaves Oxford, someone follows him." She fluttered her eyelashes at him. "I hoped you might accompany me."

"I presume you'll not obey me and stay away."

"I don't take orders from any man. Now or ever. I'm asking you as a friend. For your help."

He inwardly groaned, knowing they were more than friends. They both recognized that much, therefore trapping him in a web of his own making.

"I can't refuse to help." He gave a half smile of resignation. "I could never refuse to help in any of your madcap schemes in the past. And I find myself unable to break the pattern of a lifetime."

He shook his head in something close to despair. "God, save me from manipulative, obstreperous, females."

"Oooh, Cayle. What a lovely, lovely word. Thank you for adding to my vocabulary for the day."

She blew him a kiss and walked off. As was becoming her habit.

Chapter 18

Each night, Becca and Cayle waited until well after midnight before doing the rounds of the clubs, using hired carriages instead of Cayle's easily identifiable ducal carriage.

Becca convinced herself that their simple plan was fail-safe. Cayle remained unenthusiastic and made it clear he accompanied her for the sole purpose of keeping her safe, while he grumbled without ceasing. She'd never admit to it, but his presence at her side was comforting and reassuring. Necessary.

"At this hour, the most dissolute gamblers will be well entrenched in every salon, betting huge sums," he informed her. "Despair over losses or joy over winnings has an identical effect. It causes tongues to loosen."

"So, I'll seek out the young men who look ripe for fleecing, or who have already lost their money to predators, and coerce them into talking."

"And I'll scour the back rooms, where women are not encouraged," he glared at her in warning, "and where you will not under any circumstances intrude, to see if anyone is throwing large sums of money around."

After four hours, they'd trolled three establishments with no sign of any men who'd come into sudden inheritances or who were looking for investors. Becca was horrified by the number of men, and women, risking their estate's fortunes on the throw of a dice. She barely stopped herself from speaking to several men she knew about the waste of money.

Cayle was more inured to the self-indulgence of the gamblers and simply shrugged. "The faintest murmur of empty pockets causes a run of bill collectors knocking at men's doors, yet even that doesn't discourage them."

"In a society that runs on vouchers and debt, discovering who has enough money to wager with is difficult. Almost impossible," Becca said in despair. "I've now realized what a difficult position this puts you in. No wonder you avoid speaking to acquaintances. It's Julia, isn't it?"

He leaned a shoulder against a wall covered in faded red velvet and reeking of stale tobacco and shrugged. "According to our agreement, Julia may not frequent high-stake gaming rooms. She knows I won't be responsible for her debts if she breaks our agreement."

"So, she'll be even angrier when she hears, and she undoubtedly will."

"Correct on both counts," he agreed with an air of indifference.

"Oh, no, Cayle. This is disastrous. I should have realized sooner."

He shrugged again, then smiled faintly and patted her hand. "It doesn't matter. I'll find another way to appease Julia as soon as this is finished and you're safe. My stepmother is governed by greed. Another gown, or a piece of jewelry, and she'll be satisfied."

"I'm sorry for causing you so much trouble. When I approached you, I was too desperate to save my own family to consider how it may affect yours."

"It's true that if Julia knows that I am visiting hells every night and losing the family's fortunes, she can decry me as not avoiding any hint of scandal. But I don't care anymore. I've done enough to appease her. Right now, the most important thing is removing the consortium's hold over your family."

"I wish I could do something to help you in return."

"Don't fret, my love. Very shortly, five of our ships will be in port and unloading very lucrative cargoes. I'll then pay Julia an annual stipend for the remainder of her life, or until she remarries, and be rid of her."

"And after the terms of your agreement are met?"

His dark eyes penetrated to the bottom of her soul as he said with the first sign of emotion he'd shown all night, "Then, little one, we discuss the future."

Becca laid her hand on the dark blue sleeve of his evening coat. The exquisite cut of his clothing told of a very expensive tailor, probably French, and set him apart even more from the dissolute state of many of the men present at the tables.

Cayle didn't belong here, shouldn't be here. She shouldn't have asked it of him. How could she have been so careless as to forget his binding agreement with his stepmother? His loyalty to his promise to her had caused him to compromise his vow to the St. Martin name and family.

Becca felt sick at heart. Cayle shrugged it off as unimportant, yet it could affect the rest of his life. And she knew without doubt that she wasn't worth that sort of sacrifice.

***

Preparing themselves for another disappointment, an hour later they entered The Red Satan, the worst they'd seen so far. It was filled with men sporting identical faces of gloom, so without doubt the house was winning that night. Many men were betting large sums and none of them looked to be prospering. She and Cayle separated to their appointed tasks and spent a frustrating hour pretending to be immersed in their card games.

Wandering back to a table where Becca had just finished play, Cayle inquired as any concerned suitor would, "Did you win, my love?"

Feigning an indifference to money she never felt, Becca replied, "Only a small loss, Your Grace. And you?"

"Enough of a loss that I feel it wise to retire for the night, my dear," he remarked casually.

Hiding their frustration, they wandered outside to hail a coachman. Standing on the footpath, they dropped their voices to a low murmur to discuss the evening more fully.

"So, did you discover anything?"

"Talk is, that several titled gentlemen have been letting it be known they recently came into sizable windfalls. Nobody seems to know how many men are involved, or where they acquired their good luck. But gossip has it that these men are preparing to outlay money into an even grander proposal, one that is expected to pay immense dividends. They're seeking investors."

"Damn it, Cayle. We've already wasted days and we're no further advanced with their names."

He put a finger over her lips and stopped her tirade. "One more interesting piece of news. Gentlemen with large windfalls usually frequent their clubs boasting about their triumphs. By contrast, several well-known gentlemen have been conspicuously absent from their clubs for several weeks. They're avoiding their other acquaintances, avoiding the wilder entertainments, and have been seen repeatedly attending the most staid events in society."

He looked at her with significance, and more than a little anger, but she pretended she didn't grasp his meaning.

"Hmm." She tapped her mouth with a finger as she pondered their next direction.

He gave her an exasperated glare. "Word is they're all wife hunting. Taking a keen interest in the doings of young ladies." He paused for effect. "The three Jamison sisters, to be precise."

"So, we're correct in our assumptions. The Baron is a mere pawn while the real man, or woman, of intelligence remains inconspicuous."

"Woman?" Cayle raised his eyebrows in query.

"A woman is quite capable of perpetrating this sham."

"Agreed. But blackmailers are more usually men."

"So, while Michael keeps delaying handing over our journals, the ones in which we detail our latest research, their hands remain tied. We need to keep them at bay until we've secured documents giving us proof of the ringleader."

"Becca," Cayle snapped, glaring at her. "You're missing the vital point here. The crux of the matter. Did you not understand? These men are particularly targeting you and your sisters."

She shrugged in dismissal. "We knew that."

"What do you mean? What did you know?"

"Well, we always keep a record of which men are following us and when."

Cayle's mouth dropped open and he gazed at her in horror. "Are you just now telling me you've so many men following you, the three of you make lists?"

"Oh, not just the three of us," Becca answered breezily. "Aunt Agatha, Michael, and Jonathon, also keep lists. We've tried to match them up, but it seems different men are assigned to following each of us.

We know that several men have been assigned to ingratiate themselves to us. To get as close as they can."

"Bloody hell. I don't know if I'm angry or terrified. Why didn't you tell me all this?"

"I thought it'd only make you more demanding, and more controlling, if I told you everything. I know you. You'd immediately expect me to remain at home, probably locked in my bedroom and lashed to a bed post."

"You're quite correct," he told her, in a threatening tone. "Chaining you to a bed is exactly what I'd have done before, had I known. And that's what'll happen. From tonight onwards..."

Cayle broke off from what he'd been about to say and looked around them. He sensed danger.

Repositioning his fingers over Becca's lips, he whispered, "Shush."

They were alone on the dark street. The coach they'd instructed to wait was nowhere in sight. The hair stood up on the back of his neck. He pulled out the thin knife he wore in his boot, ignoring Becca's gasp of surprise. He wasn't frightened for himself. Cutthroats abounded in every major city across Europe, and he'd not only done business with people of all walks of life, but had been involved in some unsavory deals.

Few knew...well, he amended that after revelations in the Jamisons' drawing room. Few outsiders knew that he and his three friends had formed an unorthodox group who shipped government documents to London under the guise of their other exports.

Many European ruling houses were in turmoil, riots abounded, and it behooved the British monarchy to keep a close eye of their dealings with each other. Alliances or pacts needed to be investigated quickly to ensure the balance of power was maintained. And what better way to achieve that than to utilize the social and business contacts of four seemingly harmless British exiles.

Four young men who, for differing reasons, had escaped family troubles in England and landed in the same sort of enterprises. Now Cayle was grateful for the skills they'd honed, because quick thinking and fast acting had become instinctive for him.

"Something is wrong."

Grabbing her around her waist, Cayle threw them both sideways so they landed in a heap against the side of the building. Becca gasped when his heavier weight pinned her to the wall, but Cayle focused on the horses careening down the road.

Over his shoulder, he saw the driver hunched in the high seat, his shape concealed under an old greatcoat. As the vehicle thundered past, the driver's face was framed in a shaft of moonlight and Cayle recognized the anger, frustration and pure evil in the look he fixed on them.

A strong blast of wind whistled past and rocked them, as the body of the coach swayed dangerously close. Pressing harder, Cayle shielded Becca's body from the buffeting rush of air that followed the bulky conveyance. The corner edge of the carriage banged into his side as it slid dangerously on two wheels.

Stiffening his muscles against the impact, he held on tighter to Becca. She felt so small, so fragile, that her body didn't seem strong enough to cope with these sorts of crises. The coach rolled sideways once more before righting itself enough to slither around the corner and disappear from sight.

Still, he held Becca clasped against his body, unable to bring himself to release her. He slowed his breathing and tried to calm the racing of his heartbeat. If he'd been twenty seconds later, the coach would have run them over; although from the direction it was steering, Becca was the main target.

"Sweetheart, are you all right?"

He moved back a space to study her face. She shook uncontrollably. A trickle of blood ran down the side of her face from scraping it on the brick wall. Using his handkerchief, he dabbed at the blood and then pressed the linen against her temple. Her lack of reply worried him and he peered closer through the gloom to check her color. Her complexion was ghostly pale but her eyes were wide and alert.

She looked up at him and gave a tremulous smile. "A little shaken but otherwise unharmed. But, oh, good heavens, you took the brunt of the carriage. Let me see your side."

She tugged on his shirt but was unable to pull it out of the waistband of his tight trousers. She pulled again, determined to uncover his wound. He covered her trembling hands with his.

"My love, once we're safe in my house at Mayfair you may remove every stitch of my clothing. But right now, we need to get off this public road."

She gave a little gasp and glanced around. Despite the gathering crowd, if he hadn't stopped her Becca would have lifted his shirt in the middle of a busy thoroughfare. Vigilant Becca, who never relaxed her guard. Brave Becca, who faced all her problems with fortitude. It frightened him to realize how badly shaken she was.

On the carriage ride home she remained silent, which was so out of keeping for her he worried more. She huddled into the corner of the seat and took care not to touch him.

***

At the house, the footman lowered the tread and Cayle bounded out and turned to assist Becca down, but she retreated even further into the confines of the carriage. The night's upheavals had shattered even her stoic nature.

Finally, she opened her mouth to speak but Cayle pre-empted her by taking her arm and firmly drawing her out of the carriage and to the ground. He knew what she wanted to say and he wouldn't allow it, especially not in the street in front of his residence.

"I prefer to discuss this inside, my lady."

"Cayle, I need--"

"Inside, please."

Giving her no choice, Cayle maintained his inflexible grip on her arm and steered her through the door and to the drawing room.

"Jenner, could you please bring refreshments. Lady Rebecca has suffered a shock."

When Jenner departed, she opened her mouth to speak for the second time. And for the second time, Cayle pre-empted her.

"Don't even bother saying it. I know what you're planning and it's not going to happen. You will not use this as a reason to get rid of me. You still need my help."

"We'll manage without you from now on, Cayle. I'll not have your safety on my conscience."

"So, if you can dismiss my assistance so lightly, can you also dismiss my body and the pleasure I can bring to you with the same nonchalance."

Becca bit her lip and squirmed under his gaze. He could read her mind too well. She was searching for a feasible excuse to dispatch him from her life. Their relationship so far had been an endless sea of highs and lows. Advancements and withdrawals.

And he'd reached the end of his tether. It needed to be settled before he went mad.

After a long silence, she spoke, but there was a catch to her voice that told of threatening tears. "That carriage was primarily aimed at me, yet it was you who got hurt. It's better to make a clean break now, before it becomes obvious that we've formed a lasting connection."

He felt elated over this one small victory. "Ah, a lasting connection. So, you do admit to the relationship we have."

She shuffled her feet. "Obviously, we're friends."

He stepped closer and was gratified to note that his proximity had robbed her of breath. It was only fair after the numerous times she'd rendered him speechless, either through anger or desire. He touched her face, keeping his caress gentle.

"Just friends, Becca? Then the time you've spent in my arms, reveling in pleasure, meant nothing to you."

She shook her head. "No, of course they meant something. But, now, it must end."

"No."

"You can't just say decide what will happen between us."

"I can and I will, my dear. I have. We will continue to be seen together, but you will only attend large gatherings. Under no circumstances will you go about unprotected. No more disguises."

"Do not issue orders at me."

"And you'll not be attending any more gambling hells."

"If those men are picking their targets in those places, then that is where someone needs to be watching for their next move."

"My brothers can do that. They're eager to be of assistance and it'll keep them out of mischief."

"No, Cayle. I'll not take that risk with your brothers' lives either."

"Stop being so contradictory. You said yourself, if Michael goes to those places, he's making himself available to more pressure. If you go, you become a target for assassination."

She gasped. "Assassination?"

"Yes, because that's what was intended tonight. That coach wasn't just aiming to maim you, it was aiming to kill you. Therefore, neither you nor your sisters will visit those hells again.

Nor will you search any more desk drawers. And you will stay as far away from Bennett as you can. I don't trust him."

"Now who sounds jealous?"

"I am not jealous of a worm like Bennett, but I will ensure that you live to see another year. So, that leaves me to finish the investigation."

"No, I will not be responsible for your life either."

"Devon will accompany me. And Henry, and Tristan as well, if it will ease your mind."

For a long moment she studied him, biting her lower lip as she did when worried. She shook her head. "No, I can't allow it. I appreciate your backing but our partnership is over. You will no longer be involved."

After that, she straightened her back and turned towards the door. Pulling it open, Becca almost fell upon Jenner who hovered outside. "Jenner, I would like to return to my home."

Jenner threw a glance at his employer, torn between obeying the lady's wishes and appeasing the glowering looks being directed at him by his employer.

Cayle threw up his hands and growled his disgust. "Very well, I surrender. For tonight."

He spun away from her in frustration. "Send her home, Jenner."

As Jenner departed to arrange the coach, Cayle followed Becca's path to the door with long determined strides.

"But, be warned, Rebecca Jamison. We're not finished. I'll call on you tomorrow and we'll discuss this. Once and for all, we need to decide where our affair is headed."

She raised a haughty brow and informed him in a cool voice, "I will inform my butler that I'm no longer at home if the Duke of Sherwyn calls."

"Dammit all, Becca. Stop being so stubborn about this."

"I am not stubborn. I'm being practical. We can't be seen together anymore."

"You," he said, pointing an accusing finger at her, "are the most obstinate, contrary--"

"Goodbye, Your Grace. It's been wonderful being part of your life, even for so short a time."

"Do not walk away from me again. If you do, I won't be crawling after you. We'll be finished if you leave now. Do you hear me?"

"Jenner, I am ready to leave, thank you."

She gave his butler a gracious smile, the sort she reserved for everyone but him and, like every other warm-blooded male, Jenner jumped to do her bidding. Something provoking and tantalizing about the Jamison women made men want to perform extraordinary feats to impress them. Cayle threw up his hands in disgust, but let Becca leave. As he watched the carriage pull into the street, he was furious, aware that once again she'd bested him.

That infuriating, condescending little minx had dismissed him for the last time.

He would waste no more of his days, or nights, worrying about her. Once again, his words sounded empty and ridiculous.

Chapter 19

Not even a full day since he'd declared himself finished with her, a seething Cayle unlocked his front door and hustled Becca through. He steered her small body, cold, shivering and shapeless under her wet coat, to the library where thankfully Jenner had left a fire burning. Fury raged through him, but his first concern was to warm Becca and see to her physical comfort. Then, he'd tear strips off her hide. Admittedly a delicious and all-too-tempting hide, but also a rebellious, nonconformist, contradictory one.

After the carriage accident the previous night and her renouncing of his assistance, of his very existence, he'd been determined to forget ever knowing this bane of his existence. Perversely, he'd spent a long sleepless night tormenting himself by imagining the sort of trouble Becca might attract when he wasn't on hand to disentangle her.

No matter how angry he was, he couldn't live with himself if anything happened to her. Becca's life always had been, and always would remain, more precious than his own.

So, early that morning, he'd penned a scathing note to her and had enclosed a long list of convincing reasons as to why he'd taken charge. Therefore, she'd had no basis for continuing to expose herself on London streets. No call to frequent gaming establishments. No rationale for searching locked drawers.

Unfortunately, he'd neglected to add brothels to his long list of places he'd forbidden her from venturing. Or entering. But what gentleman could imagine that the lady he'd sworn to protect would even consider entering a brothel. Of course, he should have considered it. With Becca, he needed to be prepared for any eventuality. He shuddered to think what the outcome of this night might have been.

To his dying day, he'd relive the horror, the utter terror, he'd experienced when she'd followed him into that building. A brothel. A whorehouse.

An establishment no decent woman should recognize, let alone enter. And one that was burning. By running inside to warn him of the fire, Becca had nearly trapped herself in the wall of flames that had engulfed the right side of the house. It had only been his training and quick reaction time that prompted him to drag her through the upper bedrooms and back down again using the outside steps on the far side of the building. The inhabitants and their customers had already used that route when the first licks of smoke had risen, but Becca had been entering the front when most were leaving out the back.

His intrepid heroine had run to that room because she'd seen him go there. And as if the fire and smoke, and her in the building, weren't enough to turn his hair white, buckets of water had drenched them as they fled. The damping down had doused the sparks lighting their clothes as they'd escaped but had left them miserably cold.

Consequently, neither of them had been prepared for the pistol shot that had whistled past their heads. If Becca hadn't bent to brush ash from her cloak at that precise moment, if he hadn't noticed the flash from the gun barrel in the streetlight, the bullet would have found its mark. In all probability, one of them would be dead. No, she'd be dead.

Cayle shivered in reaction to that terrifying idea and shook his head several times in a futile attempt to clear his mind. It was unbelievable. Even at the worst the carriage accident would have only maimed Becca, perhaps broken a limb, and prevented her from visiting the Exchange, but not kill her. But a gunshot, accurate enough to have been fired from one of the new Colt revolvers, became an attempted murder. A very accurate and very nearly successful attempt. For the second night in a row, Becca stood as frozen as a statue in his house, in shock, though still braced for his outburst. He felt unsure whether she was more concerned with his imminent flare-up or with what had occurred. Her face was pinched with cold and pain and he needed to act quickly before she became ill.

Cayle had observed it firsthand many times. Danger brought a new strength to people yet when it passed, they floundered in a sea of despair, regrets, or horror.

"Becca, you need to get warm."

She didn't move a muscle, just stared at him.

"Sweetheart, take off your coat."

With a groan, he realized the only way her sodden clothes would be removed fast enough would be if he did it for her.

"God must be punishing me," he muttered under his breath.

Puzzled, she turned her face to his, as his fingers reached for the clasp of her coat, now so laden with water it almost dragged her to the floor.

"Why would God punish you? You saved me. You're still my knight in shining amour."

The look she fixed him with was one of awe and wonder. The hand she reached up to touch his face felt cold and blue though she failed to notice.

"Damn it, Becca. I'm no knight. And you're trying to distract me again. Just last night you announced we were finished. Despite which, I still worried about you. Enough that this very morning I sent you a note expressly forbidding you to go to any more unsavory places." He threw his hands up in the air in frustration. "I even wrote lists. Named specific places."

"But I went there tonight because I was worried about you. I saw your face when Arthur danced with me at Lady Moreland's. And when he threatened us both. I knew that when you met him there tonight, at that place, there'd be trouble. I saw the coldness in you, Cayle, and it frightened me."

"I assure you, I'm capable of dealing with a miserable wimp like Bennett, without your interference."

"I wasn't sure what you'd do, although I do understand what you're capable of. I've seen that look in your eyes, on your face. I already know you did more than export goods while you were away. But the explanation is in the lethal knife you carry in your boot. It tells me that you didn't merely dance with merchant's wives and flirt with diplomat's daughters. I imagine that, when necessary, you also took lives."

He gulped and nearly choked. Hell, Becca's astuteness would be the death of him. Knowing he'd never be able to hide anything from her was an unsettling thought and he couldn't decide how he felt about her knowing him through and through. It seemed that only in the matter of his feelings for her was she oblivious, or at least she pretended to be unaware. For what reason he wasn't sure, though he held his suspicions.

He studied her feigned innocence with mistrust.

"Damn! You knew I was meeting Bennett and his cohorts there, at Mistress Duval's, didn't you?"

"I may have spoken with Arthur tonight, briefly," she remarked, with a pretense of detachment. "He dined at the Markhams'."

"Correction. He followed you to dinner again. He admitted that much. Flaunted it in my face, in the front vestibule of that brothel. Your precious Arthur deliberately stirred my anger."

"He is not my anything. Besides, he was with Miss Johnston."

"Her presence didn't stop his accosting you, did it?"

"Arthur is no more than an irritating flea in my life. What matters is what you learned tonight about the conglomerate's plans."

Cayle hesitated, but after a sigh of resignation told her. "I started out tonight hoping to convene with Mitchell and Melrose. And I wanted to warn Bennett away from you, frighten him enough that he'd notify the others too. They need to know whom they're now dealing with. But then at that brothel, I decided the only way to rid myself of the torment of one redheaded termagant was to bed another."

After his cruel taunt, he waited for the meaning of his words to hit her, waited for the shock and revulsion any young miss would exhibit. He waited in vain. Becca never did the expected. Or, said the expected.

"There, there, Cayle. Don't berate yourself for a moment's passing fancy." In a gesture of comfort, she patted his chest as if he was a child who'd attempted to steal a lick of the jam spoon. "I know you weren't long enough inside the parlor to do anything unseemly. When Mistress Duval sent me the message, I hastened straight there and watched."

He was aghast, so beside himself with rage he could hardly speak. "Watched? You watched me? From where?"

"From a carriage on the street. You see, Mistress Duval is a cousin of Madame Faberge's."

"You mean ... You're telling me, just now, that you're acquainted with other, more than one, brothel mistresses?"

"If you would let me explain, without interruption."

She tapped her foot in that repetitive movement he found so annoying, the one she did when she was irritated. Well, her irritation was nothing compared to the desire he felt to wrap both hands around her neck, her slim, pale neck, and ...

Oh, hell, whom was he fooling? The only thing he wanted to do her neck was kiss it, maybe give tiny little nibbles up one side and down the other. He was doomed; without a doubt, doomed.

"Arthur was already inside and I was frantic. It was completely insane of you to even consider fighting with him, over me."

His wits reeled, her words leaving him flabbergasted. She'd been at a brothel, apparently not for the first time, and she was irritated with him. The situation was spinning out of his control, again. Stamping down his raw emotions, he returned to undoing her wet clothing, struggling with buttons and ties taut with water.

"Oh, please, do continue. I eagerly await your convoluted explanation of why you followed me. And why you were outside a brothel. Alone. Although, it is insanity to listen to any of it. I should just lock you away somewhere until all this is over."

Her glare silenced his outburst. His stiff fingers eased away wet garments, yet she appeared unaware of his actions or that her own fingers were mimicking the procedure on him. Without being aware, she shed him of his great coat and helped him shrug out of his fitted evening jacket. One by one, his shirt buttons were being opened.

"Madame Faberge and Mistress Duval are cousins. They're both customers--"

"Customers!"

"Eh, no, not customers, more associates, in financial matters."

"In general, brothel owners have customers," he snapped. "They're not customers themselves."

"Just let me finish. We've collaborated on several matters. And in return, those two women and several others--"

"Others! How many others do you know?"

"Without seeming immodest, I'm acquainted with most of the proprietors of that category of establishments in central London. Naturally, I don't visit all of them, especially the ones situated in the seamier parts of the city."

"Oh, naturally." At his sarcasm, she merely raised one haughty brow. "That could sully the reputation of a constrained and reputable gentlewoman, such as yourself."

"Oooh! In return for my assistance in managing their funds, these ladies graciously gather evidence for us. I have, on occasion, visited their premises. More often, we meet with their friends in the park."

Cayle, in the midst of slipping the saturated gown down Becca's arms, felt himself pale. "You and your sisters meet with street girls, in the park?"

She ignored his irate questioning. "Please don't refer to them by that lowering name. It's not their fault they were forced to seek such occupations. They prefer to be called gentlemen's friends."

Cayle grabbed his head in frustration and groaned. "Jesus, Becca. What next? Your family is involved with men who think nothing of snuffing out the opposition. You consort with working girls --" He sucked in a gulp of air. "Pardon me. Gentlemen's friends. You visit brothels. The wonder is that no one's shot at you long before this."

"Oh, they have. Shot me, that is."

Without a care, she tugged the gown off her waist where it had caught as it fell and stepped out of it, dropping it in a soggy heap on the floor behind her. In an instant, his mouth turned dry. He couldn't swallow for the lump in his throat.

Now he was the one frozen to the spot as he watched her, all conversation forgotten in the delight of seeing her unclothed. Her wet chemise clung to every lush curve and the enchanting pink of her nipples was clearly visible. Just as his hand reached out, her words registered in his slow-witted mind.

"Did you just say you've been shot? Before tonight."

"No. Tonight I was shot at, not shot. There's a difference."

Through gritted teeth, he asked, "Where were you shot?"

As from a distance, he watched her hand reach up and hook her fingers under the edge of her chemise and pull it down to expose creamy skin; soft skin that he dreamed of incessantly.

"There."

Belatedly, he realized she wasn't fulfilling his ultimate fantasy of undressing for him in the soft glow of firelight, but was indicating a puckered scar on the outside of her left arm. Although he must have been blind to not notice it before, it was a gunshot wound, and he should know. He'd suffered one himself and tended to others. Having suffered one, he understood the pain. Yet, this tiny bundle of womanhood exposed her wound for his examination as if it was an insect bite.

Before he could stop himself, he bent and gently kissed the scarred flesh, then lapped it with his tongue to soothe the ache and save her any more pain. The idea of anyone hurting such a wondrous creature frightened him. Even more than before, he wanted to swathe her in the thickest of furs and hide her in an enormous bed where he'd guard her with his life.

"Who shot you? Why?"

Whoever had done this to her would be in fear of their lives if he caught them. And he would.

"Oh, this one happened--"

Incredulous, he asked, "This one?" He was ready to commit murder himself, yet he wasn't sure if the majority of his anger was directed at her assailant, or her.

"Well, yes." Her voice wavered at his unconcealed horror. "But I think one should only count being shot if you've a wound. After all, men who go to war are wounded constantly and don't regard mishaps as important enough to recount. Unless you're Major Townsend, of course."

"And who is Major Townsend?"

He knew he was snarling but he couldn't help himself. Never before had he been jealous, yet in his short re-acquaintance with Becca, he'd become jealous of every male she mentioned. Wanting to do harm to his fellow man was becoming a common occurrence.

She was driving him to insanity.

Demanding an accounting of meetings with the opposite sex was the prerogative of married couples. It wasn't something he'd ever done before. His mistresses, as Becca insisted on calling them, had been women with whom he'd enjoyed brief dalliances, without involvement. Once emotion was involved, women became paramours and he'd never had time for that. Never had the inclination.

"You've no need for jealousy. The major could never be my

heroic knight like you. He's far too stuffy. And he's the only gentleman I ever encountered who regales people with tales of his injuries. Mind you, I know that his falling down when inebriated caused several of his so-called war wounds. Which is often. Anyway, between my catastrophe prone siblings and me, we devised a system--"

"A system?"

His heart pounded in a painful thump against the wall of his chest as he braced himself for her answer.

"A categorizing system, to evaluate the severity of wounds. Falling over when cup shot being taken is a two. Being thrown from a horse in full gallop is a four, because of the danger factor, you understand. Being threatened with a knife rates an eight."

Unable to believe what he was hearing, his voice came out as a hoarse whisper.

"How many have you ... you suffered? On your scale."

"Well, I'm not known for being a cup shot. So, only some others. That may account for why my family considers me the most accident-prone. If you remember when we were younger, I seemed to get into the most scrapes. But my aunt assured me I'd grow out of it." Her head fell to one side as she contemplated that. "I don't seem to have grown out of it though, do I? You're still rescuing me as you used to do years ago."

"I'm almost ashamed to admit this, but I'm starting to follow your perverse reasoning, and your roundabout conversations."

She smiled and patted his hand. "I'm not at all surprised, Cayle. You're actually quite intelligent. Brilliant, in fact."

Under his breath, he muttered, "It's not brilliant to look at you and feel the way I do." Out aloud, he said, "Becca, what am I going to do with you?"

A tongue poked out to moisten her lips in that way she must know drove him to distraction. Fingers danced down his chest to hover around his waist, sliding back and forth in a seductive motion.

"I can think of a few things you could try."

Damn! He never knew whether to thank Madame Faberge or murder her. With her education of the Jamison girls, she'd unleashed their powers as women. Richard had best beware when

Laura stopped arguing with him. The attraction those two avoided like the plague would explode and his cousin would be caught up like he was, in a Jamison whirlwind.

Becca's dark red hanks of hair dripped water onto her already sodden undergarments and adhered them to every generous curve of her body. A lone rivulet escaped confinement to trickle under lacy-edged pantaloons, over the length of a stocking-covered leg, and spilled over dainty toes to pool, unheeded, on his stepmother's Turkish carpet.

His mouth dried. He longed to follow the water's meandering path with his tongue, lap up any moisture clinging to her shapely legs, and suck her damp toes deep into his mouth's drying heat. Hell. Nothing had changed. Looking an almost caught-in-a-brothel-fire-mess, this lady still tantalized him far more than the well-groomed and well-schooled mistresses he'd passed time with during the four years he'd been abroad.

He swiveled, swallowed, and stepped away to retrieve a cover from the settee. Not allowing himself to move closer than his outstretched arm, he dangled the rug before her. "Remove your wet things, then wrap yourself in this." He swallowed, hard. "I'll turn away."

"What if..." Her fingers played with the shoulder ties of her chemise. "If I don't want you to turn away?" She tugged and one bow unraveled.

With a groan, he spun away to face the wall. "Becca. Behave yourself, as I'm trying to do." To distract himself from the thought of her undressing behind him, he picked up the thread of their earlier conversation. "Tell me what happened at the brothel. Before the fire started."

"Must we discuss this now?"

"Yes. I need a distraction." He gave a low growl. "To stop thinking about you wrapped only in a blanket."

She giggled, the high-pitched girlish sound making him smile. Lady Jamison, who'd relinquished her dreams to support her family, tutored streetwalkers on investing money and dodged bullets, still remained a young girl at heart.

"Is distracting yourself working?"

"No, it's not." This growl was deeper, pained, as he listened to her wriggle inside the coverlet. "So." He cleared his throat. "Explain what happened tonight."

"I received a message from Mistress Duval saying you'd followed Arthur to that...house. I'd asked her to inform me whenever Arthur met with consortium members, but when you followed him there she feared trouble and sent word immediately. While I was sitting outside deciding what to do, a man slipped into the alley. Naturally, I followed him."

"Naturally," he muttered.

"The arsonist threw lighted rags through the windows. The coachman spread the alarm and called for fire buckets."

"So why in hell didn't you run back to the carriage? Stay on the other side of the street."

"I was terrified you'd be trapped inside. I ran to the door. Called 'Fire'. You came out. Someone fired a pistol and ... That's all."

"That's all? If not for your calm thinking, and the heroic actions of you and your coachman, those inside would have been trapped. Many would have perished."

"I wasn't calm in the least. Not picturing you trapped inside that brothel. Oh, Cayle, if it weren't for Mistress Duval, I might not have arrived in time."

"I don't know whether to murder her, or thank her. The same way I feel about you. Frequently. Following me to a brothel, Becca? What were you thinking?"

"As soon as your spies informed you Arthur dined with me, I knew you'd follow him."

"My sp --. What do you mean?"

"You paid men to follow me."

"Yet you said nothing? Amazing restraint."

"I understood. You were protecting me. But we can discuss it later. Turn around, Cayle."

He muttered, "I hope you're covered," though it was too late. He'd already turned.

For the second time, she stood proudly naked before him. Though the blanket was clutched in both her hands, she held it below waist level so it drooped on either side of her bare feet to pool in folds on the floor. Her breasts, full, high, and bared to his view, robbed him of breath. Cool air pebbled goose flesh over her arms and her nipples stood to rigid attention while he stared, open-mouthed, awed, and reverent.

A tiny tremor rippled down her exposed body, yet she proudly presented herself, a mix of sweet innocence and knowing seductress, while he satiated his hungry senses with the sight of her. He muttered a grateful prayer he'd been granted the chance to gaze upon the perfection of her body. The first time he'd seen her like this, he'd prayed for the fortitude to refuse her offered innocence. This time, he wasn't strong enough to resist. He was merely a man and she was ...Well, she was a beautiful siren.

She swayed and he automatically reached out for her. Being with her would drive him insane. Yet, at the same time, he craved this madness.

"You should sit down. Here, move closer to the fire. Are you warm enough?"

She chuckled. "Cayle, I'm hot. Burning hot."

She took his hand and placed his palm over her breast, holding it there. He traced the shape of her curves with his fingers. Slowly caressed, worshipped them. With his other hand, he mirrored the movements on her other breast, delighting in her panted, "Yes, yes."

"Is that good, sweetheart?"

"Cayle..."

"Yes?"

"If you stop this time, I swear I'll shoot you."

His hands still caressed her breasts. "This time, I can't stop. I really can't. I want you so much."

"Thank heavens."

"And thank God you want me too."

Other areas of their relationship remained uncertain, as only the night before she'd declared their association finished. Yet in this sensual area, he felt no hesitation. Becca wanted him, and that was all that mattered at this particular point in time. Tomorrow would come soon enough.

He felt her echoing need in the short pants of her breath against his chest, smelt it in the scent of her arousal. He bent his head and covered her mouth with his, kissing her as he'd wanted to for far too many weeks. With no hesitation, and happy to at last reveal the depth of his about-to-be unleashed passion. As he slid down to draw one pouting nipple into his mouth, to suckle her breast with a strong and unvaried rhythm designed to make her knees quiver and her body shake, his own body shuddered.

He loved knowing he could do that to Becca, knowing his touch could make her shiver and shake with need. The force of his own desire could have come as a shock to someone who'd tried to deny his own emotional entanglement for the first weeks of their re-acquaintance, but he was past denying anything now. He needed her returned caresses and the touch of her hands on his bare skin so badly he could think of nothing else. Not the consequences, nor the problems they would have to face on the morrow. Desire had driven all rational thought from his mind. As a gentleman, he swore to make it right for his lady tomorrow before society. For tonight, he simply wanted her, man to woman.

Laying her on his thick carpet before the fire, he threw off the remainder of his own clothing. At last, he felt free to worship every inch of her delectable body. He licked and sucked each delicious part until she writhed and chanted his name in small tense gasps. With questing fingers, he tested her readiness, running his fingers through her soft red curls and her swollen cleft. Over and over again, he touched her until she clutched at him in desperate urging.

"Please. I need you. Now."

Ignoring her pleas, he concentrated on her pleasure and stamped down his own fast rising desire. He touched her in ways that made her hot, made her squirm, made her his pupil. When he drew forth her first climax, she screamed.

A sound of total release and joy emitted from her throat in a long keening cry before she collapsed back in a spent heap on the rug. The heavy droop of her lids fascinated him. The look of satiation on her face increased his desire threefold.

"Don't imagine that's all you'll have tonight, sweetheart." He nuzzled her cheeks, kissing her chin, her brows, the soft lids of her eyes, until he focused on the lobe of her ear, kissing, then tonguing it. "There's more." He dragged the sensitive lobe between the rough edges of his teeth, nibbled and worried it until she squirmed beneath him. "Much, much more."

Chapter 20

Becca stared up at him with awe. Aware of nothing but the startling shivers of need spearing through her, gathering again in a sphere of heat deep in her abdomen. She moved restlessly beneath her lover, unable to keep still beneath his experienced touch.

Her gaze wandered down the length of him as he held himself suspended above her. Everything about Cayle excited her. The smoothness of his tanned skin and the firm muscle beneath, the hard lines of his rib cage, the tapering of his body from wide shoulders to a narrow waist. She wanted to feel every part of him pressed against her, male to female.

He lowered to her, pushed one of his legs between hers and spread her apart. Taking his weight on his forearms, he pressed down against her torso. His erection pulsed to match the throbbing of her own rapid beat in her hidden tender place. He was hard and heavy and pulsing. And hers. Totally hers.

As he kissed his way down her neck, one large hand curved around her aching breast to pluck at the distended nipple. The sensation was a mixture of pleasure and pain so intense she didn't think she would survive. Yet, when he moved lower to trail his warm lips over her chest, she moaned, pushing him closer to her breast. Needing his mouth sucking on her tingling nipple, long and hard.

Her unspoken command was ignored so she nudged his face even closer to where she burned. Only his mouth, hot and wet could soothe the fire that raged inside her. Only Cayle could make her feel whole again, complete.

"I have to have you, all of you. Now, Cayle."

To demonstrate, she zigzagged her nails lightly down his back and ended by digging her fingers into the tight flesh of his buttocks. Cayle exhaled a low groan, giving in at last and pulling her nipple into his mouth, rasping it with his teeth, soothing it with his tongue. As the heat built in her loins, she sobbed.

"Little one, are you all right? Should I stop?"

She groaned, arching up against him. "Do. Not. Dare. Stop,"

she hissed out at him. "You've stopped twice before. The aching was so intense that I almost died of the pain when you left me last time. Do you understand me, Cayle?" She took a firm grip on his head and spoke inches from his face. "I can't stand that again. Never again."

"There'll be pain, my love. A little."

She nodded. "I know about the pain. Now show me the pleasure. All of it."

Her knowledge of intimacy went beyond that of most ladies her age. Madame Faberge believed that married men wouldn't visit her girls if well-bred ladies weren't so ignorant in the bedroom. They knew nothing of sex, apart from a rudimentary knowledge that pregnancy was achieved after furtive visits from their husbands in the darkness.

Becca wanted to learn it all, to experience every exciting moment.

Cayle moved again, shifting until the tip of his shaft probed her center. "Tell me what you feel, sweetheart, so I know how much to push."

"I can feel you spreading me."

He pushed in another inch. "And now?"

She gasped. "You're so big."

She halted him with her hand and peered down between their bodies and was stunned by the size of his shaft, half embedded in the opening to her body. "Cayle, will this work? Am I too small for you?"

He held still, and then laughed. "No, my love. You're just right for me. Perfect."

He shifted to one side and took her hand from where she pressed tightly against his chest to guide it between them, until she touched his rock-hard shaft. Two fingers lightly grazed him. He jerked and swallowed in a hard gulp but didn't move away.

"Feel me. Hold me. You'll see I was created this way just for you. To fit inside you. To fill you. And give you pleasure."

"Oooh."

She gave a moan, long and low, almost a growl, as she wrapped her whole hand around the width of him. His penis felt hard, yet soft. Strong yet gentle, just like the man himself.

Cayle held himself still with the tip of him jutting just a little into her cleft, giving her time to explore. Giving her permission to trace the long blue veins with a finger.

She felt his erection twitch and jerk in reaction to her touch and she giggled, making him laugh. His reactions were so enthralling that she was reluctant to release him. But he pulled her hand away and muttered huskily,

"Enough, enough. You can touch me as much as you want after. Just not now. I'm too close to the edge."

Parting her legs, she lifted her hips up to encourage more of him to slip inside her. He moved again, thrust a little. At the flash of pain, she let out a startled cry and Cayle paused, his body trembling above her with his effort. But she didn't care about the pain, couldn't bear the waiting, so she rubbed her hands up and down his arms, and nodded.

He plunged fully inside her and she gasped, amazed and delighted as Cayle filled her, stretching her to the limits. When he began to move within her, she realized this was exactly what she'd wanted. Needed. She hungered to hold him deep inside her hollow places, to possess him and be possessed by him.

"Yes, reach for it, sweetheart. Stay with me."

Bliss came in a rush, pleasure sizzling through her, white hot at her center and exploding in red bursts to shoot to every part of her body. She cried out, giving another buck towards him as he pushed further in four deep, fast thrusts until his own hoarse cry overlaid hers. Together they rode out the sunburst.

At the last second, she'd felt Cayle jerk back and spill his seed in a warm spurt on her thighs. After a moment, he rolled to the side, taking her with him to wrap her closely in his arms.

With his first thrust inside her tight passage, Becca knew her life was changed, forever. She smiled, the timeless smile of a girl who has become a woman.

"I've never been with a woman who was without any experience before," her new lover murmured in absent-minded reflection.

"You mean a virgin?"

"Yes, a virgin."

"Did I ... did I disappoint you? Did you expect it to be more?

For me to be more?"

She felt vulnerable as never before. The part of her that she denied -- pushed aside the sexual part of her, needed the reassurance of her first lover. She wanted him to hold the memory of these moments in his heart, as she would always do.

"No, sweetheart, no." He kissed the top of her curls. "It was wonderful. More than I dreamed it would be, and believe me, I've dreamed of it often."

"You mean us. Together. In bed."

He laughed. "In my dreams, my little innocent, we're not always in a bed. We're outside on the grass, in a cool pool, we're ... Well, never mind where." He bent forward to kiss the tip of her nose. "Perhaps soon, I'll show you all the places, and all the ways I want to take you."

She grinned. "So, if our first time was that wonderful, what will our second time together be like?"

He raised an eyebrow in query. "Very recently, in fact, mere minutes ago, you were a virgin. And yet, you're already contemplating the second time." He laughed again. "I don't know whether I should be flattered that you want more, or apologize to you because I think that the first time disappointed you."

"Surely Cayle St. Martin isn't doubting his expertise as a lover? From what I've heard--"

"No!" He covered her mouth with his hand. "I don't want you discussing me with any more of your--friends. Especially not at any brothels."

"Even if one of the women at one of those places told me that, when she was a young girl there, you used to be very adept at..."

Leaning forward she whispered in his ears, shocking him enough that he shot up and glared at her.

"Hell! You are a redheaded devil. You shouldn't even comprehend such explicit lovemaking."

"Ah, but I'm a scientist. I love experimenting with new things."

"Huh! That sort of experience will be best left for another time." He studied her more seriously. "Sweetheart, you do realize that Madame Faberge and her girls were teasing you, when they spoke about me. I was a lot younger when I visited brothels. My friends and I were always out for the latest escapade. The sort to be bought at those sorts of establishments. I'm now older, and a hell of a lot wiser."

She gasped as he lifted her over his groin and then slid her down to relocate his semi hard shaft at just the right point between her thighs.

"But in a short time, when my stamina is recovered, perhaps you'll not be too sore to enjoy a little experimenting."

He moved upwards until his length slid through the folds of her sex, still swollen and tender, but still wanting him. "Like this."

He slid up and back several times until she threw back her head to groan in a mix of ecstasy and agony. "Or like this."

And he did it again, slowly.

"Oh, yes please."

Becca purred like a cat as she wiggled in a frantic attempt to gain an even better position. She hoped to increase her knowledge every time they were together but, for now, she was content that the intense dark stranger who'd returned from abroad had disappeared. Forever she hoped. In his place was the man she'd known from their youth. Carefree, mischievous, and wonderful.

His feelings were not as hers, may never be, so she'd enjoy every minute together, knowing it wouldn't last. Sprawled on top of him, she wiggled again, adoring how her naked playfulness aroused him.

The signs were there. His indrawn hiss of breath, the hardening of his muscled body, and the more persistent propelling of his erection up and down between her legs.

"You want me again," she said.

With startling honesty, Cayle admitted, "Sweetheart, I think I was born wanting you.

When you changed into a woman, I forced myself to stay away. My father warned me--"

"Your father?" She looked at him with bewilderment.

"He noticed when we visited that my interest in you changed. From friendship for a girl who spun dreams in her head, to obsession with a beautiful butterfly on the cusp of emerging from her golden cocoon. Ready to dazzle the world. I wanted to be the only one you alighted upon."

Touched by his poetic and romantic words, Becca leaned

closer to brush her lips in a slow sweep across his. His arms tightened around her.

"I didn't think you noticed me any more after you turned twenty. Your interest was entirely focused on Annie, the blacksmith's daughter." She growled. "And that total wanton, Polly."

He laughed out loud, the vibrations rubbing against her breasts. "I remember the blacksmith's daughter. Or at least I remember her--" In the air, his hands formed the shape of two ripe melons. "Her unforgettable attributes."

Balanced on his chest, Becca rolled her eyes in mock disgust and punched him lightly on the arm. "So does every other man in the district."

"But I can't recall a Polly."

She snorted with disgust. "Polly was the chamber maid you cornered in the linen closets at your country home. You kissed her. Often."

Cayle smirked. "Ah, yes, Polly. Now she could really kiss."

Incensed, Becca glared at him. "I can kiss. I kiss very well."

He arched an eyebrow lazily. "Really?"

Realizing he was teasing her, she muttered, "Oh, you're impossible."

He kissed her, and then grinned unrepentantly. "I thought I was heroic, gallant, and chivalrous."

She smiled at his list then added her own, "Don't forget arrogant, immodest, annoying." She stilled as she stared down into his beloved face, "And utterly adorable."

Even as he gathered her up into his arms, Cayle warned in a soft whisper, "Becca, clinging to romantic notions of me as a white knight, your ideal man, is a mistake. I've changed in the past four years. Life changed me, hardened me. I became more black knight, than white."

He kissed her again.

"But from now on, I want to be the man who offers you the future you merit. You deserve the best that life has to offer."

"I deserve a man who accepts me as I am, nothing more, nothing less."

Seeing the worry etching his face, she searched for something to relieve his distress. Something to reassure him that she was no longer a starry-eyed girl. Nor was she a title-chasing chit or a clinging mistress.

"If I never find him, my white knight, my perfect man, then I shall be content to travel the world. I'll become an aunt to my nieces and nephews. Unashamedly eccentric. They'll call me Batty Aunt Becca."

She watched his eyes cloud over but was unsure again what it meant, what he wanted her to say, to admit. At present, he wanted her body, her passion. That was enough for now.

There would be time enough to feel the pain when he left her, as she was sure he would. Like before. She leaned in to kiss his firm mouth with enough enticement to distract him from his troubled thoughts.

Enjoying these moments of harmony and happiness, she trailed her fingers over his body. At each new discovery, she lingered, savoring the feel of his contours, so different to her own. She licked each new spot with measured and teasing consideration, reveling in her new rights and powers as a woman.

Cayle remained perfectly still under her methodical onslaught. He managed to hold himself in rigid check for several minutes, before greed overcame him. He'd seize all she offered him and hope it became more.

He needed her. Needed that indefinable energy inside Becca that lit his own fire and made him feel alive. Alive as nothing in his recent life had, and he wanted to savor each moment of it. Savor the call of the siren who kissed him with eagerness and passion, yet with the contrast of innocence to sweeten every touch.

He pulled her bottom deeper into the cradle of his thighs, letting her feel his intensifying desire by sliding along her cleft, through her cream, and readying her. She was as eager as he for the fulfillment that only came when they joined completely, body and soul. Using his fingers, he stroked her with concentration and with a rich, never-changing rhythm, until she wriggled and panted and sang his name. A siren's song.

Never would he tire of the way she called to him, urged him on. Finding her wet opening, he spread her thick milk, parted her and thrust upwards. Deep and straight, this time he risked filling her to the hilt.

Tossing back her long red hair, Becca arched and accepted him, sucking his pulsing arousal into the walls of her womb.

Here he'd found his home, his salvation. Pleasure washed them, sucked them in as she found her rhythm and rocked against him where he was embedded so deeply.

She writhed against his dark nest of pubic hair. Tickling, tantalizing. Taking them up. And then he jerked, unable to hold back the spasms as he yelled her name with masculine possession. Her nails dug crescents into his shoulders as the first powerful waves of his release rippled through him.

"Come for me, sweetheart," he ordered. "Now."

In this private arena, he commanded and she obeyed and he was gratified when a shuddering orgasm grabbed her and sent her spinning. Her inner muscles squeezed like an iron fist around his cock and the warm flood of his stream spurted ever upwards. He filled her body as he yearned to fill her life, her mind, her heart.

He tried to jerk out but she clamped her thighs tightly. Her recently awakened body was not ready to liberate him when she was at the peak of such new pleasure. With each contraction, she drained him more. Over and over. And still she held him tight. Eyes still closed, she slumped forward onto his chest. Spent.

Heedless of how her tears were flowing down her face to spread wetly over his chest, Becca sobbed. He brought his arms up to encircle her, wanting to enclose her in a cocoon of comfort, one from which he hoped she would never fly. She cried even harder. They lay entwined until her sobs subsided.

Brushing her hair back from her face, Cayle watched her. "I made you cry. Why?"

"It's not ... not you," she sobbed. "It's the sheer beauty of it. Us. Together. It makes me feel powerful. Whole."

After a minute's silence, Cayle groaned and shook his head. "Damn! You didn't give me a chance to protect you. And I was too carried away with wanting you to stop."

Wide eyed, she pulled back. "Protect me from a child, you mean."

"Yes. A child. I've always taken extreme care not to bring a bastard into this world. There's enough strife in people's lives as it is, without careless idiots adding to it."

Nevertheless, seeing the emotion in Becca's eyes, Cayle knew exactly what he wanted. Something he'd never let himself admit to needing before. Something that was crazy in his present situation.

He wanted to make love to a woman for more than money, for more than a night's pleasure. To a woman who was his friend, a woman who made him laugh and long to live life to the fullest. A girl he'd known all his life and obsessed over as she blossomed into a ravishing beauty who unwittingly bewitched all around her. He wanted to make a child with her, to see her belly grow round with their baby.

Jesus, he liked her. Adored her. There'd never been another who sparked his humor, occupied his mind, and stirred his body to molten heat. Effortlessly, just by being herself, she managed to do all three at the same time.

He wanted Becca. Desperately. Hungrily. He could admit it now.

"Becca, when I was nineteen I kissed Polly. Yet in my dreams, I imagined it was you. I flirted with Annie, knowing I couldn't do the same with you. All the time, with any other woman, I saw you, only you."

"I thought I wasn't pretty enough for you." She twirled the hairs on his bare chest around her finger. "I thought I didn't have enough bosoms."

He laughed and kissed the top of her head. "If you're fishing for compliments, let me reassure you, your bosoms have matured nicely."

He squeezed one globe of her rounded bottom, savoring the weight in his hands. "As have all your other female assets. But back then, you were a young sheltered girl. Far too good for me. Far too innocent. That's why I stayed away until you were older, until that night at the stables. Even then, I resisted coming to your house, knowing how I'd feel once I saw you again. It was always the same."

He saw the startled expression on her face as she digested his disclosure. She'd obviously never known how deeply he felt about her. He considered how she'd react if he told her now. If he revealed everything he envisaged in the future. Of how he was even now conspiring to make it happen as he wanted, to fall into place at his command.

"Cayle --"

He placed a finger over her lips. "Shush, sweetheart. It's of no importance. Now, we need to get you home before you're missed."

He knew she'd gnaw over what all this might mean, but his own feelings were still too new, too raw, to set her mind at rest. To convince her of his sincerity after rejecting her so many times.

Becca was different from other women. Her scientific mind would theorize that he'd made love with her because he was physically unable to resist the allure of her body. The male of the species mating with the female. Could she believe in a man who led a woman on and then rejected her, not just once but several times? No, she'd reiterated she didn't want him permanently. Not just him, but any man. A husband didn't figure in her immediate plans.

What she wanted was it. The extreme pleasure she'd found that had turned her into a demanding wanton. The wild passion that boiled under the facade of a conforming lady had been uncorked. It was far too late to put the stopper back.

He'd caused the revolution and he wanted nothing more than to reap the benefits every day for the rest of their lives. But this was his second chance with Becca and, this time, he was determined to get it right. However, all that would have to wait. Other problems hung like black clouds over their heads. His conscience tugged at him and resolutely he moved her aside and arose, muttering, "I need to get you home. We've much to face tomorrow. The authorities will question me regarding the fire, and the gunshot, but I'll ensure nobody remembers you were there."

Donning his garments was far more difficult than it'd ever been before with any other woman he'd lain with, no matter how beautiful or sexually enticing. He walked to the door to summon Jenner and the carriage.

But at the door, he made a mistake. Instead of seeing Becca home, he looked back at her. She stood before the fire, shrugging into her damp gown. The light picked up the fiery sheen of her hair and showed the swollen pout of her lips where he'd kissed her, repeatedly.

While he watched, she reached up to touch her lips with a look of wonder and amazement on her face. And he was lost. He could no more control the wanting that racked his body than she could, and he'd gained a lot more experience in lessons of control.

"Bloody hell. Michael will shoot me."

She laughed. A full-throated gurgle that enthralled him with its joyous release of feelings. His Becca, normally so worried about her family and never harming or upsetting them, decided that her own pleasure should come before theirs.

She looked happy, free, as if she was reveling in the moment and their shared intimacy. As if she was made for his loving. Tonight, he'd helped her forget their problems and think only of her own pleasure. He'd released the sensuous side of her nature so long hidden.

When he hovered beside the door, undecided of whether to go or stay, she took control. With a seductive swish of her hips, she sauntered towards where he stood paralyzed, hand on the knob.

"What Michael never knows, will never hurt him. This is between you and me, Cayle, for whatever time we have left together."

Before she could utter another word, he swept her up into his arms and crushed his lips to hers as he launched them back to the rug in a whirlwind of action. Clothing flew around the room in a flurry of activity as they both strived to get the other naked in as short a time as possible.

Chapter 21

The next night, Becca pushed open the door to her bedroom and sighed tiredly. She'd told her maid not to wait up for her and Laura had already opened her gown's buttons. As she walked, she undressed, so exhausted she could hardly take the time to shrug off her gown before she dropped into bed. Her chemise followed her gown onto the floor in a puddle.

She was untying the ribbons for her drawers when she stopped, sensing a presence in her room. Her mouth opened on a scream but when she recognized who'd invaded her private sanctum she managed to shut it again with an annoyed snap before she'd roused the household. Both hands clutched her chest where her heart pounded at a frantic rate.

"God almighty! You scared me."

"Oh, I promise I'm going to do a lot more than scare you."

A dark headed, dark eyed, and glowering giant rose from his concealed position in a chair near the fire and stalked towards her. He wore only a fine lawn shirt hanging loosely over trousers and each time his huge fists clenched and unclenched at his thighs, muscles rippled in tight waves up his equally hefty arms. With the aristocratic Cayle covered by civilized accoutrements and his raw character tamed and masked, it was easy to disregard how powerful he was, how dangerous.

The resemblance to the panther he'd referred to the night Becca had braved entering his lair was striking. So much had happened since then, it resembled a lifetime. Yet, it was mere weeks since she'd disguised herself to visit Mayfair. Tonight, this prowling panther intimidated her far more and she backed away, knowing the words about to explode from his mouth. Knowing the reason he was so angry with her.

"Where are you going, my beloved? Surely you can't have forgotten me already? I'm the man who made love to you last evening. The lover who's going to throttle your deceitful, contriving, miserable little neck."

Her eyes went wide and she stopped breathing as she searched her mind for something to appease him. "Please stop." She held up a hand as she glanced around for an escape route. "I promise, it's not what you think."

"Oh, do tell me what I'm supposed to think then. I've called here at your house three times today."

"I can explain."

"Each time, I was told you weren't available to callers. At first, I thought you were avoiding me. That perhaps you were embarrassed about seeing me again, after what we shared last night."

"No, it wasn't that."

He shot her an angry glare as he continued following her around the room, circling the bed, and shaking his head.

"Of course, then I remembered. How blind of me. What a ridiculous assumption. I wasn't dealing with any ordinary woman. Not one who might blush and simper after rolling naked--"

"Shush!" She hissed, putting her hand over his mouth. "Someone might hear you."

He pulled her fingers down and glared again, keeping a tight hold on her wayward hand. "And what would that matter at this stage? Laura already listens to everything we do and say. Your aunt already reports every move we make to Michael. Lottie has Tony so twisted around her little finger, she only has to smile and he'll spill every secret known to the foreign office. And to the St. Martin family."

He released her to wave his arms in the air in a wild gesture and raised his voice to almost a shout. "Keeping quiet about us now would be like bolting the stable door after the horse has bolted."

"I thought you were worried about scandal."

He bent over to grasp her forearms and hold her still. "Not anymore." He gave her a little shake.

"Avoiding scandal was impossible the moment I became involved with you! And your confounded risk taking. As of now, I've given up caring. It's too distressing for my nerves. As are the mindless risks you take."

"I do not take risks." She backed out of his grasp. "On occasion, I become involved in incidents, minor incidents, only by accident."

"Minor? Such as what I was told happened today? Clued-up at my clubs. Informed by at least a dozen people on the streets. Told that my betrothed--"

"We're not marrying."

"--involved herself in a public disturbance. I demand to know--"

"You demand to know?" She glared back, undaunted by his black mood.

"--where in hell you've been. All damn day. Every minute of it. And whom you were with. When you should have been with me."

"What gives you the right to demand anything from me?"

Perhaps if she'd had the sense to not confront Cayle at this late hour, in her bedroom, and when he was undoubtedly angry, nothing would've happened. Maybe he'd have turned and walked away, or run away, as he'd done before. Instead, he grabbed her almost roughly and pulled her to him before she had a chance to argue or lecture him.

As he'd done many times before, he assumed immediate control of her mouth, smothered her protests, swallowed her words and kissed. Kissed her the way they both savored, and then drew back to suck in a ragged breath and assess the fire he always ignited in her with so little effort. Each time they came together, it was a mix of anger and joy, fire and water, and the inevitable explosion that left them weakened and stunned.

"That!" He gave her another little shake.

"That gives me the right. This thing, this wild attraction between us. You can't deny we want each other."

"You're the one who decried anything but friendship between us. Several times in fact. Not me. It was never me."

His large hands plunged through his thick hair, upsetting even more his mussed style, making him appear younger yet also frustrated and confused.

"I've always, always, acknowledged the power of these feelings between us, Becca. The difficulty has been that I couldn't act upon them. Not four years ago, and not even two weeks ago. My life was too complicated."

"Damn you, Cayle, for doing this to me again. That part of your life, all those family complications, they haven't changed.

Julia's still pulling your strings."

"No, not any longer. Things have changed, Becca. You've changed them. Changed me."

In a slow and seductive motion that she was always powerless to resist, Cayle pulled her towards him and bent his head to nuzzle the sensitive skin behind her ear. She shivered, knowing she'd give in to his caresses, even if she hated herself for it the next day.

"Now, tell me about today. Please?"

"You already know," she snapped, demonstrating she wasn't a complete ninny who would fall for this change of tactics to entice her full disclosure. "Your informants will have given you a full report by now, so what do you want from me?"

He stilled, an abnormal tension in his voice. "Are you using Bennett to get back at me, for my leaving four years ago?"

"No, of course not. I'm not that petty, as you very well know."

When Cayle heaved out a deep relieved sigh, Becca realized he'd truly been worried and wasn't quite sure what to make of this latest revelation. "I'm only using Arthur as a speedy way to obtain information."

"Ha! Anyone can see he's using you for that very purpose."

"I'm not an idiot, Cayle. While Arthur and I went to the railway tracks, the others visited Margaret."

"About that, why the railway tracks? As several vicious busybodies delighted in pointing out to me, a railway station isn't the most salubrious place for an assignation with one's paramour."

She aimed a small kick at his shins but forgot she was barefoot. "Ouch!"

He chuckled. "I could say it serves you right, but I'll kiss your toes better instead."

Squatting on his haunches, Cayle lifted her foot and sucked her biggest toe into the wet heat of his mouth. Becca grabbed his shoulders for balance and moaned. Her legs wobbled and she almost missed the rest.

"If you give me an honest answer."

"We needed confirmation of Arthur's precarious financial situation. He's spent widely and unwisely. I distracted Arthur by asking him to escort me to the time trial for our new locomotive." To Becca's disappointment, Cayle released her foot and stood, waiting for her to continue. "If we're permitted to build The Great Western line, our locomotive needs to reach average speeds of over sixty miles per hour. As one of the engineers, Jonathon's directive is to reduce travel for the fifty-three miles from Paddington to Didcot to less than sixty minutes--"

Cayle burst into peals of laughter that had him bending to his knees. Becca rolled her eyes and snorted. "See! This is why I don't tell people, especially you, where I go. All you do is scoff."

"No, please go on." He waved his hand at her in encouragement. "But it does strike me as amusing. Hilarious, in fact. Half of London was watching you today. The syndicate, my men, Bennett, and me. All waiting to see what sinister events unfolded around the infamous Lady Rebecca. And you, with your scientific obsessions, stood in a grass field beside a rail line and timed a train." He laughed again.

"Our engineering schedule is important!"

"Important?" He sobered and shook his head. "Men are trying to kill you, my hair's turning grey at a rapid pace, your friends are whore--" She poked him in the ribs.

"Ouch!" She put her hands on her hips and gave him a defiant look.

"Damn it, you poked me."

"You said something despicable about my friends."

"I said your friends, your gentlemen's friends, are in a whorl, a spiral with their finances."

She wasn't fooled by his innocent look for a moment.

"Hmm, anyway, Margaret's father is paying to acquire Arthur's title for his daughter, but this money hasn't come from him. So, the consortium is paying Arthur, and handsomely, to fawn over me."

"You mean he's being paid to keep you under control. I hope you didn't imagine he'd break his betrothal for you." She knew Cayle was trying to warn her of Arthur's lurking evil but, once again, he'd wounded her. "You're not that gullible," he said, twisting the knife deeper.

"Thank you so much for pointing out my shortcomings."

"Oh, God, I'm sorry. You turn me so inside out that I consistently do and say the wrong things around you."

The heat in his look reminded her of the times when things

were very, very good between them. When she was in his arms they connected like bees with flowers and when they made love, he found exactly the right words to whisper in her ear. Those words of loving and endearments revealed his true feelings, so why did she bring out the worst in him at times like this?

"Cayle, even now you order me about, and I won't be treated like an inferior. I want a man who sees me as an equal."

"Bennett will never do that! He uses women up, then throws them away."

"He wants me to be his mistress."

"I know that already. Why do you think I was so angry today?" His yell was so loud that the vase on the shelf shook. "I wanted to kill him when he told me last night."

"You made me your mistress."

"I also asked you to marry me."

"So did Arthur. Ask me to marry him."

"But I meant it! I want to marry you." She looked at him with scorn. "All right. I admit it. Perhaps not at the time," he tried again. "At first, I only asked to protect you. But later, when I thought about it, I could see the advantages."

Once again, she glared at him.

"We suit, in the bedroom. We could have children."

"What? Children who never see their father as he's in London and they, and me, will be in the country. No thank you. My own father deserts us whenever possible and I wouldn't inflict that pain on any other child. At least Arthur professes to love me."

"Love you. He's obsessed with you. Dangerously so. And that's why I told you to stay away from him."

"How do you know so much about him?"

He rolled his eyes but then pulled her to a seat, retaining a hold on her hand. "It's time I told you the truth about some things. When I was at school with Arthur, several times he was in trouble over matters with women. Women he'd seduced, made promises to."

She interrupted him, "Yes, yes, you told me that. What haven't you told me?"

"Arthur's preference was always for women who resembled his dead mother. She had red hair, green eyes, pale skin, and freckles. Like you."

Frowning, she tried to make sense of this. "Madame told us several men who visit her establishment have preferences. Blond hair. Large bosoms. How often does this happen?"

Cayle shook his head in bewilderment. "I just told you that the man you went out with today, against my express orders, has a deviant preference. And you, you want to research how often it happens."

On the defensive, she pulled away from him. "I'll not apologize for the way my mind works."

Taking back her hand, he smiled and kissed her fingers. "Sweetheart, I love the way your mind," he looked down lower, "and every other part of you works."

He kissed her nose and moved lower, covering her lips. It suddenly occurred to Becca that he'd become expert in kissing her at the exact moment her mouth opened to launch another tirade at him. When their latest kiss finished, she sat back with a little huff.

"And, you know, you can't always settle our arguments with a kiss." He grinned, highly amused but not in the least repentant at being caught out. "But, minx, it's the most effective way of silencing your active little mouth, plus your extremely busy mind."

"Hmm. If you've finished trying to distract me, tell me what else happened today to put you in such a sour mood."

He sighed. "When I couldn't find you today, when I was told you were with that madman, I went a little crazy. Like him, I've developed an obsession with redheads."

"And you don't want to share his women."

"Mother of God! How can an intelligent woman be so dense about how I feel about her? I don't want to share you, Rebecca Jamison. Memories of us together haunt me. When I close my eyes, I see your hair spread on my pillow, your mouth on my body. I feel the warmth of you enclosing me and I know no one else will ever satisfy me."

"Oh!"

"Exactly!" He nodded and gave her a despairing yet resigned look. "But to save what's left of my sanity, you'll at least agree that after we're married, you'll stop going to unsavory parts of the town."

"See," she hissed at him. "That's why I can't marry you. One moment you say things that make me feel special, wonderful. Then you spoil it being arrogant and overbearing. Those women need me."

"Damnation, Becca! I need you!" He stood to tower over her, pointing a finger down at her. "And you need me. My name and my protection. We must marry."

Jumping to her feet, Becca faced him squarely, hands on hips. She enunciated each word as if speaking to a particularly deficient child.

"I. Do. Not. Need. To. Marry. We earn a substantial income. That's why I went out today. If you want a complete recording of my movements, I went on the omnibus to Exchange Alley and visited my contacts."

"Exchange Alley isn't a part of the city you should visit alone either."

"I wasn't alone, I was with Ada."

"Ada, Ada Lovelace? Byron's daughter? Is she part of your madcap group at those coffee houses?"

"Ada is a genius. She is devising a program for an accounting machine that--. Oh, never mind. And my friends are not madcap. All those women have normal scientific interests and we meet other traders and scientists."

Clenched fists on his hips, he glared at her. "And normal people--"

"Huh! You mean women! Normal women. Bowing down to husbands, staying at home, holding afternoon tea-type of women. I knew it!"

"Knew what? If you always claim to know what I'm thinking before I even manage to think it, perhaps you'd be good enough to explain it to me and not leave me floundering to keep pace with a woman, whose astuteness is so far superior to mine that she leaves me breathless just being in her presence."

"There! See. I knew sooner or later you'd perceive me as others do, as a peculiarity."

"I've never thought that. Never! I admire in you the very things others may find intimidating. How shrewd you are, how conspicuous, how dedicated. And I cannot consider your Midas touch an oddity when my entire family suffers that affliction.

Matrimony also involves more than money, you know, more than stock markets and interest rates and taxes. What about children?"

For a moment, hope blossomed as Becca envisioned a noisy brood of children clambering over her skirts, calling for their papa. Children who'd have black eyes the exact shade of their father's. The boys would have truant locks of hair constantly being pushed out of their eyes and the girls would have mischief written all over freckled faces.

As a little girl, she'd dreamed of a husband who adored her and a house full of children. She'd given up those dreams to give her sisters and brothers the futures they deserved and if she could finish this one accomplishment, formulate her next railway coup, her family would be forever financially solvent.

Therefore, she swallowed her hopes and dreams once again and told him, "Some things are never meant to be."

"Then what about the joys of a marriage bed? You're a sensual woman. That's already proven. Are you prepared to forgo pleasure, the sort we shared last night, for the rest of your life?"

He stepped closer and ran a finger down her cheek, making her shiver. "What'll happen when your brothers and sisters no longer need you? Will you remain a shriveled up old spinster, performing the role of doting aunt, always on guard to preserve propriety?"

"Be that as it may, I'll not be forced into marrying. When I marry..."

His smile was smug, frustrating her.

"If...I marry..."

He groaned, pleasing her.

"I'll do the asking. That way I'll know the gentleman accepts me as an equal. That he respects me enough to do things my way."

"Good, ask me now. I'll accept."

"However," she continued, ignoring him, "I won't be the cause of more scandal in your life. If I married you, a duke, people would talk. I run a society for women that investigates scheming men and makes investments. Polite society would crucify me, and you, if the extent of my involvement in the Stock Exchange becomes public knowledge."

"And that's another thing," Cayle yelled. "It's way past time you disclosed the full extent of your involvement to me. How many of the decisions does Michael make? For your family and the other ladies."

"Decisions are often discussed at meals in my family."

"That's enough! You've avoided my questions for the last time. I want the complete truth. How much of the railway expansion planning do you do alone?"

"It really is none of your concern."

He looked appalled. "None of my concern? If we marry--"

"We're not marrying."

"Let me rephrase that. When we marry, your concerns become my concerns."

"That's why I can never marry you."

"I don't comprehend why we keep arguing about this. Don't you trust that I can handle things as well as you?"

"Don't play the idiot. You're an intelligent man."

"Obviously not intelligent enough to be a match for a bluestocking like Lady Rebecca."

With a frustrated groan, she spun around and put her small hand in the center of his large chest.

"Believe me, if there was any way around this, I'd marry you."

He grinned down at her, all earlier anger evaporating. "Really? Cross your heart and hope to die?"

"No, damn your childish impudence. Can't you see it's impossible? No matter what I want, or you."

Becca put her hands to her head and groaned. This confusing man's ever changing emotions would be the death of her.

"Too many innocent people would suffer if we were to have a permanent association, of any sort. You'd regret it, within weeks, days probably, when rumors spread about me and my strange ways. I'll not cause more harm to you, or your brothers. As soon as we've destroyed this syndicate, our lives can return to normal. You need never see me again. It's for your own good."

Cayle stepped closer, towering over her and poking his finger in her chest this time. Heavens, what a pair they were.

"How dare you state what's good for me."

Becca took a step back, unnerved by the sudden upswing of his anger once again. Over the years, she'd viewed Cayle at his best, and his worst. Happy and sad. Teasing and tender. Even when he was eighteen, inebriated and casting up his accounts. She'd never seen him in such swelling rages before and it made her balk slightly. His finger jabbed.

"How dare you decide what I want, or, what I need, in my life? As you keep pointing out to me, I'm now the Duke of Sherwyn. I have a duty to my family. To marry, and produce an heir. But that, my sweet, is as far as my duty goes. Other than that, I'll choose whomsoever I please."

The finger prodded her chest again. Gently yet insistently. But his voice softened. "And I, the man, and the duke, choose you. You, Lady Rebecca. Do you think I can't decide for myself, for my family, for you and me, what's best?"

"But that's what I've always done. It's always been up to me to work out the best plan for everyone and then make it happen."

"In the past, that's what happened."

"But even now, it's up to me to keep everyone safe. You said yourself that neither my family, nor the society, could go on without my making these types of decisions. I'm always the one with the clear head. In time, you'll see that I'm right to walk away from you when this is finished."

"No, no. This isn't finished by a long shot, sweetheart. There has to be some consolation in my life for taking on control of Julia and my brothers, for assuming the family titles and topping up our coffers."

"I know how hard you're working to succeed. But it'll never work if you have someone like me in your life."

"I don't want someone like you, Becca. I want you." This time his kiss was tinged with desperation.

"Answer me one thing." Her eyes widened. "Do you love me, minx? Do I still hold your heart?"

"Stop! It's unfair to ask me that. Leave, please, just leave."

Turning away, Becca wished him gone before he glimpsed the fat tears collecting in her eyes. It was crucial that she remain strong. Even if it broke her heart to do so.

As he reached the door, Becca heard Cayle mutter, "I will have you, Rebecca Jamison. I will not stop until I find a way."

She didn't know whether it made her happy, or if it simply terrified her.

Chapter 22

For Cayle, the journey to the Hetheringtons' country seat was long and testing. A first class compartment for the train journey ensured time and seclusion for the combined Jamison and St. Martin families to plan their next strategy.

Staff had been sent ahead with the luggage to prepare for their arrival, and Cayle anticipated a few moments alone with Becca before they faced their next dramatic incident. To his dismay, the constant presence of Aunt Agatha and Becca's sisters allowed him glimpses of Becca's scowling face, without any opportunity to speak with her.

She was troubled by their relationship; he knew that she was convinced it'd be a disaster. So, he planned on snatching any opportunity to spend time alone with her at this house party. Smugly, he reminded himself that's what country weekends were about, rendezvous in bedrooms with paramours. Though the word paramour grated on him the way mistress did. For Becca, he wanted something more. Not so sordid. Something more permanent. Something to proclaim her as his.

The Jamison family had closed ranks after he'd upset Becca and concocted some nefarious plan to keep them apart. Her sisters shot arrows at him with every glance, as if he'd committed a criminal atrocity, instead of asking for Becca's hand in marriage. It was obvious his hit-and-miss attempts had been discussed and they weren't impressed. At their brief luncheon stop, Aunt Agatha hustled her nieces inside the station's dining room, without so much as a glance in his direction. Lottie hissed at him, the first angry words he'd ever heard her speak. "You ham-fisted idiot. You made my sister cry."

Of course, Laura refused to mince words either. "You've only three days to make this right with Becca. Don't make a muddle of it again. If you're going to endanger both your reputations by seducing her, at least do it properly."

The women flounced past him with their collective noses in the air, leaving him gaping after them. Beside him, three men doubled over with laughter. His brothers stood with their cousin,

Richard, enjoying his discomfiture immensely.

He nodded at his cousin. "Winchester. Glad I could be of entertainment to you."

Richard chuckled with absolute delight. "Having recently renewed my own acquaintance with the middle Jamison sister, possibly to the permanent detriment of my manhood, I'm relieved to discover it's not just my charms they find lacking." As the two other St. Martin men agreed in a collective silence, the Earl said, "Although, I feel thankful that they've yet to give me such a group set down as they just delivered to you."

Brian took pity on Cayle and led him to the far end of the room where it was blessedly Jamison free. "You need some advice on bedding a woman, big brother. Particularly one who isn't ashamed to use her mind, considering that all the ones you've been with in the past had breast sizes bigger than their brains."

Cayle bristled with indignation, despite knowing that his family was taunting him.

"I can handle a seduction quite well by myself. In bed, Becca lets me take charge."

When the others roared laughter at his expense again, he muttered, "Sometimes, anyway."

The serving girl who brought drinks bent low and directly in front of Cayle's face, exposing enough pink flesh to excite any red-blooded male. Winchester's eyebrows rose when Cayle showed no reaction at all to her enticing display.

"Good, God! You're in a bad way. But, cousin, there's nothing wrong with letting Becca take control of some aspects of your life. An energetic romp with a willing woman cures many ills."

"I'll thank you to speak with a lot more respect of my future wife."

"Future wife? Are you really going to risk asking her to marry you?"

A gleeful Anthony chimed in, "He already has. Several times. She keeps turning him down."

Winchester smirked. "I, myself, have been on the receiving end of countless proposals in my time."

Brian added, "Yes, but not proposals of marriage, I'd wager."

"Nonetheless, avoiding marriage is my forte. So I can advise you, in reverse, of how to handle your possibly, maybe, future wife."

"Becca is different," Cayle protested. "She doesn't respond well to handling. She's more intelligent than any other woman. More beautiful, more spirited, more--"

Brian interrupted with a long groan that was echoed by the other two men. "We get the idea. No need to expand on any more of her wonders."

Winchester looked amazed as he turned to his cousins. "He's completely besotted."

They nodded agreement and eyed Cayle, as if gauging whether his disease would be catching.

"Besides my wedding plans--"

"What wedding?" Tony asked. "The woman you wish to marry has refused you, how many times is it now?"

Cayle felt blessed when Winchester saved him from further embarrassment, by directing their attention back to more pressing matters.

"We're going to be occupied enough for the next three days trying to catch out the syndicate leader. Cayle's wedding crisis will have to wait. At least until we're sure his bride to be isn't likely to be murdered in her sleep."

"God almighty!" Cayle yelled.

"Good grief, Winchester," Tony said. "Did you need to add the murdered bit? Cayle's turned as white as a ghost."

Winchester gave Cayle a brief look. "He must be the one to guard Becca. We've other tasks to take care of. I've already had word from the advance staff. Five men we've narrowed it down to will be sleeping in chambers in the guest wing at Hetherington's."

"But the leader amongst them has too much animal cunning to reveal his face," Tony remarked.

"If we're to draw him into the open and reveal his identity before the aristocracy present, we need a lure."

"Something to use as bait."

"I was thinking more," Winchester looked at Cayle, "of, someone. A lady, one the syndicate wants rather desperately."

Cayle stared at his cousin, appalled at who he was suggesting. Oh, God, no. He couldn't be suggesting they dangle Becca like a worm on a hook under the leader's nose. Few knew it, but he and Winchester's names had crossed paths on British Government correspondence over the years, even though they hadn't re-met in person until recently.

Although Winchester cultivated the impression of a well-to-do lord with little on his mind, his mind resembled a steel trap, making him an ideal government envoy. Snippets of information about foreign alliances that Cayle had recognized as written in his cousin's hand had been forwarded to him in Europe by the foreign office, so he knew he could trust his cousin's logic. But it still terrified him.

The guard blew his whistle and shunted them back to the carriage and still Cayle had no opportunity to attract Becca's attention. Noticing the savage expressions on the women's faces as they conferred in a corner, terror struck him. Tony leaned over to say close to his ear, "They're probably plotting ways to string ignorant, arrogant and unbending men up by their fingernails."

Cayle shuddered at the truth in his brother's words and slumped back to endure the rest of a long miserable day. The tension in the train compartment became so thick, he was sure it could be cut with a knife; certainly daggers were being thrown his way by every Jamison on board. It was a blessed relief to reach Hetherington House. Lord and Lady Hetherington rushed down the steps to greet their guests in a warm fashion, appointing maids to show the ladies to their rooms to refresh themselves. Winchester slipped away to quiz the staff about the gentlemen in residence, and which rooms they'd been allotted.

Slipping a gold coin into a maid's hand, Cayle uncovered the direction of Becca's room. With great impatience, he waited until the ladies retired to rest before dressing for dinner, then slipped into her room. She lay on her back, her eyes closed. Making no sound, he sat on the edge of the bed and watched her.

This bluestocking was so beautiful that his heart skipped a beat. He'd told others his proposals to Becca were for her protection. It was only partly true. When he saw her, reposed, relaxed, her expression unguarded, he ached. He wanted her hand in marriage for far, far more than that; yearned to possess her, body and soul; longed to have her as his duchess standing beside him for a hundred years.

"Sweetheart," he whispered, rimming his tongue around the shell of her ear. "Open your eyes, my love."

Keeping her eyes shut, she said in a drowsy voice, "I told you not to call me that."

"Then stop pretending you're asleep and listen. I can't linger in your bedchamber for long. I dare not be discovered."

"Ah, but if you're discovered here, surely it would only aid your cause. We'd be forced to marry. Against my will."

"Touché. Being discovered together would certainly force you into making the correct decision."

"By correct, I assume you mean the decision that best suits your purpose, no matter what it costs me."

"I want you, Becca. Don't doubt that for a minute. I'll also take great care not to damage your reputation."

He bent to kiss her--only a light brush of his lips upon her -- until she moaned.

And wriggled, and reached up to curl her arms around his neck. She entwined her fingers in his hair, touched her tongue to the racing pulse in his throat. And, as quickly as a breath, he was undone. She aroused him so easily. He couldn't hover this near to her without his smoldering desire catching alight. Their kiss deepened and deepened. Everything outside her room faded away in their mad rush to be closer still, skin to bare skin. Her dress hit the floor with a soft swish to join his already discarded coat and waistcoat. Within minutes, the air was thick with the scent of dual arousals.

Becca clung to him with remembered passion and he couldn't resist. Even though he'd wanted their next time together to be a leisurely joining, slow and sensuous as befitted a novice, neither of them could wait. No matter how much they disagreed, in this arena they were always in agreement. He slid down her body, planting tiny kisses over all her bumps and curves as he went. When his mouth tickled the clutch of soft curls between her thighs, she squealed and jumped, clenching her thighs against the invasion. He chuckled and lifted his head.

"Trust me, my love. If you liked what we did the first time we made love, and the second, and especially the third, then you're going to love this." Pushing apart her legs, he bent again to his task and applied his tongue to both soothe and excite her. He licked roughly up through her crease and swirled the tip around her swollen bud until, in very little time, she writhed and squirmed. He chuckled again. "I can't decide if you're trying to get closer or escape me."

"It feels ... strange."

"Strange in a good way, or bad?"

"Good. Oh, so, so good. But should we be doing it this way? What about you?"

"Relax, little one, let me do this for you first. My turn will come."

He took her up little by little, controlling her escalating pleasure like a master with an apt pupil. Each time he felt her tremble beneath his tongue, he pulled back to muzzle the sensitive skin of her inner thighs. When she climbed down from that new level of sensation, he ratcheted up the tension by plunging two fingers into her tight passage. He knew from before just where to touch her, where to tease to give her maximum gratification. Then, without warning, the pleasure became too much for her body to suppress and she lurched and screamed.

Her womanly crevice was impelled even further into his marauding mouth, which dragged every nuance of ecstasy from her extended climax. As her warm liquid flowed and ebbed, he sucked in the flavor of her by licking his lips to catch every drop of syrupy juice dribbling down her reddened thighs. The essence of her lingered in his mouth as he rose up to greet her begging mouth and he gave a long deep growl of bliss.

His open-mouthed kiss was given so that she could also taste herself in his depths, the same way he'd sampled hers. So she'd know that what they shared was deeper, more intense than a superficial friendship. Or even the light passion of an affair. It was vital to make Becca understand the pinnacle they could reach if they trusted each other enough to combine their goals for the future. He knew time was against them.

"Why are you willing to lie back and let me assume control here, yet during the day you still fight me, every step of the way?" he asked.

"I don't know. Perhaps it's because here we're in our own world. Here, my gorgeous lover, we have the same goals, the same providence. Nothing else exists. There're no conflicts, no differences."

"Whatever you want from me, love, whatever you need, take it. Tell me your deepest wish for us?"

"To give each other peace. To surrender to our deepest longings. To have each other."

"For me, I crave long, passion-filled days and nights in the future with you in my bed, when you yield to me as willingly as you surrender to me now. I want more than anything to be your strength, as you're mine."

"Kiss me, Cayle. Enclose me in your arms. Love me.

Make me feel safe, at least for now." Too choked up to reply, unable to even vocalize what he felt, Cayle demonstrated with deeds what he couldn't express in mere words. He closed one hand around his swollen cock and opened her still soaking sex with the fingers of his other. Slowly, with great care, he claimed her. Took her to the heights. Showed her what peaks they could reach. An hour later, they lay wrapped around each other in a tangle of bedclothes. A noise sounded in the passageway, and they jumped apart.

Becca gave a breathless gasp. "Did you lock the door?"

"Damnation! I forgot, when I caught sight of you. Spread like a delicious banquet on the bed. You're too bloody distracting." She giggled.

Cayle grabbed the coverlet with one hand and reached over to snatch up his discarded clothing with the other, tossing his garments under the bed. With quick thinking, Becca jerked the sheet higher over his head just as the doorknob rattled. The door was flung wide and Laura rushed in. She jumped on the end of the bed, making its two occupants bounce and nearly causing Cayle to be tipped to the floor.

"Good afternoon, Cayle." Laura addressed the large hump lying in concealment next to her sister. "Do I take your presence in my sister's bed to mean that you've mended your differences and are once again friends?"

As Cayle struggled into a sitting position, he took care to keep the sheet pulled high over their bare shoulders. A quick glance revealed Becca's swollen lips and tell-tale heightened color. He sighed, resigned.

"Yes, Laura. Your sister and I are ... friends. More than friends. Before this month is out, I'm going to make her my wife."

"How dare you!" Becca gave him a punch on the shoulder. "I haven't agreed to marry you. I haven't agreed to anything."

Cayle scowled at her, his expression set. "My first priority, Rebecca Jamison, is to ensure that you're kept safe over the next few days." His eyes narrowed to slits. "But then, my stubborn little amour, we'll make appropriate plans for the future. Our future. Is that clear?"

Laura glanced between the two of them and snorted. Then laughed. "I'm glad you're in such total agreement, as usual, because tonight you need to present a united front. You are betrothed, after all."

"We're pretending to be betrothed," Becca corrected in a haughty voice.

Cayle bent his head until his nose touched hers.

"We. Are. Marrying." Not caring of Laura's close observation, he pressed his lips to Becca's. "Later tonight, sweetheart, I've more to teach you. A lot more."

For once, Becca was speechless, although Laura wasn't. "By the way, I came to tell you that we're all gathering in the garden to discuss our strategy."

"How did you know I'd be here?" Cayle asked.

Laura grinned again. "Oh, I asked Tony and Brian, and your disgusting cousin, and we all agreed that you'd be unable to resist sneaking in to see Becca after we'd managed to keep you apart for the entire day."

Becca regarded her sister in a mixture of horror and amazement. "Oooh, you're all as interfering, as irritating, as..." She waved her hand in Cayle's direction, "As him."

"I'll be there in an hour," Cayle announced. He pointed a finger at Becca. "And so will you. We need to draw up a roster to ensure you're not left alone at all tonight."

Laura flicked a telling glance at Becca, who nodded.

"Is there something else?" Cayle demanded.

Becca bit her bottom lip. "Actually, if what we suspect is true, you mustn't be left alone tonight either, Cayle. Or you may find yourself engaged to be married, in truth. But not to me. To another woman."

Cayle groaned. "Blast! I was so worried about your safety, I'd forgotten about the other side of our bargain. Where you protect me from some scheming hussy who's after my money and my titles."

He studied the two women. "Are you going to tell me who you suspect?"

Becca and Laura shook their heads in unison. "Not until we're certain."

Laura flounced out of the room, her message delivered. Cayle reluctantly left Becca's room and went in search of his brothers and cousin.

***

An hour later, the group gathered in a secluded part of the garden. The men went over every part of their plan twice, wisely including the Jamison women.

"Bennett being here is both good and bad," Cayle said. "We need his help, though after our conversation I thought he might turn tail and run."

"What did you say to scare him?" Laura asked.

Cayle glanced at Becca. He didn't want her to know about the redheads.

"Bennett promised to lure Mitchell into a public disclosure. Some of our peers will be on hand to overhear. In return for Mitchell's confession, I'll not reveal another, more personal, matter concerning Bennett. "

"I'll invite Arthur to the gardens," Becca said. "Tell him the Baron's threats have worn us down. We'll hand over our predictions if they'll leave us alone. That'll draw out the Baron, and whoever is pulling his strings."

"No," Cayle argued. "Too dangerous. You'll be playing into their hands."

"Dangling Becca like a juicy worm might be the only way," Richard said. "Their controller runs a tight ship. Not a single gentlemen is brave enough to speak against him."

"Or his underlings are as clueless about his identity as we are,"

Brian said.

"Cayle," Laura said, laying a hand on his arm. "We hate involving Becca, but this is our last chance to expose these men. Becca plays the overwrought lady. Tells them they're too clever for us. Begs them to let us peacefully retreat to the country. And, hopefully, draws them into revealing themselves. In front of witnesses."

"We don't have any alternative," Tony said. "One of us will stay close to Becca during the ball. When she goes outside, we'll already be in position on the terrace and in the gardens."

Becca placed a hand on Cayle's arm. "It's the quickest way to end this. I want it finished tonight."

With great reluctance, Cayle agreed and they departed to their various chambers to dress for dinner.

***

At eight o'clock, Cayle hovered near the ballroom entrance, awaiting Becca's arrival. As soon as she'd made her bow to the host and hostess, he took her arm and led her to a darkened alcove, desperate for a moment alone with her. He tried a last ditch attempt to change her mind.

"This is crazy. You can't keep putting yourself into danger like this. My nerves won't stand it." Unable to help himself, he pulled her to him and kissed her, hard.

She patted his hand. "Your nerves are fine. They always are."

"Not around you. Promise you'll be careful."

"You'll be close by. I trust you to protect me, as always."

"Sweetheart, when this is over, later tonight, we must talk."

"When this is over, our families can relax. Our lives will resume as before, as if nothing has changed."

"You're so, so wrong." He closed his eyes and prayed for strength in the face of her stubborn refusal to accept his change of heart. "Everything has changed."

When Cayle opened his eyes again, he was talking to empty space. He strained to see Becca stride purposefully across the foyer and into the ballroom. Her evening gown of amber washed silk shone as lustrously as her hair as she marched, for it couldn't be termed a walk. She surveyed the rapidly filling room like a general quartering a battleground.

His stomach knotted at the thought of the battle looming later that night, and of Becca being involved. If Bennett followed his usual pattern, he'd have already sniffed out a chambermaid to share his bed, a redhead, and would have downed several large brandies.

Their plan depended on Bennett being mellow enough to follow Becca like a lamb to slaughter. Counted on other higher-level syndicate members pouncing on this golden opportunity to seize Becca while she strolled the garden with one of their number, though Bennett couldn't be trusted by either side. Becca's powerless position rattled Cayle. A hundred things could go wrong.

He envisioned her on the ground, injured and bleeding, and him not being fast enough to reach her. He couldn't blame Becca for being confused, or for rejecting his proposal. Repeatedly, he'd swept her close and then rejected her, swinging between needing her in his bed, wanting her as his mistress, and wanting to marry her to protect her.

His desperation to have her in his life wasn't for the mundane reasons she imagined. Yes, a duke needed a duchess to manage his households and carry his heirs. But his reasons for wanting Becca were far more personal. She met, and surpassed, any of the normal requirements in a duchess. But apart from being well bred and well connected, the lady he'd set his sights on would make every day of his life exciting. Every night in his bed unique.

Though even thinking of Becca permanently ensconced in his bed made his head spin, his heart race and his body tighten in readiness. Perhaps it was the height of arrogance, but he believed he could persuade the stubborn woman to change her mind if he had a chance to use his full arsenal of seductive tactics. His humble side prayed she might declare her love for him. Four years ago, he'd pretended they'd shared a lighthearted flirtation.

Deep down, he'd understood their relationship had meant much more to her. Circumstances might have driven him away, but the moment he'd seen Becca again, all his old feelings had surfaced. Physically, he longed to make her his, only his. Emotionally, he'd kept her at arm's length in a futile attempt to stick to his bargain with Julia. And to keep his heart safe. By protecting his own stupid hide, he'd hurt the person most precious to him. Tonight, he'd rectify his mistakes.

As the musicians warmed up for the first dance, Cayle hurried after Becca into the ballroom. Bowing before Aunt Agatha he asked, "May I lead your niece away for a dance?"

Becca avoided his gaze as, for the first time, the older lady didn't return his smile. She raised an imperious brow and looked down her nose at him. "I assume you mean my eldest niece?"

Hell. He had more than one fence to mend within the family. He leaned closer. "For appearance's sake."

"Of course." The older lady nodded. "We must appear happy. Becca, dearest, smile for the duke."

Becca's look was more grimace than smile. More irritation than affection. But he'd accept any scraps she tossed his way with good grace. Having her in his arms, reluctantly or not, was enough for now. Their dance finished and the usual line of worshiping swains rushed her to claim the next dances.

A frustrating two hours later, Cayle snarled at the latest man to clasp Becca to his chest in an attempt to peer down the scooped neckline of her bodice. Why hadn't someone warned him? When he'd encouraged his contrary lady to discard her old wardrobe and purchase new garments, he'd not considered the rakish attitudes of his peers. Apart from those rushed but enjoyable times when Becca was naked with him, he should have insisted her new gowns had conservative necklines, high ones. Winchester teased him unmercifully, yet Cayle realized with satisfaction that his cousin's eyes had a dangerous glint each time a young buck embraced Laura too closely. It was comforting to know he wasn't the only man twisted into knots by the antics of the untamable Jamison sisters.

A minute later, Winchester echoed his sentiments. "Thank heaven it's supper. If young Murchison leaned any closer to Laura's chest, he'd have toppled in. I'd have been forced to challenge the idiot. Hurry, Cayle. We'll claim the ladies before those young pups come to fisticuffs over who will escort them."

Supper, however, proved as hard on all the cousins' nerves as watching the dancing. Tony fended off Lottie's would-be suitors. Winchester panicked when Laura disappeared to the retiring room with a torn flounce.

***

Becca stood alone watching the evening's chaos, normal by Jamison standards. She noticed the footman slip Cayle a note, and his frown, before he spoke a few words to Winchester. When Cayle hurried through a side door, Becca's spine tingled with apprehension.

They'd focused so intently on the syndicate that they'd ignored Cayle's original problem: being snared in an unwanted marriage. Nothing untoward had occurred at recent social events so they'd stupidly dropped their guard

Becca rushed into the corridor to find Laura running and beckoning her. "Hurry, Becca," her sister called, holding her skirts high and not caring that her ankles were exposed. "Sybila and Julia set Cayle up. He's about to be discovered in the library with our despicable cousin for a second time."

The library door was locked but Laura, having spent the afternoon sleuthing, knew another entrance.

"Laura, go for reinforcements. We need witnesses if Sybila makes wild accusations again."

Becca pushed open the hidden door in time to hear Cayle's angry voice. "Is this a repeat of four years ago, Sybila? I refused your offer then and I'm even less interested now. You'll not force me to leave England again, no matter what you say."

Sybila smiled, a cat with the cream smile. "I don't want you to leave. As my husband--"

"Husband!" Cayle threw back his head and laughed. "Don't be ridiculous. I can't be accused of preying on an innocent this time, can I?"

"No, but if you break your agreement with Julia, she'll take so much of your money that you'll end in pauper's prison. Unless you marry me."

Becca gasped at her cousin's cunning. She'd always known Sybila and Julia were schemers, though she'd never imagined they'd go to these lengths. She clutched the door and willed Laura to hurry and to bring help.

***

Cayle stood in the middle of the library and stared at the bitch who'd destroyed his life once and was trying again, for a second time. For a terrifying moment he saw his future with Becca slip away. Paying Julia would cut the heart out of his export business, just as his innovations were about to pay dividends. If their investments didn't have this chance to bloom, he'd not be in a good position to support his brothers, as well as a wife and the children he now knew he wanted.

However, Sybila hadn't finished. "Oh, and if you think of refusing, remember this. I'll make your little escapades with my mathematical cousin common gossip. Her family will never be received after it becomes known she's your mistress."

Fury such as he'd never felt before consumed him. It took extreme effort to remain calm. "No one will believe you."

"Oh, but they will." She smirked again. "Especially when Julia finishes spreading her gossip, the same way she did before."

"What do you mean, before?"

"What? You still didn't realize? It was due to Julia's scheming that your father reviled you and that my dear, late departed husband challenged you to a duel."

Cayle felt sick. Deep down, he'd known Julia had instigated his problems four years ago, but this confirmation was still a blow.

"I'm no longer that same naive man. I'll not be caught here with you, Sybila." He strode to the door and searched for the key. When Sybila followed and ran her hand down his back, he slapped away her hand in disgust. "You've lost your mind."

"Oh, no, my darling. I've planned this for a long time. You slipped away last time, but this time I'll have you and your titles. You were supposed to kill my miserable viscount so I could become your wife without the scandal of breaking my vows. Not run away for four years."

"My God. You'll never be my duchess. Nor will I ever let you hurt Becca."

Sybila laughed, a sickening, high-pitched wail. "How revoltingly sweet. You really imagine you love her, don't you?"

Cayle refused to answer, but she didn't seem to care. She didn't seem quite sane. "It matters not a whit to me. My only concern is the title and your lovely, lovely money. Once Julia has her share of the family fortune, we'll be rid of her. The rest will be ours. Perhaps we'll arrange for your little friend to have another accident."

"It was you! You tried to kill Becca."

Once again, Sybila touched him and he recoiled as if from a serpent, which, at this moment, she resembled. "If you want to keep Becca unhurt, or alive, you'll marry me." Her gaze drifted over his lower body. "And you'll share my bed. Willingly."

Sickened, he realized the best way to protect Becca was to pretend agreement until he could resolve this. Sybila was mad. Totally insane. And probably Julia, too. Greed had turned both their minds. And his life had become even more complex.

"Fine. We'll be married. I'll never see Becca again."

He'd say anything to placate the madwoman standing before him. "I'll tell her I don't want her." Swallowing his pride, he begged, hoping to gain some time. "Just leave Becca alone. Promise me."

Julia spoke from the main doorway. She relocked the door she'd just entered through and pocketed the key. "Such touching devotion to your little mistress." She smiled with evil intent. "And felicitations on your betrothal to Sybila. This time, I'll not even need to inform other guests that I surprised you on a desk. Or that you were trying to toss my skirts, Cayle."

"You bitch, Julia. Both of you. You're both as mad as each other."

Julia threw back her head and laughed. "Just for that, Cayle, you shall beg us to spare her life."

Becca quivered with rage on the other side of the smaller door. She'd heard enough. Not waiting for Laura, she swung open the door and strode into the room. For a moment, her arrival stunned the two women but she faced them without fear. Her work involved dealing with the best and worst of humanity, and it had given her a new pride in who she was and what she'd become. Jamison women were, after all, renowned for forthrightness and were unafraid to admit it. Julia and Sybila, convinced of their triumphant outcome, recovered with such ease that Becca was staggered to realize she faced two of the most devious women she'd ever encountered.

"Cayle, remember, you're the Duke of Sherwyn. Don't humble

yourself before these two traitors. Especially not for me."

She saw the tension leave Cayle's body and he stepped towards her, smiling, hand outstretched.

"We've proof they tried to kill me," Becca said. "They'll not compromise you into a forced marriage. I heard it all."

Julia threw back her head to howl her derision, a mad, hysterical note to it. "Oh, you foolish child. After I devastate your reputation, your word will be worthless. I am the Duchess of Sherwyn. You are nobody and there are no other witnesses. When the St. Martin ships dock from the East, our family will be rich again and I will be compensated for all these wretched years."

"I'll not let you do that, Julia," Cayle said.

Julia spun towards Cayle with wild eyes. "No! I was forced to suffer the attentions of your father for years. Because of you, I was exiled to rot in the country like an unmanageable child. With Sybila's help, I shall have my revenge by squeezing every penny from you and the estate."

Cayle stood before his stepmother and let her see the determination in his face.

"I've heard enough of your boasts and idle threats," he said in a calm voice. "You'll not make paupers of the St. Martin men ever again."

He turned his icy gaze on Sybila, who appeared aware now that this wasn't going to her plan. She looked frozen, as if she were unable to decide if she should flee or stay to support Julia, her fellow conspirator.

"Sybila, I'm giving you a chance because you're Becca's cousin. Leave this room without fuss and retain your dignity. Otherwise, I'll reveal to the authorities how you thought to use me to relieve you of an unwanted husband."

Julia's cackle of laughter sounded even more frenzied. "Once again, Cayle, you've no witnesses, no proof. At any minute, Sybila's mother will arrive to feign disbelief at finding her daughter discomfited by your attentions, by a peer of the realm dishonoring her."

Several people streamed into the room through the main library door, their very presence disclaiming her statement.

Julia pulled a key out of her pocket and stared at it. "But I ... I locked that door."

The group of new arrivals grinned, enjoying the chaos their entrance created.

Laura held up a piece of twisted wire. "But Julia, the ridiculous Jamison sisters, as you've repeatedly labeled us, are all able to pick locks."

Lined up beside Laura, Brian and Anthony were frankly admiring of such a matchless skill from such an extraordinary woman. Winchester looked ready to worship at the feet of anyone capable of besting scheming Sybila. Lottie looked as complacent as if housebreaking was part of her daily routine, and Aunt Agatha as contented as if partaking of tea in a duchess's drawing room.

Julia and Sybila were beside themselves. Sybila almost frothed at the mouth, as she demanded, "Where's my mother?"

Lottie answered with a disarmingly sweet smile, "I fear Lady Townsend is slightly indisposed. In the downstairs water closet."

Sybila screeched, "You locked my mother in a water closet?"

Lottie shrugged nonchalantly. "I think the lock must be faulty. It secured itself when she stumbled into it."

Sybila, her plans in ruin, swooned in a dead faint.

Cayle took control of the situation, giving concise and quiet orders to Winchester to dispatch Sybila before her absence was noticed. Her mother, freed from her prison, rushed headlong into the furor and with a wild scream, fell to her knees beside her prostrate daughter.

"Julia," Cayle said, ignoring the two women on the floor. "You'll return to London only to pack enough to take with you to travel. As long as you go to the Continent and don't return, I'll pay you a stipend each month. Take your current lover, whoever he may be, with you, or not. I don't give a damn. But stay away from this family."

"No." Julia screamed like a fishwife. "You broke our agreement, not me. You promised to remain scandal-free for three months." She glared at Becca. "But you've been bedding this whore."

Becca blanched under the force of Julia's vitriol.

Cayle stood firm. "I nearly gave up everything I cherish, everything that makes me happy," his glance met Becca's, "in order to honor that ridiculous agreement. We made a pact to bring honor back to the family name. Yet, you'd no intention of keeping your half of our bargain."

"You were seen bed-hopping with this little slut."

Cayle took a menacing step towards his stepmother and addressed her in a quiet voice. "Be very careful, Julia. A room full of my peers will bear witness that the grief of losing your husband has unbalanced you. Bedlam's a cold and miserable place for someone accustomed to every luxury."

Julia launched herself at Cayle. "You wouldn't dare. I held the purse strings before you returned and I will again. Mark my words, we're not finished."

"Ah, but there you're wrong. You're dependent on whoever controls the finances now, and I'm that person. My father cut you off when your gambling was out of control. I'm merely following his dictates."

"I'll employ a solicitor to fight you."

"On the contrary, Julia, our family solicitor will draw up papers to prevent you extorting money from us in the future. Your treachery has been exposed tonight." He narrowed his gaze at his stepmother who quivered with her first sign of fear. "My brothers and I are now free of any obligation to you."

Brian looked relieved. "I'll be happy to escort our stepmother to collect her belongings."

Tony looked just as delighted. "And I'll arrange her carriage."

When Laura and Lottie were ready to sneak back into the ballroom, Cayle took Becca's hand and kept her beside him. Aunt Agatha commiserated with Lady Townsend over her poor daughter's nervous disposition. Patting her contemporary's hand, she suggested, "Dear, dear, Joan. Sybila would fare far better if she retired to fresher country air for a long rest."

"You cannot tell us what to do, Agatha," Joan said in her haughtiest manner. "You forget, I, too, am an aunt to these girls."

Aunt Agatha's smile was bland as she again patted Joan's hand and spoke as her great confidante. "My dear, dear friend, I heard it whispered that you admitted not one, but two, footmen to your bedchamber. How devastating if your Presbyterian husband, a supporter of strict morality, caught wind of such untoward behavior."

Aunt Agatha's unwavering look withered Lady Townsend and, ignoring Sybila's complaints, she hauled her daughter to her feet. The pair hurried away to inform their hosts of their departure.

Becca, Laura, and Lottie paid amused homage to their aunt's tactics.

"You were wonderful," Becca told their aunt. "But did anyone truly see footmen entering Aunt Joan's chamber?"

Aunt Agatha chuckled. "Joan has entertained footmen in her bed since her seventeenth birthday. I'd no reason to assume things had changed in recent years."

"She'll be too timid to ever visit our house again."

With Winchester paying homage to the Jamison women and still awestruck at Laura's lock picking skills, the group walked to rejoin the ball. Cayle took Becca's arm, drawing her back into the empty library and gathered her into his arms, pressing her close to his heart. "Thank you, sweetheart, for rescuing me from such a close call. You and your entire family are miraculous."

"I couldn't let Julia reduce you to begging because of me."

Lost in their embrace, they didn't know someone had slipped in through the French doors, until the sound of clapping startled them into breaking apart.

"What a touching scene." Leaning against the door jamb and looking very relaxed, Mitchell laughed. "Better than a theater evening." He signaled to the Viscount, who lifted his pistol and pointed it at Becca. "Take her to the carriage," Mitchell ordered. "Tie her up with that sniveling Bennett."

Cayle stepped in front of Becca and pulled her behind him. "You'll not touch her." He shielded Becca from the gun with his body, but she dodged under his arm and faced the Viscount.

"Melrose, please," she said, holding out pleading hands to him. "You're not a criminal." The young man blanched and his gun hand shook. "Put the gun away. We'll talk about your problems and I'll help you sort out your debts."

"Mitchell," he said, "why, why must we abduct Lady Rebecca?" The Viscount's hands trembled so badly he needed both hands to grip the pistol butt. "She's a lady."

"Because, you dimwitted fool, she's no mere woman. It's taken me until now to discover that she's the brilliance behind their prosperity."

"A woman?" The Viscount gaped at Becca who'd been pulled back out of the line of fire by an irate Cayle. "I ... I understood it was her brother."

"No. After some wine, rather a lot of wine, Bennett revealed some new information. This lady isn't just a bluestocking. She's a mathematical marvel. I'm taking her to meet her brother."

Cayle held Becca firmly behind his back and squared off with the Baron, ignoring the Viscount's wavering gun. "You're not taking her anywhere."

"Oh, but you're wrong, Sherywn. You see, we have the guns and the brawn."

The Baron indicated the doorway behind them, and they spun around to discover four burly men blocking their escape route and thwarting Cayle's plans. Each man carried a weapon.

"I'll barter the lady's journals, and her calculations, for her life. Then, in exchange for not killing her brother--"

The Viscount gasped and fell to his knees, hands raised in an imploring gesture. "No, Mitchell, no. Don't do this. I'll not be involved in murder."

The Baron threw back his head and laughed. "She'll write down in detail everything I need to purchase, and when. I'm going to be rich; rich beyond my wildest dreams."

"Mitchell," Cayle said. "Let's settle this between ourselves, like gentlemen. I'll give you money. Whatever you need."

The Baron smirked, "Without doubt, Sherwyn, I'll be taking your money." He chortled long and loud, sounding like the cackling of a caged hen demanding to be released. He signaled to the men behind them, before pointing his gloved finger at Becca. "But, I'm still taking her," the lunatic announced.

Cayle held Becca behind his back and yelled, "Over my dead body!"

"That can be arranged." The Baron cackled again.

Cayle grabbed Becca's arm and tried to run, but before they'd managed two strides, one of the Baron's henchmen stopped them. He raised his thick arm and swung a lump of wood down towards Cayle's head. With a twist to the right, Cayle avoided the full impact of the club but it slammed into his neck and shoulder, barely missing his skull. And, thank heaven, any connection with Becca. When he fell to the floor and clutched his shoulder in a blinding roar of pain, Becca dropped to her knees beside him. The last thing he knew before he lost consciousness was Becca screaming next to his head, an ear-splitting screech for someone whose head was about to burst open.

"Cayle, Cayle. Answer me!"

Chapter 23

Becca turned Cayle's head in her hands, trying to assess the extent of his head wound. Blood rushed from the gash on his head to pool on the carpet. But, before she could stop the flow, another of the men dragged her upright. He forced her arms behind her back, battling to secure her hands with rope. Becca struggled, kicking and punching and trying to scream. The brute slapped her hard enough across the face to make her ears ring, but she fought on until two men wrestled her to the carpet. Looking up from the floor, Becca pleaded with the Baron.

"Help Sherwyn first. If you call someone, I'll go with you without a struggle."

The Baron sneered with contempt. "Such sickening sentiment has no place in commerce, my dear, which is why I detest dealing with a lady. At present, you are needed, though I care not one whit what befalls your lover."

Mitchell raised his pistol and leveled it at Cayle's head. The tip was wrapped in a cloth to muffle the sound, so Becca knew the Hetheringtons' other guests would remain oblivious to their plight. Cayle might die from blood loss if no one found him, but at least he had a chance of surviving. If the Baron shot him, he'd surely die. The best, most vital, part of her life would be over.

"No, no." Becca yelled as loudly as she could, in the vain hope that someone might hear. "Don't shoot him. Spare his life and I'll tell you whatever you need to know. I can make you a very rich man. Just let Cayle live."

The Baron glowered at her with obvious contempt. "It disgusts me to see you beg for his life. Sherwyn used you as all the others did. None of those men sniffing around your skirts want you for yourself. They want your journals, the same as I do. Past transactions, and those copious notes you make on new railway tracks."

"None of that is true. Cayle loves me."

The Baron threw back his head and laughed. "More sentimental drivel. Even if it were true, my dear, it's too late. For both of you."

Once again, he raised his pistol towards Cayle, but was interrupted when a man burst through the door. "Ye lordship, there be no time to waste. Got to be going 'fore the wagon's noticed."

The Baron's arm dropped. "Your lover's fortunate, my lady. We're out of time. I can't risk someone hearing, or discovering our mode of transport."

Becca tried to grab Cayle's hand, but the men pulled her away from his inert form. "Cayle," she screamed. No answer. He was either unconscious or dead. The Baron signaled and one of the men stuffed a vile smelling cloth into her mouth, gagged her, and dragged her to the patio. Her kicking and struggling earned her a second slap to the head. Momentarily stunned, she lost sight of Cayle as they pulled her into the garden. His body lay as still as a statue on the carpet. The woven fibers beneath his head had blended from yellow and rose to bright red. Blood red. All she could see was blood. He hadn't moved. And he looked as if he were dead.

A cart was pulled up close to the garden gate and the foul-smelling louts dumped her onto the floor, where she landed with a bruising thud. Before she could right herself, the wagon rocked into motion and tossed her against the high wooden side. And against a leg, a human leg. The gag that sucked into her mouth on each indrawn breath muffled her screech. The stench was so foul, she retched behind the filthy material and began to choke.

"Rebecca, don't struggle." Hands tugged away the offending material.

"Arthur?" The binding half covered her face so she was unsure if it was him.

"Yes, it's me. Hold still. My hands are tied, but I can pull out the cloth if you don't move." Forcing herself to remain motionless, Becca felt his hands touch hers in the dark interior. "I'm sorry, so sorry." Arthur's voice was a weak and pathetic wail. "I didn't intend for this to happen."

Bracing herself against the side, she wriggled until she was upright. She stared at Arthur. His face had a long smear of dried blood and one eye was swollen partially shut.

"What have you done?" Even in the dark his misery was

evident. "You told them about me didn't you, you fool?"

When they'd become affianced, Becca's honesty had required her to enlighten her fiancé about the depth of her involvement in Michael's stock dealings. Stupidly, she'd trusted Arthur. Until now, he'd honored his vow to never inform anyone else.

"They plied me with wine. Got me intoxicated."

"You broke your vow." She sighed, long accustomed to the vileness of men in their cups, after dealing with the scum of society in her work.

"I'm sorry, so sorry. Sherwyn warned me this would happen but I didn't listen."

"Do you know where we're going?"

"I heard them say they're taking us to a cottage a few miles from here. They've sent word to Michael to meet them there with the journals."

"Michael will refuse to hand them over to these cutthroats."

"Not if your life is at stake. These men will murder all of us to get what they want."

"I imagine they mean to kill us as soon as Michael arrives regardless."

A shaft of moonlight lit the carriage and she saw Arthur gape at her with shock. Like the ineffectual wimp her brothers had always declared him to be, he started to cry. Uncontrollably.

She may have sounded resigned to their fate, but she'd fought her entire life and she wasn't about to surrender now, not when she and Cayle had unfinished business. Earlier that evening, he'd begged for her freedom. Had been willing to marry Sybila, whom he loathed, to save Becca's life. When Julia had laughingly accused him of being in love with his mistress, with her, she had been behind the door and couldn't see his eyes.

Each time Cayle had mentioned marriage, she'd rejected him, unable to believe that he could truly love her. Now, she needed him to survive so she could ask him herself. Before, she'd laughed off his proposal as ridiculous senses of duty, honor and necessity; she'd yearned for Cayle to desire her for herself. Her only chance to have the happy life she'd dreamed of was to escape, and with great haste.

For if Cayle survived, and she refused to consider the alternative, he'd chase after her, her knight in shining amour charging to her rescue. This time, however, the foe wasn't an imaginary dragon, but flesh and blood men whose only thought was wealth. Even more dangerous was the power that such immense wealth brought with it.

Becca adopted her no-argument voice that she used to command and organize her family. "Arthur, pull yourself together. Pretend you're the gentleman your mama raised you to be. We need to escape." Her words shocked Arthur into sitting straighter in his corner, his crying subsiding into sobs.

"We're bound with ropes. How can we escape?"

The indrawn breath he took after every sob irritated her so much that she lost her temper. "Damnation, Arthur." Shock at her dockside language ceased his sobs. "Do you have a knife in your pocket?"

Once again he looked horrified. "A knife? What sort of gentleman carries a knife upon his person?"

She glared at him. "The sensible kind. Cayle carries one."

"I'm nothing like Sherwyn."

"That's been obvious for quite a while. Now, pull yourself together. We need to improvise. We need something sharp."

She heard him grope beneath the seat and she did the same, running her hand over the uneven wagon floor.

"There's a jagged piece of iron here," Arthur said.

"Perfect."

She twisted and wiggled enough to reach the short piece of metal protruding from the wagon lashings and backed up to it. Rasping the rope was a laborious task, because she was thrown off position several times before the strands broke. Her hands were rubbed raw and the pain brought her to tears.

"I'm free." She reached down and stripped the bindings from her ankles, and then did the same to Arthur's. "We need to jump out as soon as we slow."

Arthur's voice was a squeak of horror. "Jump? We could be killed."

Becca grabbed his face between her hands and fixed him with her fierce big sister stare. "We're going to be killed if we don't save ourselves. Do you understand?"

Looking close to tears again, he managed a nod. "Yes, I

know."

The wagon swayed then eased. In the moonlight glow, the narrowing road and close growing trees were visible as the wagon crept down a steep incline. "This is our chance," Becca hissed at Arthur. "When we reach the bottom, hopefully there'll be a ford. It's the best place to jump. There may be enough water that our landing will be softened."

Arthur's hands shook but he knelt beside her and peered over the lip. The carriage slowed even more down the steep slope.

"Now," she said as she leapt out. Arthur's larger body knocked her flat into the shallow stream when he landed on her. "Oooh!" The wind was knocked out of her and she gulped in water, but at least she was still alive, as was Arthur if his loud moans were an indication. He recovered first and staggered to his feet, extending a helping hand as her waterlogged gown weighed her down.

Before she was completely stable on her feet, Arthur groaned again. "Oh, no."

Using his arm for support, she pulled herself upright in time to understand the cause of his distress. The driver had noticed their leap of faith and pulled the horses to a stop. Two men trotted down the hill at a fast pace, moonlight shining on their weapons.

 Becca recovered first. "Run. To the trees."

Grabbing handfuls of her dragging skirt, she ran as fast as she was able in the direction to the darkened stand of trees, Arthur panting along behind her, dragging an injured left leg. Two lengths from the trees, she caught her foot in her flounce and landed face down on the ground. Gallant at last, Arthur tried to lift her.

"Stop! I'll shoot." The Baron, riding close behind, had reached them.

His pistol leveled at their heads as he slid from his horse. Becca watched her executioner tether his horse and walk towards her. Her thoughts flickered to Cayle. Imagining him still lying wounded on the library floor, or perhaps even worse, twisted her stomach into knots.

Becca, the redheaded and fieriest of the Jamison sisters, felt her temper fray and split beyond repair. Cayle was her future and without him nothing was worthwhile: not the intricate planning of investment strategies, nor the Women's Society, or even the joy of seeing her sisters launched. She wanted to share her life with him, share their families, and most of all she wanted to share his bed. To love and to be loved.

Her duke had taught her pleasure, passion and the joy of being with someone you loved. She'd proved a willing and able student, but she'd become greedy. She wanted time to learn much more from the master. She pushed aside all thought of personal danger and instead concentrated on survival.

Beside her outstretched hand were rocks, a solid round arsenal awaiting scientific calculation. She calculated which angle would inflict the most damage and upon which of her attackers she should concentrate her weapons.

Arthur's outstretched hand resolved her inner debate. Reaching over, she slipped the rock in her palm into his, while her other hand closed over another smooth and hard river stone. Making a slow pantomime of her movements, she lifted from the water and leaned towards Arthur to hide their makeshift projectiles.

The Baron stepped closer and Becca waited, her breath held. She only had one chance. She needed to be accurate.

"So, Lord Mitchell," she hesitated, hoping to draw him nearer still, "if you intend killing us both anyway--"

"Not me!" Arthur gasped beside her. "He can't kill me. He promised me things. Girls."

Becca's gaze swung to face Arthur. "Whatever it was, you'll not live to collect it."

"Mitchell promised that if I informed him of your daily activities, I'd profit from your new schemes. A large enough profit for marriage, while still allowing me a mistress."

The Baron sneered in disgust. "Tell the lady who was to be your mistress?"

Becca paled, already guessing. "How could you think that after you jilted me?"

The Baron said, "When we have your five-year projections, we'll have no more need of your family. You'll be destitute."

"I knew you'd be glad to turn to me," Arthur said.

Becca brought her free hand up and slapped Arthur's face. When the Baron stepped into the breach to stop her, Becca took her chance. She lifted the rock up behind the Baron's head and slammed it into his skull as hard as she could. For a moment he tottered, but then fell to the ground like a sack of potatoes. Becca turned to push herself out of the water, not caring now what befell the witless Arthur. A familiar voice stopped her in her tracks.

"Not so fast, my dear lady. Stop right where you are."

Becca wavered, surprised and shocked, then turned in a slow circle to discover yet another gun barrel pointed at her. The second in under an hour. This time, the hand wielding the gun belonged to Lord Hetherington, her esteemed host, for what had been touted, on the surface at least, as a peaceful weekend at his sprawling country estate.

"You!" Becca gaped in bafflement at the balding, bulkily-built, but basically insignificant man. His lordship had emerged in society as such a boring nonentity that now, even as he waved a weapon and threatened her life, her mind could not grasp the reality of it. How could she have been so stupid as to miss all the clues?

"Of course, my dear. You didn't really believe a man of Baron Mitchell's pathetic ilk was responsible for our large organization.? He waved his free hand towards the direction where Lord Arthur Bennett still cowered, of no help to Becca at all. "And you can't seriously consider that idiot to have commercial expertise. His only concerns of late have been pursuing redheaded whores with a striking resemblance to you, and to his addle-pated mother."

Becca looked at the transformed man threatening her and shook her head, trying to clear her bewilderment. "I don't understand. Why me? Why my family? If you're as intelligent as you seem to think, then why do you need to steal our strategies?"

"Because for some reason, your brother is able to predict possibilities better than anyone else. Either it is his vast network of spies, or an astute grasp of trading. And since we've watched you and your family, I discovered to my surprise that his network of spies consists of you and your sisters--"

He gave a strange hiccupping laugh, rather like a sick braying donkey, and Becca felt her first real frisson of fear ripple up her spine. Lord Hetherington was either an extremely brilliant man, who'd pulled the wool over all their eyes, or--and this, to Becca, was the most worrying part--the big man towering and swaying before her and moving closer every second, could be absolutely, completely and terrifyingly mad, with all the self-obsession of someone heading very quickly on the slippery slope to insanity.

"-- not forgetting, of course," he brayed with that shiver-making laugh once more, and Becca used the cover of her long-skirted gown to inch her feet backwards, one by one.

"-- your doddering aunt. Who is not incompetent at all, but quite, quite astute."

Becca halted, frozen to the spot by his threatening words. She heaved in a deep hitching breath and then spat out at him, "Leave my family alone. Or, you will regret it."

He raised one eyebrow that, even in the half-gloom, looked strangely threatening, as everything he did now seemed. Why had she not seen this side of him before? She must have been blind. It all seemed so obvious now. His bullying of his wife when no one was paying any attention; his estate workers hovering at his elbow at all times and jumping to attention whenever he spoke.

"Are you trying to threaten me? You're forgetting. I hold the gun. Arthur," he called to the sniveling coward Becca had once been engaged to, "take this rope and tie her up."

"No. You intend killing me anyway," Arthur protested with a childish pout.

Hetherington turned the gun to Arthur's chest without speaking a word. Arthur quickly changed his mind. On the ground beside them, Mitchell groaned and tried to sit up.

"Stay where you are," Hetherington warned, waving a second pistol in the Baron's direction.

Regardless of this order, the Baron attempted to rise, but was thrust back to the ground by one of the hovering men. "What the hell do you think you're doing? Let me up."

"Oh, I don't think so, Mitchell. You've outlived your usefulness."

"We're partners. Besides, I have information that you don't know about this lady."

Becca's breath caught. It was obvious he hadn't yet been told about her abilities.

"If you try to exclude me," the Baron said, "I'll go to the authorities."

"Not if you're dead." With a casual air, his lordship raised his pistol and fired. Surprise flowed over the Baron's face as he clutched his chest and slid to the ground. In the half-light, Becca saw the stain spread over his coat, directly over his heart as his cold-blooded killer sauntered over and kicked his lifeless body. "Stupid fool to imagine that I needed him as my partner. I need no one." To his two men, he said, "Light that lantern and bring more rope. We follow our plan and take these two to the cottage."

As one man moved to secure a lantern, the heftier of the two brutes asked, "Why don't we kill them here as well?"

"No, we need them as hostages. Jamison's a stubborn bastard." Peering down at Arthur, he smirked. "I'm not sure Bennett's life is worth anything to him." Spinning towards Becca, he said, "But his redheaded sister will make him willing to produce the correct journals this time. The bastard tricked us once. Never again."

When Becca gasped, he peered through the gloom. "Oh, didn't you know? Your brother tried to fool us by handing over fake ledgers. To buy himself more time. All he accomplished was angering me. I need the profits from those rail lines. In England and in France."

Two men brought rope and secured their hands behind their backs, then prodded them towards a waiting carriage. His lordship climbed in to join them just as Arthur gathered courage for another escape. He leapt for the door and rolled but, despite their size, the men were quicker. A heavy blow to the head was his only reward for that effort and his limp form was dumped back onto the seat, where he moaned from time to time but didn't rouse.

Becca knew there'd be no help from that quarter. She must depend on her own wits until help arrived, in the form of her white knight on a white charger. Her knight, her savior. She attempted to buy herself more time by taunting Hetherington with his failures.

"Ah, so the rumors we heard of your dire financial straits weren't exaggerated?"

She heard his sharp his of breath and knew she had found his Achilles' heel.

"Indeed, I find myself a trifle short of funds. Women are exceedingly expensive."

"And does your wife know where you acquire funds to support lavish entertainments?" She asked the question as the carriage jolted into motion, to keep Hetherington distracted in case riders approached. In the carriage lights, her kidnapper sneered.

"Of course. I couldn't entice so many unwitting gentlemen into my schemes without the support of my wife. She adds such a semblance of wealth and prosperity, these men are overwhelmed with jealousy and greed. They practically beg me to take their money."

"And when they lose money investing with you? Do they question your motives?"

"Oh, no, my dear. You see, by then, we've enough shameful morsels about each gentlemen, that mere threats of announcing their sins in a broadsheet ensures cooperation."

"What sort of morsels?" Keep him talking. Allow Cayle time to follow. But, also, morbid curiosity compelled her to question how he'd controlled so many men from good families.

"Acquiring enough filth to blackmail people is so very easy in such a depraved society. Both men and women change beds with reckless abandon, without giving any thought to others who might be watching. Others are willing to be paid for what they see."

"You pay household staff to report on liaisons."

Lord Hetherington laughed again, an evil chortle, and, in the light from the lantern, Becca noticed the signs of dangerous lunacy on his face. "Not just to report, my innocent. Morally righteous men and women need a push in the right direction, if we're to catch them sinning."

"You arrange for them to be caught in suggestive circumstances, then blackmail them?"

"You'd be surprised how many women are willing, eager even, to bed a fellow aristocrat in exchange for tearing up gambling vowels."

"Of whom are we speaking?"

"Why worry? You've no need of that information. Dead women tell no tales."

Another screech at his own joke, sounding even more like the howl of a wild animal.

"Perhaps because I can understand how much work it's taken you to reach your goals. How great your mind is to be able to control so many people."

He eyed her narrowly, considering his options, as the carriage slowed and came to a shuddering halt. They'd been gone under an hour, so, allowing for the time wasted in their escape attempt, they couldn't have traveled very far from the house. That realization gave Becca hope. The closer they were, the faster they'd be discovered.

The door was pulled open and Arthur dragged to the ground. With rough disregard for their wellbeing, the men hauled Becca out and tossed her in Arthur's direction beside a small cottage, hidden from view by large hedges on three sides. From the outside, it appeared well maintained, giving Becca another glimmer of hope that Hetherington House was still nearby.

Becca took her time coming to her feet, then staggered, giving the impression she was too weak to stand. Or run. "Continue, my lord. You were telling me of your ingenious plans."

"Yes," his lordship mused, "perhaps you can comprehend my genius. At first, I thought you nothing but a meddling fool. Another stupid woman. But now I hold greater admiration for your mathematical understanding. The way you plot the intricacies of commerce."

Becca frowned, and then her eyes widened in horror as she recognized her careless slip-up.

Damn! All along, he'd known who made the decisions about their share purchases. She'd made a gross error by underestimating him, a costly miscalculation.

"It can do no harm telling you. You'll not live long enough to share it with anyone."

Becca pretended to keep her gaze fixed in an enthralled manner on his face, but her glance slid to the side, seeking any sign of Cayle. If he was alive, he'd save her, she was positive. As certain as she was that what they'd shared was something rare. They'd both been living half-lives, awaiting the fall of an axe. Being with him completed her, made her whole. He saw into her soul, could see her for what she really was and still wanted her.

While Becca's sideways glance probed the bush around them, his Lordship had been doing the same. Suddenly, he peered into the gloom and smiled, crying out, "Ah, my love, just in time."

Julia stepped into the clearing.

Becca failed to contain her shock when Julia sauntered over to Hetherington and put her arms around his waist. She reached up and kissed his cheek.

"Good evening, my darling. What a beautiful night it is here at our little meeting place." She looked Becca's way and giggled. "Oh, yes, you redheaded witch. Bertie and I've been meeting here in secret for a long time, whenever I spent time at his house visiting my dear friend, and, of course, Bertie's wife, Celeste."

"You've been having an affair under the very nose of your wife?" Despite all that had occurred, Becca was stunned a second time by their behavior. "But you told me she assists you in your schemes."

"And so she does. But what Celeste doesn't know, doesn't hurt her. She's squeamish about indulging my more deviant sexual needs." His leering look in Becca's direction made her stomach roil, but she fought down the rush of bile in her throat, determined to show him no fear. "So, Celeste turns a blind eye, while I enjoy that kind of satisfaction with others." Hetherington used his free hand to squeeze Julia's rump through her skirt, hard.

"Of course, Celeste doesn't realize that it is I, her closest friend, who lures men into bedrooms for romps. So we can blackmail them." Julia beamed up at Hetherington. "Neither does she realize that Bertie joins me in threesomes, or foursomes, with these men."

"And how long do you think it will be before Celeste finds out?"

"Never!" Julia sounded so haughty and smug that Becca itched to step closer and punch her in the nose, but she controlled her impulses to surreptitiously check behind her to see if she dared shift that way. Even a little. Being so close to these two made her feel ill.

"We cover our movements too well," Julia boasted. "In another year, we'll not need Celeste. Then Bertie will arrange another accident. He's done it several times before."

Becca stared at Hetherington, her mouth open in shock. "You'd murder your own wife?"

"When it's necessary." He gave an uncaring shrug. "When she's no longer useful."

"Silly, silly Celeste," Julia giggled. "Thinking she was cleverer than me."

"Oh, but I am," a shrill voice called from the trees, making them all jump in fright. Lady Hetherington stepped into the light in the clearing. "I'm much, much cleverer than you. You stupid fool. I always knew what you and Bertie were doing. It suited me to let you play the whore with those men. And the women. After all, being a whore is what you do best, Julia."

Bertie's face, even in the yellow light, appeared bleached of color as he tried to pull away from Julia's tight grip on his forearm and move towards his wife.

"Stay back, Bertrand. I've men surrounding you. They'll shoot to kill."

"What men?" Bertrand yelled, spinning around to peer at the tree lines.

"Men from our estate."

He pulled harder and managed to loosen Julia's death grip on him, and started edging away out of the light as he blustered, "But...but they all work for me."

"Oh, Bertrand. Really, you're such a fat fool. Did you really believe you were smart enough to do all this?"

Lady Hetherington's hand waved in the air, the hand that held her pistol, and everyone in the circle gasped in fright and by instinct, ducked to the ground. "I've engineered every move you made, you and that schemer. Even Mitchell."

Julia shook her head. "No, no, Celeste." She raced towards her, fists flailing. "This isn't fair. First Cayle, and now this. I suffered your pitiable husband's groping. I bedded those others for blackmail. Without me, none of this would've been possible. You need me."

"I need neither of you. You thought yourselves better than me. Now you'll suffer an unfortunate accident and I'll be left to mourn, quite bereft. And quite, quite rich."

"No," Julia screamed again.

In a moment of blind rage Julia lunged at Celeste, causing her pistol to discharge. For the second time in an hour, somebody fell to the ground. Unlike the Baron, Julia had survived. Ear-splitting shrieks and the blood running over the shoulder of her gown were a testament to the fact that she was wounded, not dead.

Even louder noises sounded from the bushes, the scuffles and loud wails almost drowning out Julia's caterwauling. With a wave of her now unsteady hand, Celeste signaled her men to investigate the increasing sounds of flesh connecting with flesh, more screams, and then silence. Another man stepped into the light, surrounded by a group of tall figures who dragged Hetherington's estate men into the clearing.

The leader's confident voice rang out, a welcome intrusion into the nightmarish situation Becca had been enduring. "Julia! Stop that noise."

"Cayle!" Becca forgot all her hard-learned lessons about being a lady as she yelled out to the disheveled man striding purposefully across the clearing, and then sagged with relief when he rushed to her side. Strong arms wrapped around her waist, pulling her close enough and hard enough against his chest that she could only breathe in the masculine scent of her hero and inhale his familiar essence.

Her white knight reeked of dirt, sweat and horse and gunpowder; his clothing was torn and filthy; but she'd never known anything so sweet. Clutching him tightly with both hands, she was able to relax her guard, finally. She was safe. He'd come to save her.

"Is this a private performance?" Cayle asked the assembled crowd in a droll voice, but still managing to keep his arm firmly around her shaking body. "Or can any amateur actor go on stage for the final act of this bizarre play?"

Lifting her head enough to glance around, Becca saw that his brothers, Winchester and three others accompanied Cayle. All of them had that same look of authority that Cayle wore like a second skin, so she recognized them as his friends from the Continent. Yet, it was obvious these capable looking men were a lot more. Associates in his trading business, yes; but Becca was certain they also dabbled in the same intrigues as Cayle himself.

Winchester surveyed the scene with amazement, watching Lord and Lady Hetherington as they stood near Julia, who lay on the ground crying and moaning about her bleeding wound. "This whole evening, this entire situation," Winchester gestured to the clearing, "has played out like a Drury Lane melodrama. There are more twists and turns in this plot, more intrigues, more dastardly villains, than even the best of playwrights could conjure."

"I never guessed," Brian said. "I knew Julia was a scheming bitch--" He glanced at Becca. "Pardon me. A *scheming woman.* But I never suspected she'd be so underhanded."

"Stupidly, we never delved into how deep her gambling debts ran," Tony added.

"If we had, we might have prevented this farce proceeding." He swept into a low bow before Becca.

Brian dipped his head as he stood beside his brother; both looked saddened and chastened. "Please, accept our humblest apologies for allowing you to become caught in this web of deceit. One instigated by a member of the St. Martin family."

Tony and Brian both bowed again before Becca, their formal movements strangely in keeping with all the other absurdities that'd happened in the space of a few hours. When they walked away to take care of their stepmother, she edged closer to the comfort of Cayle's hard body, reveling in the warmth and strength emanating from him.

"Sweetheart, tell me, did they harm you?"

For once in her life, Becca couldn't speak. She simply shook her head and gazed up at him with wide-eyed, blatant, open-mouthed admiration. Squeezing her arms in as tight a clasp as she could manage around his lean waist, she flattened herself against Cayle's body, content for once to let a man take total charge.

This man. Her man, her warrior, her savior.

Winchester snapped out several orders and the others rallied. When the chaos and confusion of figures settled, Becca noticed both Hetheringtons being led away by men in constabulary uniform. Cayle's brothers helped Julia to her feet and attempted to staunch the flow of blood from her shoulder.

Becca unfurled herself from Cayle and went to his stepmother, who flinched. But instead of delivering the blow Julia expected, Becca bent to the hem of her own gown and lifted the wet outer garments away to grasp her petticoat. With a loud wrench, she ripped a strip of lawn from the bottom and stood to face Julia.

Wadding the linen into a ball, she pressed it to Julia's shoulder.

"Flesh wounds bleed profusely and hurt like the devil, but at least you won't die from it."

Overcome by the dire situation, Julia sobbed even louder. Raising one arm to her stepson, she begged, "Please, you have to help me. We're family."

His face hard, he wasn't the Cayle that Becca knew, but a stern Duke of Sherwyn, who addressed the woman his father had inflicted upon his family. "You will be fortunate if I can keep you out of prison for your part in this sordid affair. Nevertheless, to protect the family name of which you're so enamored, I shall endeavor to do all in my power to see that at least you do not go to the gallows."

Julia keened and wailed even louder. "No, I'll do anything. Go anywhere. You are Sherwyn. You can save me." The younger St. Martin brothers watched. Julia turned her pleas to them. "Brian, Anthony, I am your mother."

"Stepmother," Tony corrected in a cold voice.

"You've never been a mother to us," Brian said. "All these years, you either ignored us or reviled us to our father. We'll be thankful to rip you from our lives."

"Here, here," Tony agreed, patting his brothers on their backs.

"You should be thankful that Becca is a true lady, Julia," Cayle said. "Any other woman who'd been so wronged by you, wouldn't trouble themselves to tend to your gunshot wound."

At his signal, two men stepped forward to escort Julia away. Everyone moved towards the carriages and horses, relieved to be leaving the cottage and its memories behind.

Cayle clasped Becca's hand again and kept it in his solid grip.

Glancing down at their entwined fingers, she recognized that she was as reluctant to release him, as he seemed to be to let go of her. She let out a long relieved sigh that it was over, finally over.

Life at Grosvenor Square could return to normal.

Chapter 24

Becca followed orders and changed out of her wet gown, before rejoining the enlarged group gathered in a secluded upstairs sitting room at Hetherington House. She felt over-cosseted when her family fussed around her, fetching her drinks and making her warm. Still, it was the sort of smothering that felt good, comforting.

Below, the house had emptied of neighbors invited for the ball, and house guests had been dispatched to bedchambers, despite their avid curiosity about the goings on. The local magistrate had attended the ball and he'd quickly asserted his authority when the miscreants were returned to the house under guard.

The Hetheringtons were sent ahead to London, while a doctor attended to Julia's superficial wound. She, and the others involved, had then been bundled into conveyances for the journey to Town. And probably prison.

"Bennett's been remanded to his lodgings to await a full hearing into his involvement," Winchester confirmed. "His explanation that the men were blackmailing him over his predilection towards redheaded women rang true, but can't excuse him fully."

With a sideways glance at Becca, who sat tucked warmly by his side, Cayle muttered, "As far as I'm concerned, it doesn't excuse him at all. The man's a danger to himself and others."

"I can't imagine Margaret will continue their betrothal when she learns of his obsession," Lottie said.

Laura glanced first at Becca, then at Cayle, and then grinned. "Although red hair is certainly worth obsessing over, don't you think, our dearest duke?"

Cayle took this good-natured teasing in his stride, bending a little to nuzzle the red hair that Laura was referring to. "Definitely my favorite color."

Becca almost purred like a well-fed kitten when he kissed the top of her head. She felt safe at last, and content.

"And what will eventuate for Lord and Lady Hetherington,"

Aunt Agatha asked Cayle.

He shrugged. "My friends are accompanying them to London and the judiciary will decide. As they hold titles, leniency may be anticipated."

"By the way Lord Hetherington was crowing and unburdening himself of his misdeeds when he left," Brian said dryly, "he may find himself in deeper trouble. Especially when those they swindled get wind of the details."

"But when they discover the large number of men of the higher ranks who were being blackmailed, the authorities may prefer to sweep the entire affair under the carpet," Winchester commented.

"I thank God that Celeste Hetherington's true nature was revealed in time."

Becca shook her head. "I was flabbergasted when she chanted like a loony about how she was the greatest queen England had ever seen. She'll probably spend her days chained to a cot in an asylum for the criminally insane."

When Lottie yawned widely, Aunt Agatha struggled to her feet, Laura rising to assist her. "It is time we retired. Before you seek your bed, Becca, could you pen a short note to Michael to be sent with a courier at daylight? If he hears of this before we can send an explanation, he'll be racketing down here to rescue us all."

Becca stood to peck her aunt on her wrinkled cheek. "I will, Auntie. And I'm certain Michael will desert Oxford for London the moment he hears the news, regardless of what I say, so we should expect a visit from him and Jonathon tomorrow evening."

Becca and Cayle said their goodnights to the others, who all made beelines for their rooms, exhaustion catching up with them.

Left alone with Cayle, Becca bit her lip in agitation. Taking his hands in hers, she started, "Cayle--"

"Yes, sweetheart. Are you sure you're recovered?" He drew her down to the settee again, pressing the back of his hand to her forehead. "Are you warm enough?"

His tenderness made it more difficult. She tried again.

"It's time, past time, that I explain the truth, the whole truth, about us, about myself."

He moved her into a long soft kiss, then drew back to look deeply into her eyes.

"Becca," he said, in a very solemn tone. "I know all I need to know about you. You're brave." He kissed her again. "And loving." Another kiss. "And I was scared to death for your safety. This time, I thought I'd lost you. When I rode to the cottage, I envisioned you lying on the ground in a pool of blood, dead. I saw Julia lying there and, at first, I thought it was you.

My heart stopped beating."

Becca groaned. He was saying everything her womanly side longed to hear, but what she must confess might ruin their relationship, shatter his trust in her.

"Cayle," she tried again, "you don't understand. I'm trying to explain that all our money, all the family's investments, future ventures--"

"Are controlled by you. Yes, I know."

"You know? You already know that I do the planning, the investing?"

"Well, of course. I wasn't going to embroil myself in any situation if I wasn't in possession of all the facts. It was easy enough for us, my friends and me, to dig it out."

"But how? How did you know it was me and not Michael, when most of the consortium didn't discover the truth?"

"Ah, but they're not trained to unravel mysteries. My friends and I are. Besides which, Michael may be a well-rounded Oxford scholar, but he doesn't have your level of intelligence when it comes to mathematics and commercial forecasting. And Jonathon is going to be a brilliant engineer, but he also doesn't hold your particular skills. I recognized at once, the first night we became reacquainted, that the young bluestocking I used to know had matured into a woman who was both shrewd and capable. And, above all, intriguing."

Becca narrowed her gaze at him. "I'm revealing my secrets, yet, I suspect that you've more secrets to reveal than I do."

Cayle smiled and shrugged. "Perhaps I'll share them with you. Later."

Becca scowled. "I was prepared to reveal my innermost thoughts, my most secret of secrets, yet you only say, perhaps you'll share yours. I don't consider that a fair exchange."

"You, my sweet little liar, haven't revealed everything to me," he said, leaving Becca confused.

"What more do you want to know? You already know about the Society, my friends, the ones at those houses gentlemen visit. And the coffee houses at the Exchange. All my deepest thoughts have been exposed."

Once more, he gave her that enigmatic look, the one that shouted to her that he knew more than she did. "A sitting room isn't the place to discuss the rest. You can whisper it to me later, in another setting altogether."

He ran his hands up and down her back, distracting her. She needed her wits about her to decide if he was urging her to reveal her feelings for him. But, even now, she worried that her relationship with Cayle had come to an end. He was free of Julia, free to pursue his life. It was time he selected a wife, and Becca fretted that his earlier proposals had been forced upon him by time and circumstance. She needed to know if he still wanted her now for anything but her willing body in his bed.

Testing the waters, she asked with hesitancy, "Cayle, by another setting, do you mean my bedchamber?"

"That's exactly where I intend for you to unburden that last secret, my love."

Automatically, she said, "Do not call me--"

"Shush! I'll call you my love, my sweet, sweetheart, and every other endearment that comes to mind. Tonight, I was terrified for you. Indulge me, come to bed with me, and let me whisper words of love in your ear until morning."

He helped her to her feet and led her along the corridor to her room. Becca felt safe and secure, warmed by his attentions. But, still, a piece of the puzzle eluded her. What did he mean? What more did he want her to reveal?

She'd faced not just one gun tonight, but three. She didn't know if she had enough bravery left inside her to expose her raw emotions to Cayle. But when he locked the door and turned to her, he was wearing his heart on his sleeve for her to see. He loved her.

It was written across his face as plain as day. Her own heart flipped over in her chest. Her breath caught. Everything she'd always wanted might still happen. She wanted it so badly.

Cayle stood with his back to the door and stared at Becca in awe. Not for his Becca had there been any faint-hearted vapors when she was kidnapped and held at gunpoint. No. She'd done what she always did. Stood strong in the face of adversity. And thank God for her stubborn will. It had kept her alive, brought her back to him. She slipped the wrapper off her shoulders to reveal an old-fashioned nightgown. There was nothing seductive about such a garment, yet the sensual picture she presented mesmerized him.

The tight band of pain around his chest finally loosened and allowed him to draw his first liberated breath since coming upon her at the cottage. Even as he'd stepped into the clearing to face Lady Hetherington and her drawn pistol, from the corner of his eye he'd watched Becca. Watched for any sign of injury, whilst the angst of thinking her harmed was unimaginably painful. The unbearable weight of the last traumatic weeks dropped from his shoulders, leaving him more lighthearted than he'd allowed himself to be for so long. In his relief, he felt almost dizzy, though, like Becca's knight of old, he also felt invincible.

With her beside him, they could conquer all foes, solve family problems, save the downtrodden of their world and still have time enough for loving. The sort of loving that would keep them together for the rest of their lives. As husband and wife. Now, he just needed to convince stubborn, freckle-faced Lady Rebecca of that.

"Cayle, you asked me once if I'd marry you."

Hardly daring to breathe, he bit into his bottom lip as joy radiated through him. Maybe he wouldn't have to abduct her, run her off to Gretna Green after all. He'd been prepared to do anything to secure her, to make her his. Even if it had meant an elopement and another scandal. All he could think about was keeping her safely with him, forever. Never again, could he remain keeping her at arm's length, and he well knew it. He needed her, desperately. In addition, he reverently hoped that she'd realized how much she also needed him.

"I do remember," he agreed, striving for a casual air. "And I asked more than once."

Inside, his nerves were strung tighter than a bow. He wanted her, yet, he also wanted to know that she came to him of her own free will, and not because she'd been forced into it to ensure her safety. Even little teeth came out to worry her lower lip, a sure sign his beautiful Becca was nervous. How well he knew her. How he wanted to ease any worry from her mind. Despite that, he forced himself to remain perfectly still by digging his fingers into his thighs.

"I ... I thought--"

"Yes?"

"I thought perhaps we could come to some arrangement."

"An arrangement?"

She gave a little nod and swallowed, visibly. "Yes."

"I offered you an arrangement once before, I recall, and you turned me down. Rather insultingly."

At this instant, she looked truly troubled. He almost gave in and let his instincts take over. All he wanted was this wonderful and enigmatic woman in his arms, warm and safe. But, for her, pride was all that'd kept her going for many long months of being gossiped about, pointed at and ridiculed. She'd been betrothed to a cad and he'd dumped her and married a richer woman. But Becca, proud and defiant, had held her head high and pretended it was of no consequence. But the rejection had wounded her and diminished her self-esteem, and he never wanted her to suffer again.

"As the Duke of Sherwyn you still need a--"

"Wife?"

"Yes, a wife."

"I do, indeed."

"And I've realized that I can't continue doing what I've been doing, with my family's funds, even with the Society, without more support. Influential support. Someone who understands the problem, but who will allow me to continue without restraint, without administering tight controls."

"You're talking about male support."

"Yes."

"Possibly from a husband."

"Yes."

"But if you can't bring yourself to voice the word wife, how will you ever be able to become one in reality?"

"I suppose I could ... I could learn, if I had to."

"It'd need to be a strong gentleman who'd allow his wife to put herself into those situations, the sort in which you habitually become embroiled."

"But you could do it."

"Could I?" he queried, still casually.

"You're certainly strong enough."

"Ah! You're speaking of physical strength."

"No. Well, yes. Partly."

"Partly?" One pretty, little foot peeped out from under her skirt to stomp an impatient patter on the rug. He smothered his grin.

"I'm talking of an inner strength. The sort only a gentleman who knows his own place in the world would have."

"And you think I have this, um," he waved his hand vaguely, "this inner something."

"Cayle, you're the strongest man I know. Your family knows they can depend on you no matter what."

"And that's important to you, because your family has always depended on your strength too?"

"Well, yes, there's that. I suppose I'm accustomed to being involved with my family, so any man I, any man who--"

"Who?"

"Who'd be prepared to take me on as a wife, would have to be not only strong--"

"And patient."

Her foot tapped out her irritated rhythm even harder on the carpet and he could almost see steam expel as she dithered around the subject, trying not to be the first to voice the solution that was glaringly obvious to them both.

"Enough, damn you. You're enjoying this moment, aren't you?"

Grinning widely, he agreed. "Immensely."

"What more do you want me to do? Admit that I can't do it without you?"

"That would be a nice place to start."

She actually gritted her teeth. God, he loved her spirit. So determined, yet so giving.

"I can't do it alone anymore. Any of it." She counted off on her fingers. "The Society. The Stock Exchange. Our investments. A woman can't do it all alone."

"So you're saying you need me for my financial involvement?

"Financial, plus other involvements."

"You'll need to spell it out for me. Which other involvements would they be?"

"Even my family has benefited from being seen with yours."

Now he laughed aloud. "You, my little prevaricator, are dodging the larger issue."

"And you're going to make me say it first, aren't you?"

Pretending patience he didn't feel, he nodded. "I am."

He could hardly suck air into his lungs as he waited edgily for her to come to the inevitable conclusion. She needed him. Not just any man, but him, Cayle St. Martin.

However, she'd swallowed her pride enough for one day. One of the things he loved about her was her ability to rationalize any situation clearly and come to a conclusion that benefited not only her, but also those around her. It was time he told her. Time that he let her keep her pride intact.

Taking a step closer he bent his head to hers, adoring the way her breath hitched whenever he pressed near her. He nuzzled her neck, luxuriating in the scent of her and the fact that he now had the right, finally, to claim her as his.

"Becca, sweetheart, I love you."

"You don't need to say that, you know. I know what I am. I recognize my good qualities and my limitations, but if you could overlook those limitations somewhat..."

God, she still couldn't see how wondrous she was. How she made the world a better place. How his world lit up when she was in it. He needed to show her. "Becca."

"Yes?"

"Would you stop thinking and talking and listen to me. Because I do love you. As Laura would say, I love you madly and gladly and passionately. And I want you more than anything I've ever wanted."

"Truly?" Her words came out on a little gasp.

"Truly! And now, if you can keep quiet for long enough, I want to hold you and kiss you and make love to you. Because I can't live without you in my life. I will not live like that ever again." Before she could speak again, he took advantage of her open mouth to press his to it, kissing her hard and fast. Followed by long and slow. And then, he settled in and did it all over again.

"Laura was right."

With a groan that turned into a laugh, he pulled back. It seemed that not even kissing Becca would keep her quiet this time. "What was Laura right about?"

"She said that when you love someone, your knees tremble when you kiss them."

"And did your knees tremble?"

"They shook. Amazingly so."

"So should I take this to mean that you love me?"

"Oh, heavens, yes!"

"Well perhaps this would be a good time for you to tell me. "Would it?"

"Mmm. Before I go quietly mad from the waiting."

She finally stopped speaking long enough to stretch up on her dainty slippers and run enough kisses across his cheeks and mouth that he ceased to breathe. The sheer force of emotion in him swelled his chest until he literally couldn't find room to put air into his lungs. And, then; then she spoke. If he hadn't loved her before, after he'd watched the way her eyes ignited with the burning passion she seemed to have reserved just for him, he'd have toppled head over heels.

"I love you to distraction. I love the way you let me stand beside you as an equal. I love the way you let me be myself. And you seem to love me regardless of who I am, or the impetuous things I do."

"I love you because of those very things."

Green eyes twinkled up at him. Red hair flew in complete disorder around her head and shoulders. Twelve freckles shone like beacons, a testament to the fact that she was always too preoccupied with mathematics and problem solving to remember her bonnet. She was so beautiful, his Becca. So very beautiful, and he'd happily devote a lifetime to convincing her of that fact. But, she had an evil glint in her eyes now. "And most of all--"

"Yes?"

"Most of all, I love that you might come in handy on long and otherwise boring winter nights, when I'm too tired to reconcile the accounts. For performing all those extremely naughty tricks you do in a bedchamber."

His extremely busy, often preoccupied little genius thought he might, only might, come in handy to relieve her boredom on a cold night? Should he be insulted? Or laugh?

Deciding that being around Becca meant ignoring what other men might take to be a blight on their manliness, he hugged her tightly against him, feeling her absorbing his strength and yet, at the same time, making him stronger. "In that case, I think we can come to a mutually suitable arrangement."

"Cayle?" He chuckled, resigned to never getting another minute's peace in his life. "Yes, little chatterbox?"

"This arrangement. I don't think I'd feel comfortable being a mistress any longer. Not that I didn't enjoy the nights we spent together, in bed, during our affair. But if we're to be partners in trade and commerce, I think we may need a more formal arrangement."

"I suppose, if you insist," he muttered, while inwardly rejoicing. "Next Saturday, we'll be married."

"Next Saturday? Oh, no, no, I certainly don't think I shall have time next Saturday. I've the monthly meeting for the Prostitute's Reform Committee, to discuss the new bill, and Mr. Brown has news about that scoundrel Miss Featherstone is betrothed to--"

"Becca!" He was losing patience. "Is this how you intend our marriage to proceed?"

One dainty finger tapped her teeth as she pondered the question. "Mmm. Most probably. Is that going to be a problem for you? Because if it is, I could probably find some other gentleman to marry. One who'd be more considerate."

"Some poor unfortunate fool who'd do your bidding, you mean. Jump when you say jump?"

With a huge grin she teased, "When you put it that way, it does have merits compared to being with someone like you who is arrogant--"

"Arrogant?"

"And controlling--"

"Enough insults! A man's ego can only take so much battering. You're marrying me, no one else. Do you understand?"

"Yes, my lord, and master." Her eyelashes fluttered.

Eying her suspiciously, he muttered, "I trust you even less when you're docile. Are you up to something?"

"Me? Whatever do you mean, Your Grace?"

"I mean that you think you can outwit me every day of the week. However, I'll not allow that to happen. Are we clear on that?"

Grinning up at him, she feigned humility. "Certainly, my darling."

A dainty hand walked up and down his sleeve and she fluttered her eyes at him. Again. Throwing back his head, he laughed long and loud.

"Becca, you're a minx. I doubt I'll ever win an argument with you."

"But you're so ... intelligent and strong and--"

Cayle didn't let Becca finish her embarrassing and overdone litany of his merits. Well, not precisely then anyway. At that moment, he stopped her speaking by taking matters into his own hands.

He picked her up over one shoulder and threw her onto the bed. And kept her occupied there all night.

Epilogue

Martin House, Mayfair, London

Taking the steps of his house two at a time, the Duke of Sherwyn rushed past his astounded butler, who stood to attention beside the open front door. The ducal carriage had just discharged them after the long journey back from the Hetherington estate, and Cayle was impatient to be alone with his betrothed.

"My soon-to-be-duchess, and I don't wish to be disturbed, Jenner. Under any circumstances. Do you understand?"

For the first time that Cayle had ever seen, Jenner opened his mouth, threw back his head and laughed. His ageless face creased under the unaccustomed strain. Several heads popped out from around other doors: servants, curious as to why a normally proper duke and a normally reserved butler were carrying on in such a scandalous manner in the vestibule.

"Oh, yes, Your Grace. I understand perfectly. And may I say, Your Grace, that you have chosen extremely well."

Jenner nodded his head to where Becca hung upside down on Cayle's broad back, her red curls swinging in disarray as she bounced. Once again, Cayle had decided the most expedient way to get Becca where he wanted her--in his bedroom--was to pick her up and sling her over his shoulder. Cayle gave him a huge grin.

"I think so too, Jenner. It's about time Martin House saw a bit more life. Time it embraced scandal, rather than hid from it."

"Indeed, Your Grace. Indeed." He peered around Cayle's side to Becca's upturned countenance.

"And may I wish your soon-to-be-duchess every joy in her married life."

From her rather indecent position, Becca managed to lift one hand from Cayle's thigh to give a little wave and splutter, "You may, Jenner, and ... ah ... thank you."

Cayle grinned again; satisfied with his world at last, and determined Becca would linger under the title of future duchess for as short a time as possible. As soon as Laura, Lottie, and Aunt Aggie could arrange their wedding, Lady Jamison would also become Your Grace. With all his heart, Cayle longed for that moment. He heard Jenner humming to himself as he bustled away to the kitchen to spread the good news amongst the rest of the staff.

Things would be different from now on. Martin House was about to gain a new mistress. And not just any mistress, but a lady known to advocate reformed conditions for working-class people throughout England. Right about now, the Duke of Sherwyn imagined his butler was informing the servants how, perhaps one day very soon, he'd whisper a word in the new duchess's ear about the sorry financial plight of some of his family in Scotland.

Continuing his hurried strides upwards to his bedroom, Cayle entered, and then pushed the door shut with his shoulder. Dropping Becca on the bed so hard she bounced, twice, he followed her down and pinned her with his weight.

"Now, repeat after me. I ... Rebecca Jamison ... am marrying Cayle St. Martin, Duke of Sherwyn, in three days' time. I will love and obey him all the days of my life."

"Hmm." Becca pondered for a minute. "I will love, and work with him..."

Cayle contemplated her troubled expression. She'd given up so much to be with him that he could at least do this for her. He amended the vow to, "I will love him, work with him, have children with him ... and make his life endlessly entertaining."

She solemnly repeated the vows and then lapsed into a tiny silence. He looked at her in amazement and was about to comment that it was the first time he'd ever been able to stop her talking, when she spoke. Naturally!

"Ah, Cayle."

He was chuckling as he complained, "Good Lord, Becca, are you ever going to let me get in the last word?"

The love of his life mulled over that possibility for a few seconds, but then shook her head and gave her usual honest reply. "Probably not. But, Cayle?"

Her petite hand in the middle of his chest stopped him from lowering himself fully to her, from feeling her breasts squeezed tightly against him, as he was now so desperate to do. Precisely three hours and twenty-four minutes had passed since they'd made love in their private train compartment and that was too long, far too long for his sanity.

After an agonized groan, followed by a resigned mindset, he asked, "Yes, Becca, my love, my adored one."

"I love you. Love you so much." She leaned up to kiss him and repeated her sister's mantra for marriage. "I love you madly, and gladly, and, without any doubt, passionately."

The rest of the chant drifted away into a whispered promise as he proceeded to make not only her knees, but also her whole body tremble with the force of their passion.

"For the rest of our lives," she murmured, giving a contented sigh.

In that moment, Cayle decided that Becca could always, always, have the last word, if she'd say those specific words to him.

Each, and every, time.

Note from author:

Reviews are like gold to authors! If you've enjoyed this book, please consider leaving a review and/or rating the book.

About Suzi Love
Tag Line- Making history fun, one year at a time

Hi, I'm Suzi Love, an Australian author of historical romances from the late Regency to early Victorian years, with a little bit of the Australian outback thrown in.

I've had a lifetime fascination with all things old, weird, and exotic. I love to travel, visit historic places, and talk to crazy characters. I also adore history, especially the grittier and seamier side, so I write about heroes and heroines who challenge traditional manners, morals, and occupations, either through necessity or desire. I hope you'll travel with me again.

If you'd like to be one of the first to know when I release a new book, plus enjoy some special 'Mailing List Only' benefits and goodies, sign up for my mailing list at the top right of my WEBSITE.

If you liked this book, I'd appreciate it if you'd write a short review or rate the book.

Or, keep up to date with what I get up to each day via my Rebel Mouse Magazine or Suzi Love Daily Gossip newspaper.

I love hearing from my readers, so feel free to write to me and tell me what you think.

Suzi Love
Cannon Hill Post Shop,
PO Box 191, Cannon Hill,
Queensland, 4170,
Australia

Where to find Suzi Love:-
Please visit my WEBSITE
Follow my books on Goodreads
Enjoy my historical images PINTEREST
Like me on Face Book - Follow me on Twitter
Email me here:- suzi@suzilove.com

Excerpt from Scenting Scandal

Please enjoy this excerpt from Book 2 in the Scandalous siblings Series, Scenting Scandal, which is Richard and Laura's story.

"Half an hour at most until we can end this farce. Then we'll be free to bid each other a far-from-fond farewell."

The Earl snorted, the indelicate sound contrasting with the refined air he presented this morning in his long charcoal frock coat with tailored sleeves displaying decorative gold buttons. A gold-threaded gray vest fitted snugly underneath, while a gold bar sporting an enormous topaz winked from the elaborate folds of his thrice-about neckcloth.

Laura twisted her neck a little more and looked lower. Immaculate trousers – with the newer style front fastening instead of a buttoned-over flap – covered an acre of legs and finished at blindingly-polished walking boots.

Living up to her family title of Miss Inquisitive, she moved her gaze higher again and back to his thigh's evident musculature, honed from time spent on horseback. The mechanics, and easy access, of one row of buttons down the simplified closing on his trousers fascinated her, purely from a scientific point of view.

Botheration. The air had warmed all of a sudden. She lifted her ivory and lace fan. Even waving the fragile creation rapidly back and forth didn't dispel her flush. Not blush, as she'd never admit to such a state. Dealing with the Earl might be a hardship, but she and her sisters had never found it taxing to peruse the Earl's decidedly-masculine physique. She risked one more peek. No, not difficult at all. When her appraisal reached his face, she saw a wide smile and a display of even white teeth, and she smiled in return.

"Uh, uh," he said, wagging a finger. "You misunderstand the reasons for my happier expression. Unlike you, I'm looking forward to the next three months and the chance to study your fiscal strategies. I'd like to compare my investing skills to those of your astute sister's."

His mouth widened into a roguish grin. "I'm also flattered by your scrutiny of my anatomy and amused by your blush, especially after your studies into animal reproduction."

Her free hand flew to her cheek and her heavy reticule knocked her arm. "I never blush." To have him observe her ogle him was embarrassing and gave her another reason to be irritated by his company, petty though her reasons might be. She tugged, but her hand was imprisoned under his. With her nose raised a fraction, she said, "For the sake of propriety, I was ensuring your garments were intact. You've a reputation for disappearing into dark corners and re-emerging with your clothing askew. As though hasty hands ripped your garments from your body."

"Tut, tut, my pet. Has jealousy driven you to spying?"

"Jealousy? Over the class of females you consort with? I was reassuring myself your clothing was intact for the sake of my elderly aunt. The entire congregation watched that woman, the Countess, beckon you to the back of the church. Heaven knows what you were doing while the bride and groom were signing the register."

Winchester chuckled, long and low. "I doubt even my sullied reputation could support the story that I dragged the Countess into a shadowy niche for a quick tumble. At least, not with my sisters watching me like hawks." He dipped his head closer. "I may excel at dispensing pleasure, but I like more than a few minutes to enjoy a rendezvous."

She forced herself to stand motionless, to not react to his latest coarse taunt. "I've no interest," she said, between calming breaths, "in knowing any details of how you entertain–"

Want to visualize Scenting Scandal?
Web Page   Pinterest Board..   Face Book Page

Want to find Scenting Scandal?
Amazon USA   Amazon Australia   Amazon UK
Amazon Germany   Amazon Spain   Amazon France
Amazon Canada   Amazon Brazil   Amazon India